Now Is the Hour

BOOKS BY TOM SPANBAUER

FARAWAY PLACES

THE MAN WHO FELL IN LOVE WITH THE MOON

IN THE CITY OF SHY HUNTERS

NOW IS THE HOUR

NOW IS
THE HOUR

TOM SPANBAUER

Houghton Mifflin Company

BOSTON · NEW YORK

2006

For information about permission to reproduce selections from
this book, write to Permissions, Houghton Mifflin Company,
215 Park Avenue South, New York, New York 10003.

Visit our Web site: www.houghtonmifflinbooks.com.

Library of Congress Cataloging-in-Publication Data
Spanbauer, Tom.
Now is the hour / Tom Spanbauer.
p.   cm.
ISBN-13: 978-0-618-58421-5
ISBN-10: 0-618-58421-8
1. United States—History—1961–1969—Fiction. 2. Triangles
(Interpersonal relations)—Fiction. 3. Gay men—Fiction.
4. Native Americans—Fiction. 5. Hitchhiking—Fiction.
6. West (U.S.)—Fiction. I. Title.
PS3569.P339N69 2006
813'.6—dc22   2005030156

Printed in the United States of America

Book design by Robert Overholtzer

MP 10 9 8 7 6 5 4 3 2 1

For my mother

Contents

Acknowledgments

My deep appreciation to my editor, Anton Mueller. Thank you for loving this book so much.

Thank you, Neil Olson of Donadio and Olson, Literary Representatives—twenty years now, Neil, can you believe it?

My thanks to Grey Wolfe and the golden catalpas, Clyde Hall *un son baisch*, Mendala Marie Graves—how old Mendy Graves? Steve Taylor, Carol Ferris, James Bolton, *El Boy* Joe Rogers and Kate Callahan, Ellie Covan and Dixon Place, Philip Iosca, Luisa Quinoy, Kathleen Lane and Jelly Helm, Geri Doran, Ken and Jane Leeson, Emily and Rachel, Charles Lawrence, Joe Modica, Paulette Osborn, Maria Kozmetatos and the staff at Multnomah County Health Services, Leslee Lewis and Corepilates, Ken Gordon of Ken's Place, Suzy Vitello, Michael Sears, Leslie Sears, Kally Thurman, Jim Erdman, Kathy Hanson, Ashleigh Flynn, Mark Weigle, Larry Colton, Diane Ponti, Ward Green, PK Kozel, Tomas and Liz, Murray Edelman, Robert Hill, Carrie Hoops, Liz Scott, Joanna Rose, Joanna Ponce, Stevan Allred, Kate Grey, Chris Fadden, Queen Butter, Muthani and Jim, Kahunya, Damani, Diane Greenwood, Martin Mueller, the Dickie family, Andre Pruitt, Stevee Postman, David Weissman, Gregory Saks, Ampersand, Jerako, David Ciminello, Ari, Pikkul and Vetivert, Shanna Germain, Jared Germain, John Hinds, Kevin Meyer, Darin Beaseley, Charles Dye, Shannon Chaffe, Tom Chaffe, Zuna, Leo Gulick, Lynn Salcido, John dePasquali, Steve Arndt, Ruth Füglistaller, Paulann Petersen, Elizabeth Snyder, Cupcake and Vicki, Alex Cadell,

David, Thomasina, Isolde, Benny Mendez, Julieta Lionetti, Federico and Isabella, Steve Dearden, Sheena, and Ella May, Eric Baudot, Eva Gastiazoro, Juan and Wilfred, Jimene, Robert Vasquez, Joe Wheat, Kerry Mooseman, and Harold Richards.

My thanks to Jayne Yaffe Kemp.

Thanks to *Tin House* magazine.

Thank you, Powell's on Hawthorne.

Thanks, Donna Meyer of Baker and Meyer Attorneys at Law, and Karen Berkowitz of Legal Aid Services of Oregon.

My thanks to the Naraya Community, the Portland Faeries, and the Dangerous Writers.

Big thanks go to the neurologists and the cardiologists and the hematologists at Oregon Health Sciences University.

Thank you, Jackie Czerepinski. Old Friends/Bookends.

And to my family—Barbara, John, and Jerry, and my father, John. Jamie and her Lily, Cody, and Nick, and their mother, Trina Green. You too, Karen.

Pocatello, Idaho, my apologies for the fictional liberties I took with my hometown.

My love and special thanks to Thomas Soames. I am blessed to have your friendship.

And most of all, my love to Michael Sage Ricci, my beautiful friend. It is my pleasure to rest in your company.

Now Is the Hour

Lonesome Traveler

PARMESAN CHEESE.

My troubles all started with Parmesan cheese.

And they ended with Parmesan cheese.

My life up to now has been one big cheese cycle.

The first grade of Saint Joseph's School was the first Parmesan cheese incident.

The last Parmesan cheese incident just happened, and what just happened is the reason why I'm a free man out here on Highway 93, a flower in my hair, hitchhiking to San Francisco.

It's all pretty clear now. Amazing how clear things can get at night in the desert. The moon, a big silver dollar, so much light there's a shadow of me across the pavement. A long shadow. My feet here on the gravel, my head all the way over there on the center line.

George Serano told me once that you can tell how you feel by how your shadow looks. Tonight in my shadow there's something about my head and my shoulders, my arms too. The way my hair is sticking up, and my T-shirt on my biceps, the daisy I picked in Twin Falls poking out the side of my head. Something inside coming out that makes my shadow look, that makes me look, I don't know, full, I guess.

Like this moon. Moon's so bright I can see the lines in the palm of my hand. I can see my bloody, bit thumbnail. If I took my dick out, I could see every aspect of it. My ass too. I ought to just pull my pants down right here, one hundred and fifty miles north of Reno, Nevada, and show that big old moon my big old moon.

Just my luck, some trucker would come along.

Just my luck.

And quiet.

Quiet as church. Not Mass or Our Mother of Perpetual Help devotions, but quiet in the empty Saint Joseph's Church. The quiet of the votive candle flame. The blue and red and yellow stained glass lying on the pew. Close your eyes and take a breath. What you smell is Catholic: oiled wood, beeswax, gold frankincense and myrrh.

The desert's even more quiet. The perfectly still sound of everything alive. Even the pavement, its dark ribbon going over the edge of the horizon, is alive. The horizon too, slow, sloping flat, every now and then an outburst of lava rock making a jagged edge. Sagebrush a darker shade of silver than the moon. Close your eyes here and take a breath, what you smell is sagebrush and bitterroot, what you smell is everything that's possible.

Two cigarettes ago, just as I sucked the yellow flame into the end of my cigarette, a coyote yelled out a big old lonesome, but not a sound since. Not even crickets or frogs. Just my tennis shoes scraping gravel. And my breath.

Maybe there was a nuclear bomb, and now I'm the only person who survived in the whole entire world.

That might not be so bad.

After seventeen years of breathing, I, Rigby John Klusener, do hereby declare there sure as hell are a few I could live without.

Why else do you think I'm out here on Highway 93, my thumb stuck out pointing to California?

What are you, six years old, in the first grade? There I was, six years old. Sister Bertha had put me on the dumb side of the room. Over on the right side near the cloakroom door in the back. Us dumb ones were supposed to be doing something in our notebooks while Sister Bertha was flashing the flash cards for the smart ones on the other side of the room. I knew every one of the words she was flashing except for *have,* and that's only because nobody'd shown me the *v* yet, plus I didn't know about the silent *e.* Anyway, Sister Bertha catches me reading the flash cards, so she says my name out loud. She says, Rigby John Klusener?

I stood up, of course, because I may not have known about *v* and the silent *e* yet, but I sure as hell knew you had to stand up straight, away from your desk, and say out loud and clear: Yes, Sister Bertha?

Sister Bertha was old and tiny. Holy Cross nun. The ones with the big halo fan thing all the way around their head. My sis, Mary Margaret, had Sister Bertha too in the first grade, and so had a bunch of my cousins. Sister Bertha was so old, she could have been the first-grade teacher for my mom and dad, even.

So Sister Bertha says, Rigby John, read these cards out loud.

I read them all out loud, all of them, no problem, that is except for *have,* and when she told me that the *v* had the *v* sound, after she told me about the silent *e,* and said the word *love* was the same way, she moved me clear across the room to the smart side, up front, right by her desk.

Been there ever since, up front on the smart side, a whole room away from dumb.

Maybe that's when Joe Scardino started to hate me. Because I got to move up front. Because I went from dumb to smart in a matter of five minutes. Plus, then I started helping Sister Bertha with extra things like wiping the chalkboard clean and getting out of class to get the chalk dust out of the erasers.

Probably didn't help.

Like there was the day Sister Bertha asked the class to point out the color orange to her. There wasn't one student who raised his hand. Maybe it was afternoon and everybody was sleepy. Maybe all the kids were just so bored they couldn't dredge up the simple answer to the simple show-me-the-color-orange question, I don't know. What I do know is that I remember thinking I was surrounded by a room full of druts, so I raised my hand, and when Sister Bertha called on me, I stood up straight, away from my desk, and said, Orange is the color of an orange, Sister Bertha. And she said, What color is that? She said, Show me where in the room you see the color orange.

The way I think of it now, that day when I looked around the room, everything was in black and white like on *Ed Sullivan* or *Bonanza.* I looked all over the room, and there wasn't one stick of orange color anywhere on anything. So I said, I have something orange in the cloakroom, Sister.

Which I didn't. I was lying through my teeth, which I think is the only thing that separates the dumb from the smart. So Sister Bertha lets me go into the cloakroom.

The door swung open into the cloakroom, and soon as that door opened, the smell hit you. Bologna sandwiches, Wonder Bread, mayonnaise, mustard, boiled eggs, ripe apples, and a kind of pee smell mixed in with wet wool, and oranges.

I searched all over that room for an orange, inside every coat pocket, inside lunch pails, brown bags, but not a single orange, orange rind, or anything the color orange.

That's when I found it, and when I found it, I remember I swore to God and went down on my knees.

It was a miracle. A true miracle. The inside lining of my winter coat was orange. I slipped my coat on inside out, stood for a moment in front of the cloakroom door, took a deep breath, then *swung* the door open.

Sister Bertha! I exclaimed. Here is the color orange!

The whole rest of the day I got to wear a gold star on my forehead. Scardino must have hated that. I mean, I don't remember if he hated it or not, but, looking back, it's amazing how clear things can get.

Something else I can see clearly now. That day when I went looking for something believing I was going to find it and did. Nobody taught me that. Sure as hell didn't get that from Mom or Dad or Sis or Sister Bertha. Or the Pope. And it's got nothing to do with smart. Smart doesn't get you beyond fear, doesn't set you free.

Looking for something you know you're going to find. Ever since that day in the cloakroom, I've been doing that. I mean when the fear didn't get in the way. The secret is not to let the fear get in the way.

Still doing it. For example, just look at me out here in this night the color of ice cubes.

Miracles are out there somewhere. You just got to find them.

It wasn't very long after that Joe Scardino asked me to go home with him after school. I don't know why he asked me. Maybe even he didn't know he hated me yet. And for some reason, I don't know why, I was allowed to.

My parents never did allow anything too different. *Differnt.* That's how my parents said the word: *differnt.*

We had cows to milk, stock to feed, chickens to feed, eggs to gather, and some kind of more specific chore depending on the season, like, say, pick potatoes, shuck corn, can tomatoes, whatever, there were always chores and more chores to do, and dinner and supper to fix. Dishes to wash and dry. Always some kind of work that was so very goddamn important to do. Plus, we had to drive twelve miles to and from church and school, and that took up gasoline, so I don't know how I ended up at Scardino's house after school.

The point is, I ended up there, and what happened next is how it all started. After that day, it became a regular thing. Joe Scardino regularly beat the crap out of me over the next eleven years.

Parmesan cheese.

Joe Scardino was Italian — the only Italian I knew besides Regina Rossi, and she was in the second grade and a girl.

Plus, you got to understand that going to Joe Scardino's after school was my first time out alone. Oh, I'd done things alone before, but always with Sis. That was the problem with me, Dad said, that I was always with Sis. Sis'd say jump, and I'd say how high. And if it wasn't Sis, it was Mom. Those females turning me into a crybaby, a wuss, a girly-boy.

Hell, now that I'm looking back on it, I agree with him. It isn't that I liked them putting me in dresses and making me tea and playing paper dolls. I would've sooner been with him than Mom or my sis any day. But I ask you, did he ever step in and say, Come on, son, why don't we do something together, just you and me?

Forget it. Never in a million years.

Walking home from school felt strange. Sis and I had to take two buses, and it took over an hour and a half to get home. For Scardino it was only three or four blocks.

I don't remember much about the walk except for the elm trees we always drove by in our Buick on our way to Sunday Mass on Elm Street, and that Scardino and I wore our winter coats and caps and mittens, and that we banged our lunch pails against the elm trees and against a white picket fence. Scardino's lunch pail was square and had Black Beauty on it, and my lunch pail was the shape of a hip-roofed barn and it looked like a barn too, red with white trim around the doors and windows and a green roof.

Then all at once, Joe and I were standing in our winter coats, holding our lunch pails in front of a white house, tall and old, with a turret

After the spelling bee was over and after I'd won, I was supposed to feel good, I guess, but I didn't feel good. I felt like I was a big showoff, plus it made me really stick out.

At recess, out of the corner of my eye, I saw Joe Scardino, Vern Breck, and Michael Muley come around from behind Monsignor Cody's garage.

I was standing by the incinerator, next to the guide wire, out on the playground, on the blacktop, waiting for Sister Barbara Ann to ring the ten bells so we could go back inside.

It was spring. I remember the trees were just starting to get green — that new green that looks like lime Popsicles.

And lilacs. The lilac bushes along the side of the school. The lilac smell I remember and the wind blowing summer vacation all through the May morning.

The way Scardino and those guys walked, I knew they were walking right to me.

There was nowhere to go. Nothing around me, just summer air and open playground.

So I just stood.

If it was a movie, the camera would go spinning around and around me.

I said my favorite aspiration: Jesus Christ, son of God, have mercy on my soul.

Joe Scardino walked up close.

It was spring all right because Joe wasn't wearing a coat, and his white short-sleeve shirt was rolled up high on his big arms.

You should wear green on Thursdays, Scardino says to me, because you're so fucking queer.

Then he just hauls off.

I can still see the toe of his black leather boot headed right for my crotch. I jumped back, mostly just threw my hips back, but it was too late.

There were kids all around playing, but no one seemed to notice me down on my knees. No one noticed I was turning green.

What I mean to say is nowhere was there help.

If I told on him, Scardino would find another way to get me.

What would Jesus do? Where was Sis?

There I was, just me and my bent-over shadow on the playground pavement.

So what do I do? I make the sign of the cross and say a prayer for Scardino's soul. He was going to hell for sure.

I managed to get to Monsignor Cody's gray stucco garage wall before I went down all the way.

In my ears the school bell. Even though I couldn't see her, I knew Sister Barbara Ann was standing like always in the middle of the playground, next to the incinerator, next to the guide wire, her right arm lifted, the bell above her head. The ten rings of the bell.

Just like every other day, all the kids stopped what they were doing, stood up straight, put their arms to their sides. Then they turned and walked into Saint Joseph's School. No one talked. You weren't supposed to talk. Girls in one line, boys in another.

The morning sun was hot against the gray stucco. I put my face into the sun. The sun on my closed eyelids made everything inside red.

That's when my eyes felt a shadow.

I opened my eyes, but all I could see was sun and somebody between me and the sun.

Rig? You OK?

I knew the voice.

His real name was Allen, but he always threw up in class, three times already that year. So we called him Puke.

Puke Price.

Puke's shoulders were high up, and his hands were in his pockets. His lopsided glasses held together with tape in the middle.

Puke stuck out his hand. The morning sun on his open palm made his whole hand glow.

Jeez, Rig, Puke said, Scardino nailed you square.

Puke squatted down on his knees, his hand still out in the sun.

Jesus would have reached out and put his hand inside Puke Price's hand, but I just couldn't take Puke's hand.

He was Puke Price, and he threw up all the time, and his skin was dry and flaky. He had bad breath. He made radios for a hobby.

If I took his hand, I'd be like him.

Forget it. Never in a million years.

So I just lay there holding my nuts.

Get away from me, Price, I said. Leave me alone.

Go puke on something.

*   *   *

My ball sack swoll up. I was black and blue down there for weeks. But I never told anyone.

Said I just hurt my knee.

I mean, who would I tell?

Please excuse me for being late for class, Sister Barbara Ann, but I had to wait for my nuts to drop back down from my throat.

Excuse me, Dad, Joe Scardino kicked me in the balls, and I'm afraid I might be hemorrhaging internally, would you please help me?

Mom, could you please take a look at my balls to see if they are ever going to go back to their normal size again?

Uh, Sis? I've got a problem with my balls. They're purple. Could you give me a hand?

Bless me, Father, for I have sinned. I made some Italian creep so mad he kicked my balls black and blue.

Mea culpa, mea culpa, mea maxima culpa.

Shit.

That's exactly it.

I didn't ask for help because I thought there was something wrong with *me*.

It was my fault.

Hell, everything was my fault.

Even the Korean War was my fault.

Through my most grievous.

Fault.

Fuck.

That's exactly the word.

Fuck.

Fuck.

Just the sound of it makes what you want to say just right, doesn't it?

Fuck. Fuck. Fuck. Fuck. Fuck. Fuck. Fuck.

Myself, I didn't say *fuck* for a long time. Mostly at first because I thought it was a sin, and then later on I didn't say *fuck* because everybody else was saying it. Got so saying *fuck* was like having a gun in the gun rack in the back window of your pickup.

It was last night.

It wasn't until last night at supper that the perfectness of *fuck* hit me.

Fuck as a way to address the world.

There I was sitting at the kitchen table. I was sitting under the bright overhead light, in the same chrome chair with its yellow plastic seat and backrest, and there was Sis sitting directly across the oilcloth tablecloth with red tulips on it in front of me, her hair done up in a French twist and Scotch tape taped across her forehead holding down her bangs. Just below the Scotch tape her swooped cat's-eye glasses. Her big black eye, more blue than black. Of course, her husband, Gene, was even worse off. Sis'd broke his arm. So much for the sacrament of marriage. But that's a whole 'nother story.

To my right, there was Dad still in his same Levi's shirt rolled up to the elbows and his big hairy hands and his forearms smelling of Lava soap. Across his forehead, the line of sunburn straight, red below white above, his black hair smashed down from his Stetson cowboy hat.

On my left there was Mom in her rummage-sale cotton blouse, her jeans, her Keds. Her almond-shaped hazel eyes behind her glasses, her hair in a hairnet up in pin curls. On her forehead were the lines, three parallel lines across, that in the middle, between her eyebrows, sunk in deep folds of skin. Her clipped-to-the-quick fingernails. Her rough, red farm hands.

A rerun of Saturday night's *Lawrence Welk* was on the TV in the front room. Myron Floren was playing "The Beer Barrel Polka," and there we all were lifting our hands to our foreheads to start the sign of the cross and the Bless us, O Lord, and these Thy gifts, which we are about to receive from Thy bounty through Christ our Lord, amen.

On the table was the same four slices of roast beef. The same bottle of Heinz 57 ketchup, the mashed potatoes in the green bowl, the orange gravy boat, the canned peas in the blue bowl, the butter plate, and the bread plate with four slices of Wonder Bread on it. The salt and pepper shakers the shape of milk cans.

A family.

Just last night. The last night of the last supper I was ever going to sit through.

The four of us sitting around the kitchen table with all that's happened since two years ago last April. Beginning with what happened behind the barn, then Mom's novena to Our Mother of Perpetual Help for my soul, and the altar boy contest and the baseball game between Saint Joseph's and Saint Anthony's. The yellow tulip sticking out of my ass. The blessed summer with Flaco and Acho. The Slit Sisters. Trying to have a very good parade. *Spineless ass.* Billie Cody, our promise. Sis's wedding. Chuck diPietro. Baling hay with Georgy Girl. Smoking is praying is waiting is trusting. Thunderbird.

Then the Grand Finale. The Big Fiasco. *All* the shit hitting the big fat fan all at once. Billie Cody pregnant. The Senior Summer All Night Party. Mom chasing me with the broom. Joe Scardino, the El Camino, and the Kraft cheese truck. Grandma Queep going to the other side. The Back Door, where men like flowers. Solitary warriors of love. Granny's funeral, digging Granny's grave, the giveaway, George's long fingers touching my hand on Pine Street. My night in the city jail. George's note thumbtacked to the apple tree.

My broken fucking heart.

Which pretty much sums up the whole story, not necessarily in that order, and brings us up to date with last night.

To Dad, all it was was nigger-loving hippie communist queers, and with Mom, it was the rosary, the rosary. Pray your rosary. The Virgin said to pray the rosary.

So with Myron Floren playing "The Beer Barrel Polka" in the front room, we did what we always did. The only thing we knew how to do. We blessed our roast beef, the canned peas, the mashed spuds, the Wonder Bread, with the same old prayer that came out of us like bad breath from a sick dog, then made the sign of the cross again.

Always the meat first, always Dad first, then me, then Sis, then Mom, is the way we passed the food. Then when each of us had our piece of roast beef, each our potatoes and gravy, each our canned peas, then Dad said, Pass the ketchup. Then Sis handed Dad the ketchup. Then ketchup for me, for Sis, for Mom. Then we all picked up our forks and started eating.

Except for me. I always asked for salt, please, because it pissed Dad off that I like salt.

No differnt last night.

I said: Salt, please, and Sis looked over her swooped cat's-eye glasses at Dad first, then molded her mouth all pulled together like a sphincter, handed me the salt shaker milk can.

So I started salting the ketchup on my slice of roast beef, my canned peas, my pile of mashed potatoes with a little crater in them for the gravy.

I started getting kind of weepy because now the Champagne Lady was singing some German schmaltzy shit. Weepy too because I was never going to see my family again, see this house, my bedroom, my bed, see the barn, the swimming hole, the Mexican house, see my dog, Tramp, ever again, never see Flaco or Acho, or Billie Cody or Grandma Queep.

Never see George Serano again.

But I didn't cry because it was just too perfect for me to start crying. I promised myself I would rather bite my tongue off, would rather put the milk can salt shaker in my mouth and eat it whole before I ever cried in front of them again. So I just ate my roast beef, my potatoes and gravy, my canned peas.

I finished my supper in one, maybe one and a half minutes.

Like always, I was still hungry.

So I said to Mom, Mom, can I have another piece of bread?

Mom didn't say anything, just raised her plucked eyebrows that for Sunday morning Mass she penciled in with her eyebrow pencil, put her fork down, picked up the empty bread plate, got up from the table, walked across the blue and white tile floor to the bread drawer, her varicose veins running down to her Keds, bent over, opened the bread drawer, took out the loaf of Wonder Bread, undid the tie, took one piece of bread out, retied the tie, put one piece of Wonder Bread on the bread plate, closed the bread drawer with her knee, walked back over the blue and white tiles to the table, and set the plate in front of me.

That's when I said it inside my head: fuck.

And *fuck* was the most perfect way to say what I needed to say.

The fucking bright overhead light, the fucking yellow chairs, the fucking oilcloth tablecloth with the fucking tulips on it, the fucking four pieces of roast beef, the fucking green bowl of mashed fucking potatoes, the fucking blue bowl of canned fucking peas, the orange fucking gravy boat, the fucking bread plate, the fucking butter plate, the fucking Heinz 57 ketchup, and the fucking milk cans of salt and pepper.

My fucking sis in her stupid fucking hairdo and stupid fucking swooped glasses and her stupid fucking black eye.

My fucking father and his fucking Lava soap and fucking red line across his fucking forehead, his fucking Levi's shirt and his fucking superior hippie communist queer less-salt-than-thou fucking attitude. Come Sunday, him either in his brown fucking tweed suit and his brown tie or his blue fucking tweed suit and his blue tie, stinking up the fucking inside of the Buick and the whole fucking inside of Saint Joseph's Church with his overdose of Old Fucking Spice.

My fucking mother with her fucking bobby pins, her fucking eyebrow pencil, her fucking Red Cherries lipstick on Sunday morning, her hair fluffed out, in one of her three Sunday dresses, the blue fucking flowered one, the navy blue fucking polka dot one, or the fucking brown one with the beads along the scooped collar, her fucking dark seamed nylons, trying to hide her fucking varicose veins, on her head some goofy-looking hat with fucking nets and feathers in it.

That moment at the table at supper in the kitchen under the bright overhead light. *Fuck* is the perfect way to fucking say it that moment, me fucking me, I was sitting in the yellow fucking chair, my feet on the blue and white kitchen tiles, shoving a piece of fucking buttered Wonder Bread into my mouth.

In that silence. That drut dead quiet of a fucking silence that hangs over the table, over our family, hangs over our fucking lives, the Holy Fucking Ghost.

The silence so loud against my eardrums since my eardrums realized they could hear.

Bless us, O fucking Lord, and these Thy fucking gifts, which we are about to fucking receive from Thy fucking bounty through Christ our fucking Lord.

A-fucking-men!

Fuck.

The pavement is hot and soft on the back of my head, hot through my T-shirt and my cutoff Levi's, hot on my bare calves.

I just yelled *fuck!* so long and hard I had to lie down. Made my throat sore I yelled so hard. Right now, I'm spread-eagle on the going-west side of the road, tensing my toes, then relaxing them, tensing my ankles, then relaxing them, then my calves tensing, relaxing, like it says to do in the yoga book all the way up your body that Billie Cody gave me this morning before I left.

Five A.M. I'm buzzing on her doorbell. It's a lot to ask, to wake a friend up so early, but Billie told me she wanted to see me before I go.

No matter what, Billie said. So I figured no matter what meant no matter what time, and I figured she owed me one, so I shut the pickup off, made sure I was done with all my crying, then walked up the spiral staircase to her mother's brick home with one of those porch lights on a pole with ivy climbing around it in one of the nicer parts of Pocatello.

Billie lives with her mom. Her mom had Billie the same age Billie is now, eighteen, a year older than me. Billie's dad is a plumber and a drunk and an asshole. Her father hasn't lived with them since her mother kicked him out the beginning of May.

Billie's dad didn't take it well when he found out she was pregnant.

Wasn't long after that, Billie and I went to the Senior Summer All Night Party. That father of hers was out looking for Billie and me in his white Ford CODY PLUMBING INC. pickup.

Said he was going to kill me.

Billie's dad and my mom.

All Mom had was a broom.

Still my money was on Mom for causing the most damage.

But the Senior Summer All Night Party and Billie's dad in his Ford pickup, and my mom in the '57 Buick, both of them out for blood, is a part of the debacle of all the shit hitting the big old fan that's a whole long story coming up.

For right now, I'll just stick with how difficult it is to raise my index finger, to get my finger to stop shaking enough to hit Billie Cody's doorbell at five A.M. standing under the lamplight with the ivy growing up around the pole.

Inside, the light goes on and comes through the two rectangles juxtaposed at an angle on the front door. I open the screen door that has a curly C in aluminum on it.

C not for *Cody* but for *cunt*. An old joke with Billie and me.

The door latch and the squeaky whooshing sound of the door opening up. Mrs. Cody's hair is up in rollers, and she already has a cigarette going. She isn't as pretty as Billie, but there's something about Mrs. Cody that is beautiful. Maybe it's just because she's one of the two or three people in Pocatello who I think really like me.

Rigby John, Mrs. Cody says, like she's saying *Pope's a Catholic* or *Mormons suck.*

She takes a long drag on her cigarette, pulls the top button and but-tonhole of her blue house robe together at her neck, leans up against the doorjamb.

Mrs. Cody always looks at me not like I'm something of her daugh-ter's. She always looks her blue eyes right close in at me, like she knows something about me I don't know yet, something that's going to break my heart.

She looked at me just that way at five A.M., deeply inhaling on her cigarette. Then she does something she's never done before. She reaches out and touches me on the forehead. Her fingertips touch the place between my eyes. Where God the Father lives. Where it's always sore. Then she brushes my hair out of my eyes, her fingertips coming down my cheek, down past my lips to my chin.

Come on in, Mrs. Cody says, I'll wake Billie.

Mrs. Cody's living room had a picture window that's aluminum with a part that slides open that has a screen. The living room was painted beige, which Mrs. Cody and Billie hated, partly because Billie's father painted it that color, and partly because it was *beige* for chrissakes. Carpet was beige too.

Mrs. Cody was going to have the room painted and recarpeted. Something bright and hip, Mrs. Cody said, with maybe a swag lamp in the corner. But then Billie got pregnant, and Billie's dad went after her with a belt, so Mrs. Cody booted her husband out, and now who knows when she'll have the money.

In the living room, there's a fireplace made of thin bricks that were brown to yellow to red with beige mortar. I sat down on the hearth, looked up at the beige paramecia on Billie's living room ceiling. *Para-mecia,* the plural of *paramecium.*

Billie always said the plaster on the ceiling in their living room looked like paramecia. Billie was smart. Straight A's. She could be a rocket scientist if she wanted, but she wanted to be a beatnik. She was too smart to be a hippie. No makeup, only lipstick, always pink, and then at the end there it was red. Can't tell you how many nights Billie and I sat in the pickup parked out under the stars, listening to the ra-dio, just talking, talking, about the universe and Jean Paul Sartre, Paul Harvey, and Sigmund Freud.

That was before she got pregnant.

I lit a cigarette, threw the match into the fireplace. With the over-head light on, the shadows from the swerved glass that was screwed on over the two bare light bulbs so you didn't see the two bare light bulbs made the paramecia look more like stalactites or the sword of Damocles hanging down over my head.

So I went ahead and flipped the switch and shut the overhead light off because I didn't want anything hanging over my head and because Billie and I never had that light on when we were in there, only the fireplace.

The moonlight was bright through the aluminum picture window onto the beige carpet and onto the back of the beige armchair. The part of the shadow where the window opened, a straight line of shadow across my tennis shoes.

Billie was in the bathroom throwing up. Morning sickness, I guessed.

I was putting out my second cigarette when Billie came around the corner of the fireplace. It was dark, but still I looked right at her belly first. She was wearing my black T-shirt. It looked like a dress on her.

You couldn't really tell. I guess it takes sometimes up to five months to tell.

Billie'd had her hair cut short, bangs, a flip just under the ear. No more hair rats. New henna. The gold loops I'd bought her when she got her ears pierced.

I could tell all that in the dark. And that she'd just brushed her teeth with Crest, and that she wanted a cigarette fast, and that she was really happy to see me even so early in the morning. I knew all that in one moment. And for some reason right then, I knew the baby was a boy and that she was going to keep the baby.

Then it was Billie's voice, deep from sleep, deep from not speaking yet, and deep Simone Signoret from too many cigarettes the night before.

Hey, Rig, Billie said.

I had her cigarette ready for her, lifted the snap of orange up to her hand, the only part of her out in the rectangle of moonlight.

When she inhaled, she stepped her face out into the moonlight. The gold earrings, the moonlight in each of her dark blue eyes.

So, she said, blowing her breath out with the smoke, you're leaving.

The only other time I'd cried in front of a girl it was Billie.

When I found out she was pregnant, and at Russell's grave in Mount Moriah Cemetery. Now that I think about it, there were other times too.

Then this morning, sitting on the hearth in Billie's beige living room under the paramecia, when I heard Billie's voice, something under her voice, low in her breath, sounded like the saddest thing I'd ever hear.

My goddamn chin started doing its weird spasm thing, and my lips didn't move the way I wanted them to.

Then we were both on the beige carpet in the moonlight, my mouth up against Billie's neck, my belly going up and down next to her belly, the baby boy in there. I tried to pull away because of all the snot, but Billie wouldn't let me go. Then I cried all the harder because Billie wouldn't let me go.

When I finally settled down, I was looking into Billie's big blue eyes.

Billie had this thing with her eyes. Her tear ducts plugged up, and the inside corners of her eyes got red and puffy.

Last time I'd seen her, her eyes were almost swollen shut. In the hospital the night of the Senior Summer All Night Party.

Tear duct cancer, Billie called it.

My fingertips wiped the tears off Billie's cheeks.

It's a cure, I said.

What? Billie said.

Your tear ducts burst, I said. It's a miracle.

A fucking miracle, Billie said.

Then Billie said something about Saint Bernadette and Lourdes and holy tears that cure pregnancy. In no time at all, that weird sound was coming up from down deep, and Billie and I were laughing as hard as I'd been crying.

Mrs. Cody made breakfast. Coffee. Two eggs over easy, a big slice of ham, and hash browns. Could have spent all morning sitting in the kitchen at the green Formica table with those two jabbering away, but when the sun pushed up a gold glow of isosceles triangle onto green Formica, I knew it was time to go.

Hugs. Mrs. Cody gave me two big hugs. Then morning breath, coffee and cigarette. I watched Mrs. Cody's lips tell me to bend down so she could kiss me.

A big smooch on my forehead. Then her hands together against my cheeks, puckering my face.

Rigby John Klusener, Mrs. Cody said, you're a brave man.

Brimming with tears, her eyes. All along the bottom lid, brimming. Then Mrs. Cody's hands went over her mouth, and she ran into the bathroom. The latch of the bathroom door closed.

Billie walked me down the spiral steps. On the third step, she slipped the book into my hands. I didn't look at the title of the book because no matter what, it was going to be the saddest title of a book ever, so instead of taking the book in my hands and saying, Jeez thanks, or something dumb, I grabbed onto Billie's arm, just above the wrist, and pulled her to me and put my arms around her.

I love you, Billie said.

I went to say it too, but I stopped. Stepped back and took a good long look at her. There she stood next to the light with the ivy climbing. She'd put on her black beret. Black beret, my black T-shirt, gold earrings, red lips. Barefoot. Short in the leg and big in the bust. Another one of our jokes and what Richard Burton said about Liz.

I thought: love.

Almond-shaped hazel eyes.

Flaco, Acho, Grandma Queep, Georgy Girl.

I thought: love. Billie Cody.

So my brain let my lips say the words too.

I love you too, I said.

Then: My best to Chuck, I said. I'm so happy he's all right.

At the pickup was the loud metal-to-metal pop of the door opening. I lifted up my leg, just about ready to slide my butt up on the seat when Billie said something. I was going to act like I didn't hear her, but I went ahead and stopped. I looked one more time at Billie.

What? I said.

Thank you, Billie said, for everything.

I'm the one who should say thanks, I said.

Then, as fate would have it, the both of us at the same time said: We made a promise.

That strange sound coming from down deep inside us.

Weird thing, laughter.

My right hand up, palm out, my two fingers up in a V.

Peace was all my rubber lips could say.

*   *   *

Sunday morning you couldn't get any decent music on the radio. It was all church music and preaching. Plus, the farther I got away from Pocatello, it was just static.

Besides the radio, Dad's '63 Chevy Apache pickup was a pretty smooth drive up Highway 93. The tie rods were loose from driving around the farm, and the whole thing started to shake if you went over sixty, but it didn't scare me.

I've been scared all my life, and today was the day I promised myself I was going to stop.

I was, though, scared. That pickup just about shook itself off the road.

Driving along with no radio, fifty-five miles an hour, just the wing window open, the sun a big orange ball in the passenger side window, I started to think about a lot of things. My whole life really. But most particular what I thought about, after I quit crying after Billie Cody, was what happened this morning before I went over to her house.

Getting up at four-thirty wasn't so differnt. Darker. I put my cutoffs on one leg at a time. My green T-shirt. My red Converse high-tops laced up halfway. My backpack was ready to go. I started to sing "Ode to Billie Joe." I tried after that to get the song out of my head because it's a sad song, but forget it: once a song's in my head that's it.

I went into the bathroom, closed the door quiet, and locked it after I turned the light on. I took a good look in the mirror. My hair was starting to grow out. Like my head had a four-day beard. Wrapped around my head was my thin red tie. On top of that, I put on my porkpie hat.

My nose was as big as ever.

My face was really sun brown from living outside those days with the Indians.

Crooked bottom teeth.

Plus at four-thirty in the morning nothing looked good.

Especially if you flicked the switch on the side of the medicine cabinet and the two fluorescent bulbs lit up.

I got my toothbrush and toothpaste out of the zipper part of my backpack. Did the same thing I always did when I brushed my teeth. Said in my head: Crest has been shown to be an effective decay-preventive dentifrice that can be of significant value when used as directed in a conscientiously applied program of oral hygiene and regular professional care.

Spit. Rinsed my mouth out with water. Spit. Put back my toothbrush and toothpaste inside the zipper part.

I was just about to shut off the light when I stopped. Stopped and looked at things.

The black and white tiles on the floor. The linoleum halfway up on the wall that looked like gray tiles with a black border of tiles at the top. Really fake. The top half of the walls lavender to the lavender ceiling. The lavender window sash and matching lavender toilet cover. The around-the-bottom-of-the-toilet lavender rug and the lavender rug on the floor below the sink. The bathtub and the lavender towels hanging perfectly on the chrome towel rack on the wall at its base. The painted lavender clothes hamper with the lavender rug glued to the top of the lid. The toilet paper roll. Lavender toilet paper. Fuck.

The medicine cabinet mirror behind the door, in which, if you moved just right and stood in front of the mirror above the sink, you could see yourself go on and on forever and ever.

But this morning, when I moved the mirror just right so I could see forever, something looked differnt. I was probably as ugly as ever, but for some reason, after all that's happened over the past two years, and because I was leaving this fucking place, it was amazing.

Not just differnt. I looked *good*.

Tilted my hat, gave myself in the mirror a big Jimmy Durante smile.

Things looked differnt if you were never going to see them again.

I was never going to see myself in that mirror again.

Or see the window shade I used to pull down so there was just enough space to look in under from outside.

Sis flushing her Kotex.

Sis's hair down there.

Dad kneeling down at the toilet to pee. Kneeling.

Dad's dick.

Mom putting Johnson and Johnson baby powder under her breasts.

Mom's breasts.

The time I put Mercurochrome in the toilet water and told Mom I'd peed blood because Scardino was going to get me at school.

All those Saturday night baths we shared the same bath water.
Never again.
Never.
I shut the bathroom light off, opened the door. The way the door
sticks.

Then in the kitchen. Fuck. I couldn't believe what was in the kitchen.
Sitting at the kitchen table.
   I'm sorry it's too hard. I can't talk about that right now.
   I'll have to tell you later.
   I won't forget. I promise.

Tramp jumped in the back of the pickup when I started it up.
   My dog, Tramp. Believe me, he was the last thing I wanted to deal
with right then. Mostly what I wanted to do was give Tramp a big
kick and tell him to get the fuck out of there. But there he sat, his long
black hair, smiling, his tongue hanging out. Above each eye was a line
of orange hair, and down his nose there was another line of orange,
then a patch of red-orange on his chin, and his whiskers were red-
orange too. Red-orange hair just on the tips of his ears. Looked like
he had a red-orange face on top of his black face.
   His right front paw was red-orange too. That right paw of Tramp's
was really something. He always poked it in the air when you sat
down close to him and you cleared your throat and you lowered your
voice and you started talking about life, trying to make sense out of it.
   His tongue hung out, he held his lips so you could see his teeth, and
that red-orange paw started going to town with the poking, poking.
Sometimes I thought I ought to stick a pen between his toes and hold
up a piece of cardboard so he could write down in dog language what
his paw was trying to say.
   Or stick a baton between his toes and put on some John Philip
Sousa so he could poke to beat the band.
   Of course, then there was his tail. Another piece of red-orange.
   When his right paw started poking away, never failed, that tail of
his started up too, flip flop flip flop, back and forth, just banging
away.
   An endless source of amusement, Tramp and his paw and his tail.
   Can't tell you how many times I've sat myself down next to Tramp,

cleared my throat, lowered my voice, and said something like: Tramp, do you think God is dead? Or: Tramp, do you think communism is a threat to the American way of life?

Sure as hell, Tramp got that look on his face, his tongue came out and he held his mouth so you could see his teeth, and then up went the red-orange paw, poking the air, then his tail, bam bam bam.

Tramp was just a pup when I found him up at the feedlot. All feet and head and hair. I knew Dad would shoot him so I threw a bunch of gravel at him and called him a son of a bitch, threw more gravel, yelled louder.

Tramp put his tail between his legs and took off running and yelping.

I thought for sure he was gone, the way he ran.

But the next day when I went up to the feedlot, Tramp's red-orange face over his black face poked out from around the corner of a hay stack.

That's the first time I sat Tramp down and tried to warn him about Dad. Said: Tramp, it's probably best for you to get your ass out of Dodge.

That's the first time I saw him start in with the tongue and the teeth, the poking-at-the-air paw, and the tail flip-flop, bam bam-bam, back-and-forth thing.

Dad let me keep Tramp because I told Dad Tramp was a good cow dog, and he was too. Had the instinct right off. A natural heeler, probably an Australian shepherd mix.

But there had been other dogs. Dad said I could keep them too.

Every day when I got home from school the first two weeks, I expected to see Tramp's dead carcass lying out on the trash heap in the dump hole next to the feedlot.

But every day I came back, there he was. Tramp. His orange face on his black face, just smiling and happy to see me.

But I still wasn't sure. My last dog, Nikki, a terrier mix, I can't tell you how much I loved that dog. Two full months I had that dog.

Then one day, out of the blue, Nikki just started shaking and foaming at the mouth. I picked him up. His body was stiff like I'd picked up a piece of wood. I put him in the back of the pickup and drove like hell to Doc Hayden's.

Nikki was dead by the time I got there.

Doc Hayden said strychnine.

Believe me, in my world, there's plenty of men mean enough to poison a little dog.

But there was only one man who did it.

Early Sunday morning, all I wanted to do was get out of there fast, and there was Tramp in the back of the pickup. His tongue hanging out, smiling, ready to go for a ride.

I opened the tailgate, hooked the chains at both sides, sat down, dangled my legs over. Moonlight all over on the dark night. The moon on Tramp's black hair, a shine.

I took a breath, leaned over. Put my arm around my dog. My face in his face, on his face. I looked Tramp right in the eyes.

I told him: Tramp, I'm going somewhere where you can't go.

His big old pink tongue poked out his mouth. Tramp started panting, his lips the way so you could see his teeth.

In his eyes, you could see he knew something was up.

Then there went his paw, his tail.

That and the piano that morning about broke my fucking heart.

I hugged him big, put my face down in his hair, and smelled it. I scratched his ears, tickled his chin the way he liked. Nobody loves you the way your dog loves you.

I stood up, called Tramp down out of the pickup. He jumped down, walked obedient alongside of me to the pickup door. When I opened the pickup door, he thought he was going to get up front in the cab with me. His face went from obedient to happy just like that. I put my body in front of the door.

Sit! I said. Tramp, sit down!

And he sat. Tramp was a good dog.

Now stay! I said.

Tramp kept sitting, smiling, his tongue hanging out. I slid my butt up onto the seat. Tramp's tail back and forth, bam bam bam.

Tramp kept sitting while I started the pickup. He kept sitting while I put in the clutch, put it into first. He kept sitting while I drove slow on past him.

Any second, Tramp couldn't stand it any longer, so I rolled down the window. Said in my deep mean voice: Tramp! Sit down! Stay!

Tramp was a good dog.

I drove past the workshop, past the wood granary, past the light pole. Tramp kept sitting as I idled along the driveway past the pole fence, the wagon wheel, the Austrian Copper rose, to Tyhee Road.

Tramp in the rearview mirror, sitting, the moon a shine on his long black hair, his tail back and forth, bam bam bam.

When I got onto the tarmac of Tyhee Road, I floored the gas pedal.

A quarter mile up the road, in the rearview mirror, the moon on Tramp's long black hair, Tramp beating it around the corner like a bat out of hell.

That's when the pickup started to shake.

It was five miles down Philbin Road at the stand of cottonwoods when I couldn't see Tramp anywhere in the moonlight in the rearview mirror anymore.

Then I drove to Billie Cody's, and I've told you everything that happened at her house.

Out on the open highway, I was doing fine, just fine. The sunrise was orange and yellow and so bright I needed sunglasses. The pickup was running good, I was safe, fine out of there, no problem. My arm was out the window, the wing window open so the morning air was coming right at my face.

Then I turned on the radio again to see if I could find something. I found something all right.

Clear as a bell.

If you're going to San Francisco, be sure to wear some flowers in your hair.

So many sad songs.

I cried all the way to Twin Falls.

Parked the pickup on Norby Street. On the corner of Norby and South Sward.

Started walking southwest. Only time I stopped was to pick this daisy.

So that's how I got here. Out here where there's nothing. Nothing but desert. Out here where everything's alive. Nothing but me and this night and this moon and stars so clear it's a Christmas card for "We Three Kings of Orient Are." Sagebrush. The smell of sagebrush and hot pavement and my own armpits. A ribbon of pavement shiny to over the horizon, and just now, out of my backpack, I pulled out my porkpie hat, brushed it off, and put it on. Put the moon behind me, lifted my chin up, and now the shadow of my head looks like my head is an alien being's big round head.

Alien.

You can always tell how you're feeling by how your shadow looks.

PART I

Unforgettable

1 The Early Days

BACK WHEN I WAS A KID, back in the early days, there was this one afternoon. I was looking out the front-room window. Blue sky was everywhere up above, the bright sun shining down, not a cloud. The wash on the wash line was flapping in the breeze. It wasn't the wash I was looking at, though. It was the shadows of the wash on the grass. There was one shadow in particular that turned into a magic black dog all afternoon doing circus tricks.

That shadow was everything to me. An ordinary white T-shirt hanging from a pair of clothespins turning into a magic black dog on the yellow-green grass was nothing short of a miracle. When you're living in a skinny white house in the middle of an alfalfa field in the middle of Idaho and all your family knows how to do is work, you learn to look for miracles. Anything that breaks the routine, anything that comes along and makes you see what's in front of your eyes a little differnt, is magic.

Myself, I've been looking for magic my whole life. Still looking. That's exactly why I'm out here on Highway 93. I had to leave Pocatello because everything I knew — my home, my family, my friends — just up and ran out of magic the way you run out of gas. All that's left to do now is stick my thumb out and start walking.

I'm not saying it's easy. Hell, I've been crying for two weeks now, still crying, wish to Christ I'd stop. Crying for Mom mostly. Sis and

Dad will be all right. I sure as hell won't miss Scardino, may he rest in peace. I'm crying for Billie Cody too. Who the hell's going to make me laugh? But most of all, it's Georgy Girl. Georgy Girl's the dark hole in my heart.

It's hard to leave your whole life. Whatever your life was. And any life, even my life, had its moments.

Especially in the beginning, before my brother, Russell, was born and before he died, before Dad bulldozed down our skinny white house, the early days, when the Portneuf River still flowed through our farm. When my mother's eyes were the only show in town, almond-shaped and hazel. What was happening in those eyes was usually what was happening in the world. And in the early days, what the world was, was me.

Mom's hazel eyes were gold when she was happy. When her eyes were gold I could find myself inside them. In those early days, I did a lot to keep her eyes gold. One time I remember I told Sis I was born in a trunk in the Princess Theater in Pocatello, Idaho. That's not the truth, of course. I was born in a hospital like everybody else. Saint Anthony's Hospital, but I said that to Sis because Mom was listening, and I thought it would make Mom laugh, which it did.

You got to understand, sometimes on the farm, finding magic was so hard you had to make the magic up yourself. A *vivid imagination*, Mom called it. Dad called it lying. He was always on my ass for showing off. Making a spectacle of myself. Me, I never saw it as lying. I was just making the world a more livable place. For her. And then of course, because of her, for me.

Plus I *was* born there, in Pocatello. The Princess Theater wasn't there anymore by the time I came on the scene. By the time I came around to it, it was the Chief Theater, and JUDY GARLAND was in smaller blue capital letters under THE WIZARD OF OZ, which was in big red capital letters on the marquee. I was wearing my brown suit just like my dad's suit with a matching hat like Dad's too, like men used to wear in the thirties and forties. The day was cold and bright, and Sis held my hand and helped me sound out the big red capital letters. That's how I learned the letter Z. Neon red and yellow arrows were going around and around the marquee, and people were everywhere. Mom bought Sis a Cup o Gold candy bar and me Milk Duds. Inside the theater it was dark. I sat next to Mom, and Sis was on the other side of Mom, and I was so little that in the seat my Buster Brown shoes stuck out right in front of me.

When the curtains opened, it was a black-and-white Dorothy and Toto and Auntie Em on the screen. A ways into the movie, in a moment, my mother put her hand inside my hand. She leaned over to me. Her perfume. The sound of her dress against her nylons.

Now watch closely, Mom whispered. This next part is magic.

When I looked back up at the screen, the black and white had turned to color.

Magic. That's just what it was. Magic.

Movies and music and church. Before Russell, mostly that's what I remember. Not so much the things themselves, but shadows, the way they were inside me, the magic of them.

Since we lived twelve miles from town, it took a lot of gas to get there and back, so we used the gas for church. Every Sunday, church — nine o'clock Mass, come rain or sleet or snow, hell or high water. The fourth commandment. Remember that thou keep holy the Sabbath day. Seven o'clock Sunday Mass during harvest.

When we did go to movies, which was hardly ever, usually it was just Mom and me and Sis after Tuesday evening Mother of Perpetual Help devotions. Tuesday evening devotions we could kill two birds with one stone, church *and* the movies, plus save on gas. But only if it was a decent movie that the *Idaho Catholic Register* said wasn't condemned and was suitable for kids to go to too, which it hardly ever was.

Before Russell, besides *The Wizard of Oz,* the only movies I can remember are *Bambi, Snow White and the Seven Dwarfs, Cinderella, Dumbo, Pinocchio,* and *Peter Pan.*

Seven years and seven movies.

Still, though, those movies were enough.

The magic feeling all through me when we walked under the bright flashing neon marquee into the foyer of the Chief Theater with its thick, curvy adobe walls. The strange Indian blanket carpet, red and orange and brown and yellow under your feet. The rows of candy bars in the fluorescent-light glass case, the smell of popcorn, the sound of ice cubes, fizzing Coke. Then through the double doors into the theater and the sloping corridor. The big red velvet curtain with gold fringe hanging in folds with the spotlights on it. Everything around you always so dark at first. Then only when you were in your chair, your butt square on the mohair cushion, did your eyes start to see the paintings of the Indians shooting buffalo with bows and arrows on the walls, and the little alcove on each side, with the red and green lights, that looked like a Romeo and Juliet balcony with a wrought-iron fence.

Magic all around you everywhere waiting for the movie to start. Magic when the lights went dark. The dimmer the lights, the more the something inside so covered up and careful in you came up and out. Sitting next to Mom, my chest got big and full of air, like I was smart and rich and welcome in the world.

The newsreel, all the people in the faraway world doing cool stuff. Then Daffy Duck, Woody Woodpecker, Porky Pig, Bugs Bunny, Mickey Mouse. Then the movie.

There's No Place Like Home. Mirror, Mirror, on the Wall. Bambi lost in the forest fire without his mother. Pinocchio a real boy. Cinderella's asshole stepsisters. Tinkerbell dust.

To this day, if I had one wish, I'd be flying.

Looks like my thumb out on Highway 93, waving down the next truck, is the closest I'm going to get.

Music's another way magic came into our life. My mother was born to make music. She could play the piano by ear. Mom was the sixth child and the fourth daughter of Joseph and Mary Schmidt. Joseph Schmidt, her father, died in 1933, the middle of the Great Depression. Mom was thirteen.

All Mom's older sisters got to take piano lessons because it wasn't the Depression yet, but when it came to be Mom's turn for piano lessons, there wasn't any money and her father was already sick.

Mom tells the story this way. She couldn't sleep because she kept having piano dreams. In her dreams, her sister Alma was playing the piano and Mom was watching her. Then, like in dreams the way things usually go, all of a sudden it wasn't Alma but Mom who was playing the piano.

Mom got up slow and quiet and slipped out of bed. She was just a girl, maybe nine or ten. It was in the middle of the night, but she had something important to figure out. She walked slow, step by step down the stairs, through the dining room and into the parlor, where nobody could sit except when there was company. Mom pulled the piano stool out, opened up the piano, and just like in her dream Mom started playing "A Bicycle Built for Two."

It wasn't until Grandma and Grandpa and all Mom's brothers and sisters were standing around her at the piano — all of them in their nightgowns and nightshirts, Grandpa holding a candle up because they didn't have 'lectricity — that Mom woke up and realized she was really playing the piano and it wasn't a dream.

Mein Gott im Himmel, my grandfather said. *Kleine Mary spielt das Klavier.*

And that's the way it was after that. All you'd have to do is sing a few lines for Mom, and just like magic there she'd be playing the song for you.

Back in the early days, it was long afternoons playing on the brown flowered carpet with my Lincoln Logs or my Tinkertoys or Bill Ding, and Mom playing her old piano, burnt black up one side and smelling of burnt hardwood, the Steinway, on the round piano stool you could sit on and spin. Wintertime, the oil stove in the front room too hot to touch with the porcelain pan of water on top. Down the hallway, in the kitchen, fire in the cookstove, and the kindling, pine sap, cut wood, and chunks of coal stacked by the stove. Always a fire in the cookstove so the pipes didn't freeze in the kitchen sink. The door open to the bathroom, always open unless you were in there, so as to keep those pipes from freezing too. When Mom was playing the piano, you didn't want to go to the bathroom. Farther down the hallway, other rooms, Mom and Dad's bedroom and the bedroom I shared with Sis, during the day the doors closed. Way too cold to go in there except to sleep. Even in the winter, though, with frost on the windows, Mom's playing could warm up the whole house.

Spring, the whole world smelled like lilac from the big old lilac bush next to the front porch. During the summer I wouldn't be on the rug but perched on the open windowsill. Like an oven inside the house. Outside at night, crickets and frogs. Inside, Kool-Aid and maple nut ice cream. At night, the smell of chamomile, fresh alfalfa, and water in the ditch. Thunderstorms at night and flash lightning like the world was some 'lectric fuse box gone haywire. One hailstorm so hard it broke the front-room window.

Always, though, and ever, those early days before Russell, come hell or high water, a hundred degrees or below zero, there were always days when Mom played her songs on her piano. Her feet whizzing back and forth on the pedals, her hands over the keys. Mom's hair pulled back from her face, her chin up, her almond-shaped hazel eyes mostly gold, a smile busting through.

Outside the house is where Dad lived. Dad only came in the house at dinner and supper to visit us, then spent the night. Machines were out there with him. The Johnny pop-pop tractor, the combine. Out past our square of lawn, out past the fence, past the gas pump, the acres of yard that spread out to the red brick barn. Next to the barn, Dad's tin square toolshed, during the day the sun so bright on it you could not look.

Lying on the front-room floor, flat on the flowered brown carpet, Tinkertoys all around, Sis with her paper dolls, Mom on the round stool playing "Cruising Down the River," my father was out there in the big world making things go. I liked to think he was circling us. The way I pictured it, our skinny white house was in the middle of a field, and Dad was out there on the fence line on the tractor, going around and around, each time around he was closer to us in the house. In front of the tractor, dry, flat, tan earth. Behind, big brown chunks of piled-up earth. The smell of the earth dark and full of worms. Around and around, behind Dad's plow a dark shadow circling. The seagulls flying about his head screaming and squawking as if the seagulls were thoughts of his that no one knew, that made him so far away. When Dad finally came in the back door, the field was no longer tan or flat or dry. The field was all shadow, and our house was in the middle of dark brown chunks of earth smelling like he smelled, cow manure and horse piss and sour milk and straw.

Those early days, all my chores were inside the house. My main job was to put the forks on the left on the napkin next to the plate. Sis set the rest of the table. Then after the meal, Mom and Sis cleared the table while Dad had a Viceroy and his cup of tea with two sugars. Mom washed the dishes while Sis and I wiped them dry. Besides making our beds every morning and cleaning up our room, that was it for our chores in the early days, except for on Saturdays, when it was our special job to dust the piano. Both Sis and I had dust rags. Mom poured a capful of Olde English furniture polish onto each of our dust rags, and Sis and I made the piano and the round piano stool shine.

The basement of the house was another special place. Above the coal-room door, lying across on two stuck-out nails, was Dad's fishing pole. Next to the coal-room door and under Dad's fishing pole was Mom's old steamer trunk. Dark, brass-bound, the two brass latches locked in place. It was the kind of trunk that stood on its end. When you opened it up, one side was little drawers and the other side was a stainless-steel rod you could pull out to hang dresses on.

Inside Mom's steamer trunk was like its very own room in the house. Not just a room. The steamer trunk was a whole world. A magic world that existed right alongside the everyday world.

The dress I remember most is the green plaid. Big plaid, maybe some brown in the plaid. There was a blue taffeta dress too, robin's-egg blue, that made a sound when you touched the taffeta or when you walked in the dress. Sis kept the jewels in the top little drawer. Two rhinestone necklaces, a pearl necklace, and a cameo on a gold strand. A gold ring. The scarves were in the second little drawer. Two pairs of high heels. A brown pair that were scuffed suede with open toes and black high heels with an ankle strap. There were hats too. Those strange kind of hats like in LeVine's with veils and feathers that Joan Crawford and Gene Tierney and Hedy Lamarr and Aunt Alma used to wear. In the third little drawer was the red purse with the gold latch and the pair of white gloves. And lipstick. Lipstick was in the fourth little drawer. Red. Ruby Scarlet. In the fifth little drawer was the Avon perfume in the bottle that was shaped like the Eiffel Tower.

When the trunk was open, and the drawers were open, the Eiffel Tower smell hit you and a light spread out magic all around you, onto you, got inside you, magic color like in *The Wizard of Oz*.

I was born in that trunk.

Scintillatingly gorgeous, Sis said.

Scintillatingly gorgeous, I said it too.

One afternoon, Mom had made cocoa and cinnamon toast and cut the toast into triangles. Sis was sitting on the green davenport and wearing the blue taffeta dress and the white hat that sat on the top of her head with net on it and a rhinestone pin. I was in the green armchair in the green plaid dress and the shiny black velvet hat with the flower brooch. Mom was on the davenport too wearing the black straw sunbonnet with the wide brim and the black lace shawl over her normal housedress. Her dangly rhinestone earrings.

Mom was talking away, sipping on her cocoa, the plate with her toast on it balanced on her knees. I was right at home with my cocoa and cinnamon toast, scintillatingly gorgeous in my green plaid dress with my mother and my sister. Those were the best of days. Magic in so many ways, but mostly because the world that we created was a secret we couldn't tell Dad.

Every Sunday we drove the twelve miles to town to Saint Joseph's Church, the house of God. Dad opened the big old wood door, the long creak of the brass hinges. The holy water font, where you dipped your fingers and made the sign of the cross. Then your hands folded, you followed Mom and Sis past the stained-glass windows through patches of blue and green and red and gold to the pew. The smell of frankincense and myrrh, the wood pews, the waxed tiled floor. You genuflected because you were standing in front of God. God up there on the altar, inside a gold box that Monsignor Cody unlocked and took the chalice out of during Mass, and sometimes put God, the Bread of Life, into the monstrance that was all gold with rays of gold spraying out in all directions, and Monsignor pointed God at the whole church, the organ playing, the choir singing, the altar boys waving the smoke of the censers and ringing the bells, and everyone in the congregation, even Dad and tall, skinny Ott Lattig, who were the ushers, beat their hearts and said, Lord, I am not worthy.

There was nothing like it. That special moment of the consecration of the Mass. No movie, no music, not even Mom's piano, nothing at all like the moment during Mass when the Word became flesh. Nothing quite like my mother in that moment when Monsignor Cody said: This is my body. This is my blood.

Mom's head bowed, her fist beating her breast, saying, Lord God, I am not worthy.

God of God, Light of Light, true God of true God, who gave us His only son, begotten, not made, of one being with the Father, by Whom all things were made, and for our salvation came down from heaven. And was made flesh by the Holy Ghost and the Virgin Mary and was made man and crucified, died, and was buried. And on the third day He rose again according to the Scriptures. And ascending into heaven, He sitteth at the right hand of the Father. And He shall come again in glory to judge the living and the dead.

Nothing, no Wizard of Oz, no Tinkerbell dust, no scintillating magic at all in the world like the miracle that happened at Mass when the water changed into wine, and the wine changed into blood, and bread became the flesh of God, and my mother was transformed.

Her high heels with the holes in the toes, her nylons with the seams in them, her violet dress with the orchid all the way down the front, her felt hat that sat on the back of her head, the net in front, the pheasant feather, a saucy whip on the side. Her eyes, my mother's almond-shaped hazel eyes, only only at that moment always soft and full of love, the glory of beholding God in them, her face all aglow like a saint with a circle above her head.

Not even piano playing could get you that.

When she played the piano, Mom was happy. At the consecration of Mass, Mom was holy.

I don't know which of those Moms I loved the most.

There were other Moms too. There was pedal-to-the-metal Mom who drove the Buick seventy miles an hour to church. You never could catch her just sitting. Always kept herself busy. When she wasn't cooking or cleaning, or baking cookies or pies or cakes, she was sewing a dress for Sis or for her, or she was darning socks, canning, or doing embroidery. During harvest, Mom helped out driving the beet truck. Then there was rosary Mom, more holy Mom, sometimes twice or three times a day.

But it wasn't so much that all these Moms were differnt because of all the differnt things she did. It was something else. What made Mom differnt was the same thing that made the world magic. All of a sudden, out of the blue, something appeared in her eyes there's no way you could figure out.

Like I said, in the early days, how the world was, which means how I was, was how my mother's eyes looked. So what I was feeling was what she was feeling and I never could keep up with all that I felt.

What kept Mom and Dad together is something I never figured out. Dad was so differnt from her. I can't remember one time he made her laugh. Not a lick of music in him. At Mass he was the usher along with tall, skinny Ott Lattig. Dad just stood there all through Mass, even during the consecration, his feet spread, his arms behind him, at parade rest like a soldier. You never could tell what he was thinking, unless he was mad.

When he was in the house, all he ever did was sit at the table and wait for her to feed him, and then when the meal was over, after she got him his hot tea, Dad lit up a Viceroy and went back to his *Idaho State Journal*.

When it was just me and Sis, when Dad wasn't around, sometimes Mom would let loose on Dad. How he came from a family of drunks, and he was a hick and he never took her anywhere and all she did was work work work.

The way I figure it, it was the Catholic Church. Mom and Dad were married in the Catholic Church. That's a life sentence. The sacrament of matrimony. Duty. Honor and obey your husband, all of that dogma crap.

Still, though, every now and then when Mom was talking, in her eyes, you could tell they hadn't always been that way.

Take for example, her favorite song, "Million Dollar Baby." You should have heard Mom play that song on her old burnt piano. The reason it was her favorite song was because Mom was working at Kress's five-and-dime when she married Dad, so you got to figure there was something special there.

In Kress's five-and-dime the windows were curved and when you opened one of the big double doors edged in brass, the smell of wood floor hit you, and knickknacks, oilcloth tablecloths, tin, the smell of aluminum pans.

The way Mom told the story, she was working her last day at Kress's. Dad drove over from Blackfoot to pick her up because the next day they were going to get married. She said Dad looked like a dream come true, so handsome in his Stetson hat and his new jacket and boots. When she saw him walk in the door she had butterflies in her stomach. It was mostly women who worked in Kress's, salesgirls, and so Dad walking into Kress's was quite a sight for all those unmarried young women. Everyone thought he looked like Fred MacMurray, Mom said, so when he walked in, there was a big sigh and giggles all around. Dad walked up to Mom, who was standing behind the table of glassware and dishes. That's when all the lights went off in the store, and all the salesgirls started singing *I Found a Million Dollar Baby in a Five and Ten Cent Store*.

I was even selling china, Mom said.

As soon as the lights went off and she heard the girls singing, Mom ducked down behind the table. And left Dad standing in the aisle all alone.

I'd say that was a romantic story, a sweet kind of story, but if there's magic in it, it's a muted kind of magic. Reminds me of the only other story I know of their courtship, a story I overheard from my bedroom when my folks had company. It too comes with a song. From the kitchen, there was a bunch of laughing, then clear as a bell, I could hear Mom:

Joe and I had been out on a couple of dates, Mom said. We were driving along between Shelley and Blackfoot in Joe's dad's Buick, listening to the radio. Then a beautiful song came on the radio. It was "Melody of Love." I said to Joe, So do you even like me a little bit?

Joe pulled the car over to the side of the road, pulled on the hand brake, and said: Like you? I think I *love* you.

I never told that story to anyone, not ever. Not even Sis. My mother a flat forty acres of Idaho field, Dad's tractor on her circling, the shadow folds of earth turning behind him, seagulls screaming. It was my secret. My secret rested in my chest, right next to my heart and was sore there. Weird magic, unspeakable.

Things are differnt now, though. A lot differnt. I can speak out loud and clear that dreaded sinful anti-Catholic word.

Sex. My mother and my father and sex. Holy shit. Can you imagine. I mean, they had three kids, right?

Those days before Russell was born and before he died, the older I got, the more I started going out into Dad's world. Mostly it was my new chores that got me outside. Sis and I had to feed and water the chickens and gather the eggs and slop the kitchen garbage to the pigs. Those chores might sound easy, but they weren't. Carrying a five-gallon bucket of water from the house past the toolshed to the barn ain't no treat. Sis and I and later just me carrying that five-gallon bucket. After I filled the bucket, I picked the bucket up and counted to fifty, and walked fast. Then I set the bucket down. Usually where I set the bucket down was right in front of Dad's tin, square toolshed. So bright in the sun, you had to shade your eyes. Inside in there the air was filled with hooks. Grease and gasoline and forty-gallon drums of oil. Wrenches of all kinds and sizes and one big ball-peen hammer, and an anvil I finally lifted to my chest when I was fifteen. Gathering the eggs was no picnic either. You had to move those old clucks off their eggs, and they'd peck at you. Chicken poop all over the eggs.

Sometimes, after supper, I'd go out and sit and watch Dad milk the cows. I never said much to him, at least that I can remember. I just sat on a milk stool in the corner by the milk cans and under the red portable radio. I was his audience. Dad making things go, it was something to watch him move. He was like a big cat but not as smooth, maybe more like a small horse, yet a horse you had to be careful of. He had the Holstein cows lined up in the barn, the shiny stainless-steel milk machines pumping away, their suction cups on the cows' teats, the pump sound, the smell of warm, raw milk and cow shit and straw, my father.

What I knew about the farm outside our house and yard was what I knew about him. On the other side of the fence, the gas pump, and beyond the gas pump, the yard, acres of gravel stretched out so trucks could pull in and turn around. Dad's bright, square, tin toolshed. The red brick barn. Inside the barn, the saddle room, the chicken coop, the calf pen, and the stanchions where Dad milked the cows. Out the back door of the barn, the pigpen, the screaming pigs who ate little boys when they were bad. The spud cellar we weren't allowed to go into. Somewhere out there too, the railroad cars. Then the Portneuf River. We had to stay clear of the Portneuf. Then beyond, somewhere far away in the distant fields, was the Mexican house, and out even farther, at the end of our farm, on the other side of the barbwire fence and on the other side of the road, on three sides of our farm was the reservation, where the Indians lived.

Dad had a map. The map was in a big book with lots of colorful maps in it. One day, under the bright 'lectric light bulb hanging over the kitchen table, Dad plopped the map book down on our kitchen table.

'Lectric, like differnt. That was the way Mom and Dad talked.

His big hands flipped through the pages. On one page Dad stopped, put his head down close, and with his big index finger and wide, heavy nail, the line of grease under the nail, Dad pointed to Sis and me where our farm was.

Sis leaned up on the table with her elbows. Across the table, I stood up on the chair and leaned in too on my elbows like Sis.

On the map it was yellow and it was red. Dad said the yellow was where Bannock County was and where the white people lived, and the red was the reservation, where the Indians lived.

Then Dad slew his eyes up at me and Sis. His dark black eyes, Roosky Gypsy eyes, my mother called them. His black eyebrows, his sunburned face, and the line across his forehead where the hat line was.

Look here, Dad said. You see where the yellow Bannock County pokes out into this square yellow patch into the red reservation?

Sis leaned down even closer. I did too.

On the map, right under Dad's finger, at the end, right where the line of grease under his nail was, I could see yellow Bannock County and how in just that one place it poked out a yellow square into all that red.

That's our farm, Dad said. Only one side of us connected to Bannock County. All the other sides, all three of them, right up against injuns.

Surrounded by them, Dad said. Surrounded by injuns on three sides.

Something fast inside me, some way my heart beat. My hands went over my chest and belly. What was fast inside my heart when Dad said *Surrounded by injuns* wasn't only fear. It was magic.

Sis is the one who asked the question, not me.

Sis's dark eyes like Dad's. Shirley Temple hair. Sis wrinkled up her nose.

Are injuns the same as Mexicans? Sis asked.

In the kitchen, under the 'lectric light bulb, Mom somewhere at the sink or at the cookstove, her hair flying, her back to us, bent over a bowl, beating something in the bowl.

Dad leaned back in his chair. Out of his Levi's shirt pocket, he pulled a pack of Viceroys. The light bulb light on the VO5 made his black hair shine. Dad pulled a Viceroy out of the pack, put the pack back into his pocket. He reached across the cookstove, grabbed the box of kitchen matches, slid open the box, took out a match, and struck the match against the cookstove. He held the flame to the end of his Viceroy.

The way the smoke curled up into his nose. Dad reached back over to the cookstove, tossed the match into the flames.

Indians are a lot like Mexicans, Dad said, because they're dirty and drive old cars and have dark skin and black hair and don't care about themselves and get drunk.

The cigarette smoke came out Dad's mouth and nose at the same time.

Niggers are like Mexicans and Indians, Dad said, only worse, a lot worse. They ain't got no morals, and they like to get drunk too, real drunk. That's how the Pocatello House over in Niggertown got burnt down and how your mom ended up with that burnt piano.

So that was Dad. Still, though, I wanted his attention and even something more. What that something was I didn't know because I never got more than bits and pieces of it. One of them, one of the most important, happened when I was around five or six. It was suppertime and the screen door slammed and Dad was inside the house again big as ever. He took off his boots in the kitchen and grabbed the *Idaho State Journal* off the table. Usually I'd steer clear of him as best I could, but that day for some reason, just as he stepped into the hallway from the kitchen, I stepped into the hallway from my bedroom. There we were, the both of us on the red linoleum surrounded by the wallpaper with the butterflies and dice. I almost ducked back in my door, but it was too late. So I put my head down and kept walking and then moved close to the wall. As he passed, my father laid his hand on my head. Just his two fingers right on the top. I stopped dead in my tracks. Dad kept going.

For the longest time after that, I waited for Dad to touch me on my head again. A couple of times I practically threw myself at him. But I can count the times of his touch on one hand. And he never did touch the top of my head again.

Another time I remember Mom was at the cookstove, and the windows in the kitchen were fogged up. Dad was in the bathroom standing in front of the mirror that was above the sink. He was just in his jockey shorts and his guinea T-shirt. The bright bare light bulb above the sink shined down onto the white of his arms.

Mom told me once that Dad didn't like his upper arms. He thought they were too skinny. So he never wore short-sleeve shirts, only long-sleeve, sometimes rolled up to the elbow.

The hot water was running on a white washrag inside the sink. The steam from the water fogged up the mirror even more than the hot water of his bath. Dad's hands were in the sink, wet black hairs, holding the white washrag, letting it soak in the hot water.

Dad wrung out the washrag with his hands, then bent down and laid the washrag over his face. When he stood back up straight, he looked down at me. Only his black eyes down at me. I was standing in the doorway on the red linoleum floor, the butterflies and dice all around me on the wallpaper.

His mouth moved under the washrag. The washrag sucked in and blew out as he sang: *You dirty little bugger, does your mother know you're out? With your hands in your pockets and your shirttail out.*

That's when he came at me, in his white washrag mask, his hands pressing the washrag to his face, his breath pushing the washrag in and out.

You dirty little bugger.

Screaming, ecstatic, the mysterious man-monster who was after me. Mom was standing at the cookstove. I grabbed onto Mom's solid leg, my head buried in the folds of her dress.

My body ached in the places where I knew he would grab me, tickle me. My ribs. Under my chin. In my armpits.

Then: Let's do it again, Daddy. Say that again, Daddy. Chase me again, Daddy.

Just once more.

Another time, just before noon. Dad was lying on the front-room floor. The red portable radio was in the kitchen window and the cowboy was singing, Melt your cold, cold heart. Mom told me to go wake Dad up. Dad on the front-room floor, his Levi's shirt and jeans and cowboy boots taking up that whole side of the room.

Dad, I said. Dinner's ready.

Dad started snoring. My feet moved across the flowered brown carpet. Dad's body got bigger and bigger. His snores louder. My feet were right next to his arm that was under his head.

Dad, I said, Mom said dinner is ready.

My hand went down slow to touch his shoulder.

That's when he jumped. He's playing, I thought, and I laughed. He grabbed me, and he was playing, and the parts of me where he'd tickle, my belly, my sides, my armpits, under my chin, ache. His Lava soap smell, dirty socks. He pulled me around, pushed me down, and I was lying under him. The whole great body of him on top of me, the pearl buttons of his Levi's shirt pocket smashing against my face. No air, no room for breath.

My hand reached out to the corner of the brown carpet with the flowers on it. If I could reach the corner of the brown flowered carpet, I'd be OK. There was only the weight of him pressing me dead and the corner of the brown flowered carpet. I was screaming, but I didn't know.

Mom's almond-shaped hazel eyes and Sis standing in the hallway door.

Good Lord, Joe, Mom said. Do you have to be so rough on the boy?

Bits and pieces scattered like crumbs that only increased a yearning. A yearning for something more I didn't know from him. And another time, a time special not because he touched me, but because I was with him, when he might have forgot I was even there, when I saw a side of my father I didn't know existed. Just me alone with my father in his pickup out in the world. Snow and ice on the windshield. The windshield wipers, the blast of the heater. My stocking cap, my mittens, my galoshes, only my face sticking out. Outside our skinny white house, no Mom, alone in the cold, white, snowy world with the big man who lived with us, the mystery. At any moment anything could happen. My hands folded in my mittens, I sat as far across the seat I could get from him.

Chains on the tires of the pickup. Clatters against the fenders. Past the spud cellar, Dad turned the steering wheel left, shifted down into first. Even back then only a child, I watched him shift the gears. Ahead of us a big drift of snow. Dad gunned the engine and let out a yahoo. I smiled and probably laughed. Everything amazed me about him, everything about him was big.

Out the side window, the three railroad cars. I didn't know the railroad cars stored grain. The railroad cars were just more of his mystery, a freight train through our farm. It made no sense, but I dared not ask.

Dad turned the steering wheel right, shifted into second, the growl of tires over the steel bars of the cattle guard. Through the windshield, through the wiping windshield wipers, ahead of us was a long road, drifted over with snow. Each snowdrift we hit full on, each snowdrift a burst of snow across the windshield. With each snowdrift, Dad yelled, Hold onto your hat! Then he'd let out a loud yahoo! All the way down the road, one snowdrift after another, Dad yahooing and yelling for me to hold onto my hat. When we came to the biggest snowdrift, my hand on my stocking cap, I quick looked over at him.

Maybe it was just the sun, but for a moment, there was a big bright shine in his eyes. Gold in Dad's eyes, the way Mom's eyes get. I've looked for it ever since, but that gold shine in my father's eyes has been a once-in-a-lifetime occurrence.

At the end of the road, on the other side of the Portneuf, at the rise of plateau that was the gravel bar, was the Mexican house. The Mexican house was old and square and gray and dirty, and nobody went in there except Mexicans, and in the summer lots and lots of brown-skinned black-haired Mexicans, who ate only tortillas and didn't speak English, lived in the house while they worked for Dad thinning beets in the fields.

After the magic had gone out of Dad's eyes, and the cold seeped back into the pickup, I remember blowing a hole with my breath and looking through the hole at the Mexican house. Snowdrifts up as high as the windows. No trees, no bushes, just alone. The old gray house looked so cold and lost in the middle of nowhere.

Now that I look back on it, my dad was like that house.

No wonder he hated Mexicans and Indians and black people so much.

Dad might have touched me on the head or put a washcloth over his face and chased me, or plowed me headlong through some snow-drifts, but the whole time I knew I had to be careful, that in a moment I could be pinned down under his body, gasping for breath, a Levi's shirt pressed up against my nose and mouth.

Mostly Dad was just far away in his seagulls, screaming.

In those early days before Russell, Dad far away, circling, circling, there were times there when the only magic we had was us. Mom and Sis and me, and that was enough. Buttering cookie sheets, making frosting, cutting out patterns for pedal pushers. Mom and Sis and me, in our sun hats and seamed hose, rhinestones hanging on our ears, scintillatingly gorgeous, cinnamon toast and cocoa, sometimes oat-meal cookies or chocolate chip, the three of us singing our hearts out: *We are poor little lambs who have lost our way.*

Out on Highway 93, my thumb out for over two hours now, I'm the little black sheep who has gone astray. I'm *still* crying. *Baa baa baa.* My mom and me and Sis — it was enough and just more than enough. I'd have written Mom off long ago if it weren't for the early days.

Mom's magic wasn't only about what she could give me, but what I felt I was giving her. It was a sense of things I'd always had, that there was something mysterious she longed for.

When the wind blew sun and shade across her face, it whispered a sound only she could hear.

Fernweh, sick with what was far away beyond the blue horizon.

Even back then, I knew that place in her. Where no one touched. The yearning she felt to be touched there.

I tried to touch her, tried to make myself a way that she could catch the falling star and put it in her pocket. No one else would do it. It's for damn sure Dad couldn't do it. And Sis didn't know. So it was up to me, and I tried and tried, but it hardly ever worked. Besides church, it was only when Mom was at her piano. Her alto voice low and sweet when she sang her romantic songs. Really, her music was her only way to carry herself to where she'd never know. How full and happy she was then, how beautiful. Her eyes closed, her chin up a little, singing her heart out.

There was a moment in time, though, when the universe conspired. It was spring, a bright day, and that mysterious place in Mom came out from inside her and stuck around all day, from sunrise to way past sunset. Such a rare day, when Mom was happy, when my whole family was happy, and we were all together as a family should be. One day of how it might have been, but wasn't. A day to remember.

My maiden aunt Alma, Mom's oldest sister, was coming to visit. Alma and her roommate, an artist from Portland, Theresa Nussbaum, were traveling the six hundred miles from Portland in Alma's new Chevy convertible coupe with a rumble seat and the top down.

We were up by the crack of dawn. Everyone in a tizzy with this visit from sophisticated city folk. That house got scrubbed from top to bottom, starting with the kitchen. Even Dad was in the kitchen, Dad wasn't out in the fields, and he was wearing an apron, his big hairy hands in the hot soapy water. Mom brought out her best of everything. Her best dishes with the Puritans on them having Thanksgiving with the Indians. Her best real silver silverware she kept in a wooden box in her cedar chest lined in red velvet. Her best linen tablecloth and linen napkins. Nothing was too good for Alma.

Sis and I vacuumed the front-room carpet while Mom scrubbed every inch of every surface of the bathroom. The bathroom smelled so much like Clorox, Mom had to open the window and spray some of her perfume in there so you could breathe. Sis and I dusted the front room. We had that old piano shining. Mom checked up on every cleaning project. It had to be just right.

At five o'clock, the Big Ben alarm went off, which meant it was time to bathe. Mom and Sis and I all used the same bath water, but Dad got his own tub of water. Mom put on her best gold dress, green and gold and kind of see-through, so she'd dyed her underwear in Rit the same color green so her underwear didn't stick out. And new lipstick, not the old red lipstick. She'd bought the new Orange Exotica lipstick on sale a month before. Aunt Alma's visit was the perfect excuse to break it open.

When I walked past the bathroom once, Mom was smiling at herself, one shoulder up a little, her head tilted back. No doubt about it, scintillatingly gorgeous.

Sis wore her yellow sundress. I wore my Sunday pants and white shirt and clip-on red and white bow tie. I polished my Sunday shoes. Dad put on his navy blue suit and blue tie and black shoes, and his dress socks and his garters. He looked like Fred MacMurray.

Six o'clock, Mom had the chicken fried. The spuds were mashed. The gravy made, the canned green beans with Campbell's mushroom soup on top. The pineapple upside-down cake Mom pulled out of the oven made the world smell like heaven.

Mom paced the rooms for anything out of place. Everything had to be perfect. Alma, Mom's big sis, who had worked her way up from a secretary in Blackfoot, Idaho, to a high-paying job in the faraway city of Portland. Alma, a woman who had made her way through the world on her own. Alma, perfectly coifed and dressed in the latest styles. Alma who rode to work on a trolley car. Alma with her important friend, an artist, was paying a visit to *us*.

When Aunt Alma drove her Chevy coupe into the dusty yard, Toby, our dog before Nikki and Tramp, started barking, and the cats started running every which way, then Toby started chasing the cats.

It was some kind of magic Aunt Alma. A whole new world we didn't know. A whole new kind of magic that wasn't my mother's. The magic of a faraway Brenda Starr or Nancy Drew, the Queen of England in a tan coupe, her long yellow scarf, her long red hair, with her friend, Theresa, the artist from Portland.

Mom was a green and gold streak into the bathroom. I ran into the bathroom after her. I just didn't know what else to do. In the mirror, Mom was smiling real wide to see if there was Orange Exotica on her teeth. Still holding her mouth that way, Mom told me to get the hell out of there. So I ran into our bedroom. Sis didn't know what to do either, so she crawled under her bed and hid. I did too.

Then we heard Mom sing out loud: *If I knew you were coming I'd have baked a cake!*

Even under the beds you could feel it. The whole house was buzzing. Aunt Alma's voice, Theresa's voice passing by in the hallway. So refined, so exotic, their laughter so gay. In nothing flat, Sis and I crawled out from under our beds.

In the front room, when I could make my eyes finally look at them, Aunt Alma and her friend, Theresa, the artist from Portland, were both wearing pants with pleats. They were smoking Herbert Tareytons. Besides the cigarette smoke, they smelled of perfume. *Evening in Paris,* my mother whispered to me when I asked, *the both of them.*

Late afternoon light through the window, dark gold. Aunt Alma's lipstick was red on her lips and red on her cigarette. Her red hair, her green sweater fit tight.

Aunt Alma took hold of my hand. Her fingernails were perfect fingernails and they were painted red.

Rigby John, Aunt Alma said, I'd like you to meet my friend, Theresa. She lives with me in Portland.

My hand was so tiny in Theresa's hand.

Pleased to meet your acquaintance, I said.

I didn't look at Theresa. I looked at Aunt Alma instead.

You have sensitive hands, Rigby John, Theresa said. Are you an artist as well?

Theresa wore no lipstick. Her black hair was cut short and came off her forehead in a marcel wave.

Her eyes were too big to look into so I lifted my hands, palms up, and looked at my hands.

I didn't know what to say.

Dad says I draw flies, I said.

After supper, after the dishes were done, when the sun got pink and behind the cottonwoods on the road, Dad walked out to the milk barn with the milk pails to do the milking.

Mom and Aunt Alma went into the front room with their coffees and sat on the davenport. When Aunt Alma reached for a cigarette, Mom asked for one. Mom leaned in close with the cigarette in her mouth. Aunt Alma lit Mom's cigarette with a silver lighter she flipped open. Mom inhaled, and a lick of smoke came out her mouth and went up her nose. I didn't even know until then that Mom could even smoke. Alma's smile was everywhere. Sis sat down between Aunt Alma and Mom, and it wasn't long before those three females were laughing so hard their gums showed.

Outside on the front lawn, Theresa and I sat at the picnic table. Her oil paints on the picnic table in two lines of round spots, colors I'd never even known existed she carried in a wooden case.

Sitting that evening in the flat world, at the green picnic table, the skinny white house we lived in, the red brick barn, the gas pump behind us, I watched her, Theresa, the artist from Portland, dip the brush in the round colors, painting what was out there, painting what I had never really looked at before, brushes of color onto the white canvas the way the world looked. My elbows on the table, her with the gold, the green, the blue, the alfalfa green blooming purple, me with the colors and her, her long body next to me, her Evening in Paris, the sun going down, sun on my neck, the purple-orange-pink-dark-gold sun on Theresa's face and arms.

It was almost dark when Theresa laid her brush down.

Is the painting finished? I asked.

For now, she said.

I touched the painting around on the four edges.

I asked: Have you ever seen *The Wizard of Oz*?

Yes, Theresa said, I love that movie.

The magic part where black-and-white turns to color, I said, is my favorite.

Who knows what Theresa said then, maybe she just looked at me. Maybe she wanted to know why I said that. All I remember is that the way her eyes looked at me gave me the gumption to ask.

At the end of the alfalfa field. I said, All's I can see out there is flat. Where'd the green and purple mountains come from?

If I wasn't up close I never would've noticed that she smiled. When she spoke, Theresa spoke the biggest magic ever. Words my mother could never give me.

The forest and the green mountains are inside, Theresa said. That's what an artist does. She travels the world looking for something inside.

*　　*　　*

Now twelve or so years later, here's me looking with these same two eyes at my two tennis-shoe feet on the gravel on the side of Highway 93 on my way to San Francisco. Right next to my feet, my backpack. The moon is so bright, the backpack has its own shadow.

When I left home this morning, besides my Levi's, two pairs of socks, my other T-shirt, a couple of pairs of jockey shorts, my tooth-brush and my toothpaste, my roll of toilet paper and sack lunch, my white shirt with the iron burn on the collar, I packed three things in my backpack.

Grandma Queep's corncob pipe.

A photograph, and in my pocket a wadded-up piece of paper and a dollar bill — I'll tell you about the photograph and the wadded-up piece of paper and the dollar bill later.

And Theresa Nussbaum's painting. A magic that long ago set me off into the world, into myself. A magic my mother never knew.

I was careful and put a plastic sack around Theresa Nussbaum's painting. Laid the photograph alongside. Tied the sack on with rubber bands. Put my socks and underwear around the painting and the photo and the pipe so they won't get squished.

Theresa Nussbaum's trees and green mountains are traveling through the world with me, an artist, looking for what's inside.

Later on that evening, after Dad finished milking the cows, Mom called out the kitchen window to Theresa and me to come in and eat dessert. Theresa and I set the painting on a shelf on the back porch to dry.

Pineapple upside-down cake and vanilla ice cream. Dad got to have two pieces, but us kids got only one piece, but I went in the kitchen anyway, and chipped away a piece of cake and brown sugar stuck to the black frying pan, and ate it.

Then it was just adults talking and smoking and then at one moment, my father said, Hey, Mom, why don't you play us a tune.

Asking Mom to play the piano was like asking Mom to breathe. But this night my mother leaned back and folded her hands, her cut-to-the-quick fingernails, her rough, red farm hands, into the lap of her new green and gold and kind of see-through dress, her slip dyed the same color green. Her mouth one thin Orange Exotica lipstick line.

And there they were. My mother's eyes. Her almond-shaped hazel eyes, one pitched a little south, the other east, every which way the light in them traveled right on past, right on through, or hardly ever settled on me at all.

The faraway place in her where no one touched. The yearning she felt to be touched there.

Dear broken Mother, here, let me hold myself in such a way that you will see me, and if you see me, if I can make you smile, the trouble will leave your eyes and your eyes will go soft and be gold.

Some other time, Mom said.

Then to her oldest sister, the sister with the piano lessons, Mom said: Alma, Mom said, the piano is old and burnt and needs some tuning, but why don't *you* play something for us.

The way Aunt Alma played the piano was so differnt. The way she played and what she played. The way she played sounded like an old lady playing, all kinds of trills and fancy stuff. The songs she played were nice enough, like "The Blue Danube," and the Northwest Mounted Canadian police song that goes, *I am calling you-ouououououououou.* And something fast called "Gloria Mazurka," but Alma's songs weren't at all like Mom's songs, "The Beer Barrel Polka," "Du, du Liegst Mir im Herzen," "Little Brown Jug," nothing like them at all.

My aunt Alma and her friend Theresa may have brought the gift of exotic sophistication into my life, but my mom could still kick ass on the piano better than her sister any day.

Everything changed when Russell came home, and the magic of that day with Alma and Theresa, and the magic that came down to grace us at other times — not as often as I wanted, but often enough — became all the rarer in our lives. Russell came home screaming, and he screamed for a hundred days, and no one could sleep, and then he died. Mom was never the same. The music stopped, and she locked herself inside her room with Dad, and me and Sis were outside her room, and her eyes were never the same. I couldn't find her anywhere in them, couldn't find me, she was so far away.

Before Russell was born, the new word that everybody said was *brood lamp.* After he was born, they said *incubator, disease,* and *cripple.* That's what the doctor told Mom, that she had a cripple, and because of his disease he had to be in an incubator. I heard those words all the time and thought about them all the time, even when I did my chores. I asked Sis to write them out in longhand. I thought about them even more after Russell came home. But he looked just like a baby to me. After all that talk, after all those words so many times, my brother looked like a baby to me.

One day I asked her to show me what was wrong with him. It was still winter when I asked, sometime within the first ten days of his one hundred days, after he got home from the hospital, before the time when she thought she had smothered him, before the time when the pigs got out, before he died in the spring, after the chores were done, and after school and before supper. Not day and not night, when the shadows were long and running in together, and when the chickens flew up to roost, to sit, and to listen to the world.

On the porch, before I went in, before I asked her, I could smell her bathing him. I took off my coat, my cap, my mittens, pried off my overshoes on the top step, and all the while in there, in the kitchen I could smell her: the Ivory soap, the steaming water in the porcelain pan, the baby oil, the clean diapers. All of those were her smell, and his. When I asked her, Mom put her almond-shaped hazel eyes onto me, gold just around the edges. Then she did something she hadn't done in a long time. She picked me up. She leaned her body so that her hip held me. Her arm was around me, the flesh of her arm against my arm, the smell from her armpit from under her red housedress. She showed me Russell's head and said, You see how his head is so much larger than the rest of him is?

And then she showed me his foot. His foot went over to the side, and she moved it up so that it was straight, and then she let it go, and the foot went crooked again.

That's his foot, she said, and then she set me on the table. She took Russell's hands in hers. They will not open, she said. I have to open them for him and put powder in there for him.

She pried open his right hand and told me to put my finger in there. I didn't want to do it because his palm looked like a terrible blossom to me, or like an egg that the rooster had got to.

She said, Come on, you wanted to know.

So I put my finger inside Russell's palm, and my brother grasped my finger.

Those days when Mom was pregnant, I don't remember much. There is a photo of me and Mom and her big belly and Sis standing and squinting into the sun that I think I remember living in. But it's hard to say which came first, the photo of me and the experience of living it, or the living of it reminded by the photo.

I do remember six things: I remember our dog Toby died, and before he died he came over to me and stood next to me for a while, and then did the same thing with Sis, and then he went into the barn and died on the hay.

I remember Mom saying that animals do that, that they say good-bye before they die.

I remember a lightning storm that blew one of the poplars along Tyhee Road over. The sky was black, and it was day, and we prayed the rosary loud and lit a candle, and Dad wasn't home.

I remember Mom taking the paring knife out of where the silverware was in the kitchen and going outside and sitting on the patch of lawn she had planted and digging dandelions out of the grass with the paring knife.

I remember the Door of the Dead. It was a game Sis and I played, and the way you played it was you would go into a room, into the room that Sis and I had together, and we'd close the door and then you'd say that the closed door was the Door of the Dead, and then we'd get scared, or I should say, I would get scared, and then after saying *The Door of the Dead The Door of the Dead* over and over again, we'd make scary sounds, and then Sis would open the door, and it was always the same thing, I always was the one who ended up yelling, no matter how many times I told myself I wouldn't yell this time.

I remember that everybody said *brood lamp*.

When Mom was pregnant and before she went to the hospital and before Russell came home, that's it. Six memories. After Russell came home, though, and before he died, those one hundred days are not just a memory, not just some things I'm recalling, and it's always been that way for me.

The house was warm all winter, that winter, and there was steam on the windows that I was not allowed to swipe through, which was ice in the morning and blue, and orange when the sun was up. Dad carried in wood and stacked it high by the cookstove and on the porch. Sometimes I helped.

Seemed like all Russell did was cry. But there were times when Russell was not crying and he was sleeping. I wasn't allowed near him because I had a lot of childhood diseases in me like measles and mumps that he could catch and make him more sick, but I still snuck in a lot and looked at his head and his foot, but most of all I looked at his hands, to see if they had opened up yet. Sometimes Russell was awake and not crying and he just lay there quiet, his eyes rolled back up a little, as if he was looking at his head too, as if he was wondering what to do with all the mucus I could hear up there, wondering when the egg would hatch, as if it was a problem and he was planning a solution, a way to make it go away, and he was trying so hard that it made his hands fists.

I woke up once.

It was spring I think by then. The river was high, and Russell was crying and I was surprised that he was crying just the same way that I had been surprised by his crying when he first got home in the winter, and then I wondered if my brother had always been crying and if I just didn't hear him anymore or if he had stopped for a while, for days, weeks, and then started up again. My brother's cries were like the sound the pipes made when you turned on the water in the bathtub, that sound, and then the sound like the pipes were singing high, off tune. Sometimes the pipes didn't make that sound, but mostly they did, and sometimes I didn't hear them when they did, and only remembered that they had made that sound when it was over.

That afternoon she ran out of the bedroom and walked around the house inside, near the walls. I was making incubators with my Tinkertoys on the brown carpet with the flowers on it in the front room. Sis wasn't back home from school, and Dad wasn't home. I could hear Mom crying and walking around and around. I thought she might run out into the field and that Dad would have to bring her back again, and he wasn't even home like the last time. I didn't know what to do when she cried but cry, and I didn't know at all what to do if she ran out into the field. And then she said, Rigby, you have to be a grownup now. I'll make some coffee and we'll put the cloth on the table and we'll have a cigarette. I've got something I've got to tell you, but you must be a grownup for it to work, and then you must never tell anybody ever. Do you promise?

Yes, I promised.

She took out the cloth tablecloth as she spoke to me, and floated it down on the table. I had seen her do that with Russell, float his blanket up in the air like that, like a fan, and then let it settle on him, and then flip it up again and then let it settle again. Russell liked that. I think I could see him almost smile whenever she floated the blanket down on him like that, floated it onto him, so soft, like a big bird flying.

Right then, I wanted to be lying on the table and let the cloth tablecloth come down on top of me, that clean wave of air, her smell, the slow, graceful descent.

She put four tablespoons of coffee into the percolator and plugged it in. She went to the bathroom and pulled the bobby pins from her hair and fluffed it out, penciled in her eyebrows, and put lipstick onto her lips, Ruby Scarlet, and blotted her lips with a square of toilet paper, and let the square float from her hand into the air, onto the floor, by her high heels with no toes in them. She had put on her high heels and her nylons with the seam in them and her brown dress with the orchid all the way down the front.

I wet my hair and parted it, and put the clip-on tie on my white shirt on the collar, and polished my shoes the way I would do if I was going to church.

Mom poured us coffee in the cups that matched the saucers, and she smoked. I smoked too. French-inhaling, my hair slick, me in my tie with her, with her having coffee in the afternoon.

But I didn't smoke.

There was her Ruby Scarlet lipstick on her Viceroy, and there was her lipstick on her cup.

Just now, when I was sleeping with Russell, she said, I woke up and I was lying on top of him. I thought I had smothered him. I thought he was dead. Rigby, you know what that means, don't you? Dead?

Yes. I lied. I didn't know.

I knew the Door of the Dead. When our dog Toby died, he said goodbye first, then went into the barn and lay down in the hay.

Mom put the Viceroy to her lips, pulled in the smoke deep.

I thought I had killed him, Mom said, and this is the part where you have to be grownup and never tell, Rigby. Rigby John?

The smoke inside her came out her nose.

I was glad, my mother said.

It was spring when the pigs got out. Some time within the last ten days of his one hundred days, and this day, the day that started with the pigs getting out, is the most important of all of the one hundred of those days.

Mom had bought a window fan for the window in her bedroom for

Russell with her S&H Green Stamps. The June grass was already going dry, and the river was back down. Dad had built a pen out of wire
fencing and old doors in the corral behind the barn, with part of the
pen in the river so that the pigs could lie around in the water and the
mud.

Those pigs were in the water all the time. Dad called them the bathing beauties. The brood sow he called Esther. Esther Williams he
called the brood sow.

That day when they all got out, it was Saturday because school was
still on and Sis was home and wasn't sick, and it wasn't Sunday because we didn't have our Sunday clothes on and didn't go to church.
Dad was usually home on Sundays because there wasn't supposed to
be any servile work on Sundays, and he wasn't there that day, and so
that was the day when Sis and I walked out the back door of the barn
and there were the pigs, out of their pen, squealing around the corral.

Pigs are out! Pigs are out! Sis yelled, and then I yelled it too.

When Sis and I told Mom the pigs were out, she flipped her fingers
the way she always does when she gets nervous. Mom went into the
bedroom and looked at Russell, who was sleeping. Sis and I stood in
the hallway with the red linoleum and the wallpaper with the butterflies and dice and looked in after Mom. The bedroom was dark and
the fan was on. Mom turned to us and put her finger to her lips and
waved her hand at us to get out of there, so Sis and I went into the
kitchen. We weren't in the kitchen for long before suddenly a streak of
red shot past us. It was Mom.

Last one out of the corral gate's a cow's tail! Mom yelled, already
down the steps of the back porch, stretching out the screen-door
screen and running out into the bright, large, flat dusty world. We
hadn't seen Mom like this since Aunt Alma and Theresa. Sis and I followed her, first past the little green square of lawn with no dandelions
in it, then past the Seven Sisters rose hanging onto the back fence,
then past the gas pump, the '48 Buick, then onto the graveled yard
that stretched out acres between us and the corral gate, Mom ahead,
the skirt of her red housedress flying up above her knees, Sis right behind her, my sister's hair blowing like Mom's, her legs like Mom's —
those females.

I stopped running.

I stopped running and stood and watched them running.

Mom cleared the three poles of the fence like a bird flying, like something wild leaping, and Sis never hesitated. My sister dived under the bottom pole and rolled and stood up next to Mom. They smiled at each other. I stood there and watched, and my mother and my sister smiled at each other. A flock of sparrows flew over the ridgepole of the barn then, between me and the sun, and I shaded my eyes and I was there watching things. The barn, the house, the pole fence, the gate, the pigs out, Mom and Sis, everything differnt, differnt and bright, nothing the same, and I felt as if I had never been anything before.

Come on! Come on, cow's tail! my sister yelled at me, waving her arm. We have to get these pigs in before they get into the river!

Sooo-eeee! Mom yelled.

Sooo-eeee! Sis yelled, and so did I.

We circled the pigs. Mom got between me and the river, Sis got in the middle, and me on the other side, and slowly, slowly, we herded the pigs back into the pen, our arms out to make us wider.

Sooo-eeee! we all yelled.

One of the doors of the pen was down, the closest door to the barn, so we had a corner to herd them into. We were doing pretty well until Sis pointed to the door lying on the ground, to the door that was part of the pigpen, which the pigs had knocked over, which was lying there like a door into the ground, underneath the dry cow manure. My sister pointed to that door and said, just so only I could hear, The Door of the Dead.

I was almost standing on it.

I was almost standing on the Door of the Dead.

I jumped right out of there and yelled with all my might, which spooked the pigs, and they ran back out into the corral, through the place where I was supposed to be standing, and went straight to the river. Esther Williams in the lead, and the rest of them after her, the rest of the bathing beauties running after Esther Williams.

When that fat sow dived off the riverbank, the same way I think a ballerina would dive, poised in the air, and then, when she hit the water, gliding like a seal, gliding as Esther Williams would glide, through the current to the small island of brambles and scrub elms some feet off from the bank, when that pig just went like that, I stopped and looked again, looked as I had looked before, stopped and looked at what the world looked like. It was a world that was suddenly full of things, mysterious things, things that weren't me.

I could see my mother and my sister doing everything they could do
to keep those pigs out of the drink. They were screaming and waving
their arms and putting their bodies in front of the pigs, but it was no
use. Mom was able to grab one pig by the hind leg and drag it away,
but the pig kicked and squealed and Mom didn't have the strength to
pull it any farther, so there they stood, Mom and the pig, in the middle
of the corral, a standoff, the pig kicking and my mother jerking with
every kick. Finally she just had to let go. The pig ran and dived, just
like the others, and swam, just like the others, to the island where Esther Williams was with the rest of the bathing beauties.

It got quiet then.

Mom just sat down right there in the manure.

They were gone.

All the pigs got wild, got crazy on us, and swam away, dived the
way they weren't supposed to, got out of there, swam like other animals, like sea animals, not like pigs, swimming, dumb farm animals
diving, swimming, escaping, showing off, making a spectacle of
themselves.

It was then I saw the owl in the tree on the other side of the river,
just above the bank, just a little ways past the island where the pigs
were. In shallow water you could wade right to the tree where the owl
was. If you moved your eyes a little, the owl would disappear like
magic, but then, if you knew how to look, it would appear again, out
of the leaves and out of the twigs, there were its eyes.

Sons of bitches! Mom yelled.

She picked herself up off the ground and picked up a hard horse
turd and threw it at Esther Williams. And then she picked up a rock.
She spun in circles, around and around, winding up for the pitch,
twirling, a dust devil, her arms in the air, her skirt riding up, a dance,
and hurled the rock with a sound from her inside, deep, a grunt, and
the rock sailed through the air and went through the window of the
chicken coop, the side where the baby chicks were. There was a little
sound, a slight shattering in the sunny afternoon, and that was all.

Sons of bitches! Mom cried, her fists, like Russell's, aimed at the
sky. Damn sows, damn sows, sons of bitches!

I didn't tell Dad about the broken window in the coop because Russell died the next day. No, actually, it was Monday that Russell died,
because the next day, the day after the pigs got out, was Sunday, and
on that day Dad got the pigs back in with our horse, Chub. Had to

lasso each pig and bring each pig across one at a time, even though it was Sunday, but it was an emergency and not that servile.

I was picking up my Lincoln Logs off the brown carpet with the flowers in it in the front room, or Tinkertoys. Sis hadn't been home long, and I had done the chores. I had leaned a board in front of the broken window and was going to tell Dad about it at supper. We were going to make cocoa because Russell wasn't crying. Mom was sitting in her special chair, her and Russell's special chair, holding him the way she always did, rocking, when she said: Go get your father — Russell's dead.

This part is not as clear as the other parts.

What happened next are these things: Monsignor Cody was there, and so were Aunt Marguerite and Uncle Pat, and more people. I was supposed to stay in my room and so was Sis. In the kitchen, on the table, was the cloth tablecloth and the percolator and the cups with matching saucers, a chocolate cake with chocolate frosting and red Jell-O with fruit cocktail in it and bananas.

They put Russell in his bassinet in the bedroom. I wasn't supposed to go in there, but I went in there when nobody was in there, even though there were lots of people everywhere, some of them crying. The fan was off and there were candles all around him and everything was white: the blankets, the bassinet, his nightie.

It smelled like him in there, like her.

Russell was just lying in the bassinet the same way I had seen him so many times, his eyes closed, the covers pulled around him. I touched him a little on the shoulder, through his nightie, and he was no differnt. But then I pulled the cover back and saw his hands. They were open, palms up, sunny side.

On the day of the funeral it rained. Sis says it was sunny, but I remember that there were umbrellas and that we all stood next to a huge elm tree under umbrellas, and that I was wearing my overshoes. I stood to the right of Monsignor and the altar boys. I got to smell the incense. My grandmother was behind me. Sis stood by me on the side, and then Aunt Marie, Aunt Zelda, Aunt Alma, Theresa Nussbaum, Aunt Marguerite, and then Mom on the other. Dad had bought her a new coat. It was navy blue with big buttons. Behind Dad stood my other grandmother and Great-aunt Monica.

When they lowered the casket, I thought about the Door of the Dead in the corral on the ground that day the pigs got out and that Russell was still alive, but this is what is most important about what happened that day and the thing that I remember most of anything, in those days, those one hundred days. It's that Dad started crying so hard that they had to wipe the rain off the folding chair so he could sit down. As soon as I saw Dad sit down like that, I was on my way to him, and I was halfway there, just past Aunt Alma and almost to Aunt Marguerite, before Grandma, the one behind me, got a hold of my arm and pulled me back, past the flowers, past the Door of the Dead, and put me back in my place, in my place in front of her, back in my place, seven females from my father.

There was a reception in the new reception hall in the basement of Saint Joseph's School.

Sis showed me her classroom, although we weren't supposed to go upstairs.

I heard Aunt Zelda say that it was such a blessing, there was so much wrong with him.

Afterward we went home. Mom drove. Sis and I started singing *Going to the chapel* like we sometimes did in the car, but Mom told us to shut up. When we got home I changed my clothes and did my chores. The board was down from the window of the coop, and all the chicks were dead.

It looked to me that those who weren't killed right off by the owl had smothered in the corner, in a heap, trying to get away.

2 After Russell

AFTER ONE HUNDRED DAYS of Russell crying, his screams, his coughs, his fists, the way he tried for air, everything was quiet. No baby screams from Mom and Dad's bedroom. At night no Mom or Dad walking up and down the hallway holding Russell. No more poopy diapers soaking in the toilet. No bottles sterilizing in the big white pot on the cookstove. No white bassinet. No baby.

Outside our skinny white house, winter set in hard, snow almost as high as the windows, bright white, white windows, ice on the windows. It hurt your eyes to look.

Inside the house, I thought the stoves were turned up too high, or bathroom steam was out all over in the house, or the wood in the cookstove was wet and made the smoke. But it was none of these things.

It was Mom. Something about her was lost, and what was lost wasn't trying to find its way back. Pray and pray and pray. The rosary, the rosary, the rosary. That's all we did.

Then there were Mom's migraines. A pain like God the Father coming down to dwell inside her head is how she said it hurt. When a migraine hit, it started with something far away, a drip, or the wings of a big bird, a sound that was low and faint and off-key. After she heard the faint and off-key sound, a couple seconds was all she had before the sound got so loud there wasn't nothing but that sound.

Dad said Mom was about to go around the bend. Dad and Sis and me had to speak in whispers and never laugh or be loud. One time I forgot and let the back door slam, and Dad hit my butt so hard I landed on the other side of the kitchen. Dad smacked Sis a couple times too. Got so that me and Sis spent most of our time in our bedroom with the door closed. It was cold in there and we had to wear our coats and mittens. We'd quit playing Door of the Dead, so Sis mostly played with her paper dolls. Dad wasn't outside circling anymore, so I didn't dare play paper dolls with her. I played with my truck.

At night, after the rosary, and Dad turned all the lights out, I lay in my bed, the covers pulled up to my chin. It was never long before I'd hear my own faint off-key sound far away. No matter what I did, praying, singing quiet to myself, counting as far as I could, then counting backward, it didn't matter, I couldn't stop the sound. Sis knew it was Russell and my questions of why did God make him be born that way and die? Most of the time, Sis had to come lie in bed with me and touch the top of my head and whisper stories to me. Haji Baba and his magic flying carpet was my favorite.

The following spring everything happened all at once.

Harold P. Endicott and his phosphate plant put in a holding pond, and the Portneuf River dried up. Then Dad got on the yellow Caterpillar, moved the blade down just so, then pointed the yellow Caterpillar at our skinny white house. Dad waved over at Mom and me and Sis, and we waved back.

The only thing still inside the house was the piano. The piano was old and burnt and came from a saloon in Niggertown, and it had no place in our new future. In just a couple of minutes, our house — roof and all, floors, walls, doors, and windows — was just dust and a pile of rubble.

When the yellow Caterpillar got to the piano, the piano made an awful sound. Far away, the sound, at first. Low and faint and off-key. Like a big bird flying. I quick looked at Mom. Sure enough, Mom's face got that migraine look to it, but I held on tight to her hand.

Mom didn't run. Maybe because she had no place to go. In the middle of the yard in the sun, the wind blowing at our straw hats, Mom pulled out her rosary, and we knelt down right there in the gravel and prayed the rosary. The sorrowful mysteries.

Dad worked day and night on the new house. At Aunt Zelda's, where we were staying, Dad was gone before breakfast and didn't come home until after dark. Mom kept his supper warm for him in the oven. The only time we saw Dad in those days was in the afternoon when Mom made Dad a sandwich, and we brought the sandwich to him and a Coke. Power saws and hammering, two-by-fours poking up at right angles into the sunny blue sky, sawdust and the smell of plywood, is what I remember. Dad and his cousin Uncle John and Aunt Zelda's husband, Uncle Bob, three big men, cussing and laughing and sweating in the sun.

By the following winter, where there had been one house was another house. The old house, long and white and wooden and skinny. The new house, modern and brick and split-level.

The way I figure it, Dad thought he could fix Mom by fixing her up with a new house. Mom liked the new house all right, at least that's what she showed Dad. But if you looked close, you could tell something important had changed. Mom was there, but no matter how hard I looked I couldn't find her eyes. And then the migraines would return, and she'd disappear altogether again behind the door to the bedroom.

Dad didn't know what to do. He'd built his family a new home, had kept the farm going, and now he had to take care of his two children. He didn't like any of it. It was easy to see how awkward he felt, it was easy to see how sad he was at the death of his son. What I saw more than anything, though, was his anger. More anger than ever. He was a big man with rough hands and grease under his fingernails, but there he was cooking dinner — scrambling eggs and frying potatoes. Dad's one of those frontier guys, John Wayne, a man of few words and a loaded gun in the pickup. He belonged outdoors, and there he was in the house doing the wash and folding his wife's underwear, making sack lunches for Sis and me and getting us ready for school. And putting up with me. As soon as he could, he disappeared back outside to the farm work.

As I look back on it, this was the time me and Sis could've got closer to my father. A shared death can do that, for some families. It would have been the perfect time to take me fishing. But not my family, not my dad. He was around the house, and we were underfoot more than any time in my life. But that didn't mean he talked any more, and he never once talked about Russell or tried to. How he might feel about it. Or how we were supposed to feel about it.

It seems pretty clear now he was determined not to feel anything, and even though day after day, night after night, we lived cheek by jowl with him, he kept his distance from us, however scared and alone we might feel. One ornery bastard. That's what Mom said about Dad's father once. So it was with my father. Cold, irritable, impatient. One ornery bastard.

In a lot of ways, Sis and I were on our own. Any mistake, any sign of weakness, and it was the ornery old bastard we had to deal with.

The trouble for me was I was afraid to fall asleep. That's what Russell'd done — fallen asleep. And that's the only explanation Sis and I had ever heard: Russell fell asleep and went to heaven.

As soon as I'd get in bed, I could hear the faraway noise, wings of a big bird, faint and off-key. No matter how much I prayed, I couldn't get the sound to stop. In our old house, Sis and I shared a bedroom, and I could sneak into her bed, and she'd hold me and tell me stories. Sis's voice and being next to her always worked, and I'd be asleep in no time, getting up at first light so Mom and Dad wouldn't find us together. But in the new house my bedroom was down in the basement, and the journey to Sis's room through the quiet, dark house was fraught with peril because I had to pass by Mom and Dad's room. Dad caught me soon enough. Maybe if he'd been another dad, he'd have asked why I had to be close to Sis. I probably couldn't have told him but still it would've been nice to be asked. Maybe he might have taken me by the hand and walked with me to my room and then he'd sit on the end of my bed after he'd tucked me in. Maybe my father alone with me in the dark could've kept the faraway sound away. But Dad was not another dad. There was him cussing me out, then there were the spankings, and because I was headstrong and liked to make a spectacle of myself, there was the trips to the saddle room with the belt. Finally, there was a dead bolt on the outside of my door. I had to pee in a Mason jar.

In Dad's world, there is no fear. No room for it. If you don't believe it's there, you don't have to deal with it. And if there's no fear, then there's no need for comforting fear. Too bad. Maybe in giving he could have got some comfort for himself. But there are some things that just aren't allowed.

*　　*　　*

Mom's way of coping with the darkness that could descend at any moment was to fall back on what she'd always fallen back on. The Catholic religion. For her, it couldn't be any other way.

Mom started going to daily Mass. Every morning, even Saturday, Mom and Sis and me got up an hour early. For breakfast, Sis boiled two eggs and boiled water and we made Nestle's Quik. Mom had just a cup of coffee, then drove Sis and me to seven o'clock Mass. Mom prayed extra-hard those days. You could see her trying. From the minute she walked into the church, everything about her was trying to get God's attention. At the consecration of the Mass, when Monsignor Cody held up the host, Mom beat her breast and said, *Lord, I am not worthy,* but you could tell. Mom didn't really mean it. Or mean it like she wanted to. Some mornings you could hear Mom crying in the confessional, and one time she came storming out and slammed the confessional door. Mom had to take me home with her because God the Father had settled hard in her head. The migraine was so bad on the way home I had to help her hold the steering wheel.

One night, after *Lassie* on TV, we all knelt down on the new turquoise flowered carpet in the living room to pray the rosary. Mom was just about to make the sign of the cross, when Sis said: Why don't we ever pray the joyful mysteries? Why do we always have to pray the sorrowful ones?

Mom kept on making the sign of the cross, but while she was making the cross she didn't say, In the name of the Father, Son, and Holy Ghost. The way her face looked right then, I couldn't have told you who my mother was. What Mom said, she said quiet: There is no joy here, she said.

Even the new piano Dad bought her didn't do much good. It was a new Steinway with a walnut finish. Looking into the surface of that piano was like looking into a pool of dark walnut water, or a piece of walnut-tinted glass. The piano sat in the corner of the living room, always shined up, on the new turquoise flowered carpet, against the wood paneling on the wall, just left of the folds of orange drapes on the aluminum window. Mom hadn't ever played that piano, not even once. One afternoon when I came home from school, I caught Mom sitting at the piano. She was staring down at the piano keys. Like it was a deep mystery that promised some answers. But Mom's hands were at her sides. She didn't even see that I was looking, and I was standing right there.

Gradually, slowly, Mom did seem to be coming back. She was up and about more and more anyway, so Sis and I didn't have to do so many of the house chores. Sometimes, I'd come home from school, and there would be the old familiar smell of cookies coming from the kitchen. A few times I can remember some fresh-cut flowers on the kitchen table. But I still couldn't find my mother's eyes, and there was something new about her, real differnt, a brittleness, as if she was a piano string strung too tight, and a finger coming down on a key a bit too hard could make her snap.

Adding to the troubles were the bills. With the new house and Dad's new '57 Buick and Mom's new piano, plus the new hi-fi, Mom had something new to worry about. How were we going to get all those goddamn bills paid?

All she did, I mean besides pray the rosary and go to Mass every morning and try and cook and clean, was sit at her new kitchen table, hair flying, her head buried in a mountain of pink slips, her new black horn-rimmed reading glasses down on the end of her nose, cussing a blue streak, her rough, red farm hands, her cut-to-the-quick fingernails pushing a pencil around on a piece of paper, her tiny Catholic numbers adding, subtracting, and dividing, always coming up with not enough.

With Mom like that, Sis and I tried to keep our distance. I don't know how Sis felt about it, but I didn't like it. Mom had always been the person who let me know who I was and how I felt. So keeping a distance was something I had to learn, and the lesson was a tough one. Our second Christmas in our new house, Uncle Pat gave me his Lionel train set. It was complete with everything — the tracks, the engine, boxcars, the red brick train station — everything except the transformer.

In Montgomery Ward, there was a beautiful transformer. It was shiny black and cost twenty-five dollars. The transformer had a dial for how fast you wanted the train to go and a red light that blinked on and off when the train came into the train station. I could curl my hands around the transformer and not touch my fingers.

Christmas Eve, when I looked down and saw the shiny black transformer in the Christmas lights under the Christmas tree, it was a miracle. Right off, I ran downstairs and hooked up the transformer. The red light went on, and when I turned the dial it was another miracle. The Lionel train started running. Round and around that train all night. Going through the station, going through the tunnel in the mountain, stopping at the signal to pick up the mailbag. The red light blinking on and off was so cool.

Some things are just too good to be true. The day after Christmas, Mom changed her mind and took my transformer back to Montgomery Ward. She said the transformer cost too much, and with all our bills we couldn't afford it. Mom bought the little transformer, the tin one that cost ten dollars and didn't have a light, and you could see how it was screwed together. It fit in the palm of my hand.

Only a nine-year-old boy used to a new pair of Levi's every year for his birthday knows what it's like to suddenly have and then lose a Lionel train transformer. I had seen my mother hunched over the bills at the kitchen table enough times to understand the connection between those piles of paper and the fifteen dollars she'd just saved. I didn't like it, but I understood.

What happened soon after, though, was something that sent me reeling. I've told you how important dress-up was. It was something Sis and Mom and I used to do together when Dad wasn't around. With Mom a bit better, Dad had gone back out to the fields, and Sis and I again started visiting the steamer trunk. Mom didn't play with us anymore, but still it was fun being scintillatingly gorgeous.

One afternoon, I stayed home with a pretend headache from school. Mom was pushing the vacuum back and forth over the new turquoise carpet with the flowers, and just like that she shut off the vacuum. She looked up as if God were speaking. She made the sign of the cross. Then it was straight to the bedroom.

My knuckles against her mahogany bedroom door made a hollow sound. You go on and play, Mom said.

Mom? I said. Can I play dress-up?

If you play downstairs, Mom said.

It took me awhile to ask because none of us had ever said it.

What if Dad comes in? I asked.

He won't be in until supper, Mom said.

The green plaid dress buttoned up, the shiny black velvet hat with the flower brooch, the black high-heel shoes with the ankle strap. The rhinestone bracelet. The cameo necklace. The pleated green scarf tied around my neck. The red purse with the gold latch. The gold ring. The white gloves.

There I was standing inside the light of the trunk, in the perfect outfit, and the light of the trunk was the whole world, the strange magic Wizard of Oz world, the world that smelled of Eiffel Tower.

Scintillatingly gorgeous.

I didn't hear the other world, the world we live in every day, coming down the basement steps.

In all my days, I don't think I've ever been so terrified.

It was Ott Lattig. Dad's tall, skinny usher friend from church. He was yelling. Ott Lattig's face was red, and he was yelling. He kicked the steamer trunk, and the steamer trunk went crashing over. He pulled the red purse from my hands, pulled the gloves off my hands, the gold ring. Yelling and yelling, Ott Lattig slapped the black velvet hat off my head, Ott Lattig put his hands around my neck, pulled at the green scarf, pushed me back, pulled at the Peter Pan collar, ripped the green plaid dress open, tore the buttons off.

I tried to hide behind the fallen steamer trunk. The straps of the black shoes were caught around my ankles.

Then Mom was standing there. With these same two eyes, I looked up and there was my mother, and she didn't have a migraine, and she had her eyebrows on, and her Orange Exotica lipstick, and her almond-shaped hazel eyes were all green, no gold at all staring down at me.

I mean, how old was I? No more than nine.

Then Mom says — you won't believe this, but my mother turns to Ott Lattig, and she says — Thanks, Ott, she says. See how my son plays. His father is so ashamed of him.

Shame.

That's the word all right.

Fuck. Who are these people?

Not long after the Ott Lattig incident, one day when Dad was out in the field, I went down into the furnace room alone. I did not open the steamer trunk. I pulled the old coal stool over, climbed the rungs of the stool, stood on the stool, and reached up and took the fishing pole down.

The fishing pole was wood and had tiny loops on it where the fishing line went through. The reel was green. The handle, where you turned, was green. There was never any fishing line in the reel.

The way the reel felt in my hands, how the reel sounded when I turned it, the feel of the wood in my hands.

Sis had a new Brownie Instamatic. At first, Sis wouldn't take the photo. She didn't want a photo of her little brother. Sis was turning into somebody I didn't know. I had to give her a dollar.

I'm standing in front of the new house, right next to the blue spruce. Squinting into the sun. I am holding Dad's fishing pole the way a soldier holds his rifle on his shoulder.

That fishing pole meant I had a father, and that I was his son.

And you can bet your life, that's the photo that went into my backpack next to Theresa's painting, which I brought along into the world with me.

School was no refuge. I was big for my age, a head taller than anybody else in class. It was hard sitting in my desk because my legs were so long. Another thing I could do was run. Running was important because being good at it meant I could outrun Scardino. It was always Scardino and his thugs, Vern Breck and Michael Muley, chasing me all over the playground. They couldn't catch me, but there was three of them and only one of me and sooner or later it was me down on the ground under a Scardino pile.

Exasperated. I could spell *exasperated* but couldn't do anything about it. No matter what I did, I always turned out the loser. I prayed and prayed, but there just wasn't any help. It was the universe, I guessed, conspiring. You'd think Sis would've helped me out after all we'd been through. But as Sis got older in the sixth and seventh grades, most of the time she didn't want anything to do with me. Insult to injury, sometimes Sis let Scardino carry her books to the bus stop at Pocatello High School.

It wasn't just me that Scardino tortured, though. Really, he had the whole class over a barrel. One time he stuck Stephanie Smith's ponytail in the inkwell. Another time he came to class with an inked-in tattoo on his hand and his hair slicked back in a duck's ass. Sister Teetha flipped because the tattoo was a tattoo of the Pochugas, a gang in LA. Sister Teetha scrubbed the ink off Scardino's hand herself, then combed his hair down straight. The rest of arithmetic she spent lecturing to the class. That day she said something to the class that's always stuck with me. She said, I may be an old nun, but I'm not stupid. Don't think I don't know what every new hairdo and trinket bracelet and ink tattoo means. I know what's going on inside those young bodies of yours.

The reason why I remember Sister Teetha saying that was the look on Scardino's face. The look that he knew what she was talking about. Of course, I didn't have a clue. But I didn't let on. I just put a smirk on my face the way Scardino had on his.

Then there was the afternoon after civics class I got a note from Scardino. It landed on my desk right next to the inkwell. After civics was over, and before reading class and Ichabod Crane, I slowly unfolded the note.

Meet me after class by the lilac bush in front of the school. I've got a question for you about your sister. Scardino.

After the three o'clock bell, after I got my coat and lunch pail out of the cloakroom, I walked outside to the front of the school. Scardino was standing by the lilac with Vern Breck and Michael Muley. When I saw the three of them standing there like that, I almost turned around and ran. But I kept walking. Tried to put an expression on my face that didn't look scared and walked right up to them.

Scardino's face could be a lot of ways. I got so I could read him almost as good as I could read my mother. I'd had years of practice. Something usually was going on just underneath the way he smiled. The way he was smiling that day wasn't good.

Hey, Klueless, Scardino said.

Over the years, Klusener had become Kluse, which became Klueless.

Then Breck and Muley said hey too.

My heart was pounding in my ears.

Hey, I said.

The three of them stood there not saying anything. Just lilac smell. Then Breck slugged Scardino on the arm, and pretty soon they were all pushing one another around. I tried to make like I was having fun too. So far none of them had hit me.

Your sister, Scardino said.

Vern Breck and Michael Muley were really laughing, so hard it got Scardino laughing too. Finally, Scardino blurted it out: Does your sister have pussy hair?

Believe it or not, I know a little about honor among men. I'd never experienced that kind of honor firsthand. Still, at that moment, I knew I should somehow defend the virtue of my sister. I wanted to smash their faces in. But what was the use. They were three, they were

Scardino, Breck, and Muley, and they were indestructible, and I was only me. Plus my sis let *him* carry her books. My hands were fists, but my fists were like Russell's, a baby's fists, and the only thing I could do was throw a big baby tantrum. So I didn't do anything.

I may not have been able to hold my own at school, but I was older and bigger and Dad thought it was high time I started pulling my own weight on the farm. Thus began our new father-son relationship, he the boss, me free labor. To keep the bill collectors at bay, Dad had expanded the farm into a bigger operation, so now we had a herd of Hereford heifers on top of the milk cows and all the crops. There was plenty of work for his new hand. I didn't mind it so much, though. With Mom's eyes still gone, and Sis preoccupied with high school and boyfriends, doing chores was a way to escape. As long as I didn't have to work with Dad, I got along just fine. I even started staying out after chores were done. What kept me out were the secret places I'd started to think of as my own.

I had differnt secret places for differnt purposes, differnt moods, differnt activities.

When I needed to feel safe, I went to the loft of the barn. Something about being on the loft floor looking up at the roof way up there made me feel like a big old pair of hands had me cupped inside. Night wind made the barn a mysterious place. Creaks and groans, cat yowls, little animals scurrying. Moonlight on the yellow straw, the quick, white flash of the dove's wing. The stars through the holes in the roof. A lick of warm wind against the back of my neck, and everything that was ordinary turned to magic.

There were other places.

When I just wanted to get away from it all, there was on top of the railroad cars. Three boxcars in a row. When you sat up top on the boxcars, on the wood walkway, especially at sunset, and if there was wind, which usually there was wind, if you squinted your eyes and moved your body like it was on a train, from up there on top of the railroad cars you could see just about everything. The Ganges River. The Vatican. The Eiffel Tower. The Golden Gate Bridge. The Chrysler Building. The Via Dolorosa. Mount Kilimanjaro. Castles in Spain. Faraway places with strange-sounding names. Sometimes all of them, one right after another after another, in the same evening.

The grain elevator was the circus. I'd go there when I wanted to make a spectacle of myself. The grain elevator set out just behind the spud cellar and was shaped like a big teeter-totter with the one end that attached to the tractor heavier than the other. At the high end, the grain elevator was the height of me four times over.

What you did was you'd crawl up the flanges of the grain elevator. When you got to the middle of the grain elevator, you'd be sitting right above the wheel, which was the fulcrum point. Each step you took out farther from there was a step into midair, really, because halfway between the fulcrum point and the grain elevator's top end the elevator started to go down with the weight of you.

The trick was to hit perfect balance. I can't tell you how many evenings after supper I was under the big top on the top half of the grain elevator, a Flying Wallenda, hanging in midair perfectly still. Still as my shadow on the ground hanging down off me.

The spud cellar was mostly a smell. Deep under the earth, dark, cool, and the smell of earth and raw potatoes. There were two big wood doors where the spud trucks drove in and out, and then there was the little door to the side.

Once inside, it was the smell, right off it was the smell. Peel a potato sometime, then put the peel up to your nose, and take a whiff. Then bite off a piece of the raw potato and chew on it. The spud cellar was that smell and that taste times a thousand.

When I walked down into the spud cellar, I was transformed into somebody else from another time, another place. Sitting down there on the dark ground, next to a spud pile, I was a Christian during Roman times in the catacombs hiding from the Romans, or I was somebody Chinese lying on my cot in an opium den, my head filled with stark blue skies crisscrossed by fluttering flags of Chinese red and Chinese gold. Or I was an American soldier in World War II, a parachuter behind enemy lines.

Then there were the granaries. Not the wood granary on the ground, but the four round corrugated-steel granaries, which Dad set next to one another so they formed a square, and then raised the four round granaries up about twelve feet on a scaffolding of railroad ties set in concrete, so you could drive the grain truck under them and all you'd have to do is reach up and pull the steel trap open, and the grain poured down into the truck and you didn't have to shovel so much. Between the two granaries that face east is a little notch up there with a welded steel-plate floor that's shaped like an hourglass. It's shady in the late afternoon and looks out over the spud cellar and the pigpens and beyond.

In that notch was also where I really learned to smoke and took to reading the first time. The Bowery Boys were boring. Nancy Drew was better. But still, you can read about Nancy in her jumpsuit, driving jauntily in her roadster, being chagrined, for only so long.

Mom and Dad wanted me reading only good Catholic stuff. The only good Catholic stuff to read are your daily missal and the Bible and *The Lives of the Saints,* so anything that was any good I had to hide. I had to smuggle Steinbeck and Willa Cather and Hemingway inside my pants. Reading made everything differnt. I was no longer stuck in a world with my mom and my dad and my sis and Catholics and Mormons on a goddamn farm out on the Tyhee Flats. Before books, my secret places were just places I could hide. Now my places were where I could go to read and find out about people who were like me. *Of Mice and Men, My Ántonia, Winesburg, Ohio, A Moveable Feast.*

The Mexican house was still too far away for me. Plus it was flat land for almost a half mile and not a damn thing to hide behind if Dad was around. Later on, though, soon as I hit five foot, Dad started me driving the pickup and every day after school, after I got my barn chores done, I had a new chore to feed twenty-five bales of hay to the two hundred head of Hereford steers Dad bought and corralled in his new feedlots up by the Mexican house.

When I first started driving up to Dad's new feedlots and feeding the cattle, during the summer, when I drove past the Mexican house, usually there was a bunch of dirty kids just in their underwear playing in the dirt. One family one summer had a skinny yellow dog that Tramp hated, so when I drove up the land, you could see that dog put his ears back and pull his tail down and run under the Mexican house.

In the fall, after the Mexicans had gone back to Del Rio, sometimes I'd walk around the house kicking up the dusty earth that turned to sticky mud when it rained. There were three windows, and I'd look in each of the windows. I didn't go in, though. It was too dirty in there.

Before I met Flaco and Acho, Mexican people were just a part of the scenery in the springtime and summer. They pulled in the yard in their old Ford pickups loaded down with stuff. I don't even know what kind of stuff. Just a pickup full of stuff and kids all over in the stuff. They moved up to the Mexican house, stayed there while there was work, while it was hot, and then they left.

They didn't speak English. They were Catholic, but they didn't go to Mass. My mother never tried to get them to go to Mass.

The best secret place of all, though, was the swimming hole. The swimming hole was as far away from the house as you could get and still be on the farm. And it was hard to get to because you had to drive on the narrow canal bank for at least a quarter of a mile. You had to be a real good driver to drive the narrow ditch bank, and I wasn't a good enough driver until I was thirteen.

There was a waterfall at the swimming hole, not like Yosemite or anything, but there was about a six-foot drop, water flowing over and through an outcropping of slick, dark lava rock. Just below, cement walls from either side of the canal came together at a head gate and gathered up the water in a pool that was six, some places eight feet deep. On top of the cement walls was the one long two-by-twelve bolted down that you could walk over.

There was one scrub cedar there on the lava rock. The cedar was across the border, on the rez, not on our farm, just a couple feet out from the yellow, planted deep in all that red. Crooked as the wind.

Sometimes, sitting up there on the bolted-down board that crossed the head gate, or swimming, or sometimes at night in summer when I hiked up to the swimming hole, the wind blowing through the cedar made the sweetest sound.

Sweet, I guess, is the best way you can say that sound. Sad too, but something nice about the sad. The way you feel after you cry hard, or sometimes after you come. "Now Is the Hour" kind of sad. And there was a secret too. The wind through the boughs of the cedar made you feel like there was a secret. A great big secret, a huge secret about the mystery of life you'll never know.

Georgy Girl told me the sound of the wind in the cedar tree was the voices of his ancestors speaking. He said if he listened hard enough, he'd know what to do with his life.

If he could only quit drinking long enough to hear.

My prayer to Georgy's ancestors was that he heard.

I had my books and secret places, Viceroys stolen from my father, and a longing I could not name. But I recognized it. The longing in me was my mother's longing. I always thought I could take hers away, and there I was with my own. Wandering around in a world I didn't make, never really where I was, dreaming of somewhere else. Still, though, I imagined that if I could find myself in her eyes, somehow she could find herself in mine.

I think it was the summer of the fifth grade that Sis and I went to 4-H camp. It was the first time Sis and I had been anywhere. I had my duffel bag packed, and I got up early. I wasn't at all afraid to leave home. After a special breakfast, I put my duffel bag in the trunk and got in the back seat of the Buick. Sis sat up front with Dad. When Dad pulled out of the driveway, I turned around and waved at Mom. She was standing alone in the bright sun at the screen door. She was wearing her other housedress, the red one. She had that faraway look in her eyes. As soon as I saw that look, I started crying real hard. Then Dad started cussing because I was crying. He thought I was crying because I was afraid to leave my momma. That isn't why I was crying, though. I was crying because she was home alone with all that work and no fun. I was crying because she wasn't going to have me to look out for her. I was crying because she was going to be alone with him.

I'd watched Mom all my life. Watched her pray. All those years praying the rosary, going to Mass, making novenas to Our Mother of Perpetual Help. All the litanies and aspirations to sweet Jesus, the only son of God, who suffered and died for our sins and saved the world from hell. Somewhere around in all that watching, I figured out that Jesus wasn't going to save Mom from anything. Unless I helped. God the Father and His Son Jesus and the Holy Ghost were a little hard of hearing. It was up to me to lend them a hand. I'd make of myself a loving-kindness for her and be that presence in her life, and her prayers would be answered. She was so alone and sad with Russell and all, she needed all the help she could get. Dad didn't really see her. She was just his wife. Dad didn't understand about her piano and her secret longing to be a star is born. And if he did, he didn't care.

There was one afternoon after school the following year. It was Friday, and Sis was staying at a girlfriend's house for the weekend. I got off the bus, and the bus drove on, and I stood on the gravel. The drapes were drawn, which meant Mom had a migraine. I went in through the back door, the way I usually went into the house so I wouldn't track mud. Inside in the mudroom I was surprised because I smelled chocolate cookies. There was no mistaking the smell of chocolate cookies.

Inside, the house was dark. Even the shade in the kitchen was drawn. On the green Formica counter, on a sheet of waxed paper, lined up in neat rows, were the dark brown cookies. The cookies weren't frosted yet, and in the sink was the green mixing bowl filled with dirty water. The rubber spatula was in the mixing bowl and the beaters to the electric mixer. The electric mixer, Mom's new Mixmaster, was still plugged into the socket.

The oven was still warm. I touched one of the cookies, and the cookie was warm too, and I ate the cookie even though we were supposed to wait until they'd cooled and were frosted.

I opened the oven, and inside the oven was empty.

Mom must have just got through with the cookies before the migraine hit.

I'd watched Mom make chocolate frosting so many times, so I decided to go ahead. As quiet as I could be, I got a bowl and put powdered sugar in the bowl, then melted a cube of butter in the flat pan and poured the hot butter into the powdered sugar. Then I added the Hershey's chocolate powder. Two tablespoons.

I didn't use the Mixmaster because noises like that drove Mom mad when she heard them with a migraine. I used the wooden spoon and folded the butter and the chocolate and the powdered sugar in together. It took awhile to get the right consistency. I was always taking licks.

When I got the chocolate frosting right, the cookies were cool enough, so with a table knife I spread each cookie with frosting.

There was over a half a bowl of frosting left when I was done, so I ate the rest of the frosting. The only sound I made when I washed the dishes was the water turning on and off.

I filled the percolator with water, put two tablespoons of coffee in the percolator in the little aluminum thing with holes in it, smoothed out the coffee, slid the aluminum thing with holes in it down over the aluminum pole, put the lid on the percolator, and plugged it in.

Pretty soon the house was filled up with the smell of coffee percolating and the chocolate cookies.

Mom liked her coffee with a little cream but no sugar. From off the top of the milk pitcher, with the tablespoon, I skimmed off some cream, put the tablespoon of cream into one of Mom's cups that matched the saucers, stirred in the coffee.

The two chocolate cookies went onto the little plate with gold around the edge that Mom got from Aunt Alma one time.

I set the coffee cup and the saucer and the plate of cookies on the

TV stand. Set the TV stand next to the piano. I opened up Mom's new walnut piano so you could see all the keys. On one white key, I pushed down my thumb then finished the chord with the rest of my fingers. The first key was middle C, something I'd learned from Mom. Mom said, If you can find middle C, you can go anywhere.

Middle C in the dark rooms of our house, coffee and chocolate cookies. I sat on the green davenport and waited.

I heard her in the bathroom first. When she walked into the living room, her face was on and her eyebrows penciled in, and her hair fluffed out. Orange Exotica lipstick.

On her second cup of coffee, I opened the drapes. Mom said I did a real good job on the frosting.

Mom played the piano, and we sang "The Bible Tells Me So." Twice. The second time Mom harmonized, which is something I could do if I plugged my ears and listened only to myself.

Faith, hope, and charity, That's the way to live successfully. Then: *Going to the chapel, and we're going to get married,* which was Sis's favorite song.

Then we sang "Now Is the Hour." I stood real close to Mom sitting on the round spindle chair, so close my arm was almost touching hers. I sang the melody with my ears plugged while Mom harmonized.

"Now Is the Hour" was just the ticket. There's something about that song. How it's sad, but at the same time it makes you feel good inside.

Mom felt better after "Now Is the Hour."

She put her glasses back on, and the gold came back to her eyes.

"Now Is the Hour" always could make Mom feel better.

For her fourteenth birthday Sis got an autograph book. The book was white fake leather with a clasp that locked and swirly gold letters that said AUTOGRAPHS. Sis wouldn't let me sign my autograph in her autograph book. Only Sis's girlfriends could sign her book and the boys she liked. Those days, Sis wore a brassiere and she wore nylons and a garter belt and she was always talking about boys. In our 4-H Club, it was Kevin Davies. At school it was Johnny Wyeth. At church she was always looking over at Mick Havorka. Sis asked Scardino to sign his autograph in her autograph book, but he wouldn't do it. But not me. Sis didn't look at or talk to me. Maybe at home she'd talk to me if she wasn't in a bad mood. But at school or out in the world, Sis didn't want a thing to do with me. Unless, of course, she wanted to borrow some money. I always saved my allowance, and she spent hers. It never failed, I was a soft touch and somehow Sis always managed to get money out of me.

I didn't really mind, though. Sis was like Mom. I knew a lot more about her than she thought I did. In school, Sis wasn't very popular. Mom and Dad wouldn't let Sis be in pep club or in any kind of club at all because it took extra gas, and there was all that goddamn work at home to do. Sis was pretty enough and smart and funny, but she didn't know it. Sis thought she was ugly and fat and her hair would never go right and Mom wouldn't let her bleach it. Plus, there weren't a lot of Catholic boys to date. Everybody and their dog was a Mormon. So the way I made myself Jesus for Mom, I started being like a boyfriend to Sis. But don't get me wrong. Not really a *boyfriend,* but *like* a boyfriend, you know? The way things were going, the way Sis wanted to be beautiful and popular wasn't going to happen. So it was up to me to help her out.

One thing Sis and I could do was dance. Sis needed a boy to dance with, and out on the farm there usually weren't any extra boys around, so when Sis learned how to jitterbug from Francie Lutz, Sis taught me how and we practiced at home.

Some days, after Sis and I got home from school, before we changed clothes and did the chores, if Mom didn't have a migraine, Sis put on our three 45's on the hi-fi. Elvis Presley singing "Jailhouse Rock," the Everly Brothers singing "Wake Up Little Susie," and Fats Domino singing "I'm Going to Be a Wheel Someday."

I was actually better at dancing than I was at running. Sis and I got so good that I could pick her up and put her on one hip and then on the other hip and then pick Sis up, then pull her down through my legs, then, if she was wearing a full skirt she could spread her legs and when her butt hit my waist I'd pull her back up, and during that last pull up, Sis ducked her head and flipped all the way over three hundred and sixty degrees and landed on her feet.

The First Annual Catholic High School Conference was held in Idaho Falls. Idaho Falls is only fifty miles from Pocatello, but back then, that was the farthest that Sis and I had ever been away alone besides 4-H camp at Palisades Park. We got to miss school for the whole day.

Which pissed Joe Scardino off.

Idaho Falls is a really weird town because there's a Mormon temple in Idaho Falls, and all the bigwigs at the nuclear power plant in Arco, the "Atomic City," live in Idaho Falls, plus all the Idaho Falls High School boys peg their pants.

All day at the conference, it was praying. Then talking, talking, then more praying, then cafeteria lunch, then more praying and talking and praying and talking, then cafeteria dinner, then more praying. But what came after the praying after dinner was what was the most important to me and Sis. The All State Catholic Teen Jitterbug Contest.

I wasn't scared a bit standing there in the middle of the gym floor with all the other dancers. I did think my body was going to explode, though, waiting for the music to start.

The first song was "Lollipop," and "Lollipop" has a good tempo to jitterbug to. Sis and I did our under-the-arm twirls, and the arms sliding across the shoulders, then the one where Sis holds onto my right hand and I swing under and around, then come up and twirl Sis around twice. We did the cross over of arms and the swing under, and when the song was over, we did a dip just at the perfect moment when the song stopped.

The judges were two teachers from the Arthur Murray Dance Studios in Idaho Falls, a man and a woman — somebody said they were actually Arthur Murray and his wife, but I couldn't imagine what Arthur Murray would be doing in Idaho Falls.

Well, the judges chose Sis and me to be one of the final five pairs of contestants.

Then the final two.

Sis said it was good luck, and I agreed. But secretly I wondered if it was because of the rosary I prayed with my special intention that the song they played to choose the grand prize winner would be "Wake Up Little Susie." Maybe God and Jesus and the Holy Ghost did listen up once in a while.

A thousand times. Sis and I had practiced dancing to "Wake Up Little Susie" a thousand times.

Sis and I weren't sure if we should do the routine where she went on my right hip, then my left, then up in the air, then through my knees, then Sis spread-legged her butt to my waist, then the three-sixty to Sis standing on her feet because we weren't sure about the spread-legged part, on account of that might have been a sin because when Sis and I did that routine, when Sis was doing the three-sixty, sometimes you could see her underpants.

So Sis and I were dancing along to "Wake Up Little Susie," and I was waiting for Sis to give me the clue to go into that routine, but she didn't. Then all of a sudden, right toward the end, right where it said *our reputation is shot,* something happened deep inside me down there, and all of a sudden I had Sis on my right hip and then my left hip, then she was up in the air. Sis was smiling big and her Roosky Gypsy eyes were wild, and her curly brown hair was flying, and she was up in the air, then through my legs, then back up in the air, and Sis had the oh-just-fuck-it look on her face, and she went ahead and spread her legs, and her butt hit my waist, and then three hundred and sixty degrees, and Sis was ass over teakettle, and the crowd was all standing up and yelling and cheering.

The breath coming in and out of both of us was so much to breathe, and we were holding hands and smiling. Sis's gums were showing, and everybody in the bleachers was screaming, and Sis and I knew it was for us they were screaming.

Then Arthur Murray said: The winners are Mary Margaret and Rigby John Klusener!

When I looked at Sis, for some reason when I looked at her, right then I could see inside her deeper than ever. Sis *was* beautiful, so happy. But more than that.

She looked so much like Mom.

Mom got a kick out of Sis and me winning the dance contest. But what really got her going was that I was going to be confirmed. Confirmation is when the Holy Ghost comes down and enters the souls of the boys and girls, and then afterward the boys and girls become men and women.

I was pretty excited to become a man. I didn't know exactly what to expect. I just figured the Holy Ghost being inside you would have to feel great, and because the Holy Ghost was inside you, you'd get strong and start acting strong and honorable, the way men act, the way I'd never acted before, which had to do with not being so afraid, the way Dad wasn't afraid and Scardino.

When I was confirmed, though, I was twelve and I didn't know about sex yet. I mean I'd heard about sex — mostly from Scardino. Plus there was sex in some of the books I read. But up to that point in my life, sex was something that happened to other people, to Sis, to Scardino, Breck, and Muley, and in books. But sex would never happen to me because — and I haven't told you this yet — I secretly thought God was going to leave me out of the sex thing altogether and that I had a vocation to be a priest.

I hadn't actually ever said it out loud. Once I talked to Monsignor Cody about it in confession. I asked the Monsignor if you could be a priest if you were the kind of person who always wondered about God. What He was up to and why did He make people suffer so much, even babies, like little baby Russell. Monsignor didn't say anything for quite a while, and then he said: That's exactly the kind of man a priest should be, but you'd better be a Jesuit just in case.

A Jesuit priest just seemed to make sense. I didn't want to be a farmer. Maybe I could be a technical engineer because I liked math. But I really didn't fit anywhere. No friends to speak of. I didn't like girls that much. Spent most of my time alone reading books. Smart, good in school. I liked to help people. I thought about God all the time. Wondered about the universe. Yet I had a lot of doubts. I'd just seen too much hope go bad.

There were a bunch of things that happened that changed my mind, thank God. First, really, it was the books. How could I go to Spain and fight the bulls if I was a priest? And falling in love. Falling in love certainly was something I'd never do, but it sounded like just the best thing that could happen. Priests couldn't fall in love except with God. Still, though, the thought of reading and writing books all day and walking around in long skirts and drinking wine and smoking and talking philosophy while you worked in a garden sounded like an ideal life.

Two things happened, though, that changed my mind real fast.

The first thing happened in church one Sunday. It all started when Mom's sister Aunt Zelda told Mrs. Di Maio that Mary Margaret, my sis, was a whore and was sleeping around. It didn't take Mom long to get wind of this. And when she did she came unglued. In no time at all, Sis was hiding under the kitchen table with a bloody nose. The following Sunday, as fate would have it, Aunt Zelda and Mom were in charge of the coffee and doughnuts after church. After Communion, Aunt Zelda got up from the pew, genuflected, made the sign of the cross, and walked down the aisle, then down the stairs to the church basement. Mom was right behind her. Then it was right there in the church basement that Mom and Aunt Zelda went at it while Monsignor Cody finished up the Mass. Mom and Aunt Zelda cussing and screaming, the whole congregation could hear.

It was pretty clear to me. Upstairs, Monsignor was saying, Go in peace. Downstairs, Mom was screaming, You're the whore.

Upstairs was all that stuff I'd been taught. Jesus said in order to enter the kingdom of heaven you have to become like a little child. Jesus said to turn the other cheek. Jesus said to love your neighbor as yourself.

Yet it was Mom downstairs I was rooting for. Mom slapping the shit out of Aunt Zelda was what I wished I could do to Joe Scardino. And how could you love your neighbor as yourself if you called your neighbors *niggers*?

It was probably right there in that moment when I started to live more downstairs than up.

The word is *hypocrisy,* and I learned to spell it around the time I learned how to spell *rhinoceros.* I knew its definition: *an appearance of virtue and religion* — but it wasn't until that Sunday, pots and pans flying in the church basement, all hell breaking loose, that I really got what it meant.

The second thing that happened was when I turned thirteen. Almost on the very day. Sex hit me like a big hot wind. And since then, being a man is something I haven't ever got over. Confirmation and the Holy Ghost were no match for what started happening in my pants.

Then again, I guess that all depends on what you think the Holy Ghost is.

Still, though, every time I jerked off I wanted to die. Always after, I promised I'd never jerk off again. Then it wouldn't be even an hour later and there I'd be. Then there I'd be Sunday morning before Mass in the confessional telling Monsignor Cody how many times I'd broke the sixth commandment.

One time when I told Monsignor how many times, he said way too loud: In one week?

Believe me, here's something I've learned so far in my seventeen years: you got to make a choice early on if you want to live in this world or the world that comes after this world.

The way I figure it, we know we got this world, so live in this one while you're here. I figure the next one will take care of itself.

I haven't always been so sure. If I'd never met Georgy Girl, I'd still be beating off with one fist and beating my chest *mea maxima culpa* with the other.

My secret places became even more important. At first, my secret places were places I could go to get away from Mom and Sis and places to hide from Dad. Then they became where I could smoke and read books and think. When I turned thirteen, my secret places were places I could beat off, but it was more than just beating off that happened to me when I was alone and I touched myself. Something differnt happened. Something magical.

When I found my cock, my body suddenly landed in the world. The real world with things in the world. Suddenly our farm, which so far had been more of an idea than a place, started to be differnt. Spring wind across an alfalfa field, water running over gravel, the way fence posts are smooth, the flutter in a horse's withers, the tiny white cloud in the clear blue sky.

When I was in a secret place, and I was safe, and no one was around, I could reach inside my shirt pocket and light a cigarette, or I pulled a new library book out from stuck inside my pants, but now I could reach inside my pants and touch my cock, my balls. The magic had returned.

It was like I'd been sleeping for a long time, then suddenly woke up. Scintillatingly gorgeous.

And the world was alive too. The loft of the barn was a great place to go. The yellow sunlight through the holes in the shingled roof, the Holy Spirit coming on to you from deep inside your bowels.

Behind the barn, out the back door, the platform of rounded gray concrete, the wood coming down the barn in little waves, the sun warm against the warm, smooth patches of gray, your bare ass against the wood.

Between the two granaries that face east, the little place between up there that was shaped like an hourglass, you could take all your clothes off and no one could see you, but you could see everything — the land, the sky, the clouds, for miles and miles.

On top of the railroad cars, three boxcars in a row, when you lay up top on the boxcars, on the wood walkway, if you squinted your eyes and moved your body like you were fucking on a train, believe me, you *were* the Eiffel Tower, the Chrysler Building, Mount Kilimanjaro, castles in Spain. Faraway places with strange-sounding names. All of those strange-sounding names on your tongue when you came.

The grain elevator, the circus, a whole new meaning to Flying Wallenda.

The spud cellar, mostly a smell, deep under the earth, dark, cool, and the smell of earth and raw potatoes. Sometimes you could burrow yourself naked into a pile of spuds and you were a Christian slave during Roman times hiding from the Romans. Or somebody Chinese lying on a cot in an opium den, the Viceroy in the dark, a hot, orange, long puff of opium. The last puff, that magic dragon, was when your nipples got hard and your head filled up with stark blue skies crisscrossed by fluttering flags of Chinese red and Chinese gold. Your breath like those flags after you came. Or you were an American soldier in World War II. hiding out in a German trench, the S.S. encampment only yards away. You sat crouched in the dark, cold, alone, slowly unzipping your fly, waiting for the right moment to pull the pin on your hand grenade and blow the shit out of Hitler's high command.

In the Mexican house, sitting bare-assed on the cold iron stove, seeing how far you could shoot this time. But that was before Flaco and Acho. After I met Flaco and Acho, that summer when I was sixteen, and after they left, a couple times I went in the Mexican house to beat off. But both times, just as I was about to come, instead of coming, I cried.

The swimming hole was a differnt matter — I can't tell you the number of times I spread myself out naked on the bleached-out two-by-twelve across the water falling down the lava rocks. Always, always my eyes up on the scrub cedar, the blue sky behind its gnarls, the sound of the wind through its branches, something so sweet like you've never heard.

Funny, now that I think of it, I always felt so safe at the swimming hole. I was sure no one could see me. Just over the fence, though, on the other side, the red side, on the rez, in a stand of cottonwoods, was the old log cabin you could barely see that I was sure was deserted. And what do you know, all along, the whole time living in there with his grandmother, was none other than the devil himself — the infamous, drunken, queer Indian, George Serano.

3 He Wore a Yellow Tulip

IT ALL MAKES SENSE when you think about it, and God knows
I've thought about it. Sex is the reason why I'm out here alone on
Highway 93.

Sex and my family just don't mix, like Mormons and Coca-Cola,
like me and Joe Scardino, like good Catholic white folk and Indians
and niggers, no way. No matter how you look at it, it's just plain
weird. God on one side, and sex and Lucifer on the other. My family
and the sex-shame-guilt thing.

Myself, I've always found sex with people more than a little confusing. It's a brave thing to have sex, to let someone get that close to you.
For the longest time I was afraid of my own shadow, let alone another
human body with a heart. So much fear and ignorance to overcome.
At fourteen I was a long way off from overcoming anything, and I'm
still not so sure about the progress I've made. Back then, sex with myself was confusing enough. I knew it was wrong, I mean, my parents
thought it was wrong. But honestly, it was as close to God as I'd ever
felt and that was my salvation and my downfall.

My salvation and my downfall started one day after school. Mom
was in her same old red housedress in the kitchen, her back to me, her
hair pin curls in a hairnet, Mom bent over some bowl like she always
was, stirring. This day it was oatmeal cookies, and the kitchen
smelled good.

After milk and cookies, after I drove up to the feedlot and smoked one of Dad's Viceroys and listened to the top-ten countdown, I busted open the twenty-five bales of hay. I rolled the windows down and, driving back to the yard, I turned the radio up real loud and sang, *Hello, darkness, my old friend* with Simon and Garfunkel and Tramp. Tramp got that look in his eyes, and his tongue went out, and he was smiling. His paw poking, poking at the air.

I carried the five-gallon bucket of water from the house and slopped the hogs and fed the chickens and gathered the eggs. It was about five o'clock. My chores were done, and the sun was still up. I was leaning up against the barn, in the sun, my bare ass against the warm red wood of the barn. I was slowly pulling on myself, feeling the deep grace of the earth and manure I was standing on coming up through me. I was just about ready, my breath was coming hard, when out of the blue, the latch on the back barn door turned, then the squeak of the hinges of the back door, then the door was open, and there she was standing right there next to me in her red house-dress, her plucked eyebrows, her pin curls and hairnet, the little lines around her starting around her mouth, her almond-shaped hazel eyes looking down at me down there red and wet and poking up, my mother.

Faster than you could say "mortal sin," Mom had closed the barn door, and there I stood with my pants down around my ankles, leaning up against the barn, cock dripping one long strand of cum down onto the dry cow manure. Just me and Tramp and the trapdoor to the underworld flung open inside my heart. I couldn't move. Really, I am not exaggerating. I just fell over, didn't try to catch myself or nothing, just like a Road Runner cartoon. One moment I was in one position standing up, the next I was in the same position lying down.

The time between when Mom caught me and supper at six o'clock was an eternity. Everybody says *eternity* like it's just another word, but that day, that hour, was an eternity, something that was never going to end, and I didn't want it to end, because the end meant I had to walk in the house and stand inside my mother's almond-shaped hazel eyes. All I wanted to do was smoke and smoke and smoke, but Dad's cigarettes were in the house, on the refrigerator, plus he would miss the cigarettes if I took more than one.

Tramp, I said, Tramp, we're in big trouble.

Tramp's orange face on his black face, his tongue went to hanging out.

Tramp, I said, what am I going to do?

Tramp got that look in his eyes.

What in the hell am I going to do?

Tramp's paw went up, poking, poking the air.

I should have started hitchhiking right then. But I wasn't ready yet. It took almost three more years before I was ready for the road.

Walking to the house from the barn, my shadow on the ground around my feet was the black hole I was walking in. All I could hear was my breath. My hand on the screen door pulled the screen door open. My hand around the doorknob turned the knob. My feet stomped off on the square of grating on the floor just inside the porch.

The hallway light was off. Mom was a tall shadow standing in shadows. Her hair was fluffed out. The feeling I get in my arms that means I am helpless. I couldn't see Mom's eyes when I looked, but still I looked away from her eyes.

She said: Change into your school clothes right after supper. We're making a *special trip* to town. Monsignor Cody was kind enough to hear your confession. The man is a saint. And a busy man, Rigby John, and he is taking extra time for you. Hurry up, we have to be at the church by seven-fifteen.

At supper, when my voice said the blessing, I sounded like a Beatles album played backward. Only the scrape of forks against the hard plastic plates with the flower gardens on them. Mom's mouth got more and more and more puckered as we ate. I looked over to Sis. Sis didn't know yet. If Sis knew, she'd have had her smirk on under her bland supper expression, and there was no smirk. Dad was scowling down at his plate, just eating his spuds like the grunting, gruff old bastard he was. Tore off a piece of Wonder Bread, sopped up the gravy. But I wasn't sure if Dad was the regular grunting, gruff old bastard, or the nightmare bastard who came out only in the saddle room when he whipped my ass.

Just before we left the house, when Mom was getting her purse, Sis walked by me with her big dark Roosky eyes. No doubt about it, she had the smirk.

Going to the chapel, and we're going to get married, Sis sang.

Outside the Buick windows, the sun was pink on the cottonwoods on Philbin Road. In the fields, still patches of snow, ice-smooth and shiny, the same pink as the sun. The red speedometer was on eighty. Usually it was sixty-five, maybe seventy, but this March evening

Mom's high heel had got the pedal to the floor. Speed, more of what was left unsaid. Mom stared straight ahead, her red lips, her warrior paint, a gash across her face. Stiff-armed, she drove. White knuckles. The sound of her legs, the rub of nylon to nylon. The heater, blasting warm air on defrost. In the air, her smell, from the dark blue bottle, her sister Alma's Evening in Paris.

My body was on the vinyl seat, in its Sunday jacket, its white short-sleeve shirt, its black oxford shoes, white socks, its Catholic school corduroy pants. But I was not in my body in my clothes. I was in the breath in my ears, out on the hood of the Buick, standing on the edge of eighty, my mother's almond-shaped hazel eyes staring at my slope of bare butt, my naked back and arms, hands clasped around my cock, a hood ornament going at it.

Twelve miles can be forever.

Eternity eternity eternity.

On the playground, Mom parked the Buick right next to the incinerator, where the guide wire of the light pole went into the pavement.

You know why I've brought you here, Mom said.

You have committed a mortal sin, and I've brought you here to confess, she said.

You must confess to the Monsignor your mortal sin and any other sins which you have committed. You must tell Monsignor everything, she said. Every detail to be sure your sin is forgiven.

Cold wind blew up the corners of Mom's tweed coat. The wind blew against my ears. The tree branches were no longer pink, only gray and darker than gray, black finger shadows that flipped against one another in the wind.

OK, I said.

The brass doorknob of the church was cold on the palm of my hand. I pulled on the door. Mom held her hand out flat against the wood of the door. Her fingers spread, fingernails cut to the quick, her rough, red farm hands stopped the door. Her red leaching lips.

Rigby John, my mother said. You must tell the Monsignor *everything*.

My Adam's apple stuck on the top of the zipper of my jacket. The breath inside there in my throat.

Even the dog, my mother said.

The dog? I said.

You were with the dog, my mother said.

Tramp? I said.

Rigby John, my mother said, you must confess every detail.

The feeling in my forearms that meant I was helpless. Inside the church, the deep wood smell, Catholic incense, beeswax. I put my fingers into the holy water font, made the sign of the cross. Past the choir stairs, on the left, the confessional. The little red light bulb above the middle door was on.

The Monsignor was in.

I genuflected. My corduroy pants made the corduroy bending sound. I made the sign of the cross again, knelt down in the second pew. The holy light of the stained-glass windows all over me on my hands and face. I was saturated. My mother knelt in the pew behind me. My cock a tiny burning piece of shame. My body the ugly casket for my smashed-flat roadkill soul.

The confessional door closed behind me. When I knelt down I heard the red light bulb outside my door click on. Hot inside the dark. Sweat drips going down the insides of my arms. Down to my elbows. I unzipped my jacket, unzipped the zipper all the way down, pulled the wool collar away from my neck. I quick put my hands in my jacket pockets, tried to get some air moving by flapping my hands.

My throat. The air stuck inside there. My right hand, fingertips, to my forehead, my chest, to my left shoulder, my right shoulder. Then my hands folded together, fingers pointed up to God, my elbows on the little ledge below the screened panel.

Bless me, Father, for I have sinned, I said. My last confession was four days ago. These are my sins.

The sunlight on the wood of the barn. It was warm there in that spot without the wind. The red paint was peeling off in places, and the gray raw wood was sticking through. The sky was bright blue, only one little putt of clouds up there. The cement platform at the back door of the barn was ground down to round curves of light gray cement with chunks of tiny rock. Manure all over on the platform. Dry manure becoming earth, rich earth, the shit smell of cows and milk and hay and bales of straw. The siding of the barn, little horizontal waves. My hand against the waves of red wood, raw gray poking through. Sun on the wood, the blue sky, the cloud, the dry manure — all these things were things outside me, yet by some miracle also deep within. Like the day was a movie connected to the place just under my balls.

I wanted to fuck the barn, fuck the manure-rich earth smell coming up in the patch of sun. The sun warm there, so warm against the red peeling wood, that place, so safe, protected from the wind. My hand on my Levi's button was heavy and deep too, everything deep and full and heavy, the pop pop pop pop of the rest of the five Levi's buttons. I was still sore and wet from the last time and I was still hard, hard and full and heavy. The palm of my hand just touching my belly, the hair of me down there, then cupping my balls, underneath, the dark, smelly crack. Just pulling down my shorts I almost came. Then my ass, my bare ass cool outside, exposed. Why did the wind suddenly find me there? The hairs on my ass stood up with goose flesh. Soft ass flesh against sun wood. How warm the red peeling waves. Big old horny red barn flirting with my ass.

Oh. Just the tip of my cock, underneath the fold of skin. Grab it there and pinch. The sun is bright and bright, and the little putt of cloud. The slide of my ass up and down on the wood, the so soft and all open of me down there. The first sharp roll of ejaculation, not a shoot-out this time, just a slow roll, the slow out of the end of so red piss slit one long drool down. My tongue loves so much my lips. My knees come unhinged, and for a moment, there is nothing. And nothing is full and round, everything round and round and round and full and deep and hard and soft and heavy and safe and warm and wet, in the sun, pressed against the red wood barn, under the bright blue sky, protected from the wind, just the cloud, the putt of cloud, up high up there floating away eternity eternity.

For I have sinned exceedingly.

My jacket was all the way off, on the floor, the wool as far away from me as I could get. My T-shirt and my white shirt were soaked through. My sweat smelled like my cum, the way my ass smells.

I committed the sin of self-abuse, I said.

Out of the dark, on the other side of the screen, the outline of Monsignor's hooked nose.

Tell me, my son, what are your thoughts while you touch yourself?

You could hear my sweat dripping.

Lewd thoughts, Father.

How are they lewd, my son?

Monsignor's ear pressed up against the screen.

Lewd and dark and smooth, hot, red, wet flesh, hairy, sticky. Where was there air?

They're just awful, Father. They're I don't know how to say.

Are your thoughts of men or women?

My open palm against horseflesh smooth along the withers. Cows eating raw potatoes. The slice of a shovel into wet sod. Water running thin over gravel. Sunlight on the water.

They're of everything, Father.

Everything?

Yes, Father.

Even the dog? Do you have sex with the dog?

Monsignor's hand up to his mouth, then just his index finger against his lips. On the ledge my elbows were wet. The ledge was a puddle. I was turning into a puddle.

No, Father.

But your mother said you were with the dog.

Mother said. How could she say? What words?

The dog was only watching, Father, I said. He wasn't doing anything.

Then out of the blue, I just had to say it. Blurted it out the way I always do:

Tramp is not that kind of dog, I said.

After my Act of Contrition, after I left the confessional and knelt down in the pew and said my five Our Fathers and five Hail Marys and five Glory Be's, I heard Mom get up from the pew behind me. I thought for sure we were going to be kneeling in church all night praying litanies for my soul, so I was surprised when Mom got up so quick.

Then at the Wyz Way Market, parked outside in the Buick listening to KWIK while Mom bought groceries, I realized something. Mom got out of church so fast because she didn't want to see the Monsignor, let alone talk to him.

A couple things about the ride home. A little thing and a big thing.

The little thing was that Mom bought me a candy bar, a Snickers, my favorite, without me asking for one.

The big thing was what she said when we were halfway home. Mom had just stopped at the stop sign on the corner of Philbin Road and Quinn Road. There were no cars coming from any direction in the dark night. The headlights of the Buick pressed against the dark, against the rough bark of the big cottonwoods that line the road there. A gust of Idaho wind blew so hard, the Buick lifted up off its springs. The heater was blowing warm air up the legs of my pants. Mom kept her foot on the brake. Behind us, in my mind, I saw the brake lights glow out red in all the dark. The dash lights were amber and green and gold on my mother's face. Behind her glasses, her al-mond-shaped hazel eyes were still not looking at me. Evening in Paris. Perry Como was singing "Faraway Places."

Rigby John, Mom said, there's only one solution. You and I are go-ing to make a novena to Our Mother of Perpetual Help. Nine Tues-day nights in a row. Starting next Tuesday.

All our prayers will be answered, Mom said. All our sins forgiven. If only we pray to the Virgin.

The next day, after school, Dad's black eyes looked at the terrible place inside me that had hurt my mother.

Dad said, Your mom says you need a whipping.

Dad said, I'll be in the saddle room. You know what to do.

What to do was wait for him to get to the saddle room, unlock it, turn the light on, pull his squat three-legged stool out from under the workbench, and set it directly under the light bulb hanging down, then sit down on it.

The walk to the barn was long, the same long as whenever I was getting a whipping. My ass could already feel the welts the belt was going to raise. But the welts weren't the worst part. In a way I liked the welts because that meant the worst part was over. The worst part was the two knocks on the saddle room door. The worst part was opening the door. The worst part was behind my eyes what happened when I saw my father on his squat three-legged stool, the light bulb hanging down directly above him, the shadow of him a dark pool on the cement floor.

The pattern in the wood of the saddle room door was a swirl of uni-verse, a red, rough swirl of wood, years and years of a tree growing. My hand was a fist. I looked over, and my hand was a fist up in the air in front of my head.

Knock knock.

Who's there?

Daddy.

Daddy who?

Daddy under the light bulb on the squat chair. Shadow Daddy. *Inner Sanctum.*

Eternity eternity eternity.

From behind the door, Dad said, Go ahead and come on in.

My palm flat up against the wood of the painted red door, I pushed. He said, Close the door.

I closed the door.

Dad said, Now lock it.

I pulled the dead bolt into its socket, then pulled the dead bolt down.

Like always, Dad's butt cheeks went side to side on his squat chair. He put his right foot out. His foot dragged along the cement. Then his other foot dragged until both feet were square in front of him, knees perpendicular to the cement floor.

Dad said, Pull your pants down and your undershorts.

My fingers went to my first Levi's button and undid it. Then the second button. When I was on the third button, I stopped.

Something like a burp, a large lump of words, jumped right up out of my chest. My mouth was already moving before I knew what I was going to say.

Did Mom tell you what the whipping's for? I said.

Both Dad and I looked around the room to see where the strange voice had come from. He seemed smaller for a moment, only a man sitting on a squat stool. When he spoke again, he was back to proportion, which was way out of proportion. My father took up the whole saddle room.

Dad said, No. And she don't need to. Now, do as you're told.

I undid the third button, the fourth, the fifth. Hooked my thumbs onto the sides of my Levi's, slid them down. I pulled my jockey shorts down.

Air all around where I usually didn't feel air.

The look in Dad's Roosky Gypsy eyes when he saw me naked down there. Dad jumped up so quick like a cattle prod jumped him up. His eyes, then his whole face, turned away, taking the rest of his body with him.

What in the hell!? Dad said.

I looked down, and there I was, my cock poking straight out.

Get me half-naked, and it'll happen every time.

My teeth in my mouth grinding.

Pull your damn pants up! Dad said. Cover yourself, for chrissakes! And get the hell out of here!

The next nine weeks happen like one long bad dream. Tuesday nights, on one side of me out the Buick's window, the twelve miles into town flew by at eighty miles an hour. On the other side, my mother was in one of her Joan Crawford church hats, the ripple going up and down her jaw. Things could not have been worse.

But then there's the universe. This time what the universe conspired was Sister Barbara Ann's altar boy contest and Monsignor Cody's baseball game.

The contest was to see which altar boy could get the most points by the end of the school year. Five points for showing up on time. Five points for not making a mistake. Minus ten points for not showing up. Plus ten points for substituting.

The baseball game came out of nowhere. Sunday morning from the pulpit, Monsignor Cody just up and says there's nothing like a good baseball game to get the religious spirit flowing and let's beat Saint Anthony's.

Mom's novena, Sister Barbara Ann's contest, Monsignor Cody's baseball game. They all came together and fucked me up in a very particular way.

Tuesday night was the night of Our Mother of Perpetual Help devotions.

Tuesday night was the night for baseball practice.

Tuesday night no boys showed up to serve Our Mother of Perpetual Help devotions. Except for me, which means I had to substitute for the three altar boys who were at baseball practice.

Which means I would win the altar boy contest. But winning the altar boy contest wasn't winning. I never was like anybody else, and during those nine weeks of the novena, I was never more not like anybody else than ever. Of course, then with what happened later on, Scardino and "Casey at the Bat" and all, I was in serious deep shit.

And, if I didn't know what was coming, Scardino would remind me. Every Wednesday morning, after Sister Barbara Ann announced the score, Scardino flipped me the bird and moved his mouth real slow to say: *You fucking queer, you are a fucking dead man.*

One long bad dream.

Plus, what did you win? The winner of the altar boy contest got to be the winner, plus got a black glass-beaded rosary blessed by the Pope in the Vatican.

Tuesday, Irving Field, just three blocks away from Saint Joe's, boys ran the bases, hit high pop flies, hit home runs, pitched, catched, boys ran around the baseball diamond having fun together, playing ball at baseball practice. Not me. In the candlelight of Saint Joe's I was kneeling in the congregation, praying for altar boys to show up. They never did. Monsignor entered the altar alone, stood there, and waited. For me he waited because he knew everything about me. In less than a minute, I was on the altar in my cassock and ironed and starched surplice kneeling next to the Monsignor. Mom was up in the choir loft on the organ, watching me.

When Monsignor Cody said: *I who am the most miserable of all* — that's when I got up and got the holy water font from inside Monsignor's sacristy. As Monsignor said the blessing, he shook the holy water font so the holy water splashed out into the congregation in drops. If a drop of holy water fell on me, I thought maybe God was touching me. But if God was touching me, why wasn't I playing baseball instead of locked up in a church with a bunch of old people.

My next job was to go into the sacristy and start the charcoal for the incense.

Don't burn the damn church down.

Outside of confession, those were the only words Monsignor ever said to me. Not hi, hello, how are you, thanks for showing up, bless you, my son. Nothing. Just: When you light the charcoal, don't burn the damn church down.

When the charcoal was lit and the edges were turning white, I put the charcoal into the open censer with the black medieval pincers, then closed the censer, then took a deep breath and carried the censer and the burning incense onto the altar.

Me doing it, and Mom watching me do it. My whole life's been like that.

The big moment of Benediction was when Monsignor turns around with the gold, spaceship-looking monstrance in his hands and points the monstrance with God in it at the congregation. Mom started playing "Tantum Ergo Sacramentum." Miss Kasiska, Miss Radcliffe, and Miss Biddle all genuflected and made the sign of the cross. I sang too, and the censer was on the second step with the smoke coming out, and my hand was ringing, ringing the gold bells, never stopping the whole time, while Monsignor lifted the golden monstrance up through the sign of the cross.

And there we were, all of us, even God, inside the slanted mirror up in the choir loft, and Mom watching.

All the while Monsignor Cody was pointing God at us, every one of us, every human-being one of us was praying, praying hard to God for things we wanted to have, or for things we don't want to have, for an old way to stop, or a new way to be, to not be sick, or not be old, or for special intentions, like my special intention, I mean my mother's special intention for me.

After devotions, the charcoal still burning in the censer, I opened the sacristy door, carried the censer outside and down the side stairs. Most nights it was pitch-black. When I got to the corner of the church, as soon as I stepped away from the church, the wind was cold, but I liked the cold wind because it had been so warm on the altar ringing the bells and looking at God. The wind blew my cassock and surplice, and I felt like Heathcliff in the olden days wearing those clothes, flutters of cloth, the sound of big skirts on women in the wind. This was the only good part of the night because in the dark, cold night, for a while there was no Mom, and only the stars were watching.

I didn't know where I was in all of this, or even if there was enough of me around to be something enough to make a differnce. I was just putting one foot in front of the other. Trying to be a good Catholic son. I didn't see I had any choice, and I did care about being a good son, if only to keep my mother close. The rest of it I wasn't so sure about. But how could I say no to my parents, my teachers, my priest? There were no words, no real options. What started it all, masturbating, the thing that they were telling me I did have a choice about, I couldn't seem to make the right choice. When that feeling came up in my balls, I didn't have a chance. Truth be told, I was worried about my soul. I didn't want to hurt Jesus with my sin, and I didn't want to go to hell either. Even Hemingway said it. What was immoral was what made you feel bad after. And after jerking off, I felt like shit. But it could be an hour, and there I'd go again.

What I did have a choice about happened around the same time, and it is something I've been ashamed of ever since.

It all started one Saturday afternoon about the third week into the no- vena. I was out in the barn, and I looked up from where I was spread- ing out straw in the calf pen, and there was a kid my age standing there. The light was bright from the open barn door behind him, so he was only a silhouette. Then when I got close and I was looking at his face, his face was a face I'd seen a hundred times, but nothing regis- tered. Then it was his pale eyes behind his crooked glasses with the white tape across the glasses in the middle.

There I was, just me with Puke Price.

I looked around. Only the chickens and the sick baby calf were looking.

Then it was weird. On a Saturday in the barn, alone without any- body else from school, Puke Price wasn't that bad.

Hey, Puke, I said. What you doing here?

Puke always wore his corduroy pants up too high on his waist. His shirt was tucked in, and right there around his waist it was a bulgy mess of shirttails, bunched-up pants, and his brown belt cinched tight.

Puke said: My name's Allen.

His shoulders went up a little, and his hands made fists.

I want you to call me by my name, he said. I don't call you names, he said. My name is Allen.

Puke's big breath of air went right up against my face and up my nose.

Fried bologna breath. The worst kind of breath. There's tuna breath, and Cheetos breath, and onion breath, and boiled broccoli breath, and each one of those breaths is bad. But the worst kind of breath is all four of them; tuna, Cheetos, onion breath, and boiled broccoli breath all in one and that's what I call fried bologna breath, and Puke had fried bologna breath real bad.

I said: Allen. Sure, I said, Allen. What are you doing here?

I liked that Allen smiled, but still I stepped back because I saw he was going to speak, and words and breath go together, and with Allen you had to be careful.

My dad's here, Allen said, shooting rock chucks. We'll be here all afternoon.

Allen was the one who suggested that we play Poison. How you play Poison is you get the most poisonous stuff and the worst awful things possible, and you pour them all together in one bucket.

The bucket was a gallon bucket of oil-base paint with about an inch of slimy red in the bottom. The weed killer was in the saddle room under the bench in a gray five-gallon bucket that said POISON on it. It was a white powder. The skinny piece of an old cedar shingle was what I used to stir the white into the red until it was pink. Next, the bucket went to the gas pump. Three seconds of gasoline into the bucket. Allen stirred the gasoline in with the pink. It smelled awful. The creosote came from the vat where Dad was soaking railroad ties. Inside the bucket it was the color of dark blood. The rat poison from the toolshed. A white powder in a red and yellow can like Kraft Parmesan cheese. Holes in the top of the can so you can shake out the rat poison. Allen sprinkled the rat poison onto what was in the bucket. The Malathion and the DDT came from in the corner of the machine shop where the sugar beet planter was. Both the Malathion and the DDT were in quart-size brown bottles with screw-top lids. The ant spray and furniture polish were from under the kitchen sink. Allen and I held our noses, and Allen sprayed the ant spray into the bucket and I poured in the Olde English furniture polish. Bluing, Clorox, and ammonia from the closet in the washroom went in next. A scoop of phosphate from the Simplot's bag. Then drops of Mercurochrome, gentian violet, Merthiolate from the medicine cabinet. Strychnine, tiny pellets in a little blue bottle from in the saddle room, from inside the cabinet Dad kept under lock and kept the key above the saddle room door. I found that key when my dog Nikki died. Battery acid from a battery from the pile of dead batteries in the weeds next to the wood granary. Really slimy gray and white chicken poop. A dead baby chicken. A mother spider and her million babies in the web in the chicken coop window with the eisenglass. A can of Del Monte lima beans. Mush would have been good in there, or a fried hard egg or a soft-boiled egg, but Mom was in the kitchen so we couldn't get to the mush or the eggs. A piece of Kotex with blood splotches on it from inside the big garbage burn barrel outside. Allen, not me, held the Kotex by one of the white flaps. One of my father's crusty socks.

I thought of asking Allen to puke into the whole mess, then thought better.

That's when Allen said, Let's piss in it.

Allen had a look. His upper lip curled up a little. Then, before I knew it, there he was, Allen Price's dick hanging out of the zipper under the bunched-up waist of his corduroys. His dick was really white, like the rest of him, and big. Well, not big. For Allen Price, big. I mean, you'd think he'd have a real tiny one. Then his white dick started peeing.

For a moment, I was a little amazed so I just watched the yellow pee from his dick dribble out and then up full force into what was in the bucket. I didn't know what to do. I just knew I couldn't let Puke Price get the best of me, so I undid my Levi's buttons and pulled my cock out.

My cock is a lot like me. It doesn't do what it's told right off. I have to wait. And there's no telling sometimes how long I have to wait, so I just wait.

Allen's dick quit peeing in spurts. He left it hanging out when he was done. That's when Allen's dick started getting bigger and bigger and pinker and poking out right at me.

What you doing, Price? I said.

Allen said: What *you* doing?

I followed Allen's pale eyes down to my own cock hanging out. It should have been no surprise, but it was a surprise. My cock was sticking straight out too. That's when Allen suggested we put another one of our body fluids into what was in the bucket, but the thought of that, the thought of jacking off with Puke Price into what was in the bucket, was just too gross, so I quick put my cock in my pants, turned around, and walked out of the barn, across the yard, and into the house. Allen zipped up right behind me. The screen door slammed.

Mom was in the kitchen, hair flying out, bent over some bowl. The kitchen smelled good.

Oatmeal cookies? I said.

Peanut butter, she said. Go wash your hands first.

After our peanut butter cookies and glasses of milk and before Allen went home with his dad, Allen and I crawled up the ladder to the granaries, then jumped down between the granaries into the secret place shaped like an hourglass.

I reached in my pocket and pulled out two Viceroys. Allen acted like it was every day that he and I smoked cigarettes. He leaned back against the corrugated-steel granary, inhaled, and didn't cough.

Out of the blue, Allen had a book in his hands. I don't know where the book came from, and I don't remember it before that moment when I was looking at it there in his hands.

It was a Nancy Drew mystery. *The Mystery of the Brass-bound Trunk*. Allen handed me the book.

Here, Rig, he said. Take a look at my book.

The book was blue-green and the regular size of a Nancy Drew mystery. It was usually in the upper right-hand corner of his desk at Saint Joseph's School. Allen always kept the book next to the inkwell, in the upper right-hand corner of his desk.

I read this one, I said. But it's the only one I've read.

I like the Bowery Boys better, I said.

Holding a cigarette for a long time in your mouth makes you cough. I was coughing. Allen took a drag on the Viceroy like he'd been smoking all his life.

Do you notice anything unusual about the book? he asked.

I turned the book around, flipped it over, patted my hand against the cover.

No, I said. It's just a Nancy Drew mystery book.

Allen pulled his legs in and sat like meditating Indians do. Then before I knew it, Allen raised his chin and was speaking right into my face. Cigarette smoke and fried bologna breath going up my nostrils.

If I told you a secret, Allen said, would you promise not to tell?

Something in his right cheek started twitching.

Sure, I said.

Promise? he said. I'll show you a secret, but you have to promise.

I sucked the smoke into my lungs, let the smoke stay inside for a while, then spit the smoke out at the same time I said: Promise.

Allen stubbed out his Viceroy onto the steel-plate floor.

Say the whole thing, Allen said.

What? I said.

Say: I promise I won't tell anyone your secret, Allen said.

A gust of wind blew up and into between the granaries. I stubbed my cigarette out, kept the filter, picked up Allen's, stubbed out his filter too.

I promise I won't tell anyone your secret, I said.

And that you won't call me Puke anymore, Allen said.

The filters went into my shirt pocket.

I won't call you Puke anymore, I said.

Promise, Allen said.

I promise I won't call you Puke anymore, I said.

Allen set the book on his crossed legs. He opened the book and turned the pages of the book, one by one, slowly, slowly.

Page forty-two, Allen said.

Allen opened the book for me to see.

The book had been hollowed out where the words had been on the pages. Only the borders of the pages where there were no words was left, and those pages were glued together. Inside in the secret carved-out hollow space of the book, there were three glass radio tubes. One short one and two long ones with skinny red parts in the filaments.

Allen's hands shook a little when he closed the book. What he said next, he said real slow.

Now remember, Rig, Allen said. You made a promise. You promised me you wouldn't tell.

There's one more thing the universe conspired on. Mom and I almost got ourselves killed by a naked man. It happened on the last of the nine Tuesdays. We were in the Buick on our way to church. It was raining. Rain like you never see in Idaho, coming down in buckets. The swipe of the windshield wipers were back and forth, back and forth, fast as they could go, but still the wipers weren't fast enough. Soon as the wipers swiped, for a moment it was clear and you could see the road, but then, splash, it was just like we were driving under-water.

Outside my window, past the barrow pit, past the barbwire fences, the harrowed spring fields were expanses of dark brown dirt filled with shiny puddles of water. Rain splashing up on the puddles of water.

It was weird too because over there where the sun was setting it wasn't raining. Down low in the west the sky was blue, then yellow, then gold, then pink. Sun shining through all the rain coming down made each raindrop into a tiny ball of light.

There we were, Mom Klusener and Rigby John in our Buick Special speeding eighty miles an hour through a mystery shower of light and shiny rain. When we got to the cottonwoods on Philbin Road, the rain let up some, but the cottonwoods, just newly leafed out, had more of a surprise for us. The line of cottonwoods, big old grandpa trees, so big around three people with their arms out couldn't circle one, one grandpa after another after another alongside the road reaching up their big arms, lumpy, graceful, fifty feet and higher into the sky, the rain shiny-slick on the bark, the yellow-gold sunset light against the wet. Not just the trees. Everything was glowing. The yellow-gold light onto the Buick, the road in front of us, the fat drops slow falling through the air from the leaves of the cottonwoods, onto the road, onto the blue hood of the Buick, onto the windshield.

The glass of the windshield glowed, the angle of the wipers, inside the Buick even my hands were glowing yellow-gold. Mom's face, those little lines around her lips, the way she held her chin up and gritted her teeth, the light on Mom's face. Everything slowed down so slow, one long breath in and out. Mom's almond-shaped hazel eyes, one pitched south, the other east, and my eyes. My eyes looking into her eyes, that moment. Mom and I, we weren't us, and nothing was familiar. Mom and I were just there, alive and breathing in the rain and glowing light.

Just in time, Mom hit the brakes and cranked the steering wheel. Directly in front of us, the old gray '49 Ford was parked just barely off the road. All around my ears was a loud screech. My right hand held hard onto the armrest of the door. Both of Mom's arms were on the steering wheel. Her hair was flying up. We were spinning. The sun was gone, and it was gray, and outside the windows of the Buick the world was spinning. We spun around for a long time. At least while we were spinning, it was a long time. Now when I look back, I wish the spinning had lasted longer. God spins you around like that only once in a while.

The Buick stopped in the middle of the road, pointing toward town the way it was supposed to be pointing. The world was back in place, regular, the way it was supposed to be. My hand wouldn't let go of the armrest. Mom's hands were shaking so bad, she couldn't get her purse open. When she finally got it open, she pulled out her rosary. Her fingers went straight to the crucifix, then started down the beads.

But Mom wasn't praying. She was cussing a blue streak.

Her hand, her cut-to-the-quick nails, middle finger, index, and thumb, sliding the beads.

Goddamn. Son of a bitch. Asshole. Bastard.

All of them. She was saying all of the cuss words.

I was waiting for her to say *fuck* or *cunt* or *cocksucker,* but she didn't say any of those.

But she did say a word I'd never heard her say before.

To the man standing out in the harrowed field, under the cottonwoods. The driver of the '49 Ford. The man whose clothes hung out of the driver's side window. The naked man in the rain. My first time, my first naked man. The long smooth muscle of him, his hairy chest, his hairline down his belly to the dark brown-black between his legs. His brown and amber glow in the last spot of sunlight, his hands held up out in front of him, cupped. Just as I looked and before I quick looked away, that moment, a big fat drop of rain slow from a cottonwood leaf in the last light fell, the splash in his hands, crooked light.

Mom's fingers were on the bead of the first mystery of the rosary.

Goddamn Indians, Mom said. Drunken bunch of no-good bastards. A menace to society. Especially that son of a bitch George Serano.

Mom's left hand quick rolled down her window. She stuck her head out, red lipstick lips, mouth pointed up to sky.

Goddamn Indian! she screamed. Where'd you learn to drive!

I'm calling the sheriff! she screamed.

Injun George, you better get your pants on fast!

Disgusting goddamn drunk, Mom yelled.

And then she said it. The word I'd heard so many times before but never heard from her.

Queer, she said. You goddamn queer. Those Indians and their goddamn queers.

I heard this story about the Pope. When the Pope is blessing the crowd, the people up front right up close to the Pope are happy they're up close, but they're also dodging around, trying to get away from something. What they are trying to get away from is the shadow of the Pope's hand. If the shadow of the Pope's hand falls on you, it's a curse. Sooner or later, no matter what you do, your fear catches up to you.

The Wednesday morning I won the altar boy contest, and was given the black crystal rosary that was blessed by the Vatican, the shadow fell on me.

The sign of the cross and the morning prayer, Sister Barbara Ann pointed the black grease pen to the box in the ninth week that was next to my name.

Class, she said. Take a look. See who loves the Virgin the most.

The winner! Sister Barbara Ann says. Rigby John Klusener!

From out of her top drawer, Sister Barbara Ann took out a red velvet box. She held the red velvet box up so the whole class could see, then slow walked down the aisle holding up the red velvet box.

Blessed by the Vatican, Sister Barbara Ann said.

Inside the box it was white shiny cloth. The rosary was curled onto itself, a shiny, black, beaded snake, the silver crucifix on top of the folds.

Hold the rosary up for everyone to see, Sister Barbara Ann said.

I lifted the rosary up by its silver crucifix. The shadow of the black shiny beads fell onto my face, just between my eyes, down my throat, onto my shirt pocket just above my heart.

At recess, there was nowhere to go but into the boys' bathroom. All three of the stalls were full, so there was only the urinal. Allen Price stood next to me. Yellow pee coming out from between his fingers.

Scardino's miffed, Allen said. He's going to kick you in the balls again.

Fried bologna breath.

Allen's crooked eyeglasses. The piece of tape across the nose. That's when the boys' bathroom door slammed open. Allen's eyes were wide open green with gold flecks in the green. Ronald Wilson, Roger Waring, Ricky Divine, Tony Smith, Alvin Gosford, ran out of the boys' bathroom, rats from a sinking ship.

The toilet stalls on the one side of them, the sinks and the mirrors on the other side, Scardino and Breck and Muley stretched their legs out wide in one combat line across the room. Price and me were hemmed in. The boys' door behind Scardino, Breck, and Muley was our only escape.

Scardino's shoulders were back, his chin up, the grin on his face, one side of his upper lip up a little. His one tooth there that was sharp. Both his feet square beneath him.

At home in front of the mirror I'd practiced to stand like that. When I stood like that, I couldn't stand like that.

Scardino's white shirtsleeves were rolled up. His arms big biceps, smooth olive skin down his forearms, something scary how his forearms flowed down to his wrists, his big hands, knuckles big from popping. Usually some kind of ink tattoo on his arm or his wrist that Sister Barbara Ann made him wash off. His dark brown hair as long as he could get away with, wavy, combed back in a duck's ass. Brown eyes that behind something was always going on. The top button of his white shirt unbuttoned. Just down below his belt, somehow perfect how that part of him down there looked. His corduroy cuffs rolled up, white socks, black shiny wedgies.

In the mirror, the three of them lined up left to right: Scardino, Breck, Muley. Breck and Muley trying to look like Scardino. Chests out. Thumbs in their pockets. DA's. Then myself in the mirror. The cold sore I'd woke up with this morning was a big yellow pus scar across my lip. A head taller than anybody in the bathroom, skinny. My long, skinny arms and skinny legs. My neck poking up out of my shirt collar, guck, guck, silly goose. My stupid Adam's apple. My hair in a crewcut because it saved on haircuts.

Nowhere to run, nowhere to hide, just me trapped in a bathroom trapped in a body that couldn't even think of making a fist, let alone make a fist, a tall, gawky tantrum with nowhere to go, standing next to a body who was something even worse than I was. A true dork. The worst dork you could possibly get in the world. Allen Fucking Price.

Scardino stepped one step toward me. Scardino's lips said *queer,* said *syphilis lip.*

My feet were stepping backward. Somewhere behind me was the wall. Scardino threw all his weight into a John Wayne punch. I moved just enough so the punch wouldn't hit me in the face. Bam, square in the shoulder. I found the wall behind me, slid my back against the wall to the corner. The smell of mothballs from the little white beehive things you pee on, water running along the back side of the white urinal.

That was the moment, the end of the rope, cornered, the feeling in my forearms that meant I was helpless. Breathless. Shit out of luck.

A real man honors his promises no matter what, but I never have been a real man, at least not until recently. As ever, honor, when faced with Scardino and his gang, turned into a shit bird and flew out the window. I just didn't know what the hell else to do. So I said it.

I said, Leave me alone, and I'll tell you a secret.

I said, Puke's got a secret, and I'll tell you if you'll leave me alone.

Allen's crooked glasses. His belt sticking out and his pants all bunched up around the waist.

Allen whispered, Rigby, no. He whispered, Rig, you promised.

Secret? Scardino said.

That's when Allen did something that surprised us all. In that place and time, when every movement was watched, where every tiny movement had meaning, Allen broke the spell and walked over to me, stepped in front of Scardino, leaned into me in the corner. His stupid crooked glasses. Allen put his hand on my shoulder, where Scardino had hit me.

Rig, Allen said, remember? No matter what. You promised.

I slapped Allen's hand away.

It's a book, I said. On the right-hand corner of his desk. Next to the inkwell.

Scardino's little smile was all the way across his face. He laid his hand on Allen's shoulder, leaned in close to me like Allen. Scardino's thumb and index finger had Allen by the ear. But Allen didn't seem to care. His eyes stayed looking into my eyes.

What kind of book is it? Scardino said.

Allen's head was slowly headed to the floor ear-first.

I'll have to show you, I said.

A lot of commotion, then pushing back and forth, and I looked, and Allen's glasses fell on the floor. Then Scardino's shiny black wedgie stepped on Allen's glasses. Glass crushed on concrete and tile, that sound. Scardino stopped, lifted up his foot. The glasses, the parts that go over the ears, twisted, crooked, sticking up every which way.

In the classroom, the sun came in through the big east windows, big, glowing, gold sun into the room, onto the desks, onto Allen's desk, onto the blue-green hardcover Nancy Drew, *The Mystery of the Brass-bound Trunk,* in the right-hand corner, next to the inkwell.

I didn't touch Allen's book, just pointed to the book.

Scardino's big-knuckled hands picked up Allen's book, turned the book over, rubbed his thumb down the binding.

Nancy Drew, Scardino said.

It's a girl's book, Muley said.

What do we want with a girl's book? Breck said.

The secret is inside, I said.

Scardino looked around the room. Ronald Wilson, Roger Waring, Ricky Divine, Tony Smith, Alvin Gosford, were all crowded in the doorway.

The black and white clock next to the American flag said 10:55. Five minutes before Sister Barbara Ann rang the ten bells.

Scardino kicked the boys' bathroom door open. The bathroom was empty. Allen wasn't lying on the floor anymore, no broken glass, no broken glasses frames. In the stall nearest the wall, under the locked door, in the mirror, I caught a glimpse of Allen's shoes poking out of his pants and shorts down around his ankles.

Scardino took hold of my elbow, grabbed it hard, but somehow because he had touched me, something inside me relaxed.

Back by the long urinal against the green wall and the white toilet stall on the end, the four of us stood there, Vern Breck, Michael Muley, Joe Scardino, and me, in a huddle, like I was one of them, like I was on their side.

Scardino's big knuckles, his big, smooth Italian hands, held Allen's book.

Turn to page forty-two, I said.

Scardino's fingers flipped through the pages, stopped on page forty-two. The carved-out hole inside the book.

Scardino and Breck and Muley started hooting and hollering, saying, Shit, look at that. Wow, how'd Puke do that? and Why is there just radio tubes in there? I'd put my rubbers in there, I'd keep pictures of naked women, I'd jerk off in there.

Sister Barbara Ann rang the ten bells. At the fifth bell, Scardino threw the book over the stalls. The book landed against the back wall, above the stall where Allen was sitting.

Radio tubes falling, more glass breaking, thin glass against concrete and porcelain. After the tenth ring of the bell, after the classroom doors closed and everyone was gone, I was alone in the bathroom leaning up against the sink, looking into the mirror at myself, and beyond, at the pile of corduroys and underwear bunched around Allen's ankles under the white stall door. Behind the white stall door, Allen was great big howls and whoops of crying. I walked up to the stall door. My hand was formed into a fist so I could knock. Then I looked at my hand as a fist, and I wondered where the hell that fist was when I needed it.

When Allen saw my shoes under the door, he quit crying. Just like when you shut the lights off or turn the water off or shut the radio off or you stop the car, Allen stopped crying.

At home that night, after the dishes were done, I went into my room. The red velvet box was under my pillow. I sat down on my bed, turned on the light on my nightstand. I adjusted the light so the light went right into the red velvet box. With my fingertips I touched each word in gold swirly letters, "The Holy Vatican."

Mom was sitting on the green couch under the standup lamp. Her hair was flying up, and her glasses were down on her nose. This time of day, she always looked tired. She was darning a pair of my socks.

I held the red velvet box out.

Her eyes, her almond-shaped hazel eyes. The look in her eyes at that moment was the look I'd forgot I'd always been waiting for.

The velvet box in my mother's rough, red farm hands.

The Holy Vatican, my mother said.

A present for you, I said.

Mom's clipped-to-the-quick fingernails.

Open it, I said.

Inside the box, the shiny white cloth. The rosary was curled onto itself, a shiny black snake, the silver crucifix on top of the folds.

The sound from out of her.

For me? my mother said.

I won it in the altar boy contest, I said. I had the most points.

Blessed in the Vatican, I said.

My mother lifted the rosary up by its silver crucifix. The shadow of the black shiny beads fell onto her face, just between her eyes, down her throat, onto her blouse pocket just above her heart.

All our prayers will be answered, she said. If only we pray to the Virgin.

As it turned out, that Wednesday after school, while I was riding home on the bus — everybody else at Saint Joseph's, even Sis, at the baseball game — at the bottom of the ninth, Saint Anthony's was three and Saint Joseph's was zero. The bases were loaded, and Scardino was at bat.

One strike, two strikes, three strikes, Scardino was O . . . U . . . T.

Scardino didn't show up for school Thursday. Or Breck or Muley. Or Allen Price.

All day I had a day I could breathe easy. Then after school, walking to the Pocatello High School, one block from Saint Joseph's School, at the intersection, there was Scardino in a red T-shirt and Levi's and Breck and Muley in Levi's and T-shirts, standing the way they'd stood in the bathroom, spread-legged, one combat line across the sidewalk. Between me and Pocatello High School. Between me and my bus ride home.

I didn't stop to think. I was the tallest in the class with the longest legs, and I was the best runner, and I turned around and started running. My red binder in my right hand, I was pumping my red binder forward and back, forward and back, grabbing at the air. Pulling the air from in front of me to behind me. I was going in the opposite direction from where I should have been going, but I tried not to think about that. I concentrated on getting my ass out of that crack even if I had to run the whole twelve miles all the way home the wrong way.

The Memorial Building is a red brick building with columns at the entrance and big trees all around it just over the Portneuf River across the Hayes Street bridge. I was midbridge when I decided I was going to run to the Memorial Building.

All around me there were tulips. Planted in the borders along the porch with the columns and along the wide cement sidewalk into the entrance, red tulips, yellow tulips, pink tulips.

How can it be so beautiful while you are so afraid?

Scardino and Breck and Muley were right behind me, yelling at me. The doors to the Memorial Building were always locked, so I didn't think of trying to get in, so I kept running by. I jumped a row of red tulips, yellow tulips, pink tulips, like an antelope. Then jumped the other row of tulips on the other side of the sidewalk. I was beating it around the Memorial Building down the slopes of the other side. Soon as I made it around the corner, I ran smack into Breck and Muley.

We played dodge and fake for a while, and just when I saw an opening between them I could run through, something big hit me from behind. It was Scardino, and I went flying. There was quite a slope there, and Scardino hit me, and I was midair, arms and legs waving around. Seemed like I was going to take off flying altogether. I landed, and there was a buzzing around me, and things weren't in focus. Scardino and Breck and Muley were on top of me. Scardino's red T-shirt, his belly, his chest, over my mouth and nose and eyes, and there was no air. Then a fist, a shoe, something hard and square hit me in the stomach.

Right before I passed out, I almost remember wondering who

would find my dead body on the green lawn with all the blooming tu-lips.

I finally opened my eyes, I was kneeling on the grass. I was looking at the grass and wondering if I was on a golf course. Big piles of puke on the green lawn, and I was barfing loud, and I wondered if the loud noise I was hearing was me. I don't know how long I lay on the green grass, even after I could feel the wind on my ass so I knew I had lost my pants. But I wasn't lying, I was kneeling, with my chest against my knees, my ear to the ground, my ear on the blades of green grass, sun-light and shadows on the green. My arms were out there somewhere, and my hands at the end of my arms.

I saw the shadow of it first. It's funny now that I say it. I mean, I can't help but see how ridiculous I looked.

There was a tulip stuck in my ass. A yellow tulip.

All the rest is just the end of the story. Nobody saw me, I don't think. My pants and my jockey shorts and my shoes and socks and my red binder were lying around me on the real green grass. When I was pull-ing my socks on, there was the hole in my sock that Mom had already darned. I phoned Mom from the Wyz Way Market. I don't remember walking to the Wyz Way Market. I just said: Mom, I missed the bus, come pick me up at the Wyz Way Market, and hung up.

In the reflection in the Wyz Way Market front window, my cold sore was bleeding, but otherwise that was me still staring back at me.

But I was differnt.

Differnt, as in changed.

Differnt, as in other.

My shadow a long, strange darkness coming out of my feet.

I had a nickel so I bought a Snickers. At the magazine stand, usually I stayed on the kids' side, the side of the magazine stand that was the comics.

That afternoon I stood on the other side, with the car mags and *True Confessions* and *Gent*. The other side with the freestanding book display that turned.

I was reading *Peyton Place* when Mom walked in. I didn't try to hide *Peyton Place*. I stood there on the side of the magazine stand where I wasn't supposed to be standing like everything was normal, and I looked up over the pages.

Mom wasn't wearing lipstick. She was still in her farm shoes. Her almond-shaped hazel eyes, squinted, green, one pitched south, the other east. No doubt about it. She was pissed.

Allen Price did not come back into class the next day. Or the rest of the week. And the end of the rest of that week was the end of school.

The truth is, I never saw Allen Price again. One day the following spring, Allen's father came to our farm to shoot rock chucks. I heard Allen's dad tell my dad that Allen had been sick, had spent some time in the hospital, but was doing much better at a special high school in California for kids who liked science.

California California California.

If you're a little differnt, if your pants don't fit and your breath is bologna breath and you like secret places inside Nancy Drew mystery books, if you're good at spelling, or you like to read Steinbeck on top of the granaries, if you're differnt, if you're a little bit queer, California California California must be the place you have to go.

PART II

Somebody to Love

4 Gringa Loca

OUT HERE ON THE HIGHWAY under a silver moon with an alien head shadow, it's only now I can see I wouldn't be free and clear and on the road if Mom hadn't busted me with my cock out behind the barn. Funny, all those years praying to God, and what gets my ass out of Pocatello is the devil. Then again, they say the Lord works in mysterious ways. Sometimes when the universe fucks you up, it's part of a larger plan.

Weird, how things seem so easy when you look back on them. Hindsight is twenty-twenty, Dad would say. The thing I needed most was somebody who could see me for who I was even though I couldn't see that person yet. Allen Price tried, but I had my head up my ass. I needed somebody who was safe. Somebody I could like too. Mom had been that for me, but now that I was older, now that there was sex, all she could see was sin and eternal damnation and hell. What I needed was a friend.

It took till the summer I turned sixteen to find true friends. Kind of pathetic, I know. But I was always differnt, more differnt than I could ever know, and maybe I just needed to wait for the right kind of differnt to cross my path. I was still scared too, deep-down real scared, so whoever differnt was, they needed to be kind. As fate would have it, my first two friends were as differnt from me as you can imagine, at least that's what my parents thought. Mexicans, like niggers, like Indians. Maybe that's why it worked out. That, and they were gentle. Flaco and Acho. They were the first, since my mother's eyes, I found eyes I could recognize something in.

That summer, Dad had one hundred acres of hay. I don't know how to tell you how much one hundred acres is, but if those one hundred acres were a half mile long and the windrows of dried hay were laid out one after another six feet apart over and over again, the hay would last so far your eyes couldn't see the horizon until you were halfway through.

The whole time behind the baler, I rode what you call a slip. I carried the bale to the end of the slip and stacked the bale, and at the end of the field when the tractor turned around, I took the iron bar and poked it into the ground in between the two middle boards, and the stacked hay went off onto the ground.

Heavy dry grass dust floated around you like a yellow cloud. You breathed the dust in, and you coughed and sneezed all the time. You were covered in that dust. Yellow scratchy dust through your top collar settled on your bare shoulders, down into your armpits. The dust even crept down into the crack of your ass. Felt like a million tiny jumping spiders in your pants. And it was fucking hot. Some days it was a hundred degrees and you were out there standing in a toxic yellow haze you could barely see through, in your straw hat, sweating, and the blazing sun was a huge yellow fluorescence, and here came another bale another bale another bale, and the sound of the baler was ka-chung ka-chung ka-chung. After a while you didn't hear the baler anymore, you just heard your own breath through the handkerchief over your mouth like you were in an oxygen tent or something. The yellow dust filtered inside your goggles, so pretty soon the world looked yellow, looked like you were looking through a yellow periscope at everything. What everything was was a bale of hay coming at you and coming at you, and your feet stumbling over four boards, and the ground going by underneath your stumbling, heavy feet.

Sometimes Mom drove the tractor, sometimes Sis. Mom always had to stop the baler, and with the pitchfork she'd walk all over creation trying to get every tiny last bit of fucking hay. Drove you nuts, that woman. Sis could give a shit, though. All Sis cared about was her tan. Plus, by then, Sis and I were sharing cigarettes. Sis would shut off the tractor, and I'd get a slug of water, and we'd each have a cigarette. Thank God for Sis.

What made the work even harder was, whatever you might think of your dad, you still wanted to do a good job for him. Maybe if you worked hard enough he'd look at you, call you *son*. Slap you on the back or touch you with his two fingers on the top of your head like when you were a kid. Never worked out that way, though.

Baling hay was a good three to four weeks straight, six days a week, eight to ten hours a day, in the dry, hot Idaho summer, out in the fucking sun, working like some fucking slave.

Fucking hay, man.

I hate fucking hay.

When the hay was all baled, finally, finally, far out, thank the fucking Lord, and the hay was stacked in stacks at each end of the field, it was time to get the '49 Jimmy hay truck running, time to start hauling the hay bales and stacking the hay bales into a haystack up at the feedlot. Sis and Mom could drive the tractor for the hay baler, but stacking hay was work too hard for the women. So that summer, Dad hired *those two Mexicans* who lived up in the Mexican house with their family.

The Saturday before the Monday we started hauling hay, I was driving up to the feedlot in Dad's Chevy Apache. I had my Viceroy, and the radio was going. I hadn't heard any of my favorite songs yet, "Summer in the City" and "Paperback Writer." I drove up the lane that connected us up to the rest of yellow Bannock County, over the old riverbed of the Portneuf River, then up past the Mexican house. I shifted into second, and this day I looked out the pickup window, and there were two young men, Mexican men, with smooth skin and shiny black hair.

One was wearing a bright blue shirt with a really white T-shirt under it and Levi's and red Converse tennis shoes untied. The other man was wearing a bright red shirt with a really white T-shirt under it and Levi's, and he was barefoot, smooth and brown. The young man in the blue shirt was playing a guitar, and the young man in the red shirt was playing an accordion, "Cucurrucucú Paloma" I was to find out later. The way they were smiling, I didn't know it yet, but my world had just changed so much that in thirteen months I wouldn't recognize a thing.

Monday morning I drove the hay truck up the lane to the Mexican house to pick up *those two Mexicans*. I was nervous in a way I always get when I'm going to meet somebody new. At least that's what I thought was troubling me. Now that I look back on it, there was a lot more going on.

There I was, the boss's son, so I had an authority that I didn't want. And also, there I was, fifteen, just about to turn sixteen, and *those two Mexicans* were much older, say, maybe even twenty years old. How could I possibly boss them around, tell them what to do and how to do it? Plus they were real handsome with black hair, so they were probably like Scardino.

Halfway down the lane, I was in the middle of thinking the universe was conspiring to fuck me up when something happened inside me that I remarked on because that something had never happened inside me before. Or maybe it had, and I just never listened.

A voice. You might call it a voice.

Just don't do it like he'd do it.

He being Dad.

Dad shouted orders and expected you to know. He waved his arms and pointed his finger and didn't listen to you. That's how Dad did it.

The place to start was to not be like Dad.

And never to treat anybody again the way I'd fucked up with Allen Price.

I revved the engine so maybe *those two Mexicans* would hear me. I thought about honking the horn, but there was no horn, plus honking the horn was something Dad did.

I shut the engine off, took a deep breath, opened the door to the truck, put my work gloves in my back pocket, and started walking up the hill. Car parts sticking up out of the weeds. The definite Mexican smell of tortillas.

Hello? I called out.

There was a bunch of voices speaking Spanish real fast. You could hear people walking around on the wood floor, lots of commotion. Then the screen door blasted open, and *those two Mexicans,* the two young men I'd seen in the blue shirt and the red shirt playing the guitar and the accordion, jumped over the two wood crates that were the front steps, jumped into the air between me and the sun, and landed on the ground.

Dad would never introduce himself, so I introduced myself. I said in English, even though Dad would use English — I mean what kind of choice is there when you know only one way to speak? I said: Hello, my name is Rigby John, and I stuck out my hand out to the guy who had worn the blue shirt playing the guitar.

Flaco's eyelashes almost covered up his eyes, but underneath the lashes were two pieces of black coal that looked straight into my eyes for just a moment, then looked away quick down at the ground. He was tall, tall as my dad, six feet at least. Real smooth, shiny skin. Long arms with that same skin. You might call him beautiful. I didn't then, I couldn't say both *he* and *beautiful* together yet. But I can say it now. Flaco was beautiful, big and strong, and kind of funny at being big and strong, but really what was beautiful about him was soft, a gentleness I'd never felt in a man before. Maybe it was because he was so polite, and the way he smiled. Like I was someone important that he would smile at me like that. How strange to be admired. He was wearing an old cowboy hat, sweat-stained around the brim, a white cowboy shirt, and the red Converse tennis shoes I'd seen him in, laced up this time. Some kind of denim pants, not Levi's. A cigarette stuck behind his ear.

Flaco reached for my hand. When we were palm to palm, I was about to give his hand a big howdy-pardner pump, but his hand and his arm just rested out there in mine, letting me hold it.

Differnt from how any man had taken my hand before. He *accepted* my hand. It was weird at first, like when you think there's another step, and there isn't, and your foot steps anyway, and you feel where the step wasn't all through your body. I almost pulled my hand away, but that's what Dad would do, so I accepted his hand as well.

Then our hands dropped to our sides at the same time.

Pleased to meet you, Rigby John, Flaco said. My name is Flaco, and this is my brother, Acho.

His English sounded like a Mexican speaking English, but I could understand him. Then I was looking at the ground, at our shadows on the ground. A polite, beautiful young man I could talk to.

Acho accepted my hand too, but his hand was not a surprise. I was getting used to these guys.

Acho's beauty was differnt from Flaco's. Acho's chest and arms were big around, and he could throw a bale of hay all the way to the top of a fully stacked truck from the ground. Not as tall as Flaco. He had a Kirk Douglas chin, and his hair was cut in a butch, straight black hair sticking up. On his cheeks, the same shiny, smooth skin with three pockmarks, two on one cheek and one on the other. His dark eyes were deep inside, under a thick brow. His nose hooked down. Shiny, smooth skin on his thick arms. More hair on his body, on his arms, and when he took his shirt off, the patch of black hair just in the middle. His straw hat looked like somebody'd stepped on it. A white T-shirt, the same kind of denims as Flaco. A cigarette stuck behind his ear too.

Skinny and Hachet. That's what Flaco and Acho's names mean in Spanish.

Hello, Acho said. How are you?

As I was about to find out, that was about it with Acho's English. He never did get my name, Rigby John, right, even though all summer long we practiced my name. The best it came out was Reegbeejoan.

Flaco and Acho were watching my every move. I turned the ignition on, pushed the starter with my right foot, put the clutch in. It took me some time getting into second gear, but I finally found second, let the clutch out, and something weird was going on, and then I remembered the emergency brake so I reached down, let the brake off, and it was a big sigh from me with all the trapped-up air in my lungs, and we were off.

The closed gate was my first problem. Dad, in this situation, would tell Acho, who was by the window, to get out and open the gate. The problem for me was *how* to tell Acho to open the gate, partly because I didn't know if he could understand me, but also I didn't want to tell Acho to open the gate the way my father would tell him to open the gate. Plus, opening some gates, this gate especially, was tricky, because you had to know how to lean your body against the top part of the end post of the gate.

So I shut the engine off, opened the door, and asked Acho to come with me. Flaco gave Acho a push and said something fast in Spanish. At the gate, I showed Acho how to lean into the top of the end post, which stretches the wire of the gate and lets the pressure off. I flipped up the oval piece of wire, pulled the end post out at the bottom, then arched the gate out of the way. After I drove the truck through the gate, I got out and showed Acho how to close the gate.

At the next gate, Acho realized it wasn't advantageous riding shot-gun. After a bunch of fast Spanish, Flaco got out of the truck, and I showed Flaco how to open and close the gate.

Mostly what was happening with the gate was I knew how it felt to be out there wrestling with something you didn't have a clue about while the old man sat in the truck and found new ways to humili-ate you.

And you know, that's no way to treat other people.

In the hay field, I made another decision: we'd take turns with lift-ing and stacking. Two of us would lift while one of us stacked. And then I hit on something that was the best idea I had that summer.

The truck was pulled up next to the first stack of hay at the bottom end of the field. First field, first stack of hay, first everything. The three of us sat inside the truck cab. I didn't know exactly how to start, so I took a Viceroy and matches out of my shirt pocket, stuck the cigarette in my mouth, lit the cigarette. Both Flaco and Acho, their faces were so surprised looking at me. They took the cigarettes from behind their ears. I lit their cigarettes too. Three on a match.

We all took drags on the cigarettes. I kept the smoke in my lungs for an extra-long time. I was waiting to say the something that I had to say. When I exhaled, the words came out with the exhale.

I said: We'll take turns driving.

That's what did it. That's how Flaco and Acho and I became such close friends. That summer they learned how to drive.

After two weeks of hauling hay, we'd all learned a lot about one an-other. Acho liked to clown around, Flaco stacked the tighter stack, and I could go all day without peeing. In the mornings, it took Flaco and Acho and I awhile to get used to one another. I mean, Christ, after all, who wants to be cheery and perspicacious at seven o'clock in the morning? First thing, after they argued in fast Spanish about who was going to ride shotgun, we'd just look at one another and say morning or hi or *hola*. Acho always said hello how are you when he got in the truck, and after that none of us said anything, and one of us lit a ciga-rette, and we'd share the cigarette. In the cab, just the cigarette smoke, our three bodies. The smell of soap, sweat, tortillas, tobacco, and in-stant coffee, the roar of the truck inside the cab. Outside the cab was the new day. The sun still pink and blue and cool shadows lying around on everything.

We got a good routine going. In the hay fields, we took turns driving the truck from stack to stack. This was some good practice for Flaco and Acho because, although they were driving in an open field and not out on a public road, they still had to do some precision driving. They had to back up close to the stack, make three-point turns, use the mirrors, plus the general steering, gear shifting, clutch, and brake.

Two of us threw bales onto the truck, and one of us stacked. Again we took turns.

We took turns driving back and forth from the feedlot, we took turns opening and closing the two gates, and at the stacks we took turns throwing bales off the truck, turns at stacking. Which wasn't without incident. Especially Acho. I can't tell you how many times I was laughing so hard I couldn't even think or stand up the way Acho gunned the gas, then popped the clutch. The truck would take off like on a drag strip, hay bales flying every which way and the truck bumping over corrugations, finally coming to rest in the middle of the field.

It *is* tricky getting the gas right and the clutch right. It took me months to get it down right. Flaco caught on pretty quick, but for some reason Acho just couldn't get it. Then I realized something. Acho was like me. He couldn't do things while people were watching, so I just left him alone. Soon as I left him alone, Acho was letting out the clutch, easing on the gas, in no time at all.

One thing in particular I learned about Flaco and Acho was how they liked to cuss. Especially Acho. *Chinga* and *chingada,* I think meant "fuck," and *puta* was "whore," and *Chingada tu puta madre* meant something like "fuck your whore mother." There was also *cabrón,* which meant "son of a bitch" or "bastard."

There was another word. Flaco and Acho also called each other *negro,* but *negro* was not a cuss word. *Negro* is pronounced "nay-gro" with the emphasis on *nay. Negro* means "black" in Spanish, and *negro* was a cool thing to say to someone, like you'd say, *Hey, buddy,* or *pal,* or *chum.*

Flaco and Acho liked it when I cussed in Spanish, so right off I started cussing in Spanish and pretty much preceded and ended everything I said with *chingada* or *puta madre* or *cabrón* or a mixture of all of the above.

I didn't use *negro* with them, though. Although *negro* was a good thing, only Flaco and Acho used *negro*. I wasn't sure why. I figured it was because I was white and American and I was differnt. I could call Flaco and Acho *cabrón,* or *chingada tu puta madre,* but I couldn't call them *negro.*

And another word. *Gringo.*

When Flaco and Acho were going at it in Spanish, that's what they called me, *gringo, gringo loco,* crazy gringo. I took it to mean they liked me.

As fate would have it, my birthday was our last day of hauling hay. What a day. It's only looking back on it now that I understand all that went on. It was the first time friends had ever asked me to do something with them, except for the time Scardino asked me to stay at his house and I said his mother's Parmesan cheese smelled like farts, and except for Allen Price the day we played Poison, and except for Sis when she invited me to go shopping so I could spend my allowance on her school clothes.

My birthday started out like any other day. The door to the truck opened, and Flaco got in first. He smiled at me as he slid to the middle of the seat. I said, Morning. Flaco just bobbed his head, then Acho got in and slammed the door. Flaco reached into his pocket, pulled a cigarette out, struck a matchstick against the bottom of the dash, lit the cigarette.

Morning cigarettes made me dizzy, still do, and although I didn't know it then, now that I look back on it, I always smoked anyway because I wanted to press my lips around what their lips had pressed around. When I went to third gear is when I handed the cigarette to Flaco. Same as ever, I turned the truck left over the cattle guard, drove past the boxcars. When Acho got back in the truck from closing the first gate, I couldn't stand it any longer.

I had the cigarette. I inhaled first, blew smoke out my nose, said: Today is my birthday.

Both Flaco and Acho said: Birthday! And just like that, it was like a whole differnt world. Funny how you don't know how things are always the same until they're differnt. Just like that. I saw it in Flaco and Acho's eyes. A whole new differnt world in their eyes. Then what was in their eyes got in my eyes too. It was still the old hay truck, it was still the same old hot-boxed cigarette, it was still right after the first gate was closed, it was still seven fucking A.M., it was still hay and Idaho and cheap labor, but everything was differnt. Differnt and bright. A whole day lit up ahead of us in our eyes, and in no time at all we were throwing our bodies around in the cab, clapping, cheering, and whistling, pounding on one another. Acho was speaking Spanish so fast it sounded like a machine gun. He started beating the dashboard like a drum.

Flaco said, This is a great day! It is our last day hauling hay, and it is your birthday. We must celebrate!

Acho said, *Aaii,* Reegbeejoan! *Chingada tu puta madre!*

Acho picked up the first bale of hay, and as he bent over he let out the longest, loudest fart I'd ever heard. *Puta madre,* Acho said, then Flaco said, *Cabrón* something or other in Spanish, and they were laughing hard, and I didn't need to know what Flaco said to laugh hard too. That started it. After that, every bale of hay that day was something funny, a new way to make us laugh. Funny all morning, funny into the afternoon.

That afternoon, at the top end of the field, on the last load of hay in the field, Acho popped the clutch and the truck lurched ahead. Flaco was standing on the back of the truck. He tried to keep his balance as the truck bounced over the corrugations, but it was too much. Wasn't long, and Flaco and the half load of hay we had on the back of the truck went flying ass over teakettle. Good thing we didn't break any bales, but it wouldn't have mattered. Acho, *cabrón, puta madre,* his driving not worth one *chingada.*

The field where we were loading hay that day was the hay field next to the swimming hole. The truck, when Acho finally got it stopped, was right next to the gate to the canal.

It was about three o'clock. Flaco was lying on the ground, his head propped up against a hay bale. Acho sat in the cab of the truck, the door open, smoking a cigarette. I'd just jumped up and was sitting at the back end of the truck, my legs dangling over the side. After laughing, all that was left was the high, hot sun, heat, and hay dust, flies buzzing, and half a load of hay to restack.

That's when we heard it. The most beautiful sound.

The waterfall.

Spontaneous combustion inside of us all at once.

Flaco leaped up like some wild animal. He said: Let's go swimming!

Acho didn't have to think about it. He was in midair, puffing on his cigarette, *puta madre negro!*

Flaco and Acho were halfway climbing over to the fence before they looked back at me.

I was still sitting on the back of the truck. In fact, my butt was welded to the back of the truck. The air inside my chest trying hard to breathe.

Come, Rigby John! Flaco said, come. Let's us swim. It is your birthday.

The feeling in my arms that means I am helpless.

You guys go ahead, I said. I'll restack the hay.

Ay! Cabrón chingada tu puta madre, Reegbeejoan! Acho said.

Just leave the hay, Flaco said. We will swim and then we stack the hay.

No, I said. You guys go ahead.

Cabrón? Flaco said.

Flaco's dark eyes trying to look inside me all the way from over on the fence.

Let's swim! Flaco said.

How do you say something you don't even know.

I can't, I said. My dad will catch us. You go ahead swimming and I'll watch out for my dad.

It wasn't long, and Flaco and Acho were standing behind the truck. Flaco had his hands around one of my legs, Acho had his hands around the other. They were looking up at me, the *gringo loco.* How could I help it, being from my family? I mean, now that I look back on it, it's true I was worried about getting caught by Dad, but, really, that day, my birthday, I could have risked that. What was scaring me, what was welding my ass to the flatbed, was something else.

I don't have a swimming suit, I said.

I mean to tell you. I have never seen two people laugh so hard so fast. The both of them, Flaco and Acho, were squirming around on the ground, in the hay stubble, yelling and screaming, beating their hats against their legs, holding their guts. Like to die laughing, those two.

And no towel, I said. I don't have a towel.

I was one fucking funny gringo, all right. I can laugh at it now, but believe me, sitting on the back of the truck that day, my ass welded to the flatbed, my hands curled around inside the slots where you stick in the sideboards, the prospect of swimming naked with Flaco and Acho was another life away from me.

So what did Flaco and Acho do? They did what any good friends would do. They helped their friend not to be afraid.

Don't get me wrong. They didn't hold my hand and say, It's OK, Rigby John, you don't have to be afraid, you're among friends. In fact just the opposite. Acho grabbed me around the middle and threw me over his shoulder. Such a surprising feeling. I am a big guy, wasn't as big then, but I was five foot ten and one hundred and sixty pounds, easy, and there I was up in the air, a sack of potatoes hanging over Acho's shoulder. I must tell you, I didn't like it. Every time someone has grabbed me like that, it meant I was nothing. It was my father or Scardino, and I wasn't considered, I was just something to throw around, to stick a yellow tulip up my ass. The fear was great in me, and I was having trouble breathing. The feeling in my arms that meant I was helpless and everything started to go black.

Flaco and Acho didn't know how scared I was. I mean, I don't think they knew. Acho didn't know for sure, he just carried me kicking and screaming like a girl to the gate. He opened the gate even with me on his shoulder. It wasn't until we got to the canal, just before Acho set me down, that my eyes happened to look over to Flaco. That moment. Something in Flaco's eyes was like Jesus. I don't know what you'd call it. His long black eyelashes, his black eyes, something in them, whatever it was, when I looked, down inside me, and quick I felt sure I was not alone. After that glance, just like that, I quit kicking and screaming. Acho put me down on the ground.

The ground, my feet were on the ground, and up through the ground some kind of solid sucked up into my legs. Flaco's eyes were still Jesus, and I got my breath back, and I was standing on my own two feet, and I was with my friends, and we were all laughing like before.

Then the shock of my life — well, that is, up until then — Flaco reached down and grabbed the bottom of his T-shirt and pulled his T-shirt over his head. Armpit hair. My God, I'd never seen Flaco without a shirt. My breath gone away again. Flaco's shoulders, his collarbone, his nipples. Then both of his shoes were off, he'd kicked them off, and his hands were around his denims, and sure enough in nothing flat there he was, all of Flaco naked right there, the black hair of his crotch, the muscles that curve down from his waist a dovetail to his cock. His cock resting on his balls, darker brown and voluptuous. I don't know what else to call it, how he was. Thick darker brown than the rest of his skin, his cock, his balls, voluptuous.

Then Acho too. Naked, stark naked. All that dark brown muscle, one long uninterrupted ripple of muscle, the hair in the middle of his chest, the little trail of hair starting at his waist, then thick down around his cock and balls. His cock and balls full, beautiful, round, like swear words in your mouth that mean "joy" when you speak in a Romance language.

Beautiful, brown, round asses. Flaco's ass something so smooth you wanted to slap hard or bite into, but instead you lost your breath, you lost your balance. And Acho's ass, smooth and round and brown too, but inside the crack a dark mass of black hair.

All in an instant.

Naked romping men, whole entire bodies, all of the body, every part of the body. Foot pads to foreskin to earlobes, totally naked, gut-wrenching, breathtaking, heartbreaking, naked.

I was lost.

My clothes were not like Flaco's and Acho's. My clothes did not come off so easy. All they had to do was undo their buttons, zip down their zippers, unlace their shoelaces, pull off their socks. But not me. Getting my clothes off me in front of Flaco and Acho was a lot dif-fernt.

I got by, though, with a little help from my friends.

Flaco started with my hat, off went my hat, then Acho unbuttoned my top button of my shirt, then on down. Off with my shirt. Flaco was kneeling down and unlacing my boots. The bounce of his balls between his legs, I couldn't look. There went my boots. My smelly socks. Down there on the ground my incredibly white feet. *Puta madre*, Acho said when he saw my white feet. Then my belt, then the five, count 'em one two three four five Levi's buttons. Then Acho divested me of my Levi's and underwear, and there was air around all around me where I loved to have air, my pants a bundle around my feet. I pulled one foot out of the bundle, then the other.

I was naked.

In the sun naked.

With all my zits naked.

My hands were fists covering my crotch.

Acho grabbed one hand, Flaco grabbed the other. They pulled my fists away.

Both Flaco and Acho put their hands over their ears. Their eyes like in horror movies when the woman sees the monster. They screamed loud screams, and they stared at my cock.

Qué horror! Chingada tu puta madre!

My head rolled down, my eyes traveled down my chest, over my belly, down to myself down there.

What I was doing was what I always do when I get half-naked, naked.

I was poking straight out in front of me.

Acho pointed at my cock and said something in Spanish that later that night in the haystacks they told me and I memorized: *El trae la verga bien parada!*

Which I think sounded like: He tries to have a very good parade.

But it was not a parade I was trying to have.

It was a hard-on.

And I was not trying.

Then it was something magical. The swimming hole was magical, and the three of us were one flying whooping hollering screaming shits and giggles, one long, smooth, uninterrupted naked thrust through the sky of the dry, hot, sunny Idaho afternoon. Suspended in the air, arms, legs, cocks, a balls-out splash, the whoosh down deep into cool, muddy, green water.

No swimming suit, water all around me touched me deep the way water goes wherever it can go. My legs, my ass, my cock, my balls, waterfall rushing water against me, better even than air. Floating low, my body a slide along dark rocks and mud, tangles of moss, gliding like a seal, some kind of sea animal, audacious pigs, Esther Williams, I was sprouting gills, breathing water. In the dark turbulence, my hands found one human leg and then another, and I grabbed the legs and pulled and from somewhere up above in the breathing air world is a holler, a high-pitched yell that turned into bubbles.

Flaco's face right up next to mine through the dark, muddy, green, Flaco all-his-teeth smile. His Jesus eyes turned devil, Flaco grabbed for me, but I was too fast. I was out of the water in one long lunge, the deep breath of air glory in my chest. In no time at all, Flaco's arms around my neck. Then Acho got my legs, and the two of them lifted. I was lifted up high, straight-armed, to the Lord, a lodgepole pine, a pyre, a wet, long body in the hot, dry air. Just like that, a splash into green again and dark. Flashes of black hair, brown skin, and differnt parts of bodies, arms, legs, shoulders, the mole on the back of Acho's neck, Flaco's brown foot poking out of the green water, the white water of the waterfall. A finger poked me in the ass, right *in* the sphincter, the same place as the yellow tulip. In an instant, how curiously full it felt in my heart that place of me touched again. This time the touch let the lead out of my ass. I let out a scream. I thought it was laughter that lifted me up, and I walked as if I were walking on water.

Flaco's broad hand, his perfect fingernails, curled around a hank of crabgrass next to my foot. I ran in the sun, naked, ran wet in the sun, Flaco behind me, Acho behind him. In my ears all I could hear was the water running out of them, my breath, Flaco's breath, Acho's. Past the cement walls from either side that came together at the head gate, my feet were splashes of wet on the dry old board, two-by-twelve, bolted down. My balls bouncing, my cock. I'd never seen my cock when I was running, how it lay on my balls when my legs were together. How it swung loose with the ball sack, my legs stretched out as I jumped to the outcropping of slick, dark, lava rock. I landed, my palms sea anemones, suction cups onto the black, slick rocks. My feet found their way up the side of the mossy, wet, dark lava.

Once up top, the flat, dusty earth was hot on the bottoms of my feet. I looked down. I was breathing hard, water running down my body. My feet were across the border, my feet were on the rez. Planted deep in all that red, as crooked as the wind, was the lone cedar tree. In the hot sun, the cedar boughs smelled of one more sweaty body. The wind through the cedar, the secret song of the wind in the cedar that moment, was something not outside me but down deep up behind and under, a fist balled up inside me opening to a hand waving in the wind.

Flaco charges from the left, Acho from the right. They jumped to nail me, but I was one, two, three grand strides and another whoop, high, high in the air, forever it seemed in the air I was falling, falling. Then the rush of water about my ears, the deep green water. In no time at all, it was Flaco, then Acho, full-body splashes. Underwater sea animals, slick, swimming along the bottom.

We could not stop. We swam, we climbed the bank, we ran in the still blazing heat, goose flesh our bodies, our feet pounded, pounded, over the two-by-twelve, jumping to the lava rocks, handholds, footholds, sometimes the moss too slick for good purchase, clambering, breathing hard, laughing always, always laughing, up to the top again on the rez in the red world, and the sweat cedar, we jumped again and again, over and over and over. In the world, there was nothing else, only our bodies propelled through the air, under the sun, in the green water, into the white rapids, the plunge.

Everything differnt, differnt and bright.

Everything possible.

Low, gold sun, driving the load home, in first gear, down the arc of the bow of the reservation. Between the two gates, on the longest stretch of open, flat land between the field and the feedlot, Flaco is driving too fast. We always drive too fast when we can, especially between the two gates. And this late afternoon, my birthday, it is the last load. Saturday night and Sunday and no hay to haul ahead of us. I am sitting in the middle between Flaco and Acho. Flaco's hat is off, and the wind from the open window is blowing his wet hair. Acho isn't wearing his shirt, and the sun is gold on his skin. Flaco shifts from third gear to fourth gear, and when the gearshift goes into fourth, Flaco's hand comes down. I doubt if Flaco even knows he's touched me. The little square inch of skin on my right leg below the knee. Everything gets slow, and I feel the scared place inside me that I don't know is scared until it stops feeling scared, and when the scared feeling stops I get a big, full feeling in my chest, and I love God so much right then. Our smell, sweat and hay and dust and the smell of the cab, gasoline, oil, exhaust fumes, cigarettes, mossy canal water, roaring down the road in a beat-up old truck. Me in the middle, Flaco and Acho and I, skin to skin to skin, my skin almost as dark as their skin. Just the three of us, close, riding in the truck, the wind blowing through. The way we are smiling we all know. This is a moment in our lives. Flaco takes a drag on the cigarette. Acho closes his eyes, stretches his neck. My exhale settles my body deep into the seat as if the seat is the only thing that holds me up. Each of us knows, and we know that we know, and without a word we bless the moment.

And now, a year later, even more, that moment is still with me, riding on my breath, in the pulse of blood, the deepened lifeline in the palm of my hand. What I have come to know as true. Moments of gesture. To know what it is to love.

Flaco slid down in the seat so his body stretched out to the end of his knees. He put his long fingers through his curly black hair.

Rigby John, Flaco said, why don't you come tonight to our house and visit us?

The big empty place just down from my throat, the sore place next to my heart. My arms got the helpless feeling in them. I thought I was going to cry. I quick made my hands into fists, put my fists up into my armpits.

These guys really liked me.

A deep breath, my mouth finally let the words out.

Sure, I said, I'll come up. After supper. But I have to change the water in the pasture first.

Birthdays on the farm were like any other day except for you got a birthday cake and a pair of new Levi's or underwear, and Mom and Dad and Sis sang "Happy Birthday" to you.

That's the way it was that night at supper. Mom had made my favorite cake, which was a spice carrot cake with caramel frosting. The cake was sitting on the blue dish on the kitchen counter, sixteen blue candles stuck in the frosting.

I was standing both feet mostly on a square blue tile. I was about to reach out and test the caramel frosting, when, behind me, Mom said, Go wash up good now. Dinner's ready.

Mom's hair was in pin curls and the hairnet over the pin curls.

Going somewhere tonight? I said. Or are those pin curls for me?

Mom's almond-shaped hazel eyes, in them a little touch of gold. Lately she'd stopped wearing housedresses and started wearing pants.

Just go wash up, she said. Make sure you get behind your ears.

The cake looks great, Mom, I said. Thanks for making my favorite.

Mom turned her back to me, grabbed the pot with the spuds, took the potato masher out of the drawer, and started mashing the spuds.

Use the towel hanging behind the door, she said. And clean the sink out when you're done.

Mom had fluffed her hair out and was wearing her new rummage-sale cotton print blouse when she sat down at the table. Dad noticed her lipstick and her penciled-on eyebrows too. Supper was fried chicken, mashed potatoes, and canned string beans. As ever, we started supper with the sign of the cross.

Bless us, O fucking Lord, and You know the fucking rest.

Same with the rest of supper. I've already told you about fucking supper.

Sis and I cleared the dishes, scraped the plates into the kitchen garbage bucket under the sink. Mom poured Dad another cup of tea. I carried the cake to the table, set the cake down on the oilcloth tablecloth. Sis brought over the dessert plates and dessert forks, set them down next to the cake. Dad reached into his Levi's shirt pocket, pulled out his matches, and flipped the pack of matches onto the table. Sis grabbed the matches before me. She struck a match, lit a candle on the end.

Mom said, Start in the middle so you don't burn yourself.

Sis brought the match to the candles in the middle. When the candles were all lit, I sat down in my chrome chair with the plastic yellow seat. Under the table, where nobody could see, I squeezed my hands tight around the seat of my chair. I was smiling too much. I know you could see my gums.

Sis started singing. It's important to get the first note to "Happy Birthday" right; otherwise the whole song is ruined. Sis started singing too high. Consequently, everybody was straining their gizzards.

That's when Mom stopped singing. She stopped singing and told us all to stop singing. She got up from her chair and walked into the front room. She folded open the piano and sat down on the round piano stool. The first note she hit was middle C. If you can find middle C, you can go anywhere from there.

Mom hit all the keys just right so everybody knew where to start singing so the song wasn't ruined. Dad and Sis sang along as Mom played the piano.

Happy birthday, dear Rigby Joh-on.

Sweet sixteen and never been kissed was what I was thinking. I was thinking Mom always looked so beautiful when she played the piano. I was thinking I was going to beat off in the pickup parked up in the pasture. I was thinking about the Viceroy on top of the refrigerator I was going to steal. I was thinking Sis should never wear her hair in a French twist. I was thinking about the best way to go about getting two pieces of birthday cake for Flaco and Acho. I was thinking, Oh, you're supposed to make a wish. I was thinking I didn't know what to wish, so quick I wished that Flaco and Acho and I would be friends forever.

Happy birthday to you.

Sixteen candles aren't hard to blow out. One big breath, and the little fires are gone and there's only smoke.

Dad reached up from below his chair with a brown sack that said BLOCK'S MEN'S STORE on it.

Here's a pair of Levi's for ya, Dad said. Happy birthday.

In the hay field where we'd finished hauling that day next to the swimming hole, on the pickup radio "Trains and Boats and Planes" was playing. Just as Dionne Warwick sang *Those trains and those boats and planes took you away, away from me,* I pulled my Levi's and my shorts down, and my bare ass was sweaty on the pickup seat. I could tell by the feeling at the end of my tongue that I was going to come like a rock. Just when my nipples started to get hard, out the windshield in the robin's-egg sky, three clouds in the sky were a pink and orange train and a pink and orange boat and a pink and orange plane. Flaco was the train, I was the boat, Acho was the plane.

Mom and Dad were sitting on the love seat in front of the TV when I walked into the house. They didn't hear me walk in, or at least they never turned around. That was good. I took another Viceroy off the refrigerator. Strange how people laughing on the television sounds in another room.

The swimming hole that afternoon and my new friends had made me feel strong. Some kind of solid up into my legs. I was standing on my own two feet. So I just went ahead and did something I wouldn't usually do.

The cake was in the cake safe, which was a red cover with stenciling on it and a wooden knob at the top. I cut a big piece of cake for Flaco and put it on a blue paper plate, a big piece of cake for Acho and put it on a red paper plate, and a big piece of cake for me and put it on a green paper plate.

I was sliding my thumb and index up the cake knife when all of a sudden the bright overhead kitchen light went on.

What you doing here in the dark? Dad said.

I didn't turn around to look at Dad. I knew how he looked.

Nothing, I said, just getting some cake.

Three pieces? he said.

I laid the cake knife in the sink, turned the hot water on, rinsed the knife.

For Flaco and Acho, I said.

What? Dad said.

Dad had his teacup in his hand, the teaspoon sticking out of the teacup. In the bright overhead light, on the top of his head, above the sunburned line on his forehead, you could see where he was going bald.

Who, I said. Flaco and Acho, I said. Those two Mexicans.

Dad jumped his chest up. He did that when something pissed him off. Poked his chest out, pulled his shoulders back. Put his free wrist against his hip, jerked his Levi's up with his wrist.

Why do you want to give 'em cake? he asked.

In my mouth I could hear my voice get high and kind of whiny, and I hated that my voice was like that. But I didn't let that stop me.

They are my friends, I said. It's my birthday. They invited me up to their house. We're going to have some cake.

They don't eat cake, Dad said. All they eat's them tortillas. They don't eat cake.

Dad set his teacup down hard on the kitchen counter. The teaspoon rattled inside the cup.

Not your mother's cake, Dad said.

Dad's body was close to me. The only times he got close was when he was mad. He never punched me or anything, but he didn't need to. All he had to do was step close. He was probably still mad that Mom had fluffed her hair out and put on her eyebrows and her lipstick for me. Or mad at something or other. Who could tell? With Dad and me, Dad was always mad.

Then it was Mom right next to Dad.

Are you having some cake? Mom said.

Him and the Mexicans, Dad said.

The bright, bright kitchen. I always hated that bright kitchen. Made everyone looked tired and weary. Under the bright overhead light, Mom's hair and her glasses made shadows down her face.

For Flaco and Acho, I said. My voice inside my mouth was still high.

It's my birthday, I said. And they invited me up to their house, and I thought I'd bring them some cake.

The bright overhead light, Mom's almond-shaped hazel eyes, you couldn't see her eyes, only bright reflected in her glasses.

You don't go in that house, she said. You'll catch fleas.

And who knows what else, Dad said.

Mom, I said.

You can't go in that house, she said.

I'll stay outside in the pickup then, I said. We'll eat the cake in the pickup.

Nobody said anything. Each of us stood in a blue tile. Like we were a game of chess, and they were the king and the queen and I was one of those pieces you don't care about. The bright overhead light in my mother's glasses pointed down at the counter, the red plate, the blue plate, the green plate.

Took me awhile to find my voice, then finally: They are my friends, Mom, I said. They're Catholic. They are always praying to the Virgin.

Our Lady of Guadalupe, I said.

Dad knew I had her.

Under the bright light in the kitchen, that moment, his black eyes Roosky Gypsy. My body thick and heavy with his hate. I mean, really. Whatever the case may be, whoever your dad may be, your dad hating you don't feel good.

Still don't. I can still feel it, all the time I feel his hatred for me, maybe it's permanent. Mostly up high in my chest next to my heart where I smoke I can feel it.

Dad couldn't stare his drut stare at me any longer. He turned away quick and left the kitchen.

Mom opened the drawer under the bread drawer and pulled out the roll of waxed paper. Her rough, red farm hands, her clipped-to-the-quick fingernails, her plain gold wedding ring, how she folded the waxed paper careful over each piece of cake on its paper plate, put each plate in a lunch sack.

Use the plastic forks, she said. You'll lose the silverware.

I put a plastic fork in each of the lunch sacks, closed each sack by making a fist.

bottle, put the neck in his mouth, and pried off the cap with his teeth. The brown bottle in his hand across to me.

Happy birthday, Rigby John, Flaco said.

The Budweiser was cold, and the bottle gave my hand a place to wrap myself around. I put the beer to my lips, took a long, long drink.

My chugalug brought up a long burp. This wasn't the first time I drank beer. Sis and I had got drunk a bunch of times. Twice.

Flaco reached into Acho's pocket, pulled the Winstons out, tapped a cigarette out, cupped the match, and lit the cigarette.

When I saw the cigarette, there was another way to be scared.

How do you say it without sounding like your father?

Cabrón, I said, I'd be careful with that cigarette in the straw.

Flaco took the tip of the cigarette and moved the tip of the cigarette close to his eyes. When he spoke, Flaco spoke to the cigarette, not to me.

Yes, I know, Flaco said, the fire. I will be careful.

Then that smile of his, and in his eyes that Jesus look like that afternoon.

I tried to imagine my father laughing like those two. Maybe if he had a beer he would laugh. Mom could laugh that way. I could still make Mom laugh. Just cross my eyes a little, curl up my top lip, scratch my butt.

Oh my heavens pretty woman so far, Flaco said.

Flaco said Acho first heard "Oh my heavens" from a *gringa* woman he worked for as a gardener in San Luis Obispo. That woman always went around saying *oh my heavens.* She was an old *gringa* lady who wore the kind of high heels you could see her painted toenails through. *Oh my heavens, oh my heavens,* all the time she said, *oh my heavens.* Flaco waved his arms around like the woman in San Luis Obispo.

Acho figured that was how you cussed in English, Flaco said. So he started saying *oh my heavens, oh my heavens* too, but it got so *oh my heavens* wasn't enough, so he added *pretty woman.* Because *pretty* sounds like *puta,* so it became *oh my heavens pretty woman.*

It is a very mysterious English word, isn't it? Flaco said. *Woman.* Sounds like Marilyn Monroe. *Woman.*

Woman woman woman, Flaco said. Pretty woman.

Through the bottle, the moon was a brown moon soaked in beer. I wanted to drink the whole beer and then another and another, but I only sipped.

And the *so far*? I asked.

When *negro* fucked her, Flaco said, when she came, that's the sound she made.

Soooo! Faaar! Flaco and Acho screamed out together, their mouths wide open on each side of me, their white teeth, the moon on their teeth.

Something jumped up into my throat when Flaco said *fucked her*. It sounded so easy. Like he had shaken her hand or something. *Fucked her*. For a moment, it made me a little crazy, and my breath started to go. But then in no time, I was rolling around in the spread straw with them laughing my ass off. Then Acho said something in fast Spanish to Flaco as Acho pointed at my crotch. Flaco and Acho screamed the way they'd screamed like in horror movies when the woman saw the monster like they did that afternoon when they saw me naked with my cock pointing out in front of me.

Flaco said the Spanish again for me real slow:

El

trae

la

verga

bien

parada.

He tries to have a very good parade.

It means, Flaco said, "He has a good hard-on."

I was glad it was dark because not only were my ears red, I think my whole body was red. I didn't know how to say what I wanted to say, what words. Plus I was waiting to see if I was going to barf or not. But then again what do you say to two men you had a hard-on in front of? *I was as surprised as you? Who knew? Please don't think I am weird.*

And then I said it.

Please don't think I am a queer, I said.

Queer, such a loud word. Soon as I said *queer*, I wanted to capture it in the air and cup it back into my mouth.

Queer? Flaco said. What is *queer*?

Oh jeez.

You know, I said. A homo.

Homo? Flaco said.

Homo, Acho said.

What is homo? Flaco said, almost yelled.

Fuck.

Shh! I said. Not so loud.

It's only the cows, Flaco said, and us.

I grabbed the Winstons in Acho's red shirt pocket and had me a cigarette out and lit in no time. I hunkered down so far into myself I almost disappeared.

Flaco and Acho were looking me in the face. The night wasn't dark anymore. It was bright, way bright, moon bright, and Flaco was on one side of me and Acho on the other. Both of them staring, staring at me.

Acho slapped me on the back and the smoke came out in one big silver billow.

A man who does it with men, I said.

Does it? Both Flaco and Acho said, *Does it?*

Has sex, I said. Makes love, I said. You know, a man who has sex with other men.

Beer and cake in my stomach. The smell of burnt plastic. Oh my heavens pretty woman so far.

Then: Fuck, I said. A man who fucks other men.

Now that I look back on it, you know, I don't think I really knew what *queer* and *homo* actually meant until that moment when I spoke the words out loud.

Flaco and Acho were trying to get air, they were laughing so hard. Snorting, coughing, they were clinging onto each other, jumping around the straw stack like jackrabbits. My breath started to go, and my arms had the weak feeling in them.

But you are not a *queer,* Flaco said. He said the word *queer* careful so he could hear the word in his mouth.

A queer, Flaco said, is a *puto* or *maricón.*

Ma-ree-con, Flaco said real slow.

A *maricón* is a man with a cock and balls, Flaco said. But really he is a woman.

Acho got up then, grabbed the cigarette from me, unbuttoned his shirt to the last two buttons, pulled his shirt down over his T-shirt shoulders like an evening gown décolletage. Acho walked through the spread straw, moving his shoulders and his ass like you see prostitute women in the movies walk in high heels. Acho puckered his lips and held his hand with the cigarette in it, wrist up, and his hand, the palm of his hand, trailed along.

Flaco was, of course, laughing. Acho too. Then Flaco had to get in on the act, and Flaco pulled his shirt down like Acho's décolletage, and they both walked, shaking their shoulders and their asses, running their hands through their hair, puckering their lips, their lips making sucking sounds.

Ai! Ai! Ai!

Oooh la la, chingada tu puta madre, maricón.

Flaco reached down and grabbed his guitar. He started playing, long dramatic strums on the guitar wires. With each strum, Acho flipped his skirt and danced like a woman with a fan dancing flamenco.

Come on, Eleanor Rigby John, Flaco said. Join us in the queer parade.

Verga bien parada.

Myself, I hadn't dressed like a girl or acted like a girl for over five years and I'd be go to hell if I was going to start *that* again, so I put the beer to my lips and took a long, long drink, swallowed the whole damn bottle of beer.

Who knows how long those two carried on that way, like girls, *putas, maricóns,* whooping and hollering, singing and dancing and shaking their asses. The beer was going to my head, and everything was loud laughing and fast Spanish. Up above, the moon, a gibbous moon, some kind of miracle hanging up there in the sky. The sun shining on the moon, the moon shining on the straw, sunlight on the moon, moonlight onto us dancing and drinking and singing, human damn fools.

Gringo loco.

Then somewhere around in there, out there, someone was out there grabbing me by the shoulder, saying something in my ear.

It was Flaco.

Flaco was back to being Flaco and no longer a *puto maricón.*

Flaco's dark eyes in the moonlight, so close to my eyes, I saw clean down to the Jesus inside his soul.

Eleanor Rigby John, Flaco said. Where are you? Are you *borracho* so soon? Where have you gone?

There were big tears in my eyes, and when I first started to speak I couldn't speak.

Finally: Where do all the lonely people come from?

That smile of Flaco's some kind of resurrection.

From God, Flaco said.

When Flaco said *God,* his whole flat palm cupped my shoulder. His palm rested on my shoulder with the intention of being on my shoulder. Then out of nowhere, Acho's big calloused hand on top of my head rubbing my hair back and forth. The moon on their hands on my shoulder, on my head.

Mira, negro, Flaco said to me.

Negro.

Moments of gesture.

It is only natural running in the sun, Flaco said, and jumping in the water to be a hard penis. It happens to me all the time.

Flaco spoke fast Spanish to Acho for a moment and then:

All all all all the time hard-on in the sun, Flaco said, and the water running. It is only natural for a man. He feels good so he gets hard. Isn't it beautiful?

Beautiful. Friends loved one another, and my friends who loved me, their hands were on my shoulders, on my head, touching me.

Beautiful.

Sí, I said. *Me gusta.*

Ai, cabrón, Flaco said. You are knowing so much Spanish!

Oh my heavens pretty woman so far, Acho said.

Quiet again all at once.

At once, Flaco's hand, Acho's hand, their fingers, their arms, moved away. On my shoulders and my head still on my flesh in my bones the palms of their hands where they had touched me.

We were out of words and each of us sat alone holding a beer, passing the cigarette, like when we hauled hay, all at once everybody talking, talking, then, just like that, the world tipped on its orbit just enough, or the moon got brighter or darker, or the sun went from high bright afternoon to the first gold of evening, or a comet passed somewhere above us, huge fire and brimstone roaring through space, and suddenly we were alone again and we didn't touch and we sat quiet.

So you liked our song? Flaco said.

I didn't say *te amo* this time.

I loved your song, I said.

Quiet again, way off no train, no cows, no crickets, just quiet.

I got to say, though, I said, Eleanor is not a name for a boy. Eleanor is a girl's name, and I thought you were calling me a girl.

Flaco snapped his long fingers.

So that's why you thought we thought you were *maricón,* Flaco said.

Well, that and the hard-on, I said.

Then: Have you ever fucked a girl? Flaco said.

Flaco's question landed right on my heart. Something stung.

The truth was, Scardino and his friends were all fucking girls. I was sixteen too like Scardino, and I hadn't even wanted to fuck a girl. I knew I should want to fuck a girl, but the truth was I didn't. Fucking was a sin, a mortal sin, same way as masturbating, but with masturbating it was just you abusing yourself, not anyone else.

No, I said.

Flaco said some fast Spanish to Acho, Acho said something back.

Would you like to? Flaco said.

I didn't know what the fuck. There I was, a man, almost a man, and the thing a man most wants to do, if he is any kind of man, is to fuck a woman.

Sure, I said.

Mira, Flaco said. Acho and I have met two girls.

Thindy, Acho said. And Cricket.

They are white girls, Flaco said.

Flaco's white teeth. Acho's white teeth. Sun on the moon and moon on their teeth.

When did you meet them? I said.

In Pocatello, Flaco said. Last Saturday when my family went shopping in the town. Flaco took the cigarette, inhaled.

Mira, Flaco said. There were two girls in the magazine section of the Wyz Way Market. Acho and I saw them and we went directly to them. Acho began to read *Hot Rod* and I *True Confessions.* Thindy has long, beautiful brown hair and was reading *True Confessions* also, and Cricket with short blondie hair was reading *Seventeen.* It is a small place where the magazines are, and as I read slowly I moved until my ass was touching Thindy's ass. Thindy didn't move. Then we started talking.

Acho took the cigarette, put the cigarette between his lips. The cigarette bobbed up and down with Acho's English.

Thindy and Cricket, Acho said, love Mexican men. They want to fuck us tomorrow.

Fuck us.

Did they say that? I said.

No, *cabrón,* Flaco said.

And what Flaco said next he said while he flipped his index finger against his thumb and middle finger. Snap.

But we know, Flaco said.

How do you know? I said.

Flaco, that smile of his.

Because we are men, Flaco said. And we know.

Perhaps we can ask Thindy and Cricket if they have a friend for you? Flaco said.

They're coming here tomorrow? I said. What time tomorrow?

They have no car, Flaco said. And we have no car also, so they are hitchhiking. They will arrive here sometime in the afternoon.

Will they walk through our yard? I said. Or cut through the field?

Flaco spoke fast Spanish to Acho, Acho spoke back. Back and forth, back and forth, talking for a long time.

They will be coming through in the yard, Flaco said.

I took the cigarette. It was hot-boxed as always. I took the last puff. A long puff, all the way to the filter.

Then Acho hit Flaco on the arm with his fist, and Flaco and Acho were laughing again.

We will fuck them right here in the straw, Flaco said.

The clock on the stove when I closed the kitchen door said eleven-fifteen. Inside the house was hotter than outside. Dad was snoring, or Mom. My room downstairs was a little cooler. Mom had opened both the windows wide, but there was no breeze. I took my clothes off, pulled the covers back, lay only on the sheet. Moonlight on the sheet.

In the middle of the night, I was sweating and woke up. In my nightmare, all around me there was smoke and the straw stack was on fire.

Sunday afternoon, it was about two-thirty when Mom turned the oven off, slipped the red-checkered oven muff over her hand, opened the oven door, and reached down and pulled the chicken out. Chicken grease and Crisco snapping and popping. On the stove, the spuds were boiling in the big kettle, in the little kettle, the string beans.

Dad walked into the kitchen in his Sunday outfit, a white shirt with rolled-up sleeves, Levi's, and his boots. He was folding the Sunday *Idaho State Journal.*

We sat down, a family, made the sign of the cross, bless us O Lord and these Thy fucking gifts and you know the rest. I got a drumstick and a wing. For dessert, we finished up the birthday cake.

Then it was the sign of the cross after dinner, the prayer of thanksgiving, the sign of the cross again.

Sis and I scraped the plates into the kitchen garbage bucket and stacked them. Mom started the hot water in the right side of the double sink and poured in two drops, only two drops and sometimes three drops, of Joy dishwashing liquid. Mom washed, and Sis and I dried. Dad went back into the front room to read the paper. He was snoring in no time.

Mom filled the black skillet with water. Sis finished drying the last knife, the butcher knife. I was just finishing two dinner forks when I looked out the window.

Just past the two corral poles, on the other side of the wagon wheel and the Austrian Copper rose, two people, two young people, two girls, Flaco and Acho's two white girls, Thindy and Cricket, walked into our yard.

Tramp started barking and in that moment everything stopped. The washing and the rinsing stopped, the drying and the wiping stopped. Mom shut the water off, and Dad quit snoring.

I quit breathing.

Mom's almond-shaped hazel eyes under her glasses.

Mary Margaret? Mom said. Rigby John? Do you know who those girls are?

Sis was looking at me, eyes wide open, mouth open, that look that says, Holy shit.

I quick gave her the furrowed brow, clenched teeth, shut-the-fuck-up look.

Sis stayed with her eyes looking right at me. As her eyes scrutinized me, Sis said in her high singsongy, best Catholic schoolgirl voice: No, Mom, I don't know who they are.

Still no breath inside me.

I'll go out and see, I said.

And before anybody had the chance to say *Arbeit macht frei*, I was down the steps and out the back door.

As I walked out on the sidewalk, Tramp came to my side, and I patted his head. It's OK, boy, I said, but really who knows what I said, it was so trippy walking out to meet the two girls, Thindy and Cricket, who Flaco and Acho were going to fuck in the straw. There I was, one foot on the sidewalk, then the other, getting closer and closer to Thindy and Cricket, while my mother and my father and my sister stood at the windows and looked out the windows at me.

As I got closer to Thindy and Cricket, a horrible feeling started coming up inside me. Thindy and Cricket were two girls from Pocatello High School. I recognized them right off. Who wouldn't. The whole town knew them.

They made Puke Price look like Steve McQueen.

Thindy and Cricket were what everybody who was anybody in Pocatello steered clear of, never spoke to, wouldn't be caught dead with, who nobody knew the real names of, and knew only either as the Slit Sisters, or by their particular names of Sewage and Slut.

For the longest time, I called them the Slip Sisters. Then Sis made fun of me and told me it was Slit, you dumb shit. And I said, What is slit? And Sis told me.

One story goes, Sewage fucked Scardino in the back seat of his '59 El Camino in the Dead Steer Drive-In on a Saturday night while a group of boys stood around the car watching.

In another story, Slut took on a whole fraternity at Idaho State University, Phi Sigma Epsilon, doggy-style, up on Pocatello Creek.

And not only were these girls nasty. They were ugly, and they were weird. Sewage wore high heels and ankle socks and nylons with a seam in them and big full skirts with lots of petticoats, red petticoats. Slut always tried to look like Sewage, or maybe it was the other way around, so that was pretty much how Slut dressed too. The differnce between them was Sewage wore cat's-eye glasses and had long brown hair that came down in ringlets, and Slut was blond, with hair cut short. She looked like a boy who pierced her ears.

That Sunday, Thindy white, Cricket light blue, in Peter Pan collars and big, wide, white shiny belts that looked like marshmallows with gold buckles, and the both of them with those little shell sweaters with beads on the shoulders and down the fronts, came around the blue spruce, stopped in their tracks, and took a good long look at me.

The wind was blowing Thindy's long brown hair, but Cricket didn't have to worry because she didn't have any hair. Necklaces, charms on the necklaces, and Thindy with her cat's-eye glasses with rhinestones at the tips. Cricket with tiny gold loops punctured into the flesh of her ears.

There was a moment there when all there was in the world was wind and sun and the scratching of petticoats against nylon hose.

Then Slut, I mean Cricket, shaking her head so her earrings shimmered, said: Hello there, cute boy, she said. What is *your* name?

Her earrings went right into her earlobes. I wondered if it hurt having pierced ears.

Rigby John, I said.

Cricket took a step toward me, but Tramp growled, and I moved one foot back and stood mostly on that foot.

I'm Cricket, Cricket said. This is Cindy.

Thindy.

We're looking for Flaco and Acho, Thindy said. Do they live here?

I pointed with my arm to the east, up past the wood granary, down the lane to the boxcars.

Just follow the lane, I said. When you get to the boxcars, turn left, then turn right after the cattle guard. Keep walking, and you'll see their house up by the feedlots.

From the windows I looked like I was doing what I was doing: talking to two girls, pointing, but what I was really doing was trying to figure out a way I could explain to my mother and father what the Slit Sisters were doing in our front yard.

The long walk back into the house, up the stairs. I put my hand around the kitchen doorknob, turned. My body slipped through the door, and the kitchen door closed behind me.

Behind me the Slit Sisters, in front of me the Inquisition.

It was the first time ever I decided to lie to Mom and Dad, and since it was my first time, I decided it had better be fucking good.

They're missionaries with some church, I said. They want to help Mexicans.

Mom's almond-shaped hazel eyes looked over her glasses at me. The wrinkles that started up her forehead.

Dad was glaring too like a Hereford steer. Drut.

I didn't even look at Sis. Sis was way too much to look at.

First Church of God in Christ or something like that, I said, Baptists who think Mexicans are equal and want to convert them.

Sis spun around so fast I thought she'd fall over. She was out of the kitchen in a split second.

There I stood on a blue tile. Mom mostly on a white tile, Dad on a white tile. The light coming in the window made her hair look really gray.

Baptists? Dad said. What are Baptists doing in this country?

That's when Mom started.

I've told you some of the things that I could make Mom do. Well, there were some things she could make me do too. And she started to do one of those things she can make me do right then.

The eyes, always the eyes. It's like she turns a huge floodlight behind them on, and in the floodlight you disappear, and all that's left of you is the big fat lie you're telling.

But inside me was some kind of solid. On my own two feet. I wasn't alone anymore. I had two best friends.

They're Baptists, I said.

Religious people, I said.

Missionaries, I said.

They want to talk to the Mexicans about God, I said.

In the kitchen, everything was clean, clean and scrubbed and swept and shining with light bouncing off because everything was so clean.

The spotlight behind Mom's eyes had me, the deer in her headlights.

I remembered to breathe. Flaco had called me *negro*. Flaco and Acho had rubbed my shoulders and my back the night before.

It was a standoff. Me in my blue square tile and my big fat lie, and Mom in her white square tile with her floodlight.

In a science-fiction movie, this part is where all the test tubes start buzzing and foaming and blowing up.

All that was in the room was the cleanliness next to godliness, the floodlight, and the breath in, the breath out, of me.

Who knows how long I stood there. A month of Sundays. Till hell froze over. From here to eternity.

But in the end, I won. Breathing and a little help from my friends made me win. Mom's almond-shaped hazel eyes couldn't see through me to the big fat lie anymore. I'd broken the spell. Something in me loved God so much right then.

I let out my breath and stepped off my blue tile and walked to the kitchen door.

Where are you going? Mom said.

To feed the chickens, I said.

You stay away from those Baptist girls, Mom said, you hear?

I will, I said. I'm just going to the barn.

I closed the kitchen door behind me, not hard, not soft, just regular like this was just a regular day and I was shutting the kitchen door. I touched my shirt pocket and touched a Viceroy. Touched my Levi's pocket and touched the matches.

Up on top of the steel granaries, where I'd read all of Steinbeck, I lit the Viceroy. From up there I could see just about everything. I could see the spud cellar, the pigpens, the boxcars, and the grain elevator. There was the lane that connected us with the rest of yellow Bannock County. I could see the light pole. Where the earth rises up and the arc of the reservation begins. I could see the Mexican house. The two girls at the Mexican house and the two boys. I could see as two girls and two boys walked to the straw stack, climbed the straw stack. I saw the two girls and the two boys sit down in the spread straw. Then after a while, I couldn't see anything, just dark spots in the bright afternoon in the spread straw on top of the straw stacks, fucking.

The Slit Sisters didn't come back through the yard until ten o'clock at night. Tramp started barking, and all the lights in the house went on.

Dad was in his light blue pajamas with the dark blue buttons. Mom was in her pink bathrobe, cold cream on her face, her glasses off.

I cracked the door to my bedroom. Mom was standing in a white tile, and Dad was standing in a white tile. Both of them were staring out the window.

Baptists, my ass, Mom said.

Then Mom went around into the front room and opened the front door. From the front porch, Mom hollered out: You two little bitches stay away from my house! We don't want your kind on our property!

Then she slammed the door, came around from the front room, and headed straight for my door. I closed the door quick, ran and jumped in bed, pretended like I was sleeping.

The light from the kitchen when she opened the door went up against my bedroom wall. Mom's shadow, hair flying around her head inside the light on the wall.

Rigby John, she said. Her voice was high and too loud and a little crazy.

Don't ever let me catch you coming anywhere near those girls ever again, she said. There'll be hell to pay if you do.

Mom slammed the door and where her shadow had been on the wall it was dark. But her shadow was still there on my wall, inside the dark on the wall. All night long, her shadow on the wall, hair flying all around, a shadow inside a shadow, always there on my wall.

I forget just how long it was before the Slit Sisters came walking back into the yard. Two weeks later, maybe three. I was putting gas into the pickup from the gas pump. It was about four in the afternoon. Dad was combining wheat, Mom was down with one of her migraines, and it was time for me to feed hay to the Herefords up in the feedlot.

I didn't see Thindy and Cricket until they were standing right behind me. In fact, I jumped and made a little scream when Cricket spoke. Damn near dropped the gas nozzle. It could have been a real embarrassing disaster.

Hello there, Rigby John, Thindy said. What ya doing?

They pretty much had on the same getups as they had on the last time. High heels and ankle socks, square dance skirts poking way out with all those petticoats underneath. The wide white marshmallow belts.

I'm just putting gas in the pickup, I said.

Duh.

Right then, I know, my face looked just like a Hereford cow's.

Drut.

Where ya going to drive that pickup when you get done putting gas in it? Cricket said.

I knew what was coming, but I couldn't stop it.

I'm driving up to the feedlot, I said.

Next to Flaco and Acho's house? Cricket said.

Yes, I said.

Thindy puckered her lips and poked her shoulders up.

Could you please give us a ride? Thindy said. These rocks hurt our feet in these shoes.

I looked down at their high-heel shoes with the holes in the toes and the ankle socks. I looked over at the house. I looked over at the barn. I looked all around the yard.

Pleee-eease! Thindy and Cricket said.

After all, it was the Christian thing to do.

Inside the cab of the pickup, Thindy and Cricket smelled good. They didn't seem at all like the Slit Sisters or Sewage and Slut doing it doggy-style. They smelled good, and they were laughing, and the skin on their necks was smooth.

I started the pickup. Thindy and Cricket were watching to see how well I could drive. I put the clutch in and shifted into reverse, let the clutch out real smooth.

Oh! Thindy said.

Oooh! Cricket said.

Then I put on the brake, put in the clutch, and shifted into first gear, no problem. I let the clutch out, turned the steering wheel, and there wasn't even the slightest jerk.

That's the way we were, Thindy, Cricket, and I, driving slow, inside the pickup, smelling good, the soft white skin on Thindy's neck, on Cricket's. Cricket's pierced ears looked cool. The round piece of gold just went right into her earlobe, no blood or anything. We hit the bump just down from the gas pump and the bump made the flesh of these girls bounce. Their breasts bounced, and because of the bump and the bouncing, the breasts bouncing, we all laughed, and because we laughed I started to tell them that Flaco and Acho were my best friends ever.

That's when the pickup door opened. It was Mom, and she had her glasses on, her eyes, one pitched south, the other east. Mom grabbed me by the hair and pulled my hair, pulled me by the hair out of the moving pickup. She was slapping me in the face and calling me names. The pickup went rolling and smacked right into the side of the machine shop and stalled. Thindy and Cricket were screaming. I think they were screaming. When I look back on that day, I can say they were screaming, but I really don't know for sure. All I remember is the slaps to my face, on my head, against my ears.

I think Thindy or Cricket said something to Mom. Said she was a crazy woman. I think Mom yelled at them to leave. Called them sluts, dirty bitches. But I really don't remember. It's only looking back that I remember that part, so that part I could be making up.

What I remember, though, besides the slaps on my face, was what my mother called me that day.

My mother put her forehead against my forehead, put her almond-shaped hazel eyes straight into my eyes.

That's when she said it. Something she said I will never forget.

You spineless ass, my mother said.

Spineless ass. In front of those girls, my mother called me a spineless ass.

*   *   *

There was a big hullabaloo after that. Lots of doors slamming and cupboards slamming and yelling and righteous indignation. I'd never seen Mom so nuts. Even Dad didn't understand what was going on with her. I mean, Dad never did understand what was going on with her, but he never let us see that. This time, though, he stared at her like Sis and I stared at her, like she was some wild woman.

That evening after supper, Mom walked up to the sewing machine, her Singer sewing machine that was a piece of furniture in the front room. She walked right up to that sewing machine, squatted down, and put her hands under the wood box of the sewing machine, and lifted. She lifted and lifted and then just heaved that thing over her head.

Singer sewing machine a big pile of kindling with a Singer sewing machine stuck up in the middle of it in the middle of the front-room floor in no time.

Finally, Dad drove up to the Mexican house.

When Dad came back, he sat at the supper table, under the bright overhead light, in his chair at the end of the table and told Mom, Sis, and me all he'd said to Flaco and Acho and their father and their mother and sisters and brothers.

The sunburn line on his forehead. Hat hair. The sideburns next to his ears going gray. His big hands, the black hairs on them, fingers spread out flat on the oilcloth tablecloth.

By sundown tonight, I told 'em, Dad said. Said they were an abomination to our good Christian values. We're good Catholics, I said. I said, We can't have no midnight shenanigans go on around here. I told them, This is our home, Dad said. And you have to show us some respect.

I want you out of here by sundown's what I told them, Dad said. Just get your things and load 'em up in your truck and go.

When Dad finished talking, I didn't know what to do. I hated him and Mom so much right then I didn't know what I was going to do. All there was was a roaring in my ears and a big lump in my chest that was going to come out with a big mess of sobs and tears.

I wished they were dead.

Nothing else in me, in my head, nothing else in my heart.

I wished the two sons of bitches were dead.

I headed straight for the kitchen door. Mom, wild-woman-crazy Mom, jumped in front of me, put her body in front of the kitchen door.

In all my years, I'd never seen her look like that. I mean, yes, there were all those things I knew so well: Her almond-shaped hazel eyes, one pitched south, the other east. The wrinkles on her forehead. The glasses that always shined in the light. The little wrinkles starting along her lips. The way she gritted her teeth. How her cheeks moved because she was gritting her teeth.

There were those things and more. Her high, arched eyebrows, her cheekbones. The tanned-smooth quality of her skin.

And more. Something impenetrable, something hard and mean and stubborn. Something ugly about her, the way she always knew she was right.

Mom spread her arms out wide across the kitchen door.

In her eyes a dare to try and pass.

Spineless ass.

Rigby John Klusener, Mom said. Get to your room and do not leave your room for the rest of the night.

For a moment, in my right hand there was a backhanded slap. First to her right cheek, then her left. There was the way I pushed her head through the glass of the door. The breaking glass, the blood.

Hey! Dad yelled. Your mother told you to do something! Now move!

So what else was there to do? I went downstairs to my bedroom.

As I look back on that evening now, I can see I had no other choice. They were my mother and my father, for sixteen years I'd known nothing else. You honor your father and your mother. And it wasn't even that I had a decision about honoring them or not. I didn't have a clue how to speak the mess inside me I was feeling. Still don't really.

So there I was, the spineless ass, walking down the stairs to my bedroom.

All's I had was *negro*, all's I had was Flaco's long fingers, his open palm on my shoulder. All's I had was Acho's thick fingers on the top of my head.

All's I had was my dark bedroom.

I didn't even have a cigarette.

*   *   *

That night around midnight, Flaco and Acho's old Ford truck, stacked with mattresses, a table, pots and pans, dishes, cups, an old wardrobe, a mirror that reflected the yard light and the stars, piles of dresses and shoes, pants and shirts, flour to make tortillas, all the stuff it takes to live in a house — seven people in a two-room house — and one guitar, one accordion, drove through the yard, the engine loud because of the bad muffler, the headlights gone dim from bad wiring.

The time it takes to drive from the wood granary, past the light pole, past the blue spruce, past the pole fence, the time it takes at the wagon wheel and the Austrian Copper rose to yield to oncoming traffic, on Tyhee Road at midnight no traffic, still the old Ford yields, the brakes squeak, the bed of the truck floats a little.

On the back of the truck, two young boys, men really, I never did ask them how old they were, Flaco in his blue shirt with the really white T-shirt under it, his denim pants, his red Converse tennis shoes untied, Acho in his red shirt and his really white T-shirt under it, his denim pants, his tennis shoes tied up, their legs dangling over the back side of the truck. Their faces, how I knew their faces, the way they smiled, the way the sunlight, the moonlight, lay on their skin. In the hay truck the smell of them, soap, sweat, tortillas, tobacco, instant coffee, cigarettes.

Chingada tu puta madre.

Sí, cabrón.

Oh my heavens pretty woman so far.

Gringa loca.

The back turn signal of the truck a spastic white flash. The brake pedal released, the clutch disengaged, the gas pedal pushed toward the floor, the old Ford leaned around the corner, the high sound of first gear, then second gear, then on down the road.

Flaco and Acho.

I never saw them again.

Not that night, or the next night, but the third night the eastern sky at night was as bright as day.

In the straw stack at the feedlot, it took the fire trucks two days to put the fire out. Spontaneous combustion, the fire marshal said. The fire had been smoldering in there for days.

5 Wild Thing

BACK IN THE DAYS before Flaco and Acho, when the only things to do on the farm besides work and do chores was to climb up the grain elevator, or sit on top of the boxcars, go into the dark spud cellar, or climb up in the steel granaries, there was a game I used to play out behind the spud cellar under the grain elevator.

I stacked two straw bales on top of each other, then spread out a couple bales of straw on one side of the stacked bales.

What I'd do was take a run at the bales, then tuck my head and flip over the bales, using my hands to push off the top bale, and then land in the soft bed of spread straw.

I usually did the flip after doing the balancing act on the grain elevator.

One day, out of sheer monotony, I decided to spice up my life by stacking a third bale on the stacked straw. It didn't seem like much of a risk. After all, I thought, what's so terrible that could happen?

I took a run at the bales, tucked my head, pushed off the top bale, went flying ass over teakettle for a while, then landed. I landed on my ass as usual, on the straw, but this time my head kept flipping while the rest of me stopped, and my face had a head-on collision with my knee.

Who knows how long I lay out on the spread straw totally knocked out, cuckoo, blood streaming out my nose. For three weeks my eyes were black. There was a week there my face was so swoll I could barely see out my eyes.

When I could see again and the swelling went down, when I wasn't black and blue anymore, what stayed and what didn't go away was I no longer could breathe out of my nose. My nostrils were plugged up with busted gristle.

That's why I went around with my mouth open all the time, because I couldn't breathe.

Monsignor Cody found something new to say to me. Whenever he saw me, he reached his hand over, put his fingertips on my cheeks, his thumb on my chin, and then closed my mouth with his hand while he said: *Halt dein Mund.*

Which is German for "shut your mouth."

One way or another, all my life the universe has conspired to shut me up.

Submucous resection. That's the name of the operation I had to have to open up the breathing passages in my nose.

As fate would have it, my stay in the hospital was quite an event. Two birds with one stone. I met Billie Cody and George Serano on the same day, in the same place, Saint Anthony's Hospital. Although Billie saw a lot more of me than I did of her. George was a differnt story altogether. It probably makes some kind of sense that I ended up fighting him that day. He was a drunk, and an Indian and in the throes of the DTs. Fear had him around the neck. As things go, I was ready to fight him, but not ready for him. It took a long time and a world of hurt before George and I stood eye to eye, that is without wanting to kill each other. You might say we had some issues. The line between our farm and the rez, the differnce between the yellow and the red, plus there I was a self-righteous Catholic boy with an ax to grind, and there was George, another mean man in my life — a no-good ne'er-do-well Indian and a queer to boot.

Amazing now that I look back on it, I got through all this alive.

Thank God for Billie Cody. I'd never have made it without her.

Dr. Verhooven told me and Mom it was a simple operation. Thursday night I'd check in the hospital. I wouldn't have any dinner, only liquids. Friday morning, Dr. Verhooven would put me under a general anesthetic. I wouldn't be awake during the operation. The operation consisted of Dr. Verhooven taking a drill and drilling two new holes through the busted gristle in my nose. I'd wake up around lunchtime. I'd be able to have a light lunch. I'd stay in the hospital for the rest of the day, I'd get supper that night, and I'd spend that night in the hospital so they could watch me, and the next morning they'd give me some pills and send me home.

It sounded simple enough.

Mom packed an extra pair of shorts, a T-shirt, a pair of white socks, my toothbrush, and my underarm deodorant in her blue square overnight case. Mom drove me to the hospital. Dad couldn't go because he was still combining wheat. As always, he had something better to do when it came to me.

Neither Mom nor I said a damn word to each other on the ride into town. Usually, what was silent when there was silence came from Mom and Dad. After Flaco and Acho, though, I discovered I could be silent too. Something real hard was in my heart for Dad, and even more for Mom. Sending a family off in the middle of the night — now there's a Christian act of charity for you. Their talk about their good name and the abomination of good Christian values had never sounded so ridiculous.

Halfway to town, Mom got her rosary out. There we were again with the sorrowful mysteries. Every goddamn Hail Mary stuck in my throat. Then after the rosary, just as we started to get into town traffic, insult to injury, Mom started on a litany.

Have mercy on us. Have mercy on us. Pray for us. Pray for us. Pray for us. Over and over and over again.

Fucking litanies, man.

Like to drive you fucking nuts.

Mom's almond-shaped hazel eyes were definitely green, and she squinted a lot, one eye gone south and the other east. Her hair had frizzed so she tried to cover up the frizz with a hat. The blue hat from LeVine's with the pheasant feather in it. Her new big plastic glasses. She wore her tan slacks with the big crease in them and the cuffs and a blue and white polka-dot blouse tucked in and no belt and her white Keds and her nylons. Really, she looked weird. When we walked in the hospital, I didn't want anyone to know I was with her.

At the admissions desk, Mom made me hold the blue square overnight case while she signed the insurance papers. It felt like I was holding a purse, so I set the overnight case on the shiny waxed lino-leum floor closer to her feet.

Across from me in the line was a girl my age from Highland High School. She was checking in to the hospital too. That girl was Billie Cody, but I didn't know it then. Billie was with her mom, and I re-member that she was short and that she smiled at me. Pretty soon we were talking, and Billie told me she was in to have her tonsils out and perhaps her tonsils out would help her tear duct thing. I noticed that her eyes were red, but I didn't ask what her tear duct thing was. I told her for me it was submucous resection and that I couldn't breathe out of my nose and the doctor was going to drill me some new holes. I re-member Billie laughed, that great laugh of hers in her big chest that seemed to take over her whole body. Billie's mom said something to my mom and my mom said something back. I don't know what they said, but that's the only time those two ever spoke to each other, let alone spent time in the same room together.

When Mom finished with the papers and it was time to go to my room, I didn't want to pick up the blue square overnight case, but I did. Billie looked at the blue square overnight case in my hand, and the way she looked at me was somehow the way Flaco had looked at me, in a moment that look that takes in the whole situation — the overnight case that looks like a purse, me holding the purse, my em-barrassment that I was holding something that looked like a purse. Billie saw the whole picture — *Gestalt* is the word Billie would use — all the levels of me and Mom. I saw it in her eyes, her tear duct eyes rimmed in red, there inside her eyes, the Jesus look.

The hospital was dark woodwork and big dark wooden doors with little windows above the doors, mostly open, and green walls. The floor made big creaks in the long lengths of hardwood. In the hall-ways, up high, you could see where the old gaslights had been on the walls. But the gaslights had been replaced by long fluorescent bulbs hanging down, which made everything have that too bright light from above. The dark woodwork had strange whanged-out shadows.

My room was room 22, and I turned off the fluorescent lights as soon as I walked in. There were three beds in room 22, and my bed was the bed by the big wood bay window. There were no other pa-tients in the room but me. The black and white clock above the door said five-thirty. I looked around before I unbuttoned my madras shirt. I hung the shirt up on a hanger in the closet, then my Levi's on a hanger. Put my wallet and my change inside the blue overnight case. I pulled off my T-shirt, folded the T-shirt and laid the T-shirt along with my socks and my underwear next to my shoes at the bottom of the closet.

There I was stark-naked in a strange place, and you know what that always does. Poking straight out in front of me. I didn't dare whack off. It was a Catholic hospital, plus I had nothing to come into. Then I saw the sink and the mirror above the sink, and I thought the sink would work. Then there was a knock on the door. I quick pulled the hospital gown over me, didn't tie the gown up in back, just jumped into the bed, lay down, and pulled my hard-on into between my legs and pressed my legs together.

Mom came in with a nurse who was a nun. Sister Angelica. A Benedictine. No big crinkled fan of starched halo across her head like the Holy Cross. Just a little white cap on her forehead called a wimple that looks like it hides horns and a white veil and white robe instead of black.

Rigby John, Sister Angelica said, do you want the lights off?

I was about to mumble some shit I hadn't formulated yet.

That's when Mom said: My son doesn't like bright light, she said. He takes after his grandfather.

In a moment, the anger I had for my mother went away, and there she was, the woman in my life I could never live without.

My body sank way down in the bed I was in, flat as the mattress. All of a sudden there I was, a part of myself I'd never known.

My grandfather. I wasn't differnt at all. I took after my grandfather.

When I came back from wherever I was, Sister Angelica was gone and Mom was at the closet. She picked up my jockey shorts from next to my shoes, folded them, and put my jockey shorts inside the blue square overnight case.

Mom didn't pull out her black beaded rosary that was blessed in the Vatican. She just sat down, sinking in that side of the bed in her blue and white polka-dot blouse and the blue felt hat and the pheasant feather staring out the window. Her new big plastic glasses on her face looked like scaffolding for her eyes. The trees outside the second-story window were big silver maples. Big Idaho wind in the trees scattering sun.

It took her awhile, but then Mom said: You'll be safe here. You'll be fine. The nuns are so kind and helpful, especially Sister Angelica.

Mom still stared out the window. Shaky shadows and sun across the white sheets of the bed. She didn't move her head, she just reached out her arm, and her hand touched my arm, which was connected to my hand, which was cupped over my other hand, which was covering the lurking evil in my crotch.

At first all I could think about was the evil under my cupped hand, but then the longer she touched me, the more the evil went away, and the more I didn't have to worry about covering anything up.

A big white room, three white beds. Shiny waxed brown linoleum. The fluorescent lights off, light and shadow, light and shadow. Everything quiet. The way Flaco had accepted my hand, it took me awhile, but I accepted Mom's hand as it lay on my arm. Rough, red farm hand, cut-to-the-quick fingernails.

Your grandfather was a frail man, Mom said.

In the room, my eyes couldn't lie on a piece of shadow or a piece of sun for even a second without the sun or the shadow going differnt, getting brighter or longer or wider, or sun changing into shadow or shadow sun right there, there in front of my eyes.

He loved to sit in his room, Mom said, and read and read and smoke his pipe. The ceiling light was never allowed on, only the reading lamp at his desk. Your grandfather sat in a dim circle of light in a room full of books. Floor-to-ceiling books. The smell of old books and Prince Albert.

Mom waved her hand in front of her nose.

My mother hated the smell of that room, she said.

She wrinkled up her nose, which made her new big plastic glasses go up and down.

On my hand, the palm of her rough hand curled, then took within it some of my fingers.

Us children were never allowed in his room, Mom said. I only went in there to clean, and cleaning only meant emptying the ashtray, the garbage can, to vacuum, and dust the lamp and the wood of the bookshelves where there wasn't any books stacked.

Out in the hospital hallway, a gurney with a bum wheel. Over the intercom, a woman with a soft voice.

You're a lot like your grandfather, Rigby John, Mom said. His eyes were hazel too. Green, sometimes gold. I loved his eyes when they were gold.

Outside the window, green leaves, gold sun. Shadows and light all over on us on the sheets of the bed, the gold band on her third finger, her hand on top of my hands. Mom stared ahead out the window, chin up, light and shadow all over her face. She took her new big plastic glasses off, laid her glasses on the bed, rubbed her eyes.

One time I walked in on him reading, Mom said. I don't know what got into me. I just opened his door and walked in. There he was with his glasses down on his nose, the room full of smoke. My father looked over and smiled at me. The way he smiled, I knew I wasn't his daughter. I was a strange visitor from one of his books.

Mein wildes Mädchen, he called me, Mom said. My wild girl.

Mom held tight to my fingers. She used my fingers to pull herself around. Her knee on the bed, her beige slacks with the crease, the cuff, nylon folds on her ankle, the white Ked. She looked straight at me. Frizzy hair, the stupid hat. No glasses. I loved it when her eyes were gold. At that moment, if I curled my lip up, crossed my eyes, scratched my butt, she'd laugh so hard she'd never catch her breath.

You've never imagined your mother as a wild girl, Mom said. Now, have you?

That night it was cool falling asleep in the big empty room. Just me in a white room in a white bed, the sheets folded down, just my arms out. Through the bay window, the moon, that same old moon shining through the silver maple leaves, like my dog, Tramp, always there ready to accompany you.

The black and white clock above the dark wood door said ten-thirty. I dangled my feet over the side before they landed on the cool, shiny linoleum. I watched my feet walk through the moonlight and the shadows of the silver maple leaves on the floor. My butt was hanging out and I liked my butt hanging out. Of course, you know what happened.

When I got to the sink, I pulled the little chain on the light above the sink, and there in the mirror, sure enough, there I was poking out in front of me.

What happened next is something that has never happened before.

When I am half-naked and poking out in front of me like that, there has never been one single time that I haven't whacked off and broken the sixth commandment.

But this night it was differnt.

The light above the sink was a tiny light globe with a glass cover that was green, and the light globe with the glass cover made a circle on the wall, around the sink, and onto my feet on the shiny floor.

I put my closed eyes into the light. Warm light on my cheeks, on my lips, on my eyes.

I opened my eyes, and there they were, looking right back at me. My hazel eyes. Almond-shaped.

Moments of gesture.

Grandpa, I said. Hello.

The next morning, some Swiss doctor guy with an accent put a needle in my arm and asked me to count back from ten.

The next thing I knew I was waking up in bed. The bed was at an angle so I was halfway sitting up. It felt like my head was in a vise clamp. The bib down the front of me was covered in blood all the way down to my waist.

Mom was sitting in the chair next to my bed. The black beaded rosary blessed in the Vatican was lightning through her fingers. I quick closed my eyes because the last thing I wanted was to pray another rosary.

Who knows how much later I opened my eyes again. Somebody'd tightened the vise clamp. Mom was sitting at the bay window, staring out at the tall silver maples. The shadows and the light all over her and all over in the room. She had her face on. Her glasses off, her eyebrows penciled on, her new lipstick Royal Red. Her hair fluffed out, not frizzed, so she didn't need a hat.

The next time I woke up, Sister Angelica was plumping up my pillow. The bib that was on me before was gone, and the whole bed, including me, was all white. Everything was bright and shiny. My eyes took awhile to see. There was something stuck up in my nose. When I moved my head, I thought it would fall off. The shadows and the light were gone, and the sky through the silver maple leaves was gray. In the bed next to me was a man with black hair. He looked like an Indian man. He was sleeping.

Looks like we're in for a storm, Sister Angelica said.

Up close her skin looked yellow next to the white of the pointy wimple on her head. Lots of black eyebrows.

I love these Idaho storms, she said. When I was a girl in Oregon, we never had storms like you do here.

Sister Angelica picked up a tray from the table between me and the Indian man. She set the tray with cottage cheese and mandarin oranges in front of me and pushed a button at the side of the bed. The bed made a sound, and I was sitting straight up in no time. On the

---

tray, there was also a carton of milk, some crackers, and a gingersnap cookie.

Your mother had to go home and cook supper, Sister Angelica said.

Supper! I said. What time is it?

Five o'clock, she said.

I was supposed to wake up in the afternoon and have lunch, I said. And dinner. Why did I wake up so late?

Dr. Verhooven is a very good doctor, Rigby John, Sister Angelica said. But he is only a doctor. These things are God's concerns, she said. God's and the anesthesiologist, she said. And sometimes I wonder about the anesthesiologist.

Sister Angelica smiled at me and looked in my eyes while she touched my forehead. Then she picked up my arm by the wrist. She held my wrist cuffed in her hand and looked at her wristwatch that looked like a man's wristwatch.

My head hurts, I said.

You're going to live, Sister Angelica said. Keep your hands away from your nose. Don't waste your food. Later on tonight I'll get you something more. Now say your prayers.

I made the sign of the cross and started in on the Bless us, O Lord, and these Thy fucking gifts.

Sister Angelica walked over to the next bed. The way she stood above the sleeping Indian man made you know she was a real holy person. She had tears in her eyes, and she held her hands bunched up and close to her heart. Then she made the sign of the cross.

At the dark wood door, Sister Angelica stopped, the skirts of her habit swaying. The long wood rosary tied around her waist knocked against the wood of the door. She looked at me as she turned off the fluorescent light.

I don't like these lights either, she said. They make everything so garish.

Is *garish* two *r*'s or one? I said.

One, she said.

Then: Rigby John? she said.

Yes, Sister? I said.

If you need anything, Sister Angelica said, just push that buzzer next to your bed.

I moved my head real slow. On the side of my bed, at the top, on the railing was a green lever.

This one? I said.

No, she said. That one is to adjust your bed. It's the button on the wall.

On the wall, behind my bed, there was a button that looked like a doorbell.

That's the one, she said.

Then: Perhaps you could do me a favor, Sister Angelica said.

Sure, I said.

If Mr. Serano wakes, push that buzzer as soon as possible, will you?

Yes, Sister, I said.

Then something quick in my throat, and I said: Sister?

Yes?

Is that *George* Serano?

George Serano, yes, she said. Do you know him?

For a while my mouth just hung open and then hung open some more.

Then: No, I said quick, I don't know him.

Sister Angelica stayed in the dark wood doorway for a moment, the white from the fluorescence in the hallway making her bright.

Then she was gone.

I was alone with a plate of cottage cheese and mandarin oranges, crackers, a gingersnap cookie, a carton of Meadow Gold milk, two buttons, a head the size of Idaho, and George Serano.

Injun George. The naked guy who almost got me and Mom killed.

The queer.

Now that I look back on it, that moment in room 22 of Saint Anthony's Hospital, the fluorescent lights off, the dark gray light through the window, the tall trees dancing up a storm, when I leaned up and turned so I could see this George Serano guy, I wouldn't admit it then, but I can tell you now, the helpless feeling was in my arms, and the scared place inside of me was scared.

That moment.

Oh my heavens pretty woman so far, what was a queer Indian doing in a Catholic hospital?

I've always said the universe always conspires to fuck me up.

But that didn't stop me from looking. In fact, I'm surprised Georgy Girl didn't wake up the way my hazel eyes were looking. Gawking.

Every aspect.

He wasn't an Indian with hair like when Indians had long hair. His hair was cut in a butch. He was tall — as long as the bed. Big hands with nice fingernails, long feet. He didn't look like most Indians I'd seen.

Then of course I'd never really *seen* any Indians yet, now had I? I mean, *looked* at them like people.

The first Indians I'd seen was way back when I'd seen Indians coming down the steps of the Pocatello House.

One time, I was driving the John Deere A up Tyhee Road and there was a bunch of Indians in an old car sitting in the barrow pit. All four doors were open and beer and wine bottles all around the old Ford on the ground. I never stopped to look at their faces. Who would? Drunk Indians are dangerous, and you have to steer clear of them.

One story my father told, there was this Indian man beating up his wife and when a white guy stopped to help, the Indian woman turned on the white guy and hit him over the head with a purse full of rocks.

Another time I saw Indians was at the Pocatello Frontier Rodeo. The lights went off and the spotlight went on a bunch of Indians dressed up in beaded buckskins and feathers, dancing a war dance, spinning around while a bunch of guys played drums and sang, Hey ya, hey ya, hey ya.

Dad was president of the Pocatello Frontier Rodeo, and he had to deal with those Indians. He said all they cared about was the money so they could go out and get liquored up.

In Fort Hall, on our way to Blackfoot to visit Grandma in the Buick, usually there were Indians who stood in front of the Trading Post. Dad told us to lock our doors, and Mom always got the rosary out — if it wasn't already out. As far as I could tell, the Indians in front of the Trading Post were ragged and dirty, but again I never got to see them up close.

I used to think Mexicans were dirty. They lived in that ratty old Mexican house, and they didn't plant flowers or try and take care of the yard.

But that house wasn't *their* house. It was Dad's house.

And look at Flaco and Acho, scrubbed clean every day with no running water in the house.

That day in the hospital, cotton stuffed up my nose, leaning over, damn near ready to fall out of bed I was leaning over so close, looking at the Indian, it was only then I realized.

I had lived my whole life — over sixteen entire years — next to the Bannock Shoshone Indian reservation, and I had never been in the same room with a human being who was Indian before.

The only thing I knew about Indians was what I'd seen from far away and stories about Indians.

Told by who?

My father.

So, since I wasn't my father, and since this was the first time for me ever to be in the same room with an Indian, and since that Indian was *asleep,* I decided to get an eyeful.

When it came right down to it, what scared me, what I wouldn't think about too much that day, that moment, what really made my heart go wild, was two things.

This *puto maricón* Indian lying in the bed next to me was sleeping.

Something about the *sleeping* freaked me out. He was just lying there, his chest going up and down, up and down, so slow. His head tilted to one side, his arms spread out, his hands, the fingers, spread out. He was somewhere else and his arms and his hands, his fingers, were wings, and he was like me in my dreams when I fly, and he was flying.

That's when I saw it, the second thing.

The Indian man, Injun George, the *puto maricón* George Serano, looked a lot like Flaco. Sturdier than Flaco, not so skinny, and older, say maybe thirty-five. His skin was smooth like Flaco's, though, and brown. Not brown the same brown as Flaco's, but close. Red-brown.

What it was, though, was the eyes. Even though his eyes weren't open, I could tell. The dark lashes and the black eyebrows and the graceful arch of the lid.

Soft the way Flaco was soft. Jesus right there behind his eyes.

I'd never eaten cottage cheese before. Cottage cheese in your mouth the first time is weird.

Outside the bay window, the silver maples were wild girls, wind whipping through them something fierce.

Somewhere way out there, a slow, low rumble so far out there, I thought it might be something inside me here in my big sore head.

It wasn't until that night, late, after Sister Angelica went off shift, that the first blast of thunder hit so hard it shook the halo off Saint Anthony.

One thousand twenty-two counts later, the bolt of lightning hit the power plant. Everything in Bannock County went dark.

One thousand four counts later, outside the bay window, the silver maple lit up an electric green.

One thousand one counts later, thunder so loud it wasn't a sound but a thick place that sucks air. Ants crawl in your ears, ants all down your chest and back. All you want is breath.

One thousand, and boom all around a bright flash the color of the moon. Then dark. Thunder is your skull collapsing. Lightning, God's long fingernails, jagged silver rips in a velvet black sky. Lightning you taste on your tongue.

Lightning was the blue arch of an electric fist coming right out at me, low on the floor, from the plug-in under the bay window.

For a moment I think, This is war. This is what we bend over and kneel under our desks for, this is Khrushchev's atomic bomb.

Another blue fist clear across the room.

That's when I look up at the end of my bed. The shape of a man in a flash of lightning.

I yell out loud, too loud like I always do, but you can't hear me yell. Hell, even *I* can't hear me yell. My legs are pulled up into my body, and my arms are around my legs. Another flash of lightning, and my bed sheets are glow-in-the-dark folds on Catholic statues.

The hand touched my leg first. The hand was hot. The hot hand on my arm. His lips were feathers against my ear.

It is Thunderbird, the man said.

Please help me hide, he said. I'm afraid. Thunderbird wants me. Thunderbird is after me, and I'm afraid.

The feeling that I can't breathe. There is a yell inside my mouth, but I don't yell.

So sudden and so natural, how the man curled into me, the way he laid his head under my arm. He pulled his legs up, and his hands, the long, beautiful fingers, covered his head.

A lightning flash. A blast of thunder. I took a deep breath.

The smell, a strong smell of burnt air, or was it the smell of the man?

In that moment, I looked around at things — the neon silver maple leaves, the strobe of bright and dark, bright and dark, all around me in my ears the sound of the earth falling apart.

At first, I couldn't figure out why I wasn't scared. Then I knew. I wasn't scared because someone else was more scared. And as soon as

I saw there was someone more scared — it was so weird — in that moment I began to accept my own fear, and by accepting my fear I began to deal with it.

I let my hand touch his fingers on top of his head, let my hand lay there soft on him.

My voice in the room: It's all right, I said. It's only a thunderstorm, I said. It will pass.

You got to understand. I'd never been around someone with the DTs before. Back then, delirium tremens was just a bad case of diarrhea to me.

So that night, lying there with a sick and terrified man, in room 22, on a hospital bed, in the middle of the storm of '66, I thought: I will hold this man until the storm breaks. That's what Jesus would do. That's what my father wouldn't do. In the morning, the sun will rise on a peaceful world.

But as I was about to find out, it was a differnt world than I had figured. In the first place, the man I was in bed with was no Flaco. He was George Serano, Injun George, drunk and delirious.

And the world was no Hallmark card.

My first clue this was no fine romance was his breath. Something sweet and sour at the same time. Something rotten. Then the terrified man raised his head up. His eyes were like Flaco's all right, dark and beautiful, long eyelashes, but inside his eyes there was something wrong. I was busy trying to figure out what was wrong in those eyes, when he raised his hand, his long, beautiful fingers.

Fucking little white bastard, he said.

Then slapped me across the face. A piece of cotton went flying out of my nose.

Speak with forked tongue asshole, he said. You made us many promises, more than I can remember, but you never kept but one. You promised to take our land, and you took it.

The last time someone had hit me in the face was Scardino. For a moment, the eyes looking into my eyes were Scardino's, but then another flash, and what I saw was something I'd never seen before. The eyes looking into my eyes were wild, gone, off somewhere else. Another blast of thunder and a flash. The storm outside was some kind of chaos.

My knee went up, and I caught George Serano in the balls, or close enough. He went flying off the bed. I sat up fast, made all of my intention one thing: the buzzer on the wall.

Of course, the buzzer wouldn't work without electricity, now would it?

In the doorway, I could make out a nurse in a white uniform. She had her hands on her cheeks. I think she was screaming.

In no time at all, George Serano was back up on his feet. All over on his head, his hair was sticking up like he'd been hit by one of those blue fists from out of the plug-in. Behind him the bay window was neon green and shafts of lightning. The shafts of lightning looked like they were coming out of his head.

Just like that, his hands were around my neck.

My hands were on his hands. You know, the worst thing for me is not getting any breath. Well, that's what I was doing, trying to get breath. I doubled up my fist, and just like John Wayne I punched this guy, a jab right into his eye, then I hauled back with a roundhouse and smacked him in the side of the head.

George Serano let go his hands from around my neck. He fell against the bedpost, then down on the floor. I jumped out on the other side of the bed from him. I started yelling, Nurse! Nurse! Sister Angelica!

The amazing thing is that all during this lightning and thunder and darkness and wrestling around and women out in the hallway screaming, there was some part of me that was saying, I can't believe this! Look! My arms are not helpless. I'm fighting back! Look at me, I'm fighting back!

From under the bed, an arm reached out and grabbed my naked foot. I let out a scream, and it wasn't long, and I was *under* the bed. This guy was all over me. I was rolling and screaming and naked arms and legs kicking and punching. All around us, shit was crashing and breaking. All hell was breaking loose.

When we finally stopped, we had rolled up into the corner to the right of the bay window. George Serano grabbed my hospital gown and his fists balled up my hospital gown around my neck. He put his face right up to my face, his forehead to my forehead, his wild eyes into my eyes.

Jeez, this guy was way beyond bologna breath. He hadn't brushed his teeth since Eisenhower was president.

Then he lets go of my gown around the neck. And what does he do? He puts his arms around me. He pulls me close into his body, so close I can feel all of him. Like there was lightning in him, the way he was jumping.

You've got to help me, he said.

Then he let out a howl. Some kind of animal howling, something awful and crazy and sad, weird the way he was shaking.

It's Thunderbird, he said. Thunderbird won't stop until he has me in his claws.

George Serano's hands had me by the shoulders. We were face to face again. I was about to push away when he shook me in a way that made me stop. His eyes weren't wild, gone-off crazy. His eyes were the eyes I always knew he had, something soft, broken inside. Hurt the way you don't ever get over being hurt.

Flashes and flashes of lightning. Sweat on his forehead, all over his face. His lips, blood on his lips, blood inside on his teeth.

Thunderbird lives at the edge of the world, he said, where the sun goes down.

I wasn't scared again. Fear was in the room, but I didn't have it. This Indian guy had it. And if he had it, maybe lots of other people did too. Lots of people must be afraid, not just me. I wasn't so differnt.

I loved God so much right then. Still, I tried to step away, but George Serano held me firm.

Thunderbird can take any form, he said.

Flashes of light. The blood on his lips. The blood on his teeth.

Human, plant, animal, he said. But all the forms are only one. He has no shape, but he has four legs or two legs or a fin with hooves, and the hooves have claws. His wings cover the world, his wings are clouds, the beating of his wings brings the thunder. Thunder is the sound from deep inside his throat, though he has no head, yet there are teeth in his beak and the teeth are wolves' teeth, rows and rows of teeth. He has one eye. Lightning comes from his eye. He sees everything. He flies through the sky searching to cleanse the world of filth.

Snot from out his nose, tears down his cheeks, snot and blood. I'd never seen a man cry like that before. Break down and cry, sobbing and snorting and making all the embarrassing sounds.

Filth, he said.

I'd seen only myself cry like that. And my father when Russell died.

The next flash, and all around us were people in white, nurses and nuns, and one bald man with a stethoscope.

Now, now, Mr. Serano, the bald man in white said. I'm Dr. Overturf, and I'm here to give you a sedative.

A flash. The crazy was back in George's eyes when he looked at the
doctor.

You have run over my country, George yelled.

Now, Mr. Serano, the doctor said. Just come over to your bed and
lie down, and we'll give you something to sleep.

Dr. Overturf talked with a singsong in his voice.

No sleep! George said. No sleep! Not now. I have to stay awake
and I have to hide.

Dr. Overturf took George Serano's one hand off my shoulder. He
held George's hand in his hand. Two nurses and a nun crowded
around George and Dr. Overturf and me. Everybody took little steps.
George's other hand was a clenched fist around my shoulder. Fear in
his eyes. I have known fear like that.

Thunder and lightning, thunder and lightning. *Donnerwetter.*

A big slap of wind against the bay windows and a falling branch.

The wind is the Thunderbird breathing, George said.

Come on, George, I said. You'll feel better if you lie down.

You have destroyed the growing wood and the green grass, George
yelled.

Our tiny steps were moving us, one bundle of people, slowly,
slowly toward the bed.

You have set fire to my lands, he yelled. You have devastated my
country and killed my animals, the elk, the deer, the antelope, my buffalo.

Karen, get the sedative ready, Dr. Overturf said.

Yes, doctor.

If I reached out, the bed was only an arm's length away.

You do not kill them and eat them, George said. You leave them to
rot where they fall.

The human wedge of us forced George against the bed. George let
go of my shoulder and sat down. Dr. Overturf pulled George's arm
out straight. Nurse Karen swabbed a place on George's inner elbow.

George looked down at his arm, the blue vein in his arm, blue even
in the dark, blue in the flash of light.

Sleep won't stop Thunderbird, George said. If I'm awake, at least I
can run.

Now, now, George, Dr. Overturf said. In just a few seconds you will
get some rest.

Nurse Karen guided the needle into the blue stuck-out river in George's arm.

George's words out of his mouth were so slow.

Thunderbird, George said, is the giver of revelation.

The wild went out of George's eyes, and his eyes closed. His body fell into itself. I helped the other nurse get George's legs up on the bed.

The sides of the bed went up fast, little jail cells about a foot and a half high. Then the strap was pulled over George's chest, another strap over his legs, straps around George's wrists, around his ankles.

It was weird, standing there, all of us around George Serano's bed. The way the lightning was flashing, the darkness, then the light, thunder, all of us dressed in white, in a hospital, Nurse Karen with a syringe, all of us white people staring down at the Indian.

Somewhere in my body, maybe not *in,* maybe *all* of my body, felt something familiar, yet I did not know what.

Another flash of lightning. A roll of thunder.

Moments of gesture.

We were a Frankenstein movie, the part in the laboratory, when all the townspeople are safe because the monster is sleeping.

Dr. Overturf and the nurses kept telling me I was such a brave boy. After they wheeled George out in his bed, Nurse Karen brought me some cherry Jell-O and a 7UP.

In the morning, the sun was shining through the silver maples. Shadows and light on the shiny waxed floor.

A peaceful world.

But the peace did not last long.

My madras shirt was not on the hanger. Inside the blue overnight case, my wallet and my change were gone. And something else gone. My pair of jockey shorts. Not the clean ones, the dirty ones I'd worn into the hospital.

George Serano was out of his straps, out of his bed, out of his room, out of the hospital.

I heard the two nurses talking.

No one in the hospital had seen him leave.

Nobody told Mom what had happened the night before. Not even Sister Angelica had the nerve.

I said nothing. I loved that I had a secret.

At the checkout window, Mom's eyes were neon green, and her hair was a wild girl's. Man, was she pissed. Her voice got high and her chin was up.

I'm here to report a theft, Mom said.

On the other side of the checkout window, the nurse was young and her cheeks were red.

My son's new madras shirt, Mom said, his wallet, and his change have been stolen.

I didn't tell her about the jockey shorts.

I paid five dollars and ninety-five cents for that shirt, Mom said. And his driver's license was in the wallet. Took him three years to get that license.

In no time at all, Sister Angelica was white flowing robes and veils around the corner.

Mrs. Klusener, Sister Angelica said, I'm so sorry about your son's belongings.

We try to run a tight ship around here, Sister Angelica said.

Sister Angelica took a deep breath. Her eyes went to my eyes, and her eyes were tears and had the holy look, the way she'd looked at George Serano.

Sister Angelica put her hand on my mother's shoulder.

Mom didn't know what the hell to do. A nun was touching her. There was lipstick on her teeth when Mom smiled.

I can assure you, Sister Angelica said, as soon as we find the culprit, we will contact you.

We walked that way down the hall to the bright outside the hospital doors, Sister Angelica next to Mom, her hand on Mom's shoulder.

I held the door open for Sister Angelica and Mom.

You take care, Rigby John, Sister Angelica said.

I turned to look Sister Angelica in the eyes, but the sun shined hard against the glass door. Sister Angelica blurred like a photograph with too much sun.

Thank you, Sister, I said.

On the stairway, the sidewalk, in the parking lot, in the street, big tree branches lying all over. Leaves on everything. I was carrying the square blue overnight case. Billie Cody and her mom were getting into her mom's white Pontiac Bonneville. I quick walked behind a car so Billie wouldn't see me carrying a purse again. Billie's face was real white, and her hair was sticking up. Her eyes were red. I don't think she saw me.

The Buick was a blue and white streak flying low over the Tyhee

Flats. Under Mom's new big plastic glasses, her eyes were still green. The ripple up the side of her face. She was grinding her teeth. The speedometer hit eighty-five miles an hour.

Gott im Himmel! Mom said, Jesus, Mary, and Joseph! Where can you be safe if you can't even be safe in a Catholic hospital?

Weird what a secret can do. It separates you from the rest of the world, insulates you because you're the only who knows. It's like you're finally somebody because you have something nobody else has. A place where nobody else is.

At first, my secret was pretty simple. I had a wild night fighting with a crazy Indian in the hospital and came out the hero. People had slapped me on the back and smiled at me special. The doctor had told me I was brave.

Something real, something tangible, something big, had happened in my life, and my mother didn't know a thing about it.

It was a great pleasure, my secret.

Always before what had kept me from my parents was some faraway unreachable place in them, in her. A place I wasn't allowed.

She was the one who decided. For whatever reason, when she decided to come back, when the light came back in her eyes and she looked at me — like in the hospital that day when she told me about Grandpa — it never failed, I was always there, the place for her eyes to land.

Then came the wild night in the storm of '66 fighting for dear life with George Serano.

After that night, what kept me from my parents, what kept me far away from Mom, wasn't something she decided anymore.

Now it was my turn. I was differnt.

I had a secret, and the secret was real.

Mostly, I kept the secret to protect her from what happened to me.

But that was only part of the truth.

The whole truth. It was the place I went to instead of her.

The whole truth I kept even from myself most of the time.

What I knew for sure was I started seeing Indians everywhere, and every time the wind blew, I thought of Thunderbird.

6 Cast Your Fate to the Wind

Saint francis de sales is the patron saint of teenagers, so that's why Sis and I got to drive the pickup into town one night a week on Wednesday. Supposedly De Sales Club provides the Catholic teenager with a social life. You know, teenagers getting together to talk about what it was like being a teenager and maybe find a boyfriend or a girlfriend. But don't be fooled. De Sales Club doesn't have anything to do with help growing up and a social life, or any life at all. Unless you call kneeling on the cement floor praying the rosary a life. And as far as boyfriend or girlfriend goes, forget it.

In fact, the only thing differnt about De Sales Club from religion class was in De Sales Club instead of the other nine commandments, what got beat into your head was the sixth commandment.

Everybody knew it, even the nuns. *Especially* the nuns. We were all in the sex years now.

The only good thing about De Sales Club was Joe Scardino never showed up.

Father Dominic Arana, a new young priest at Saint Joseph's who was a Basque, was the priest in charge of De Sales. He lectured to us about what a venial sin was and what a mortal sin was when you were making out.

As far as I could tell, kissing without tongue and hugging were venial. Everything else was a mortal sin.

Same old thing, we studied *The Lives of the Saints,* but hip saints like Saint Dominic Savio, and Saint Theresa of Ávila, and Saint Sebastian, who was tied naked to a tree and pierced with arrows. There was even homework sometimes, but nobody ever did the homework, which was a discouragement to Father Arana because he was trying to be a good influence.

What a sorry sight he was standing in the sophomore classroom at the blackboard under the bright fluorescent lights, a heavyset man, sweating hard, smelling of garlic and incense and altar wine, with his white handkerchief in his big, black, hairy hand, wiping the sweat off his forehead and around his neck, his thick neck bulging out over his tight Roman collar, the pointer in his hand pointing at the words *venial* and *mortal* he'd chalked onto the blackboard.

You had to hand it to him. Father Arana tried hard to reach us. He used words like *cool* and *what's happening* and *can you dig it,* but really we couldn't help it, none of us, no matter how hard we tried, none of us could give a shit.

He lasted only one year. Right after Christmas, Father Arana ran off with *some woman. Some woman,* Mom said, who he was giving marriage counseling to.

Mom and us must have prayed a thousand rosaries for that guy. And the *bitch* who led him astray.

Father Dominic Arana. One big Basque, sweaty, hairy example of walking, talking mortal sin.

As it turned out, though, in the end, Father Arana helped me out a lot. I figured if he could run off, so could I.

Wednesday nights. There was no better feeling than Wednesday night after supper, Sis at the wheel of Dad's '63 Chevy Apache pickup, cranking the wheel and spitting gravel out of the driveway, KWIK on the radio, the windows rolled down. The first Wednesday of De Sales was hot, late September and warm air blowing all around us, the sun-baked soft, gold world speeding by, Sis still in her off-white spaghetti-strapped summer dress and tanned legs, me in my clean Levi's and blue T-shirt, a fresh pack of Marlboros on the seat between us, Sis and I smoking away, the twelve miles to town ahead of us, twelve miles of top-ten rock-and-roll hits blaring freedom, freedom, all the way to town.

Those twelve miles of freedom got us hooked on freedom, Sis and I. We got so free during those twelve miles, the second Wednesday of De Sales we didn't show up at De Sales Club at all. As soon as we pulled off Main Street and headed down Hayes, soon as we saw the cross on the steeple of Saint Joseph's Church, we just couldn't help it. Sis and I had to have another cigarette, we had to listen to more top-ten hits, we had to drive around some more.

At the Snatch Out, around the corner from the Dead Steer Drive-In, across Pole Line Road and from the Portland Cement Company and the Kraft cheese factory, is where we ended up. Parked in the Snac Out Drive-In everybody called the Snatch Out or the Red Steer Drive-In everybody called the Dead Steer, watching everybody else drive by.

I mean to say, *I* sat and watched everybody drive by.

It was just too queer, Sis said, a brother and a sister sitting together at the Snatch Out.

I couldn't have agreed with her more.

Sis took off with Gene Kelso, going from venial to more and more mortal sin in the back seat of his red '56 Mercury.

And I sat, just sat, sat and smoked, and even though I'd had my nighttime driver's license for a whole week, I didn't drive. To tell the truth, I was afraid to drive but wasn't about to let myself know it.

It wasn't so bad being alone. Scardino wasn't around, and I had enough money for French fries, and I sat behind the wheel so it looked like I was driving. I got to listen to the radio. Plus Gene Kelso gave me a Budweiser.

For holding down the fort is the way he put it.

Somewhere in there, as I was sitting and smoking, drinking my beer, listening to the radio, watching the cars go by, a '67 green and white Cadillac with wire wheels pulled in. When I looked to see who was driving, what I saw was a car full of Indian kids my age.

Jeez, even in the Snatch Out, Indians.

It was that night, the last Wednesday night in September, parked at the Snatch Out holding down the fort, right after the Cadillac full of Indians, that I met, *really* met, Billie Cody.

"Cast Your Fate to the Wind" by Sounds Orchestral was on the radio. It was my favorite song.

Maybe it was fate, I don't know. Billie says so. Billie always says, *As fate would have it.*

Anyway, out of the blue, the pickup door opened, and up stepped a girl with dark red ratted hair. Pink lipstick. White plastic sunglasses, dark green glass. When she got her butt on the seat, she reached back and slammed the pickup door behind her. A white shirt, a man's oxford shirt with a buttoned collar. Around her neck, a tiny gold necklace that looked like a hand, an open palm facing out. The hand hung down between what looked like two cantaloupes underneath her white shirt. Black pants with stirrups around the feet. Her bare feet barely touched the pickup floor. She pulled one foot up, cupped her foot in her hand, turned and leaned against the door. Her tiny toenails were painted dark blue.

Outside all around us, kids lined up parked in cars. The kids in the parked cars looking out at the cars passing by, a slow idle through the Snatch Out. Across from me in the cab, Billie's eyes were dark behind the green glass of her white plastic sunglasses. The sun was setting in through the back window of the pickup. The whole inside of the cab was Technicolor, how gold and pink can be sky blue. All the sunset colors on Billie's skin. Wind, just a little for a moment, just enough wind to feel on your skin.

Billie pointed her tiny blue toenails at me, then pulled her legs under her, knelt on the seat. She reached up, pulled off her white plastic sunglasses, folded them, put the glasses in her white oxford shirt pocket. The white oxford shirt at that moment a Technicolor illumination out of *Gentlemen Prefer Blondes*.

Something about her eyes. She looked like she'd been crying, but she wasn't crying, she was smiling. Like a little kid, the way she was smiling. In all that Technicolor, those sad bloodshot Billie Cody eyes looked close at me for the first time. Jesus.

Tear duct cancer, she said. You got a cigarette?

What? I said.

My eyes, she said. I have a condition. The tear ducts get plugged up. The tonsillectomy didn't do shit. Do you have a cigarette?

It's cancer? I said.

No, silly, she said. I'm being affected.

Sis had taken the Marlboros with her and left me with four cigarettes. I had two left. I reached in my shirt pocket, pulled out a cigarette, handed it over to Billie, then pulled out the other cigarette for me. I pushed in the cigarette lighter.

Billie and I sat looking down at the cigarette lighter, waiting for it to pop out, both of us with cigarettes in our mouths looking, waiting. For some reason I had forgotten my native language. I couldn't even remember if it was English.

Besides the cigarette lighter, the only other thing in the pickup was a beautiful smell. Really clean like soap but not Mom's White King or Sis's White Shoulders. Some smell so fresh and differnt, it smelled French. This girl smelled French.

Myself, I'd been transformed into a wheelbarrow of Redi-Mix cement, either that or a big block of Kraft extra-sharp Cheddar cheese. When I looked over at my arm and hand, they were ridiculously poised just above the front edge of the seat, my middle finger and my index finger and my thumb perfectly formed waiting to grab the cigarette lighter when it popped out, and my little finger, there it was, how embarrassing, sticking up the way English people drink tea.

Then outside just like that, it wasn't sunset. It was dark, dark inside too, headlights passing.

On the radio, the guy was singing *So tired, tired of waiting, tired of waiting for you.* So I started singing *So tired of waiting* too.

That's when it happened all at once, the way it does with laughter. Coming up fast from so deep and hard your belly hurts. When the lighter finally popped up, my whole body spazzed, which made Billie let out a little scream, which made me let out a little scream. She cut a fart too, which was so fucking funny. Even with Sis, I'd never heard a girl fart before. We laughed for I don't know how long for a while there, just staring at each other no sound coming out of us except for gasps.

When Billie had herself calmed down, and she thought she could speak, Billie said: *Waiting for Godot.*

Billie spit *Waiting for Godot* out of her mouth more than said it, and maybe you had to be there, but she barely had *Waiting for Godot* out of her mouth, and we were holding our stomachs again, our bodies slamming around inside the pickup, arms flailing, feet kicking, high screams, laughing like a couple of damn fools.

Billie Cody. Laughing is how I met her.

I got my hand steadied enough, and I held the lighter to the end of her cigarette. Billie puffed away, and the end of the cigarette started fire, and the smoke started.

In the orange light of the cigarette lighter, behind the bloodshot tear duct cancer, it looked like Billie's eyes were blue.

After our cigarettes were lit, and after laughing like that, it was real quiet again like before when we were staring at the cigarette lighter. I thought maybe we might start in on it again, but this time we didn't laugh. It was just the radio and some song and us in the dark smoking. I was back to being Redi-Mix cement or extra-sharp Cheddar. Billie looked down at her fingernails. Her fingernails were small too, like her toenails, and they were painted dark blue too.

Can I have a sip of your beer? she asked.

Billie's red hennaed hair rats poked up through the white neon light of the Snatch Out sign. I handed her over the Budweiser. Billie tipped up the bottle, took a swig, handed the bottle back to me. When I put the bottle back to my lips, I tasted pink.

Say, I was thinking, Billie said. You want to go on a date?

My tongue on my lips, beer mixed in with pink.

Sure, I said.

You would? she said. Even after I farted?

Before that night, I'd never heard a girl fart, and I'd never heard a girl say *fart*.

I wanted to say *yes* right off, and my mouth was right there, but I stopped. The reason I stopped was because even though I didn't know her name, I knew she was a junior at Highland High School. She was a year older than me and wasn't Catholic, and I was just a sophomore at Saint Joe's.

Then: Sure, I said. But, I mean, are you sure you want to go out with me?

I'm only a sophomore, I said.

This was the moment when everything stopped, and all there was was Billie Cody and her cigarette. You know how each of us does things over and over, things nobody else does, or if they do they don't do it so particular? For instance, the way Mom gritted her teeth, or her eyes got gold, or Sis always stuck the fingernail of her index finger between her two front teeth, or Dad pushed back his black hair off his forehead.

Here's something Billie Cody always did. With the cigarette. I think she knew she was doing it. Bille was into theater, and I think she practiced. Then maybe at some point, she'd done it so much she didn't know anymore.

Anyway, that evening in the Snatch Out was the first time I saw her do the cigarette thing.

Her left arm across her belly under her breasts, Billie cupped her right elbow. The cigarette was always in her right hand. Her right hand connected to her right arm, her right arm connected to her right elbow, her right elbow rested in her left-hand palm, Billie Cody's right arm connected that way at the elbow, came to life as something of its own. A windshield wiper, a wand, a pointer, a metronome, the minute hand of a ticking clock, one of those lawn sprinklers that spurt spurt spurt, then razzle razzle, back to spurt spurt spurt again. A jab, a poke, a twirl, a wave of disgust, any kind of emotion really, sarcasm, joy, terror, surprise, the fuck-you finger, a blossom bursting forth in the morning dew, a fist and forearm up your ass, you name it, Billie's right arm could do it. Always, always with the cigarette in her hand at the end of the arm, the exclamation point to whatever it was Billie had to say.

Plus her mother was half Italian and half Jew.

Like I said, theatrical.

Billie's right arm, the hand, the cigarette, did a little tornado by her ear, then she lowered the cigarette to her knee. Tapped the ashes off the cigarette onto the floor with her index finger.

You're old for your age, Billie said. And besides, I liked how you handled that guy in the hospital.

The scared place in my chest jumped up into my throat.

What guy? I said.

You know, Billie said, the Indian guy.

You saw that? I said. How did you see that?

I was standing at your door with everyone else in the hospital, Billie said.

Everyone else? I said. Who was that?

Billie inhaled, Bette Davis, on the cigarette, blew the smoke out her nose. I could blow smoke out my nose too now that I had my nose drilled.

Three nurses, the doctor, Billie said. The woman next to me with the gallbladder, and the candy striper.

I inhaled, blew smoke out my nose.

What did you see? I said. The lights were out.

The cigarette in Billie's hand, the way Monsignor sprinkled the audience with the holy water font.

I saw a lot, Billie said.

Those hospital gowns, I said.

Yes, Billie said, I saw that. But I'm talking about something else.

The smoke in the cab, the headlights of the cars, "My World Is Empty Without You" on the radio, the big rats of Billie's red hennaed hair sticking up through the neon of the Snatch Out sign.

Finally.

Finally somebody saw and somebody knew the worst thing, the most shameful, the curse of my soul my life gathered around.

Who knows where my breath was. My shoulders were up around my ears. The helpless feeling in my arms. I braced myself for what Billie Cody was about to say.

But Billie didn't say what I thought she'd say. Billie didn't say I saw into your soul when you fought George Serano, a queer man, and you're queer too.

Billie said: I saw somebody scared. I saw somebody defending himself and yet, Billie said.

Billie's arm went down like a speedometer going from eighty to zero. She stuffed out the cigarette in the ashtray in the dash.

You were kind, Billie said. Very human.

Maybe tears couldn't come out of her eyes, but that doesn't mean Billie Cody couldn't cry. I don't know if she cried right then, but I remember her as crying. Maybe I'm remembering with what I know now, and she didn't cry.

What I know she did was put on her white plastic sunglasses with the dark green glass. Pushed them up on her nose.

My heart felt so wide open, and the scared place in me wasn't scared, and I loved God so much right then, and out of the blue the whole world was crying.

Then: You're a Cancer, Billie said. Aren't you?

I swear, this girl was magic.

How can you tell? I said.

At the hospital, she said. On the insurance papers. June 30, 1950.

Then: I'm Pisces, Billie said. Water signs. That's good. Pisces are the most beautiful women, except for me.

Meet you here? she said. Seven-thirty?

The way I looked at Billie. That great laugh of hers in her big chest that seems to take over her whole body.

Our *date,* she said. Next Wednesday.

Yah, I said quick. Yah, Wednesday for sure. Seven-thirty's cool.

The quiet again. Quiet and dark, we were both sitting in again. Billie quick reached around, pulled on the door handle, opened the door. When she reached back like that, just then the headlights of a passing car, and I saw the size of her breasts. They were enormous.

By the way, I said, have you noticed that all of a sudden there are Indians everywhere you go?

Billie got out and slammed the door behind her hard.

Technicolor Pisces, theatrical smoker, woman of mystery, kneeling beatnik, blue-toed existentialist, intellectual snob. In her heart of hearts, Billie Cody was an Idaho girl.

Only an Idaho girl can slam a pickup door like that.

We're surrounded, Billie said.

An empty cab, the French smell going with her, I snuffed up all the clean fresh French that was left. Outside the window just her face on that side of the pickup. Billie's big red hennaed hair rats, white plastic glasses over her plugged-up tear duct eyes. Billie's big smile all over her face.

Who are you? she said. General Custer?

Just curious, I said.

Then: Say, what's your name? I said.

Billie, she said, like in Billie Holiday. Cody.

I reached across the seat and stuck my hand out through the window for her to shake.

Billie Cody, I said, Rigby John Klusener.

But Billie didn't take my hand.

Rigby John Klusener, she said. Yes.

On Pole Line Road, a cop car flashing red and white.

Red and white flashes on the world, headlights, dark. With the tip of her finger, Billie ran her finger along the ridge of my red-and-white-flashing knuckles.

I know who you are, she said.

All week I looked forward to next Wednesday.

There was a couple of times, though, I freaked out about going out on a date with a girl, and how should I act. After all it was my first time, and there was nobody to talk to about what happens on a date. In fact, I couldn't even tell anyone I had a *date*. Father Arana would've said something hip and cool, then asked if my parents knew, then he'd have started in on venial sin and mortal sin and what the differnce was. Mom would've run screaming for the rosary. And forget about Dad. Sis would've laughed and then probably threatened to tell Mom and Dad. But I had my bases covered there. Sis still hadn't told Mom and Dad she was dating Gene Kelso. Sis's excuse was De Sales Club too.

With the money I had saved that Sis never got to, I bought some English Leather and new Mennen underarm deodorant and some Barbasol shaving cream and my own Gillette razor, even though I really didn't need a shave — still don't really, only on my chin and upper lip, and I think now that I'm a free man I'll let my mustache and goatee grow.

But I did try shaving that Wednesday when I got home from school. Dad wasn't home so he couldn't show me, even if he was home he wouldn't show me, so Sis and Mom showed me, and they didn't know shit about shaving your face. They just knew about armpits and legs.

Mom's eyes got a real weird look when she first saw my face lathered up. I hadn't seen that look in her eyes ever before, so I didn't understand. But now that I look back on it after all that's happened, it's pretty clear. There I was, her little boy, doing something she'd seen only grownup men do.

In the bathroom, the fluorescent lights were on. Mom was on one side of me, and Sis was on the other, and the three of us were all looking in the bathroom mirror. Mom's almond-shaped hazel eyes, mine, Sis's black eyes she got from Dad. Mom and Sis were making faces in the mirror like they said you're supposed to make faces when you shave. Both Mom and Sis had their heads tilted left, and they were pulling the skin taut on the right side of their faces by screwing up their lips. But when I tilted my head left and pulled the skin taut on the right side of my face by screwing up my lips, when I pulled the razor the first swipe down my cheek, instantly that whole right side of my face was blood, blood mixing in with the white Barbasol shaving cream, everything pink.

Mom and Sis went screaming females out of the bathroom. They were covering their heads, covering their eyes, screaming. Then they both fainted. I haven't told you that yet. Something both Mom and Sis do when they see human blood. Mom was the first thud. Out like a light right there on the blue-and-white-checkered floor. Sis made it to her bedroom, crawled under her bed, and *then* fainted.

There I was a bleeding face like in a horror movie, and Mom was lying on the blue and white squares of the kitchen floor, twitching, and I didn't even *know* where Sis was.

No wonder I turned out the way I did. Just look at the help I got. What a fiasco.

When I got in the pickup to go to De Sales Club, I had pieces of toilet paper stuck all over my face. Sis wouldn't even look at me. Don't ask me how I'd done it, but I'd even cut my ear.

Billie didn't say anything about my face right off. You know that first moment when you first look at somebody, and you can catch what her reaction to you is? Well, I looked at her hard in that moment when Billie rolled down her window and looked up out of her mother's white Pontiac Bonneville and saw my face.

Billie's face, no grimace, no horror, no holy shit, what the fuck happened to you.

Then, after Billie looked at me, I thought maybe it was all in my head that I looked like I'd took a bite out of a chain saw, so I quick reached and turned the side mirror so I could look at myself. It was not pretty.

Billie opened the door to the pickup, stepped up, put her butt on the seat, slammed the door. It was all I could do to look at her. She looked nice. She had her hair pulled behind her ears. No tear duct cancer, her eyes were clear and blue. A blue oxford shirt this time, the same gold chain necklace with the open palm hanging between her breasts. I tried not to look at her breasts, but with Billie you had to look at her breasts because, well, there they were. Two large melons just down from her chin. The black pants with the stirrups, black strapped shoes with a low heel. Blue toenails. The French smell.

I was a bag of Redi-Mix cement again, a forty-pound block of extra-sharp Cheddar. Big nose, crooked bottom teeth, and a face full of bloody toilet paper.

Billie was acting cool, like she had it all together, but she was just being an actress. Inside, her stomach was grumbling and she was afraid she was going to fart again, plus she had her period, and she thought she smelled bad.

We got to all of this later in Mount Moriah, but as it was happening, Billie and I, the both of us just went along, pretending everything was cool.

Two weeks I had my nighttime driver's license, and it was my first time driving out at night alone, and nobody, not even Sis, knew I was doing it. I didn't know what the fuck, so I did what everybody else did — drove the loop. Slow idling through the Dead Steer past the parked cars and the kids in the cars, then out across two lanes of traffic onto Pole Line Road. Cars lined up at the stoplight, squealing tires on the green. Then across from the Portland Cement Company and the Kraft cheese factory, turn signals flashing, and I was back across two lanes of traffic again, the cars, the kids in cars, slow idling through the Snatch Out, then the loop again, cruising the Snatch Out, the Dead Steer, over and over.

Billie wanted a Coke, so I drove through the Snatch Out where the cars went through where you ordered food. Into the speakerphone, Billie ordered a cherry Coke Ironport for her and a vanilla Coke for me and a large French fries for both of us. I pulled up to the window, and we got the French fries and the Cokes, and I gave the money to Billie, and she paid the cashier. When the cashier saw my face, she looked at me like I was the Blob or the Monster from the Blue Lagoon.

We drove the lower end of the loop, onto Ashby Street, then right to the stop sign on Hall. Across Hall, then into the Dead Steer. I reached over for a French fry and instead I picked up the ketchup cup. For some reason, I don't know why I didn't know it was the folded extra-thick heavy-duty waxed paper ketchup cup, but I didn't, and then what do I do but stick the ketchup cup in my mouth.

When the ketchup cup is in my mouth was when I knew it was a ketchup cup. But what do I do? I was afraid Billie would think I was a dork so I swallowed the ketchup cup.

That was when Billie looked down at the French fries and said: They didn't give us any ketchup.

So I made a big scene of going back to the Snatch Out and telling the cashier she didn't give us any ketchup. I went to the walk-up window, not the drive-through, and the cashier, when she handed me the ketchup out the window, she said, Did a porcupine get you?

We cruised the Dead Steer, then I crossed the two lanes of traffic, no problem, onto Pole Line Road. I drove down Pole Line Road and stopped at the red light. Everything was going fine. We were eating the French fries with the ketchup, drinking our Cokes, the music on the radio "Little Deuce Coupe." The light turned green. The car next to us squealed out, but I didn't squeal out.

It was when I went to turn back into the Snatch Out, it was when I flipped the directional signal, and the signal was flashing right, it was when I turned right across the two lanes of traffic of Pole Line Road, that I looked up and from out of nowhere there was a pair of headlights headed right for us.

The long, high sound of brakes and squealing tires. The car behind the headlights slid and fishtailed, a swerve all over the road. Either I had to gun the engine or put on the brakes, but I didn't do either. The moment before the shit hit the fan — in the cab of the pickup — the dashboard, the windshield, my hands on the steering wheel, the radio "Little Deuce Coupe," the knees of Billie's black stretch pants — everything got real bright. Billie's hand was on my arm, her tiny blue fingernails. The open gold hand on the gold chain against the skin of her neck. Together Billie's eyes and my eyes stared ahead at the same air between us. That was when I threw my whole body up against Billie Cody. The incredible softness of her. My neck against her neck, my shoulder and my arm up to cover her face.

In my ears, it was that awful thwump and then broken glass. Billie Cody and I were catapulted into the air. We landed all broken and bloody on Pole Line Road.

But none of that happened.

The first thing I knew was I was the closest to a human being that I can ever remember. Billie's breath in and out, her breasts against my chest and her heart. When I could, I turned my head and looked out the pickup window. Below me was the hood of a red '56 Mercury. Its bumper was so close to the pickup's running board I couldn't open the door.

In the car, it was Sis and Gene Kelso.

Then everything was as fast as it was slow. Sis's head out of the window started in yelling at me, cussing a blue streak.

You dipshit, you almost got us killed, and I'm going to tell Mom.

Then Billie got into it, saying, Go kiss Old Rose, and Up yours, you stupid asshole. Gene Kelso and I, we were just looking at each other, going, Holy shit.

Fiasco.

It took me awhile to get the pickup started because my hands were shaking so bad. I couldn't get the clutch right, the gas. The whole Snatch Out was watching. I don't know which was worse, almost getting killed, or driving through the Snatch Out after almost getting killed. All the parked cars we drove by, you could tell, everybody in them thinking: Rigby John Klusener is one dumb ass.

I tried not to show how freaked out I was, but it wasn't just my hands that were shaking. All the way through the Snatch Out, the muscles in my legs and my back, even my neck muscles, were shaking.

Don't ask me how, but the pickup stopped on Ashby Street. On Ashby, the way you always turned was right and then drove to the stop sign on Hall, then across Hall to the Dead Steer.

Billie said: Turn left.

Billie's face was pure white and not just from the Snatch Out neon. We were both train wrecks.

Billie laid her hand on my leg and left her hand on my leg.

The pickup turned left.

You got a cigarette? she said.

The cigarettes Billie pulled out of my shirt pocket didn't look so good either. With her foot, Billie pushed the cigarette lighter in and then Billie was lighting my cigarette. Who could tell which of us was shaking the most.

A fucking fiasco.

Billie threw her head back, inhaled, exhaled through her nose, then inhaled again.

The cigarette was a little orange whirlwind by her ear, then the dive to the ashtray, the flick of the ashes with her index, then up again, the cigarette pointing off into the distance, Billie said — like big deal, so what, who cares — she said: I've got a grand idea.

Windshield wiper, the cigarette, back and forth.

Let's smoke all these cigarettes, she said, one right after the other, then buy some more, and we'll go to my most favorite place.

Billie's pink lipstick lips were a little screwy off to the side. She poked the cigarette in there. In the dash light, Billie's face right then looked like my first best friend.

And park, she said. It's my most favorite place in the whole world.

Mount Moriah is Pocatello's cemetery.

When Billie said, Turn in here, I said, We can't go in there. And Billie said, Sure we can. And I said, It's the cemetery. And Billie said,

So? And I said, It's night, and Billie said, So? And I said, You're not supposed to drive in there at night. And Billie said, But this is my favorite spot.

As fate would have it, Billie's most favorite place in the whole world was an important place for me too. I didn't have any idea how important. I'd been there only once before when I was just a kid.

Billie's favorite place in the whole world was in Mount Moriah Cemetery. Who was buried in that cemetery, in that particular favorite place of Billie's, was a baby boy I hadn't thought about in a long time.

And something else. I probably would never have recognized Russell's grave if it wasn't for the wind. Where we were parked in Billie's favorite place was toward the back of the cemetery in a little cul-de-sac. The lights were off, the radio was on, and Billie and I were smoking, smoking. Clueless. I was fucking clueless. The only thing on my mind was how was I going to get my forty-pound-block-of-Cheddar-cheese arm up over Billie's head and around her shoulders.

Then the universe conspired, and I looked up just as a gust of Idaho wind hit an elm, and the elm branches shook, then swayed slow back and forth. The way the elm tree moved, I could feel the way it moved inside my stomach.

The wind was Thunderbird breathing.

My eyes followed the sway of the elm from the top branches in the moon, down and down through its candelabra arms, down to its thick trunk, down.

Sis says it was sunny, but I remember that there were umbrellas and that we all stood under umbrellas, and that I was wearing my overshoes. I stood to the right of Monsignor and the altar boys. I got to smell the incense.

Then it was the Door of the Dead and them wiping the rain off the folding chair because Dad has to sit down he was crying so hard.

Just like that, I was out the pickup door, running to the elm tree. Billie was yelling something, but I didn't pay her any mind. Then my back was smashed against the elm tree, and I was walking around the elm tree always with my back against the elm tree. Around and around until I found in my mind how I stood that day.

Then I was standing in that same spot, then kneeling, cleaning away the leaves and grass of all the years.

Nobody, none of us in my family, ever came back to visit his grave.

A piece of moon came through right onto the metal plaque.

Russell Thomas Klusener. 1955–1956. *Agnus Dei.*

Billie knelt down next to me. She had her hand on my shoulder. Something about the way her hand was on my shoulder.

My first date with Billie Cody. It was in the middle of the night, next to a big old elm tree, I was kneeling in a cemetery, Billie's hand was on my shoulder, and I was crying. Weird, deep sobs in me the way you throw up. My face was down in the grass, I was eating grass, digging down, trying to get to dirt.

The whole time, Billie's hand tender, the way I'd never known, right there on my shoulder.

How can we carry pain around like that and not know it?

That was what I said in the middle of the third cigarette. Snot was still hanging out of my nose, I kept trying to snuff up.

How can we carry pain like that around and not know it?

Billie sat cross-legged on one side of *Agnus Dei,* I sat cross-legged on the other side.

Who was he? Billie said.

My brother, I said.

It's so weird, Billie said. This has always been my favorite place.

I ate the ketchup cup, I said.

I know, Billie said. I'm so glad we came here.

My face, I said. I tried to shave today. Did I freak you out?

No, Billie said.

I look like bloody murder, I said.

People stare at me all the time, Billie said. So I don't ever stare.

Tear duct cancer? I said.

No, Billie said, boobs.

Oh, I said.

Billie, I'm so sorry about back there, I said. I almost got us killed.

Who was that bitch in the car? Billie said.

My sis.

Then I said, Were you embarrassed? The whole Snatch Out was looking.

When I said Snatch Out, Billie laughed that great laugh of hers that took over her whole body. Her cigarette was italicized language and quotation marks.

We're still alive, Billie said.

Then: Billie, I said, I've never been with a girl before, I said. I mean, this is my first time even on a date.

Me too, she said.

Really? I said. So you still like me?

Like you? Billie said.

On the pickup radio, out through the cemetery, around the trees and headstones, Donovan's "Mellow Yellow." The cigarette in Billie's hand was hot-boxed, a big orange fire sucked all the way up to the filter. The slow exhale from her lips was a cloud of moon.

I think I love you, Billie said.

Like you? I think I love you.

Oh my heavens pretty woman so far. The same thing my mom and dad said, Billie and I said. Only it was the other way around, who said what to whom. They were sitting in a car listening to "Melody of Love." Billie and I were next to the pickup listening to "Mellow Yellow." No idea what the fuck this means, or the implications, other than it's the universe saying the apple don't fall far from the apple tree.

That's something hard for me to believe, though. I've always been so differnt from them, my parents.

But then, so far the universe has had a lot of surprises for me, what I thought wasn't at all the way things were, and after all that's happened, I wouldn't doubt for a moment there's a couple more surprises coming down the road.

Highway 93, my getaway route to San Francisco, is one long shiny black ribbon of tarmac. From the east, the alternating white line in the middle of the road comes right up to me, goes right on past me, then heads west on up the road and disappears. Somewhere in the direction of the Pacific Ocean.

California California California.

Since the semi truck, there's been just one car passed, a convertible yellow Buick, going at the speed of Mom, going eighty. One big flash of noise, headlights bright and dim, bright and dim, a yellow streak, horn honking. Somebody with long blond hair in the passenger's seat, waving at me, flashing me the peace sign. Or maybe it was the bird.

Whatever it was that happened, it was loud and bright and didn't last long.

I was standing at the time. For a while, there I was back up standing, the perfect picture of a hitchhiker, on my feet, my thumb out, poised and ready to go. You got to think positive. You know, like the color orange back in the first grade when I found the color orange on the inside lining of my jacket.

Faith, hope, and charity.

Flaco, Acho, and Billie Cody.

Just having these three people in my life is proof enough for me my life's been lived successfully. Plus then there's George. Cost a lot, though.

Trouble is, in the yoga book Billie gave me, there was a joint and I took a couple tokes on Billie's joint, and no time at all here I am on my ass, somewhere between standing and lying, between waking and sleep, between gravity and levitation, between here and there, hope and despair, between my second-to-the-last and my last cigarette, Rigby John Klusener one big lump of slow-moving land mammal sinking into the gravel strip between tarmac and barrow pit. Sparkly gravel running through my fingers.

This gravel is beautiful.

I'm talking to the still air, to the sagebrush, the moon, to whoever it is out here who'll listen.

The first thing about Billie I loved so much was that she was so damn smart. There was nobody in the world I could talk to like Billie Cody. And laugh. Man, we could laugh.

It was on our second date when we first started talking. Really talking. Billie had asked me why I hadn't called her, and I told her Mom had a five-minute limit on the phone, plus we had a party line, and who knew who was listening. But the real truth was because when I was around my mother and father I wasn't something. I mean, I wasn't me, a human being, I was theirs, and when I was around them I felt like theirs, so there wasn't any me here to talk.

Billie totally understood when I told her that. Her blue eyes lit up, and Billie's big smile went all across her face. We both went for the cigarettes and started in talking. For two hours, all Billie and I talked about was how we disappeared around our parents. For me, both my parents. For Billie, just her father.

Billie really loved her mother. Her mother had Billie when she was only eighteen, so they kind of grew up together. They were more like sisters than mother and daughter. In fact, at one point, Billie actually said her mother was her best friend.

Hard for me to believe.

No religion, no weird trips about sex and sin. Billie and her mom shared the same clothes. They even drank beer together.

Billie couldn't wait for me to meet her mother, but there was a logistical problem, because I had to meet her mother when her father wasn't home. You see, as cool as Billie's mother was, her father was that much of an asshole. Her father was a plumber and liked whiskey too much and guns and sports and liked to get drunk and break things. Macho stuff.

He isn't going to like you, Billie said. We'll have to play this one carefully.

Which, as you'll soon see, as things turned out, Billie was right on.

Besides her father, everything else about Billie was damn near perfect. I knew everything about her. Jean Paul Sartre was God, but God was a She, and She was an atheist. Her favorite color was black. And blue because of her eyes. She got A's in all her classes except PE, but she hated all her classes, especially PE, except for drama and English lit. She hated Elvis Presley, loved the Beatles, loved Dylan. She hated her big boobs. Her feet were too small, her toenails too tiny. She was too fat, too short, she had no hips, and there was not one particular quality to her face that was important — except for her tear duct cancer, which was a curse. When she graduated from high school she was going to some college in the east, Smith, Brown, Wellesley. After college, she was going to get a breast reduction and move to Paris. She didn't like men, most men, except for me and her drama teacher, Mr. Woolf as in Virginia. She had a lot of friends, even the popular girls, who were a bore, but Billie could put up with them. She felt sorry for them because most women weren't really alive as people yet. She was for integration. Malcolm X was her hero, and Martin Luther King and John Kennedy and Robert Kennedy. The only thing good about Idaho was that nobody in the world knew about it yet. She loved hippies and was considering becoming a hippie herself. As Thomas Jefferson said, she said, a revolution every now and then can be a great thing. She had to have at least three cups of coffee in the morning before she could even think. Then toast. The toast had to be buttered right out of the toaster, and the butter couldn't be soft. A morning without a cigarette was a morning without sunshine. She liked body hair on men and women, but she herself hadn't yet arrived at the place where she could not shave her armpits. Her legs were no big deal because at the most on her legs it was peach fuzz. She loved gold and silver jewelry, and especially gold and silver together, like the Bedouins. The gold open palm that hung around her neck on a gold chain was the Hand of Fatima. She didn't know what that was, but it was

Arabic. Bananas and chocolate milk were her favorite foods, and peanut butter. She was a vegetarian, but sometimes she ate hamburgers and hot dogs. Especially hamburgers from the Dairy Queen, and hot dogs that were Jewish hot dogs, kosher, that didn't have all that crap in them, the rabbi saw to it. She thought reincarnation was a lovely idea, but probably just an idea because mankind found it so hard to face death. She never wanted children. Henry Miller and James Joyce were overrated tap dancers of the English language. Hemingway sucked except for *A Moveable Feast*. Sylvia Plath was self-indulgent. *Breakfast at Tiffany's* was her favorite book so far. Tennessee Williams was a fucking genius. The C on her front door didn't stand for *Cody,* it stood for *cunt*. She wanted to smoke marijuana and take LSD, but she didn't know any dealers, and it was important that you knew your dealer.

That's a lot to know about somebody, especially a girl.

And Billie knew everything about me.

I thought I was ugly. My mom was really weird. My dad was weird too. My sis was weird. I was raised Catholic, but like Teilhard de Chardin I believed that God was the process of the evolution. My whole life at school was trying to stay clear of Joe Scardino. When I was five, my brother, Russell, was born. He screamed for a hundred days, and then he died. His hands were open. I hated mush. Mush constipated me. Besides mush and my egg thing, there wasn't any food I knew of that I didn't like.

Every story I've told you, I told Billie, except for dress-up and the sex stuff.

Billie loved to hear me talk and tell my stories. She'd stare up into my eyes, and her blue eyes made me feel like what I was saying was important, and funny. I could really make Billie laugh. The story of Dad and Mom and Sis and me in the early days going to the Spa Plunge, the public swimming pool, in Lava Hot Springs, made Billie laugh her ass off. And the story of Mom buying her blue felt hat with the pheasant feather at LeVine's, the fancy shop her sister Alma shopped in when Alma and Theresa were in town. The first time I tried to shave. How all of a sudden there were Indians popping up everywhere. Really, I didn't know I could be so funny.

There was one story, though, an important story, I couldn't share with Billie.

Why I couldn't bring myself to kiss her.

Flaco and Acho could have helped. For sure, they'd have some good advice for me on how to kiss. It wasn't the *kissing* so much, though. I'd tried kissing my pillow, and I did pretty good. It was how to work up to the kiss. What to do with my arms and hands when they turned into forty-pound blocks of cheese, and should I close my eyes or keep them open. How do you know if your breath is bad?

There was nobody else around to talk to. Sis had gone AWOL years ago. Every time I talked to Tramp about kissing Billie, he just raised his paw and poked the air. Who else was left? Mom and Dad, Monsignor Cody, Father Arana. No thanks.

And something else. More something I couldn't talk to anybody about. The more I got to know Billie, the more I got scared.

When Flaco and Acho left, I felt hurt in a way I didn't have words for. With Billie, the stakes seemed even higher. On the one hand, with Billie I was feeling strong like I'd never felt. On the other hand, there was that sore place in me next to my heart. What would happen if Billie decided to split?

So many times I'd gone to kiss Billie, but something always happened. Some nights, sitting there next to her, my arm just on her shoulder, her French smell and her pink lips, I really wanted to kiss her, but for the life of me, I couldn't imagine that Billie wanted to kiss *me.* I needed to be bigger, stronger, needed to go home and do some pushups, or maybe I had a zit and I couldn't kiss her with the zit, or she was so much smarter than me, or I'd probably miss her mouth altogether, or I'd forget how to breathe out of my nose again.

Truth is, I was afraid to kiss Billie because a kiss would make us so close, and already I was so close.

Billie Cody. Love.

The story I told myself, though, was a differnt one: the reason it took us so long to kiss was because we liked to talk so much. Every Wednesday night in September, October, November, and December, Billie and I parked in Mount Moriah. We had only two hours Wednesday nights. With Billie at Highland High and me at Saint Joe's, we never got to see each other. It took us two hours just to say hello and catch up on all the shit that happened the week before. Really, we needed another couple hours to get through all we wanted to say. Then before we knew it, it was time to leave each other at the Snatch Out and go home.

Don't get me wrong, though. Talking was important. The Lord

knows I needed to talk. To Billie especially. Billie helped me with shit I hadn't even thought about yet. Before Billie I was thinking some pretty stupid things. For example, I thought John F. Kennedy and Martin Luther King and Robert Kennedy and Malcolm X were killed by communists.

Communism was a discussion Billie and I went back and forth on. One Wednesday night, I said: If we don't fight communism in Vietnam, then the communists will take over Southeast Asia, and then India and Africa, and then they'll take over the whole world.

Billie's drag on her cigarette was long. Scary long. The cigarette poked up out of her fist like the finger finger.

Isn't your fear of communism like something else you're afraid of? Billie said.

There I sat like a dumb drut, trying to figure out what else I was afraid of. I couldn't think of anything I was afraid of right then, except that I wanted to kiss her and I couldn't kiss her. All the air went out of the cab, and the sweat started going down the inside of my arms. I thought for sure that was what she was going to say and I knew if she said it, it would ruin me.

Like what? I said.

How about Joe Scardino? she said. Don't you think your idea of communism is a world where the Joe Scardinos run amok?

A deep breath came back to my lungs, and I was breathing again, but it wasn't long before I felt something that scared me even worse.

I hated that I'd told Billie about Scardino. What had I done that for? What kind of guy went around telling girls he was afraid of other guys.

Dizzy in my head, and I felt the puke come up in my chest. I didn't know what the fuck to say, but I had to say something so I didn't look like a total dumb ass.

So I said: Scardino's Italian.

That made Billie laugh, and thank God she laughed, so I laughed too, and I was off the hook.

But no, no, not with Billie.

That's when, for the first time, Billie looked at me in a way I'd come to know her looking at me. Her eyes opened wider and she seemed to take in all of me for a moment, and in that moment while she was taking me all in, she was thinking of just the right way to say what she had to say.

Billie's cigarette was between her fingers, in her hand, her hand on her knee.

Don't you think, Billie said.

The cigarette came up to her ear, an orange whirlwind.

That your fear of communism comes from your Catholicism? Billie said.

The cigarette was between Billie's puckered pink lips. Breath-in inhale.

Don't you think you've been brainwashed to believe there is an evil force in the world? Billie said. Breath-out exhale.

The cigarette was a slow arc down to her side. Her head turned, blowing the smoke up and away.

Aren't you just substituting communism for the devil? Billie said.

I opened the pickup door, got out, slammed the door, and stood out in the winter and smoked a whole cigarette. It was that night, during that cigarette, that I looked out of my eyes, these same two eyes I'm looking out now, and when I looked, I tried to imagine a world that had no devil, no eternal hell and damnation, no punishment, no doom.

I could not do it. But the fact that I could not do it said a lot to me.

So I opened up the pickup door and got back in. Billie was on the other side of the pickup on her second cigarette. The radio was back on, and it was some commercial, so I turned the radio off, turned the key off. I lit up my third cigarette. I didn't say anything for a while. Sitting in the pickup, no radio light, in the dark and the silence, I knew I wanted to say something, but I didn't know what, and I didn't know how. When I finally spoke, my voice was high and weird. It seemed like someone else was speaking.

I said: Maybe you're right, Billie. It seems like all I'm ever doing is waiting to screw up. Or waiting for the universe to conspire to screw me up. I wish I was differnt.

Even if it was dark, I could see Billie's face light up, that big smile of hers, her blue eyes blue even in the dark. Billie came sliding across the seat. She put her palm against my cheek, the fingers of her hand soft across my eyes.

Billie's voice was deep. We called Billie's voice like that her Simone Signoret voice.

Rigby John Klusener, Billie said, I love you so much.

Or at least I thought that's what she said.

I pretended I didn't hear her, and still I didn't kiss her.

Then, still in her Simone Signoret voice, Billie said: What are you going to do about the draft? Have you thought about it?

Thought about it? I couldn't stop thinking about it. And the only thing I could think about it was stop thinking about it.

I wouldn't even make it through boot camp, I said.

Before I knew it, my lips were on Billie's lips. It was the only thing that could stop me from crying. I was breathing through my nose, and my mouth was exactly on her mouth — maybe a little off to start with, but everything slid into place.

In an instant, my body was just my two lips. Two lips against two lips soft with a kind of suck, tobacco, and the taste of pink. Something inside fell away, something that was holding me up, a scaffold that held my head up and made my shoulders square, crash, a high-rise building in a city blown up, falling in on itself.

Billie's breath, my breath. Breath suddenly a remarkable thing, how it happens without you.

It was still winter when our lips stopped kissing. In a cemetery in a pickup right next to Russell's grave. Our breaths, puffs of steam in the cab.

Around the dark round center, the blue of Billie's eyes a hundred differnt blues. White outside the round of blue.

Promise me something, Billie said.

Billie's best Simone Signoret.

All the tea in China. An audience with the Pope. The moon.

Here was where I wanted to stay.

Promise me, Billie said.

Her lips against my lips on the *pr* and the *m* and the *m*.

What? I said.

No bones in my neck to hold up my head.

That no matter what happens, Billie said, we will always be friends.

The moon, the goddamn moon, up in the branches of the elm, the light of it through the back window, the frost on the glass, little diamonds of moon onto Billie's face.

I promise, I said.

Some time in January, I finally got the gumption up.

Mom was in her red housedress, her back to me, her hair hanging down in her face. Oatmeal cookies or peanut butter cookies or chocolate cookies or pound cake, eggs and flour and sugar, there she was bent over a bowl, beating things into shape.

Can I have the pickup Friday night? I asked.

My feet were exactly in a blue square of the kitchen tile. I was sitting in Dad's chair at the head of the table.

Where are you going?

To a movie.

Which movie?

A Man for All Seasons.

You better check with the *Idaho Catholic Register*, she said. Is it condemned?

It's not condemned, Mom, I said. It's about Saint Thomas More.

Oh.

Who are you going with?

A girl.

Mom stopped beating the bowl and set the bowl down. She didn't turn around. Some of her pin curls had come undone. She stood up tall, reached up, and touched the back of her wrist to her hair.

A girl? What girl? What's her name?

Billie Cody.

Is she Catholic?

She goes to Highland High School.

What religion is she?

Mom poured the yellow batter in the bowl into the cake pan, wiping down the sides of the bowl with the rubber spatula.

What I said next, I said slow because I didn't know how the words would sound in the kitchen with Mom.

She isn't sure, I said. Her mother is a Jew who was raised Catholic, and her father is a Mormon who's Italian.

Mom didn't have her eyebrows on, but if she did, they would've been two Joan Crawford swoops high up into her forehead.

Good Lord, she said. She made the sign of the cross.

Mom set the bowl down, wiped the spatula end with her finger.

Where did you meet her?

At De Sales.

Oh.

Can I have ten dollars?

Mom walked the green bowl across the blue and white tile.

Is she converting?

She set the bowl with the spatula in it right in front of me.

She's into it, I said. Can I have ten dollars?

Ten dollars, Mom said. You can go to a movie on five.

There was a lot of yellow batter in the bowl and on the spatula to lick.

But I want to buy her a Coke and some French fries at the Snac Out.

Well, six dollars then, she said.

Pound cake. It was lemon pound cake.

Then, can I go? I said.

Ask your father, she said.

That Friday night became the first of the every other Friday nights I got the pickup.

Now it was Billie and I every Wednesday and every other Friday. First thing Billie and I did was beat it to Mount Moriah Cemetery and park.

That's all I wanted to do was sit close to Billie in the pickup in the dark with the radio on, and smoke, and kiss and kiss and kiss. It felt like home kissing Billie. Her lips on my lips, French-kissing too. Billie's kisses on my neck, on my ears, on my face. Billie even kissed my eyes. One time, she kissed my hands, each finger on both hands, the palms of my hands.

Her body right up against mine on the seat, the French smell of her, how her shoulder fit just right under my arm, I felt so solid, yet at the same time so floaty, like sitting next to Billie and kissing made us into a dream.

One night I remember, Billie had just turned "The Ballad of the Green Berets" off, and outside the pickup the snow was melted down and it was gray slush. We'd just finished about three hours of kissing, and we'd lit cigarettes. I was going on and on about this guy I'd read about in a psychology book who said that everything we do is sexual. How we eat, and drink, how we relate to others, how we stand, sit down, lie down, how we pray, even how we believe in God, is sexual.

So I was going on and on about this guy, showing off about how much I knew, the ramifications of this and that, and so on and so forth. At some moment, I realized there was something about Billie's face. When I stopped and looked into her blue eyes, she couldn't stand it. She burst out laughing.

The guy's name I'd been talking about was Sigmund Freud. But I hadn't been saying his name right. I thought the *eu* in Freud sounded like *oo*. So I had been saying Sigmund Frood.

Froid, Billie said, as in *oi*.

What a dumb ass I can be. Really I just wanted to die or something. So many times I'm like my father and mother or sis, and I don't get words right. Fuck, even when I think about it now, it just makes me want to cover my head.

But Billie did something very cool. She put her hands on my face, the palms of her hands on my cheeks. She squished my cheeks together, and she kissed me a big wet smooch, and then she put her face right up to mine so that blue was locked into hazel.

Rigby John, Billie said. How you are is just fine with me.

Billie kept holding my face like that, holding it and holding.

God, she said, if you could just see yourself right now. Did you know your eyes have flecks of gold in them?

I went to speak, but I couldn't because my face was squished.

I love it when your eyes are gold, Billie said.

I wondered if Dad had ever said that to Mom.

On Billie's birthday, February 28, Billie got her ears pierced, and with the allowance I'd saved I went to Molinelli's Jewelers and bought her a pair of fourteen-karat-gold thick gold loops for her pierced ears. That night, parked in Mount Moriah, when Billie opened the box and saw the gold earrings sitting inside the box on the blue velvet, Billie made the happiest sound. I had to open the pickup door so the dome light would go on so she could put the earrings on in the rearview mirror even though she was supposed to just leave the gold posts in.

You should have seen Billie that night. The thick gold loops in her ears were gold sparkles of moon. Her blue eyes a couple of stars. She put her arms around me and held on to me so tight.

Life was sweet. There we were kissing and making out. The moonlight through the elm tree on Billie's skin, the warm cab of the pickup, only the radio light on. Billie was my girlfriend, and Billie and I were safe and warm.

We were close like that all that winter. It seemed like Billie and I together made something totally new in the world. We weren't just two kids from Pocatello, we had something special. We read *A Death in the Family, The Dharma Bums,* and *Native Son* at the same time. I can't tell you all the hours we talked about those books. I mean really talking, like our lives depended on it.

Talking like that with Billie made me differnt. Pretty soon I was speaking my mind all over the place. Not necessarily at home — Mom and Dad were as weird as ever — but in class. My English teacher, Miss Barnett, couldn't believe her ears when I spoke up in class one day about the Reverend Dimmesdale in *The Scarlet Letter.* First A I ever got in high school. Plus Scardino had flunked out, and I started to breathe in the hallways between classes.

Then there were the movies. Billie and I loved movies. Not your regular kind of movies like *Beach Blanket Bingo* or *Harum Scarum.* I mean real movies. Movies you had to stop and think about. Movies I'd never have gone to without Billie. *A Man for All Seasons, Georgy Girl, Alfie,* and *Who's Afraid of Virginia Woolf?*

And instead of just parking in Mount Moriah, Billie and I started going to the Shanghai Café. It was real old, with old dark wood and Chinese lanterns. We sat in a red booth in a bright, bright room and drank Chinese tea and ordered pork and seeds — what Dad would call *gook food* — with hot mustard. Billie and I'd pump a couple of quarters in the jukebox that was on the wall by the table. Billie couldn't shut up long enough for me to talk, and vice versa.

The night we walked out of *A Man for All Seasons* I felt like I'd been in a philosophy class. Billie and I forwent kissing altogether that night.

Billie was smoking a Winston Long with one hand, and her other hand was around a white Chinese cup without a handle when Billie said *authenticity.* The light was so bright you needed a pair of shades.

What do you mean by *authenticity*? I said.

Billie's cigarette, the Queen of England waving to a parade.

By *authentic,* Billie said, I mean people like Thomas More or Rosa Parks who stand by their beliefs no matter what, imprisonment or even death.

I made a mental note of the word *authenticity,* and when I got home that night, I got out my dictionary and looked it up. *Authentic* wasn't hard to find because it's spelled pretty much like it sounds, and what it means is this: being fully trustworthy, not imaginary, false, or imitation.

Billie and I spent days and days in the Shanghai talking talking about *Alfie* and *Georgy Girl* and *Who's Afraid of Virginia Woolf?* And men and women, and women and babies, and babies and abortion. Billie thought abortion should be legal. She said if she got pregnant, she'd get an abortion, even if it was illegal.

Myself, I'd never thought about abortion, really, but what did I do but open up my trap, and of course, what did I say but:

I think abortion is wrong, I said. Because that's a child you're killing.

That's because you're a Catholic, Billie said. And a man.

That don't make no differnce, I said.

Billie's cigarette was a spurt spurt spurt, then razzle razzle razzle, then back to spurt spurt spurt again.

The hell if it doesn't, Billie said.

Then Billie launched into an argument there was no way in hell I could keep up with. Just the way her chin got and her eyes so blue, you knew Billie Cody knew what she was talking about. So in the end I ended up agreeing with Billie because I figured it was like me and communism. Abortion was something I'd never really thought about in any way that was real. I was saying only what I'd heard other people say. Catholic people, that is.

That's what Billie did for me. She showed me I didn't have to think like everybody else. I could have opinions and I could back them up. And I think I did something for Billie too. She started out knowing she was smart, but somehow in there, maybe I gave her confidence.

Billie and I were for peace and love and integration. Not a whole hell of a lot of people in Pocatello like that. It wasn't that everybody was mean and stupid. They just never stopped to think is what I decided. Most of the kids who sat in their cars at the Snatch Out thought getting drafted was cool. The only other things they thought about was getting drunk and getting married. Like Sis and Gene Kelso. Seemed like all they did was drive around town in his red '56 Mercury, buy beer, smoke cigarettes, and end up in the back seat parked up in the cedars.

Weird. Usually something shows up in the world, and then you start talking about it. With babies, though, Billie and I were talking about babies long before any babies showed up. At least in our own personal lives. How the fuck were we to know what the universe had conspired to do.

It was a real long while, maybe three, even four, weeks, after Billie and I had talked about abortion, after another Wednesday night when Billie and I'd sat and kissed and talked about more stuff, and Sis and I were headed home in the pickup. It was nine-thirty and we were supposed to be home at nine-thirty, but we never got home at nine-thirty, we'd only just get started going home at nine-thirty. We were smoking. The windows were up, and the heater was on because it was March. The song on the radio was "Something Stupid."

Rigby John, Sis said.

Rigby John. When Sis said my name like that, it meant only one thing. She wanted to borrow some money.

I don't have any money to lend you, I said. I need my money. I've got Billie now.

Sis's dark eyes, Dad's Roosky Gypsy eyes, looked across the dark at me.

Are you having sex? she said.

Sex?

Billie and I were Frenching. I'd touched just the top of her boobs. Really just the lower part of her neck.

Sex?

My mouth was a bowling alley. A bunch of words stacked at one end, the rest of me throwing a heavy ball at them. Sooner or later something would come out.

Sis stubbed out her cigarette in the ashtray, pulled the ashtray out from the dash, opened her window, then poured the cigarette butts and ashes out the window. Tiny orange sparks in the night.

Sis was holding the empty pickup ashtray. She looked inside the ashtray and took a deep breath. Ashes blew up and out.

Rigby John, Sis said.

This *Rigby John* was differnt. *Rigby John* said that way accompanied by a sigh meant only one thing. Sis had a secret.

Sis shoved the ashtray back into the dash.

I'm going to tell you something, Sis said, and you got to promise not to tell Mom and Dad.

I reached down, shut the radio off.

Promise? she said.

I promise, I said.

At the corner of Philbin and Tyhee, nine-forty-five, ten till, after Sis shifted into second, slowed down to twenty-five, turned the steering wheel to the right, and we were in good purchase on Tyhee Road, Sis said:

I'm pregnant.

Holy shit. For a moment there, everything stopped. Breath, movement, the whole world went black. Deep in my bones, in my blood, a fear so vast, I don't know what happened. Perhaps I fainted. All's I know is, when I came to, the pickup was off on the side of the road, Sis was crying and crying, trying hard to get a cigarette lit. I was in the middle of the seat, and my arm was around Sis's shoulder.

Are you going to get an abortion? I said.

Sis's mascara was mud all down her cheeks. Her dark Roosky Gypsy eyes. Sis inhaled deep, turned her head quick, looked over to me, and said: What in the *hell* are you talking about?

The bowling ball a long, thunderous roll down my tongue. The words in my mouth never seemed to come out right.

Abortions are cool, I said. Abortions should be legal.

The way those Roosky eyes looked at me, I should've curled up and dropped dead.

Abortion! Sis screamed. Do you think I'm going to kill my unborn child? What are you, nuts?!

My arm wasn't on Sis's shoulders anymore. I was sitting across the cab, lighting my own cigarette.

Well, I said. What you going to do, then?

Well, duh? Sis said, like I was so stupid. What do you think? Gene and I are getting married, Sis said.

Just then, headlights from a car came around Philbin onto Tyhee. The headlights filled the cab up with light. The headlights on the rearview mirror pushed the rectangle of headlights right onto Sis's eyes.

Everything was in Sis's eyes right then. The day Russell died, the Door of the Dead, how much she hated her brown patch of birthmark on her thigh, how when we were kids I chased her with the dead mouse, the baby inside her, dress-up, the night we won the jitterbug contest.

Gene wants to marry you? I said.

The old Ford passed by slow. The horn beeped.

A bottle out the window, broken green glass.

Indians.

Of course he does, Sis said. It'll just take some time.

Time for what? I said. You only got nine months.

Six, Sis said.

Sis was crying again. Holding her belly, crying. Crying so hard she wasn't just crying for herself. She was crying for her baby too.

I haven't told him yet, she said.

Who? I said.

Gene, she said.

Kelso? I said.

Gene fucking Kelly, you dumb ass.

The first time I heard Sis say *fuck*.

When you going to tell him? I said.

Tomorrow, Sis said. Or soon.

Sis reached down, turned the engine off. She was crying so hard, she had to lie down with her head on my lap. She pulled her legs up into her chest and put her hands up across her eyes.

On the Tyhee Flats, in the middle of all that dark, there was Sis and I on the side of the road, the headlights still on, poking a hole in the night. The last time I'd seen somebody cry like that was me with Billie, hunched over Russell's grave.

I put my hand on Sis's hair, rubbed her bangs from off her face. Sis looked differnt now that she was pregnant.

We should have been home an hour ago. Mom and Dad were going to be pissed. I really had to pee.

But what was an hour late compared to a pregnancy?

Einstein was so right on with his theory of relativity.

Still the cigar was only a cigar, and the shit was going to hit the fan.

It was still a while of Sis crying. Finally, she snuffed up, pulled herself together. She sat with her back to me, staring out the driver's-side window.

Can I borrow some money? Sis said.

She wasn't even looking at me.

All I need is ten dollars, she said. I promise I'll pay you back.

Mom and Dad were waiting up. They were sitting at the kitchen table under the new bright light that pulled down. The clock that looked like a black cat with big back-and-forth eyes and its tail wagging above the refrigerator said twenty to eleven.

Mom and Dad sitting at the table that night is a photograph in my mind that I don't think will ever leave. Dad in his baby blue pajamas, Mom in her pink quilted robe, her hair in a hairnet. The way they sat stiff there in the circle of bright light in the quiet house, just Grandma's clock ticking. Sis and I had just entered the *Inner Sanctum*. Suddenly we were all an Alfred Hitchcock movie. Everything was normal — a kitchen, a table, a light above the table, the blue and white squares of the kitchen tile, the table with the oilcloth tablecloth, the yellow plastic chairs — but inside everything, such terrible fear.

You've got some explaining to do, Dad said.

A school night, Mom said. Damn near eleven o'clock.

Nine-thirty, Dad said. You were supposed to be home at nine-thirty.

My knees were buckling. I was leaving my body. I looked over at Sis.

The shower scene. A pregnant Janet Leigh in *Psycho*.

I could tell Sis was going to spill the beans.

If I were a better person and a better brother, I would have stayed there with Sis, walked down the narrow, dark hallway hand in hand with her, but really, I had to pee. Plus, the breathing thing I do. I wasn't breathing.

I gave Sis a look, touched her light on the shoulder, said too loud: I really got to use the bathroom.

Frankenstein words in the Alfred Hitchcock kitchen.

I ducked my head and made a beeline over the blue and white tiles, past Dad sitting there in his blue PJs at the end of the table. In no time, I was around the corner. My shoulder pushed the bathroom door into the jamb, and the latch clicked. My hands turned the lock. I pulled on the switch of the fluorescent lights on either side of the mirror. The light flipped and spazzed and made the buzz sound. Out of the dark and into the fluorescence, I appeared.

There I was, still me, still with this family still in this house.

I didn't hear Sis actually say the words, but she told them, all right. On the other side of the locked door, the silence of the deep.

Then screaming and yelling like thunder and lightning. Sis getting smacked around good. Mom cussing a blue streak. Sis was really wailing.

My face up against the mirror, I looked at everything about me so close. Somewhere in there, in me, there was a person who Billie Cody found interesting and smart and handsome, said she loved. All I could see was the bad lighting. All I could hear was the war going on in the next room.

My big nose, my crooked bottom teeth, funny ears, curly hair. Zits, always zits on my face. Clueless. How I wished for something more, something *else*. In my life, in *them* — the people who reared me, molded me, showed me the dimensions and the qualities of the world.

Oh my heavens pretty woman so far.

How I wished I was someone else.

From someone else.

Authentic.

Up close to my eyes, my almond-shaped hazel eyes, inside deep in the mirror, I looked for something graceful, true, beautiful. I looked for God.

The only thing I saw was the fickle fucker who gave us our five senses, gave us sex, *some* smarts, and then set us loose. It was up to us to do the rest.

Frood had a theory. Jean Paul Sartre had a theory. Saint Thomas More.

Theories, fucking theories, man.

Two hours ago, I felt so warm and floaty kissing Billie, and now in this mirror in this moment, screaming and yelling and crying, punishment, exploding hell and damnation.

The sex-shame-guilt thing.

Doom everywhere.

Maybe there was no God, but I still had Billie.

7 Going to the Chapel

MERCIFUL LORD, HOLY LORD, Son of the Father, Prince of Peace, Lamb of God who takest away the sins of the world, Sis was pregnant, and for a while there the whole world went crazy, and nothing made any sense.

Sis had committed the gravest of sins.

She'd sinned against the Holy Virgin.

And raised the devil.

That very night, Mom made us drop to our knees. Not one, not two, but three rosaries we prayed, all sorrowful mysteries. Then an endless string of litanies.

Fucking litanies, man.

Sis cried most of the way through the first rosary and only stopped after Mom got up after the fifth sorrowful mystery, the Crucifixion, and slapped Sis silly. You can be sure that after that, there wasn't a peep out of Sis. We were on our prayer bones till almost two A.M.

Bright and early the next morning, Mom and Sis were doing eighty to the confessional and a private audience with the Monsignor. Sis was going to get married and fast.

That first week, I thought for sure Mom was going back to the Russell days. That migraine look was in her eyes. The rosary, the rosary, the rosary, pray the rosary. Out loud in her bedroom, whispered in the living room, her rough, red farm hands going over the beads. Once she even ran out in the field, and Dad couldn't find her anywhere, and

I found her in my secret place on top of the granaries. She was lying prostrate in the little place that's the shape of an hourglass, her arms out like a cross. She didn't move, only the wind in her hair. Then I saw her fingers, slow rolling over the beads.

Dad totally disappeared. Too bad he didn't drink, or he could've got drunk, but his dad was the drunk, so Dad didn't drink, he just acted like a drunk. Gruff old bastard. And he was spoiling to get into it with me. I had to watch every move I made. All of a sudden I had twice the irrigating to do, and weeds to pull and ditches to burn, and the Augean calf pens I had to haul shit out of. I was fucking Hercules, man.

I felt sorry for Sis. She was alone with her sin. Not that it was a sin, but she thought it was. My attempts to talk to her went nowhere. She was pregnant and scared and alone, and all I was was her little brother. Strange, though, what another life can make you do. As the days went on, Sis with her baby inside her, slow but sure, a change started to come about. It was as if the baby growing inside her was growing a place for Sis too, a place to come out on her own.

Mom didn't speak to Sis, not once, the whole time before the wedding ceremony. When Mom wanted to say something to Sis, she said it to me, then I told Sis. Can you imagine — the dress, the fittings, the invitations, ordering the cake — the whole schmeer? All Mom did was mumble litanies under her breath, and never once looked up at her pregnant daughter or said a fucking word to her.

At first, all Sis could do was keep her distance from Mom. After a while, though, Sis figured out that two could play that game. And the Mom-Sis War began.

I wish to hell I'd have done some figuring myself. How to get my ass out from in between those two.

The night Gene Kelso came over for cake and ice cream, there was no shotgun loaded by the dinner table, but there might as well have been. Everybody had their Sunday clothes on, and it was Tuesday. Sis looked particularly nice, tanned in her yellow summer dress and blue eye shadow. Mom had never allowed blue eye shadow. Even Gene, who always wore Levi's riding low on his hips and a white T-shirt with KELSO PLUMBING on it every time I'd ever seen him, wore a shirt and tie. It was an ugly tie. Green and gold with a weird pattern. Looked like butterflies and dice.

It was weird, all of us sitting at the table. No one moved. I mean, our arms moved and our mouths opened and closed, but our bodies didn't move, and when they did move, our bodies looked like in our heads we'd been practicing how to move, and then all of a sudden decided it was time.

When Gene got up to leave, it was the sound of the chairs scraping the floor. All of a sudden everybody came alive.

Mom said: Joe has spoken to Monsignor about the special dispensations.

Dad said: They just have to announce the wedding banns three weeks in a row.

Mom said: It wasn't easy.

Dad said: Monsignor owed me a favor.

Mom said: It took an arm and a leg.

Dad said: You'll have to pay us back.

Mom said: You're the ones who got yourselves into this mess.

Dad said: Hell of a way to start out a life together.

Mom said: You think it's easy. But it isn't easy.

Dad said: You'll need all the help you can get.

Mom said: It isn't easy at all.

Dad said: You're going to find out.

Mom said: Your work is cut out for you.

Dad said: You got to make a life for yourself and your family.

Mom said: At first, it's all lovey-dovey. It's all music and laughter.

Mom said: At first, you have no way of knowing how hard it's going to be.

But there's more. As fate would have it, a lot more. When Sis fucked Gene Kelso and got pregnant, a crack opened up in the world we thought we lived in, and nothing was ever the same again. Sis didn't just break a commandment, she went right to the heart of the matter and banged on the door. The Joe Kluseners went from a family who never could talk about sex to a family whose sexual secret became the sole conversation of Saint Joseph's Church. Really, they might as well have announced it in the Sunday bulletin. Mom said she couldn't show her face at Mass again, and both those Sunday mornings before the wedding it took all Dad had to get Mom in the car. Then at church to get her out of the car. I swear, if Mom and Dad weren't Catholic and knew only one way, their marriage would've been toast. Then the night after the wedding dance, what happened between my mom and dad I'm still trying to figure out.

Then to top it all off, with the sin against the Holy Virgin, and the wedding and the Mom-Sis War, somehow another female got sucked into it.

Billie.

Thank God for promises and good reefer. Without them, Billie and I would never have made it.

My own part in the drama began one evening in the kitchen. Mom at the counter beating away at some batter in a bowl turned her head over her shoulder, and said: What about the girlfriend? It would be nice to finally meet her. What's her name? She's got a boy's name.

Billie, I said.

Why don't you invite the girlfriend to the wedding? Mom said.

That was the moment right there when all the chaos whirling around outside me wasn't outside at all anymore. It was inside.

That night, Billie and I in the Shanghai Café, Billie was acting a little strange, but then everything was a little strange with the wedding and all.

The ashtray on the table was full of cigarette butts and ashes. Billie's last cigarette was stamped out in the ashtray but still smoking. When I looked at Billie, there was something in her eyes. I guessed it was tear duct cancer, or the smoke from the cigarette, but just then a tear busted loose and rolled down her cheek.

Why don't we go to Mount Moriah anymore? Billie said. I miss being close to you.

Right then, there was something awful got inside me. I had no idea what it was. Butts and ashes, smoke from the smashed-out cigarette. As I look back on it now, if you don't ever stop and take a good look at yourself, your fear can wear just about anybody's face.

As I sat there looking into Billie's blue eyes, suddenly Billie Cody, my best friend, turned into something awful.

Billie had ugly red, weepy eyes and cigarette breath and tiny fingernails and stupid hair. She was just another female who wanted to make me do stuff I didn't want to do.

I couldn't put a name on what I was feeling, but right then I wanted to get away from her.

Then I hated myself for feeling that way, so I tried to cover it up.

I reached into the ashtray and crushed the smoky cigarette out.

I'm sorry, I said. It's this wedding, I said. And Sis.

My hand was squeezed around my clear plastic water glass. What I wanted to do with that glass was throw it against the wall.

Instead, I poured water from my water glass into the ashtray. The quick hiss of water on fire.

I haven't told you something, I said. Something important.

A big mess of ashes and floating butts over the side of the ashtray, a puddle onto the table.

Sis is pregnant, I said.

And Mom won't speak to Sis.

Sis doesn't have anybody else but me, I said.

Wet black ash in my nostrils. My paper napkin on the puddle, wet and black soaking up through.

Sis is so alone, I said.

And now Mom wants me to ask you to the wedding, I said.

Billie's hands came across the table. She folded her hands around my hands. I wanted to pull my hands away, but I kept my hands under Billie's.

When I looked back up into Billie's eyes, Billie was the old Billie. There she was again, not ugly or sniveling, but my friend, looking at me, deep inside at me.

Rig, Billie said, I'm so sorry. Of course I'll go to the wedding with you.

The awful scared feeling inside me went away, and I loved God so much right then.

Billie took her hands away and made herself busy lighting a cigarette, inhaling, exhaling.

There's just one thing, Billie said.

I could tell the way Billie said *just one thing* that she was going to say something a whole lot smarter than I was.

Billie's cigarette was the whirlwind by her ear.

Do you want me to come to the wedding, Billie said, because *you* want me to come to the wedding?

Her right arm down to the puddle around the ashtray, the speedometer needle going from eighty to zero. Her index finger knocking off the ash.

Or do you want me to come, Billie said, because your mother wants me to come?

Inside me and outside me, all over everywhere, and Billie was ugly again.

Sirens and horns and alarms going off. Or some deep, low sound, a fart or burp. The fear I'd never looked at wanted to get the fuck out of there.

I pushed a Winston up out of the pack. Put it in my mouth. Lit it.

Inhaling is breathing.

If I waited long enough, some kind of words would come out of my mouth.

Billie Cody and I sitting in a pew together in Saint Joseph's Church was impossible to imagine. Kneeling and praying and genuflecting and sitting and listening to the sermon, impossible. Billie and Mom and Sis all in the church all together during Mass, impossible. Dad ushering Billie and I to a pew, impossible. Going up to receive Communion while Billie sat in the pew, impossible.

It's impossible, I blurted out. I don't want to be in that church with you.

Billie's cigarette a windshield wiper back and forth, back and forth.

Maybe, Billie said, you should ask a girl more suited to the festivities.

Billie's eyes were blue and clear. I'd never seen her angry before.

I was in some kind of quagmire I didn't know.

More breath, I inhaled cigarette smoke.

On the exhale: It isn't *you,* Billie, I said. I just can't imagine doing all that Catholic shit in front of you. I'd feel like a big fucking phony.

And then a little light came inside my darkness.

It's hard enough to put that act on for myself, I said. Every Sunday. But to do it in front of you, I couldn't do it.

Billie looked a lot like Mom sitting there, something tight in her, Billie's face somewhere behind the smoke she was exhaling.

The Shanghai got even brighter. I don't know how that is possible, but the place got even brighter. Billie smoked. I smoked. We just sat there like we weren't ourselves anymore, like we were Mom and Dad and Sis and Gene Kelso at the dinner table that day.

Absurd. Theater of the absurd.

The fear inside me was that I had lost Billie and at the same time the fear was that I'd never lose her.

When Billie spoke, she was Simone Signoret.

You say you love to dance, Billie said. We've never danced.

Billie's eyes were blue and not red, and she wasn't ugly.

What do you say? Billie said, I meet you at the reception dance at the Green Triangle. That way I don't have to go to Mass, you and I get to dance, and I can meet your mother.

A genius.

Billie Cody was back to being my best friend and a genius.

Later on that night, when I walked Billie up her windy front steps, past the lamp with the ivy growing on it, I kissed Billie open-mouthed and hard, lots of tongue.

I didn't really want to kiss her like that. I just wanted to kiss my friend and hold her. A boy was supposed to kiss a girl hard after what Billie and I had just been through.

Billie looked up into my eyes. Her blue eyes were looking into my eyes trying to find something.

I opened the aluminum screen door.

The C's not for *Cody,* I said.

No, Billie said. It's for *cunt,* she said. And you'd better not forget it.

Sis just barely fit into her size ten wedding gown. I should know, I was the one who had to zip up the placket in the back. Sis had stood in front of her mirror in her bedroom all morning, crying and crying. Totally freaked out. About everything. Getting married, being pregnant. Gene Kelso and his white socks. All the people coming to the wedding, you name it. But mostly what freaked Sis out was that the baby showed. The truth is, though, what was really bothering Sis was Mom.

The morning of the wedding the Mom-Sis War was no differnt. Mom wasn't with her daughter. Mom was knelt down in her bedroom praying the rosary.

I told Sis. Sis, I said, don't worry. I said, It don't show that much. Hardly at all. It's fine, I said. Don't worry, nobody can tell.

The church was crowded with aunts and uncles and cousins and members of the congregation. A solemn high nuptial Mass. One of those Masses that goes on forever. Organ music and the choir.

The theme of the wedding pretty much was daisies. White daisies with a yellow center. Mom's hat was a swooping bonnet with white daisies, and her dress was yellow, and so was Francie Lutz's, Sis's maid of honor. Francie wore a swooping bonnet with white daisies too, and she carried a bouquet of white daisies. Sis's bouquet was white daisies and yellow roses. Two big bouquets of white daisies on the altar.

Gene Kelso looked really hung over. His duck's ass was dragging. He wore a black suit, but not like Dad's. Gene's was shiny, and he wore a skinny, shiny black tie. He didn't wear Levi's, but when he knelt down everybody could see his white socks.

Gene's best man was a guy named Chuck diPietro. He was as hung over as Gene. Chuck had a cherried-out '57 Chevy pickup and was friends with Joe Scardino. Chuck was a big guy, big arms and chest, curly dark hair. One time in grade school, he threw a snowball at me and hit me right in the eye. Another Italian. He worked at the Sinclair station on Fifth Street, but back in high school, he played quarterback on Highland's football team. He had a white daisy boutonniere too.

Remember this guy, Chuck diPietro. Believe me, we're going to come back to Chuck diPietro.

The Wedding March. The one that in your head you always sing: *Here comes the bride, all fat and wide. Here comes the groom, skinny as a broom.*

Sis taking a long step, then a short step, alongside of Dad, holding onto Dad's arm. It was quite a sight, Sis in her white gown and veil and white daisies and yellow roses. Sis smiling so big her gums showed. And something else showed too. Sis's breasts were almost as big as Billie's, and down around her stomach — no doubt about it — it was a baby down there all right.

Myself, no way I wanted to be best man, or flower boy, or ring bearer, or whatever the fuck things you can be in a wedding. Sis wanted me to be one of the altar boys, but after that novena to Our Mother of Perpetual Help, I'd sworn off the altar boy shit. Sis threw one of her fits and would have gone crying to Mom, but of course it was the Mom-Sis War, so that was that. My job at the wedding was to sit in a pew. And wear a white daisy in my lapel.

It was better than having a yellow tulip up my ass.

Mom was in the choir, up and far away. Dad was giving away Sis, and when he wasn't doing that, he went back to his old job as usher. I was alone because I wanted to be alone, that is, not with Billie Cody.

Sis was insulted that my girlfriend wasn't going to come to *her* wedding.

It just confirms, Sis said, that your fucking girlfriend is a bitch.

Sis had met Billie just that one time, if you remember, not in the best of circumstances.

She's not a bitch, I said. She's a cunt.

Sis was in her bedroom trying to get her veil on straight.

Oh! Sis said. I hate that *word*. Don't ever say that word.

You said *fuck,* I said.

That's differnt, Sis said.

No it's not, I said.

Yes it is, she said.

No it's not.

Yes, it is.

They're words, I said, just like any other words.

Four-letter words, Sis said.

Like *love*? I said.

That shut her up.

Monsignor Cody said: I now pronounce you man and wife.

Sis lifted the veil and looked up into Gene's eyes. Actually, Sis looked straight across into Gene's eyes because Sis was almost as tall as Gene, and she was wearing low heels.

When they kissed, the organ started in, and all of us heard the organ, and I guess we expected the song to be some Catholic song. But then when our ears finally heard, we heard something we didn't expect to hear.

It was Mom. Mom was singing soprano, and she was singing alone.

Sis looked up at Mom, and so did Gene, and then everybody in the congregation looked up. There was Mom in her yellow shiny dress and her big swooping bonnet with daisies on it, both hands folded into a bouquet of white daisies. Mom was standing alone right up against the choir railing.

For a moment there, I thought she was going to jump.

What she was singing — none of us, not Sis, not Gene, not Dad, not nobody, let alone Monsignor Cody, had any idea Mom was going to sing:

> Going to the chapel and we're gonna get married.
> Going to the chapel of love.

Sis's favorite song. Oh my heavens pretty woman so far. I got to tell you. My mother up there in the silly swooped daisy hat, the shiny yellow dress that made her arms look fat, her penciled-on eyebrows, her rough, red farm hands, her cut-to-the-quick fingernails, clutching not a black Vatican full-length rosary but a bouquet of fresh white daisies, singing not "'Tis the Month of Our Mother," not "Tantum Ergo," not "Sanctus Sanctus Sanctus," but "Chapel of Love."

Really, you had to be there.

Bela Lugosi singing "Itsy Bitsy Spider."

Then Sis.

Sis at the altar, dressed up in a beautiful white wedding dress, her long white veil, finally Sis like in *The Wizard of Oz* when everything went to color, the world smelling of Eiffel Tower in the old dress-up trunk, scintillatingly gorgeous, smiling, smiling, my big sis, finally pretty, walking down the aisle with her husband, Gene Kelso, Mrs. Gene Kelso, *Here she is, Mrs. America.*

What a trip.

Then Dad.

At the back of the church, next to the confessional, just under Mom up in the choir loft and to the left, standing at parade rest in his new black suit, Dad saw me look over at him, and he quick looked away.

My father was going to cry if he looked at me, so my father looked away.

It was later, at the reception dance at the Green Triangle, things started heating up. Technically speaking, Mom had ended the war by singing Sis's favorite song, but soon it got pretty clear Mom was going to do more than make a truce. She was going to break an unspoken rule between her and Dad. Mom was going to let loose and get a little drunk.

Then there was Billie. Who knows with all that happened next how much of it Billie planned. The way it turned out, though, when Billie walked in the Green Triangle, the chemistry of the night changed. Sex hung in the air, and the war started all over again, but on a differnt battlefield.

Wild and weird this night. Dancing and singing and drinking. Liberation for Mom, at least for a night. A rite of passage for Sis. A chance for Billie to step into her body.

All bad things as far as Dad was concerned and maybe for me too.

The Green Triangle Bar and Grill is a bunch of old army barracks tacked together and painted green. There's a café part, a restaurant part, two banquet rooms, and a bar.

It was always a big deal for my family to go eat at the Green Triangle. It was a big deal to go out anywhere, but especially a big deal to the Green Triangle because they served shrimp cocktails and fried shrimp dinners. Plus Dad didn't like bars, even though the restaurant and the café were separate from the bar. Plus we never had the money, and there was always the goddamn work to do.

The Klusener-Kelso party was in banquet room number one, the banquet room closest to the bar. Between the banquet room and the bar was a big beige folding door that was one whole wall. After dinner, the folding door was opened so that the adults could go dance to the band playing in the bar, Rob Roy and the Cougar Mountain Four.

It was a weird feeling, in the parking lot of Saint Joseph's Church, to get into the back seat of the Buick with Mom and Dad up front, and then look out the window to see Sis getting into Gene Kelso's '56 Mercury.

Sis was mostly a pain in the ass, but that day when she was pulling the folds of her big white skirt into the red Mercury, her and Gene laughing in a way that didn't mean anybody else, deep down inside me something wanted to cry.

Then driving over to the Green Triangle, something else hit me like a ton of bricks.

Now it was just me and them.

As Mom and Dad and I were going in the Green Triangle's double doors, three Indians, two men and a woman, were coming out. The Indians were laughing and the woman was tall and had one tiny braid in her hair tied with a red ribbon. The men both had long hair and wore big black hats with silver headbands. They were real polite and said good evening and how are you tonight? but Mom just held on to her purse. Her teeth were grinding. Dad got the drut cow look on his face and quick stepped between the Indians and Mom and me and ushered us in.

First off what hit you was the smoke and the smell of liquor and fried food and sweat and how all those smells were in the red carpet and the red drapes and the flocked red wallpaper on the walls.

A quick scan of the room told me Billie wasn't there yet.

Dad walked up to the blond-hair-piled-up hostess just like he was still the usher at Saint Joseph's. Mom stood next to me, stiff as a board in her swoopy daisy bonnet, her shiny yellow dress, her yellow-dyed high heels, and the brown purse because she wouldn't buy a new purse just for the daisies. Mom's big arms, her leathery hands, her fingernails. Her eyebrows and her almond-shaped hazel eyes underneath her big gray plastic glasses.

In a public place wearing that hat, that yellow dress, those dyed-yellow shoes, Mom made herself disappear. When her eyes glazed over like that, she was a goner. Nobody could get through to her.

Only I knew how to get through to her.

I curled up my upper lip, crossed my eyes, made like I was going to scratch my butt. In nothing flat, there was Mom, her hand over her mouth, trying to hide her gums because she was laughing so hard.

You big dumb lug, she said, and slammed me with her purse. Quit acting like a hick. We're in public.

Mom's voice was serious, but she couldn't keep a straight face.

I liked the song you sang, Mom, I said. You made Sis real happy.

Just like that, Mom's face went serious, then she smiled a little bit but not much and not for long.

The banquet room's this way, Dad said, and stuck his arm out, showing which way to go.

About then, Sis and Gene came through the door. Sis in her big white dress, making a spectacle of herself. The people in the dining room, air jumped up in their throats and the whole room let out a big sigh. Then everybody started clapping. I've never seen Sis look so beautiful. With all that attention on her, it was like sun on a rose, a daisy, the way Sis bloomed.

Mom quick pulled her brown purse in close to her and ducked behind Dad. Sis walked over to Dad, her Roosky eyes into his Roosky eyes, grabbed Dad's arm, grabbed her husband's arm, and stood there in the middle of her men, smiling, proud, and tall, and a whole lot pregnant for all the world to see.

The tables were set in a T-shape. At the head table, from left to right, it was Mr. Kelso and Mrs. Kelso and Chuck diPietro and Gene, then Sis, Francie, Mom, and Dad. I sat just where the vertical part of the T goes into the horizontal head table part. The chair next to me empty.

Still no Billie.

Everyone was seated and the waitresses had served the dinner salads and set down the trays of Thousand Island, blue cheese, Italian, and French dressings on the table. I was halfway through my salad with a mixture of French and blue cheese when Billie Cody walked in the banquet room.

Holy Shit. Billie the Cunt Cody.

Her hennaed-red ratted high hair, big gold loops in her ears, her black eyeliner and red, red lips, in a low scooped black sequined top and black velvet miniskirt and knee-high black leather boots.

Every eye in that place on Billie.

Every eye in that place on Billie's tits.

The universe has always conspired to fuck me up.

The look on Sis's face, the look on Mom's face. I'd never thought Sis and Mom looked alike, but at that moment Mom and Sis were the same face.

And Dad. A snarl in his upper lip and his Roosky eyes pitch-black.

The scrape of my chair against the fake hardwood floor was the only sound in the room. I slapped a big smile across my face, stood up, walked the mile across the banquet room to meet Billie. Say cheese. A big block of Swiss cheese, big holes shot through.

Billie was a black hole in the bright Green Triangle fluorescence.

Some guy whistled, and people laughed.

I was a big smiling gawky big nose stupid ears Pinocchio. Somebody pulling my strings, making my arms and legs, making my body, flail around like a spineless asshole. Not authentic at all.

Really, I was trying hard to find my friend, but the Billie, the Mount Moriah–soft Billie parked in the pickup listening to the radio, the girl who held my face and said, *The way you are is just fine,* where was she? I knew she was in there somewhere inside the shiny black and red and gold package standing in front of me, and in my heart of hearts, I trusted I would find her. But meanwhile, I was all arms and legs, shits and giggles.

I grabbed Billie's hand and held her hand tight. Billie's blue eyes were looking in my eyes. But my eyes couldn't look her back. The sex of her was too strong.

Sticking out above Billie's low scooped neckline was three inches of cleavage.

I leaned down to her and whispered, *Hi, Billie,* in her ear. Then my arm was around Billie, and together we about-faced, and Billie and I, arm in arm, started the long trek back to the table.

The cocktail waitress in her Green Triangle short green skirt and halter top ensemble was at the head table getting drink orders. I heard

Dad say, Just a Coke please. The cocktail waitress and Billie and I arrived at Mom about the same time.

With that big swoopy bonnet on, all you could see of Mom was daisies.

What would you like to drink? the waitress asked.

Mom, I said, I'd like you to meet Billie Cody.

When Mom turned her head, Billie's black sequined boobs were eye level to Mom's almond-shaped hazel eyes. Mom's big plastic glasses slipped down her nose. She pushed the glasses up with her index finger.

Rum and Coke, please, Mom said. Make that a double.

Dad quick looked over to Mom with that look of his. Mom pulled the daisy bonnet down on that side of her so Dad was out of the picture.

Billie, I said. This is my mother.

Mom put her hand on the daisy bonnet and turned her face up and around. The grim line that was my mother's mouth broke out into a smile that was way too big.

The Klusener smile. You can be sure if our gums are showing, we either love you or hate you.

With Billie it was not love.

So nice to meet you, Mom said.

Mom's rough, red farm hands stayed in her lap holding her brown purse.

Billie's hand in my hand, one of us was sweating or both. I don't know who was holding on tighter.

The bald spot on Dad's head. He was drumming his big hairy fingers on the table.

Dad, I said. This is Billie.

Dad didn't look up.

That's quite a getup she's wearing, Dad said.

Billie's hand, my hand, squeezed tighter.

Then Sis — lots of gum showing — Sis said: Hi, Billie! So nice you could come to our wedding!

Sis stood up and acted cute and made a big show of hugging Billie. Big white pregnant dress hugging the shiny black slut dress. Sis should never act cute. Especially pregnant.

This is my husband, Gene! Sis said. Her voice sounded like it was full of bubbles. And this is my maid of honor, Francie Lutz!

Francie was still gripping the wedding bouquet she'd caught at church.

Gene and Chuck diPietro stood up so fast their chairs collided.

Gene's eyes, Chuck's eyes, started at Billie's chest and worked their way up.

Yah, I know Billie, Gene said. Man, you look great tonight.

Pleased to meet you, Chuck said. Nice dress.

I stuck my hand out to introduce myself to Chuck, but Chuck didn't see my hand so I let my hand drop.

Chuck's eyes looked at Billie the way men are supposed to look at women.

You going to be dancing later? Chuck said.

Billie's black eyeliner eyes looked up at me. If I looked anything like Billie right then, the way I looked was, Where the fuck am I?

Sis, still cute, still full of bubbles, said: The folding door opens at eight o'clock!

Sis laid a hand on Chuck's shoulder, one on Billie's.

Sure she'll dance with you, Chuck, Sis said. Won't you, Billie?!

Will someone please turn off the fucking bubble machine?

Then: I'm Gene's father, Gene's father said. Kelso, Jim Kelso.

I stuck my hand out to greet Mr. Kelso, but his hand was already headed for Billie.

Mr. Kelso gave Billie's hand a big Howdy Doody shake.

Mr. Kelso had a Wyatt Earp tie and turquoise belt buckle so big it looked like a dinner plate.

Mrs. Kelso stuck her blue hair around Mr. Kelso's potbelly.

In a voice that sounded like a baby kitten, Mrs. Kelso said: Pleased to meet you, I'm sure.

My oh my, Mr. Kelso said. You sure enough are an attractive young lady, isn't she, Pickles?

Mrs. Kelso's blue hair around Mr. Kelso's belly again.

Yes, dear, she said. She's a very pretty young lady.

I stepped around Mr. Kelso to shake Pickles's hand, but she was embroidering a blue bunny onto the end of a pillowcase.

Standing there at the head table in the bright Green Triangle fluorescence in a mess of people I didn't know, I brought my hand up close to my face.

Looked like nobody wanted to shake it.

But in my other hand, holding on tight and true, her fingers and her little blue fingernails wrapped inside mine, was the hand of Billie Cody.

There she was, my friend. I knew I'd find her.

I pulled Billie's hand up to my heart.

You *do* look great, I said. When I first saw you, I didn't know what to think.

Oh shit, Billie said. Do I look too?

No, I said. No. It's just that you look so.

Sexy, Billie said.

Yes, I said, sexy.

My breath wanted a cigarette.

It scared me a little, I said.

If Billie had a cigarette right then, it would be a whirlwind around her right ear. Yah, Billie said.

Me too, Billie said. Tonight, when I looked in the mirror, it scared me too.

Sure enough, at eight o'clock the beige folding wall opened. The spotlight went on Rob Roy and the Cougar Mountain Four. Rob Roy was in a blue Elvis jumpsuit, and the Cougar Mountain Four in white jumpsuits.

Everybody under twenty-one had to stay on the wedding side of the beige folding door — which meant everybody in the wedding party but the parents and the aunts and uncles.

By nine o'clock, though, nobody gave a shit.

It was so crowded in banquet room number one, you couldn't tell the banquet room from the bar, the wedding crowd from the bar crowd, one side of the beige folding wall from the other, your ass from a hole in the ground. Billie and I were undercover where the beige folding wall came together with a green wall, leaning together in the corner holding hands and sharing the bottomless glass of beer the cocktail waitress kept filling up and setting on the end of the banquet table. The band was on a break, but it was still real noisy. People all around us laughing and talking and smoking. Everyone having fun except Mom and Dad.

Dad was off in the corner by the bus tubs, talking farm stuff to Clyde Schoonover, who had a place over on Rio Vista. Mom was sitting alone at the banquet table, still in the daisy bonnet, sipping on her double rum and Coke.

Sis had drunk about twenty bottles of champagne by then. She was standing in the middle of the dance floor with Gene and Chuck diPietro, and Francie. Sis wasn't really standing, Sis was trying to stand. Sis reached inside Gene's jacket pocket and pulled a pack of Marlboros out of Gene's inside pocket, tapped a cigarette out, and lit it. Sis spent a lot of time clearing away the netting of her veil so she wouldn't set the damn thing on fire.

The next thing you know, Sis in her big white dress is weaving across the dance floor, the pack of Marlboros in her hand, headed straight for Mom

Billie scored a cigarette about then, and Billie and I were puffing like mad on that cigarette. When Sis gets to Mom, Sis clears away a bunch of chairs so she can sit down. Sis lays the Marlboros down on the table, takes a big drag on the cigarette, her head and head-dress bobbing around, leans in, and says something very particular to Mom.

Mom's almond-shaped hazel eyes all the way across the room. Even Billie saw Mom's eyes light up. In no time at all, Mom's lighting a cigarette, and there they were, the two of them, Mom and Sis, those females, smoking.

That's when the cocktail waitress in her Green Triangle short skirt and halter top ensemble comes by with two shot glasses filled with something clear and sets the shot glasses down in front of Mom and Sis. Sis reaches down, smells the shot glass, smiles, then holds the shot glass up to Mom. Mom doesn't hesitate. She takes her shot glass, and then, there they were, Mom and Sis, here's mud in your eye. Mom had to hold on to her hat; Sis, her veil. They tipped their shot glasses up.

It wasn't long after that, Mom pulled her hatpin out and took her swoopy daisy bonnet off. Mom spruced up her hair, put her cigarette out, spread some lipstick across her mouth, then stood up and walked across the banquet room and into the bar.

The way Mom walked, you could tell she had a purpose. When Mom walked like that, she had one thing in mind. That day she walked out of church after Aunt Zelda, then beat the crap out of her: Mom walked like that.

Up onto the empty stage and straight to the piano, Mom sat down. She started right in on "Chapel of Love," then after that "Red Roses for a Blue Lady."

It didn't take long for the bar to quiet down. Pretty soon, you couldn't hear nothing but Mom's piano. Must have been a hundred people standing silent.

Billie passed the cigarette to me, and I was into a deep inhale when all of a sudden, Billie grabbed my hand, and I looked, and there was Dad standing real close. I mean almost shoulder to shoulder. I quick opened my mouth and let the cigarette fall from my mouth and onto the floor. He didn't see me, though. Dad was just staring through the crowd at Mom up there in the lights on the stage. I never saw my dad look like that. He looked so young, like a kid like me.

Pretty soon people in the crowd were singing along, then everybody was singing.

When Rob Roy and the Cougar Mountain Four came back from their break, they didn't go into their regular set, they started playing along with Mom. She was playing "Darktown Strutter's Ball," and the drummer was drumming and the fiddler was fiddling and the guitar guy was playing along and the bass. Rob Roy grabbed the microphone, said: Come on, everybody, sing along! Pretty soon, the whole room was singing: *I'll be down to getcha in a taxi, honey. Better be ready 'bout half past eight.*

Dad wasn't standing there anymore, and I looked around but didn't see him.

Billie and I started jitterbugging the way Sis and I danced. Billie caught right on. There was this one dance move where Billie went under my right arm and started twirling, then I, holding tight onto Billie's left hand up high, started twirling too, and the two of us were twirling, twirling, then we came together face to face and started dancing just like we'd been slow dancing. We did it just perfect.

It was right then things got slow. There was Billie, so happy to be dancing with me. Then through the crowd, across the room, when I looked over, there was Sis in her big white gown. She had bent over and picked up Gene, and Gene was in her arms the way the bride is supposed to be when the newlyweds cross the threshold. Gene was acting like a fainting bride, and Sis was growling like a horny guy. Everybody over by Sis and Gene were laughing their asses off. Then, when I looked, up on the stage, there was Mom playing "We Got to Get Out of This Place," for chrissakes.

You can play anything as long as you find middle C.

Mom's hair was flying back, and her rough, red farm hands, cut-to-the-quick fingernails, were playing the piano, her stocking feet banging the pedals. Mom was up on the stage playing with the band.

Looked like Grandpa Schmidt's wild girl was having the time of her life.

If it's the last thing we ever do.

Mom's almond-shaped hazel eyes — that shit you thought was in them for good was totally gone, and Mom was smiling, smiling. In the middle of a bar, the world bright and loud and a little drunk all around me. People sweating and dancing and drinking. Everybody so happy. Mom was happy. Sis was happy. Billie was happy. Why couldn't things always be this way? I loved God so much right then.

The only time Billie and I stopped dancing was so she could dance with Mr. Kelso, and Gene, and of course Chuck diPietro a couple of times.

Billie's who pointed him out to me, though, through all the music and the noise and the smoke, Dad sitting at the banquet table with his Coke. He had his drut cow face on. My father, without his wife, so out of place in all the drunken fun. Mom up there in the spotlight and Dad cold and way off and alone, the old Mexican house out in the snow.

Who knows how long that song went on, everybody singing and dancing. *We got to get out of this place* must 'a been a hundred times. Then "I Want to Hold Your Hand," then "Jailhouse Rock," Mom playing right along.

The whole bar cheered, clapped, for Mom when Mom got up and took a bow. Still smiling ear to ear, Mom walked offstage, carrying her dyed-yellow shoes, like she was walking on clouds. At the banquet table, she sat down. But Dad wasn't sitting there anymore. Mom lit another cigarette, and it wasn't long, and the cocktail waitress set another double rum and Coke in front of her. The waitress leaned down and said something into Mom's ear, then handed her something.

In no time at all, Mom's yellow-dyed shoes were back on, her swoopy daisy hat was in her hands and her brown purse. Mom walked right up to me and Billie. Her almond-shaped hazel eyes were green. She didn't say a thing to Billie, didn't even look at her.

Rigby John, Mom said, come with me. You've got to take me home.

Then Mom was out the door of the banquet room just like that, leaving me standing there wondering what was what.

Billie went right for a cigarette. I was lighting Billie's cigarette when Sis came up to me.

Sis had an aura of tragedy about her. When Sis ain't being cute, she's being tragic.

Dad's gone missing, Sis said. He left the keys to the Buick with the cocktail waitress.

Her dark Roosky eyes, breathing fast bad breath, tears rolling down her cheeks. Tragic.

Where'd he go? I said.

Who knows? Sis said.

You better take Mom home, Sis said. She's had a lot to drink, and she shouldn't drive.

As if *he* hasn't, Billie said. Meaning me.

What? Sis said.

I had to step in or there'd be a bitch fight right there and then for sure.

I've got to take Billie home, I said. My voice was high, and I hated it.

Sis said: I'm sure Dad is probably home. My God, what if Dad isn't home?

Sis looked over to Billie the same time I did. The cigarette was a whirlwind by her ear.

Gene and I can give Billie a ride home, Sis said. Is that OK with you, Billie?

Billie was just about to say something. Who knows what. There was a lot going on with her face, and I couldn't tell.

Just as Billie was about to speak, as fate would have it, Chuck diPietro stepped up.

He smelled of sweat and Elsha. Across his shoulders, he made two of me.

Don't worry, Chuck said. I can take her home.

It was strange driving home in the Buick. I hardly ever drove the Buick, and never with Mom sitting next to me on the front seat. I drove forty-five miles an hour, the speed limit. Mom sat with her knees curled up under her. It was a warm night for April, and Mom had her window open, her hand out the window, rolling her arm along in the warm night air. Her new perfume smelled nice.

It wasn't like Dad to do anything spontaneous, and I was worried.

But Mom wasn't worried. I hadn't seen her so exhilarated since Aunt Alma came to visit with Theresa, her artist friend from Portland. On Philbin Road, Mom reached down and turned on the radio loud to KSEI. They were playing Mom's old songs. She still had a cigarette going, and right at the moment when the song on the radio said, *Just let the smoke rings rise in the air, you'll find your share of memories there,* the smoke from her cigarette rose in the air. Mom laughed a little then at the smoke, then let the wind come in onto her and blow her hair.

The house was dark when Mom and I drove into the yard. The way the headlights hit the house, the house looked haunted. Tramp started barking, and the cats ran out of the garage.

I followed Mom up the four steps into the kitchen. The kitchen door, how it always sounded opening. When Mom went to hit the light switch, from out of the dark, Dad's voice was too loud: Leave the light off, Dad said.

Sudden quiet in us, Mom and me.

I've got some things to say, Dad said. And they're better off said in the dark.

The kitchen door closed behind me quiet. For a moment, Mom's shoulders went down, and she turned in toward me like she was a kid too, afraid of Dad in the dark. Her daisy bonnet and her brown purse in her hands went up to her breast, and she held them there.

Out of the dark, Mom's voice was low and whispery: Rigby John, Mom said. You go down to bed.

Then Dad too loud again: No, let the boy stay. What I have to say is for him to hear too.

The moon and the stars made light that came in the kitchen window. Dad still in his new black suit sat in his chair at the head of the table. His elbows were on the table, and now and then his hands came up to his face and covered it.

Come over here and sit down, Dad said.

Mom and I both had to pass by him so we could get to our chairs. I tried to think of a way of getting around him, but there was no way.

Mom laid her daisy bonnet on the table, her brown purse. The sound of Mom's chair and mine against the blue and white tiles.

Mom sat in the chair that usually was Sis's chair. She moved slow and careful. I sat in my chair across the table from her. In the dark she was inches deep, soft.

Mary, Dad said still loud, I want a divorce.

Shock and surprise in me in a way I'd not known in myself yet. Crazy weird.

The shock of Mom without Dad.

But other things weird in my chest too. Old hunks of stuck shit, gray old bats hung upside down, sudden butterflies, hummingbirds, shit exploding, flying up and out of me, fireworks.

For Mom and for me.

At last she could breathe.

What Dad said next, he said in one long stream of words, like he'd been sitting in the dark and practicing the words. Not just all night, but for a long, long time.

Mary, Dad said. You're too headstrong. You've always got to have things your way or else. And I'm tired of it. I'm always pussyfooting around here, wondering if something's going to tick you off. Walking around here on eggshells half the time, always afraid that you're going to have one of your migraines or one of your menstrual cramps, your change of life, or who the hell knows what can go wrong with you. There's always something.

Dad put his head in his hands. His black hair was shadows on his face.

Grandma's clock ticking, ticking.

The light from the night in through the window on Mom's face and shoulder.

You're a hard woman, Mary Schmidt, Dad said. I knew that when I married you. But I thought you'd change. But you haven't. You turned out the spitting image of your mother. I've worked hard for you and these kids, and I don't get any thanks for it. I get my dinner on a plate, but I don't get a smile with it. It's all gloom and doom to you, and hard luck. Ain't no relief from it. We're always kneeling down praying our asses off for some kind of calamity or another. A man can't live like that. He's got to have something besides cake to keep things sweet. And these kids. Look at the way they've turned out. Spoiled rotten. I've told you over and over again, but you won't listen. Hell, all their lives, you've been herding them like a sheep dog, always at them to be special and differnt. Well, they're differnt all right. A knocked-up daughter and a momma's boy.

Momma's boy.

Spineless ass.

Grandma's clock ticking, ticking.

All because of you, Dad said. You're always talking about God and praying to God, but you don't have a ounce of faith in you. If you did, you'da let these kids be and trust in the ways of the Lord instead of riding them to the ground.

Dad's fist came down hard on the table.

Saddle-room Daddy, the shadow of him a puddle around his feet. Some part of me jumped right out of my skin. Another part had never sat so square in one place.

Tonight at the bar, Dad yelled.

His voice was too high and sounded like my voice when it went high.

You were drunk as a sailor, Dad yelled. Son of a bitch this, and son of a bitch that, it's downright embarrassing. What self-respecting man lets his wife act like that? You ain't never had any respect for me or for your children, it's always you, you, you. Well, I'm tired of it. I want a divorce. Monday morning I'm going into the lawyer's office, and I'm going to sign the papers. Make myself a free man for once. For once, I can live my life the way I want to live it, instead of yoked up to a willful woman who won't have things any way but hers.

That night, the silence behind Mom and Dad's bedroom door, silence in the hallway into the kitchen, silence across the blue and white tiles of the kitchen, down the stairs to my bedroom door, the silence of Sis gone. Silence at my bedroom door pressing hard up against it. Kept me awake all night.

Sunday morning, that very next morning, the three of us in the Buick driving to church for nine o'clock Mass. Same as ever, Dad drove. Same as ever, Mom sat under her church hat and big plastic glasses. Nobody said a word. Usually driving to church, that's the way things were, nobody saying a word, but that Sunday, all that was unspoken was so full on, you liked to suffocate.

Inside the Buick it still smelled like the night before. Despite Dad's Old Spice, despite Mom's new perfume, inside the Buick smelled like the Green Triangle. Sex and booze and rock and roll.

When we parked in the Saint Joe's parking lot, when Dad got out of the car, I took a good look at him. His face was drut cow face, and he was feeling stupid. You could tell.

After church, when Mom was making breakfast, the pots and pans were getting slammed down extra-hard, the silverware drawer was getting slammed shut, and the refrigerator door slammed shut, the mush a big lump of glue, and the eggs were cooked hard, and when I asked for more toast, Mom said: Get your own damn toast.

When I left the house to go do the chores, as soon as the screen door slammed behind me, inside the house, all hell started breaking loose. Yelling and screaming and things getting thrown around, dishes breaking, you name it.

Damn hick! Mom yelled. What did I do but go and marry a damn hick!

The chores took me extra-long that day. After my Viceroy, after whacking off and breaking the sixth commandment, after listening to the top-ten countdown, after I fed the cows their twenty bales of hay, I didn't have anything better to do, so I went into the Mexican house. The wood box that was the front step, the blown-out screen door, the two bare rooms smelling of cookstove, tortillas, sweat, cigarettes, and instant coffee. I sat on one of the two double beds, then lay back. The springs made a *pinche* racket. The sun from the window was warm on my face and red in my eyes when I closed them. I wondered which bed Flaco and Acho slept in. I wondered where they were now. I wondered if the stain on the ceiling looked like a terrible blossom to them.

That night, Dad didn't come in to watch *Bonanza*. He stayed out in the machine shed and didn't eat dinner. There wasn't any dinner to eat. I had a bologna sandwich and a glass of milk. I tried to call Billie, but there was no answer. Dad didn't come in that night at all. Slept in the truck, I guess.

It was weird lying in bed thinking about Mom lying in bed alone, and Dad outside in the machine shed or the barn lying alone somewhere.

Monday morning, Dad didn't go to the lawyer. He sat at his end of the table, sipping his hot tea with two sugars, reading the *Idaho State Journal* same as ever. I looked hard across my mush at Mom. Behind her big plastic glasses, her almond-shaped hazel eyes weren't giving up a thing.

It went on all week like that. One evening, walking down the hallway, the bathroom door was open. Dad was standing at the sink with his long johns top draping down over his Levi's. From his shoulder to his Levi's was a long scratch. When I looked at the scratch, Dad was looking in the mirror at me to make sure I saw that scratch.

Billie still wasn't answering my calls, so when Wednesday came along, I drove to Billie's house and parked and walked up her windy sidewalk past the lamp with the ivy growing on it. When the world falls apart, you can pretend it's not and make it look good from the outside, or you can try and move forward, even if all you take is one step.

I rang the doorbell.

C not for *Cody,* but for *cunt.*

The man who pushed open the aluminum door wore a gray work shirt with CODY PLUMBING on the pocket and a matching pair of gray pants. He was short like Billie with big shoulders and chest and arms. A way of staring that made me forget what I was going to say.

All I could think was, if I married Billie, both Sis and I would be married to plumbers.

Billie's dad had a toothpick stuck between his lips, and he was chewing gum like he had a wild animal in his mouth.

What can I do ya for? he said.

His left arm with the gray sleeve rolled to the elbow, the dark hair on his forearm, held open the aluminum door.

Is Cunt here? I said.

Yes, it's true.

Really, that's just what I said.

I said, *Is Cunt here?*

I know. I know. Can you fucking believe it? Even now, just thinking about it, I have to put my arms over my head.

Homer Cody's index finger drilled his ear. He took his finger out of his ear, looked at his finger, sniffed his finger.

Then: Speak up, son, he said. *Who* you looking for?

Billie! I blurted out. I'd like to see Billie!

Homer Cody's eyes looked at me the way you look down the sights of a gun.

Young man, he finally said, I don't like you.

Sir? I said.

Then over his shoulder, Homer Cody yelled: Hey, wife! Someone's here to see you.

From the back of the house, a woman's voice: Who is it?

Homer Cody's blue eyes were square into my eyes when he yelled:
Some dipshit!

Mr. Cody turned back into the house, and then it was Mrs. Cody at
the door. Her brown hair cut short in a bubble around her face. She
pushed the aluminum door away, and I was freestanding again.

Bare feet and little toenails. Thirty-six years old. Twice the age of
Billie. The cigarette in Mrs. Cody's hand.

Hello? Mrs. Cody said.

The conductor of a symphony, the cigarette and Mrs. Cody.

He's looking for the cunt of the house, Mr. Cody said loud from
back somewhere inside the house.

So I called for you, he said.

Mrs. Cody took a long drag on her cigarette. She was looking at me
and back behind at her asshole husband at the same time. There on
that day was the first time she looked at me the way Mrs. Cody did
sometimes. Not like I was something of her daughter's. Her blue eyes
right close in at me like she knew something about me I didn't know
yet and when I knew, it was going to break my heart.

You're Rigby John, she said.

Her blue eyes more gray than Billie's. The reason I know is because
it was such a long time since I looked into them. Pain in those eyes
too, same way as my mom's.

Then out of the blue, Mrs. Cody said: Billie was right.

I said: Mrs. Cody?

You *are* lovely, she said. Never seen anything like it.

Mrs. Cody smiled big, so much like Billie when she smiled. She
bowed a little and rolled the cigarette starting at me, then out, like she
was introducing me to an audience.

Dramatic.

Come on in, then, she said. Wait in the living room. I'll tell Billie
you're here.

I stepped one foot inside the house. Four empty Budweiser cans on
the counter. Two more on the kitchen table. Suddenly the house got
real hot.

I said: I don't think Mr. Cody wants me in here.

The quick puff on her cigarette.

Neither does Billie, she said. But you're in here, aren't you, at least
halfway.

I stepped my other foot inside.

Mrs. Cody put her hand on my shoulder, then let her hand roll down my arm. It was nice the way she touched me, soft. In all my years, my mother had never touched me like that.

Her voice went low. She was telling me a secret.

I'm glad you've come, Mrs. Cody said. It's the right thing.

Her hand went up to my shoulder again.

It shows Billie that you care, she said.

Then the cigarette the way you play with sparklers on the Fourth of July.

And don't mind Billie's dad, she said, her voice still low.

He's a damn drunken fool, she said. So don't pay him any attention.

Billie! she yelled. Someone here to see you!

In the living room, I quick sat down in the beige armchair. Outside, through the aluminum picture window, Mr. Cody was zipping up his bomber jacket that said UNITED STATES MARINES on the back. He was flipping the bird at the house, flipping the bird at me. The way he walked down the steps was like a soldier.

Billie came around the corner into the living room pulling a black sweater over her head. I quick stood up. I thought it was weird that when she said, Hi, Rig, I couldn't see her face. Now, as I look back on it, I understand why Billie was doing that. But that day, I just wanted to look into Billie's eyes and see myself inside them looking back.

When I spoke, my voice wouldn't come out at first. But I had to speak. I wasn't going to end up like Mom and Dad.

Where have you been? I said. I've been calling and calling.

Billie's eyes got red, not from tear duct cancer, and they were full of tears. Her face was in the buttons of my shirt in no time.

Oh, Rig! she said. I've been feeling a little weird.

The palm of my hand on the back of her head. Billie's smell clean, something French. Her body up next to mine like that in somebody's very warm beige living room with the lights on. I started to sweat.

I said, Let's go park in the cemetery next to Russell and listen to the radio and smoke and kiss.

Let's smoke here, Billie said. Do you have cigarettes?

Here? I said. You can smoke in your house?

Dad's gone, she said. That's all that matters. I smoke with Mom all the time.

In my shirt pocket were four Viceroys. I pulled out two cigarettes, gave one to Billie, lit hers, mine.

Billie's inhale was a gulp of air. Her blue eyes were looking up the way Mom looks up when there's a migraine.

Don't you think the ceiling looks like paramecium? Billie said.

Then she said: The plural I guess would be paramecia.

I said: Billie.

Billie kept her chin lifted up at the beige paramecia and took a long drag.

When I looked down, Billie's other hand was gripping the lip of a green glass ashtray. Something so sad right then the way her fingers and her little blue fingernails were shaking.

Above us, the beige ceiling paramecia were moving slow.

Very slow like what Billie said next.

I've been seeing Chuck diPietro, she said.

Everything very slow, slow and thick, the way my stomach feels when it's full of mush.

Seeing him? I said. You mean dates?

No, Billie said. Just at the Snatch Out.

So weird smoking inside somebody's house where everyone can see.

More than once? I said.

Twice, Billie said.

Two beige ceiling paramecia above the aluminum window slid down onto the wall.

Seeing him, I said. What does seeing him mean?

Paramecia down the wall around the aluminum window out onto the floor into the beige carpet.

Driving around, she said. Having a Coke.

Paramecia under my feet, under the beige carpet.

He's got a cool pickup, I said.

The next thing I said I couldn't think about very long. But I had to say it. Somebody in my family had to say things.

Did you kiss him? I said.

Paramecia, the whole damn beige room was crawling.

Rig. Billie's voice was low, an especially low Simone Signoret. She was still looking up at the ceiling.

I looked up too.

The paramecia that ate Pocatello.

Do you remember that promise we made to each other? Billie said. That no matter what we would be friends?

My heart was slamming in my chest, in my ears. Sweat rolling down my sides. I crushed my cigarette into the ashtray.

Well, Billie said, this is one of those times.

Seems like I sat on the hearth forever, the paramecia that ate Pocatello eating at my heart. Sat and smoked. Everything all at once going around in my head, and that everything was loud.

How long did he kiss her, where were they when he kissed her? What kind of girl would go around kissing two boys at the same time? Was I doing homework, doing the chores, having supper, watching *I Love Lucy,* when Chuck diPietro was kissing Billie? Beige paramecia crawling inside my pants like hay dust. We sat on the hearth for an hour, maybe longer. A couple of times, Billie went to touch me, but I wouldn't let her. Each time I scooted away, Billie scooted over to me. It went that way, Billie going to touch me, me scooting, for the whole length of the hearth.

When I finally let her touch me, my butt was hanging off the end.

We promised, Rig, Billie said. We promised to be friends no matter what.

My mom and dad had made a promise too. Look where it got them. But Billie and I were differnt. We could talk to each other. We weren't trying to hide.

I reached down and took a hold of Billie's hand, pulled her hand up next to my heart.

I'm still your friend, I said.

Billie closed her eyes and kissed me, two lips against two lips, soft with a kind of suck, tobacco, and the taste of pink.

Promise? Billie said.

All the tea in China. An audience with the Pope. The moon.

My voice was low. Yves Montand, we called my voice when it was low.

I promise, I said.

Back home, same as ever, breakfast was served at eight o'clock, dinner at noon, and supper at six. Mom still cooked, and Dad and I ate. After supper, Dad had his hot tea with two sugars and his Viceroy and read the paper. Everything was back to the way it had always been, except Sis wasn't there to help with the dishes. Like to drive you crazy. Same as with Russell, Dad's threat to divorce was something scary that was going on, and everybody knew it was going on, but nobody had the courage to talk about it.

Things were differnt this time, though. All that was beneath the surface of things and not talked about was gaining velocity. All you had to do was scratch a little bit, and there was pandemonium.

The little things. Mom burning the cookies, Dad running out of gas in the field, me riding the fucking bus to school, weren't just the miserable things they were, but misery itself. The whole world was against us except we weren't even an *us*.

That whole spring, Mom and Dad stuck to the script so close I started to believe it myself. Divorce seemed to be off the table anyway, which was a strange kind of relief to me. I'd considered the idea that divorce might be a good thing for Mom, but finally I just couldn't imagine anything that differnt. Their papered-over stalemate was awful to be around. But I understood stalemate. Billie and I had patched things up our own way too, and we were back to our routine of Wednesday and Friday nights at Mount Moriah. Things were the same and weren't the same, but parked under the elm tree, spring outside, the bushes and trees and flowers blooming, everything coming back to life again, all around us so much hope, Billie and I looked into each other's eyes and talked as best we could about what was inside.

Then Billie and I got some unexpected help.

We discovered something new, something differnt.

Actually it was Billie's mother who discovered it, in fact she bought it, for herself and for Billie and me.

A lid of marijuana.

My mom would never go out and buy a lid of marijuana.

As soon as Billie told me about the marijuana, I got a fear inside me that damn near stopped my heart. I didn't know it then, it took me awhile, but I came to see my fear as the same fear as my mother and father's. My mom and dad were afraid of anything new. Marijuana was new, that's for sure. But after I let the fear settle down and took a good look at it, I decided it might be just the thing. After the fiasco of Sis's wedding, my parents, and Billie and me, I was ready to try something new, really new. Not something outside me like trying out for sports or buying a car, but something inside. Marijuana held the promise of breaking down your inhibitions, a promise of actually changing your consciousness. Like Huxley's *Doors of Perception* and

Heaven and Hell, marijuana was going to crack my world open, and at last I was going to face the fear in me. Scardino, the sex-shame-guilt thing, the fear that made my arms weak. Really, I was so tired of being a wimp.

Looking back on it now, it was the marijuana all right, but even more than the marijuana, it was my determination to change things. Some famous guy that Billie knows the name of said, Be careful what you wish for. Better said, I think, is, Be careful of what you decide to go after.

Whoever that guy is, he's right. Look at me out here on the highway alone in this silver desert with just the moon. And it's not the universe that's to blame. When you go after something you want, and you end up fucked up, nobody's to blame but yourself.

And you know what — fucked up is just a part of it. As a matter of fact, things *have* to get fucked up if you plan to go anywhere new that your parents haven't. Maybe that's why the universe conspires.

And that's what we did one night in late spring in Billie's house with Billie's mother while her father was off at a plumbing convention in Boise.

We got fucked up.

There's a beer in the fridge! Mrs. Cody yelled from the bathroom. Make yourself at home!

It was weird just pulling a can of beer out of a refrigerator. I popped the tab and sat down at the kitchen table as if I walked in the house, opened the fridge, got out a can of beer every day. Billie and her mom in the back rooms, mother and daughter more like sisters, laughing and talking, the water in the bathroom sink, the hair dryer, one of them brushing her teeth. From the back rooms, the clean smell, something French. Females, how they always sound and smell like they know they are a comfort.

Onto the green Formica kitchen table, Mrs. Cody's hands, her tiny fingernails, set down a rolled-up plastic bag that was full of something dark green.

Mrs. Cody, Billie, and I all sat there staring at the plastic bag, trying to find our breath. Mrs. Cody lit a cigarette first, then Billie, then me.

Nobody touched the plastic bag. It just lay there next to a cut-glass ashtray like some strange new British movie you wouldn't understand.

We didn't know yet, what it was, how it would make us feel.

Weird, how a plastic bag could be all I'd never done and was afraid to do. And more. What was in me, I didn't know and was afraid to know. Who it was, I wasn't and was afraid to be. All that in a plastic bag on a green Formica tabletop.

The smell. Something pungent. Dead weeds in a pile by the fence.

Moldy hay. Just my luck if marijuana turned out to be moldy hay.

Billie laid a pipe on the green Formica next to the plastic bag and the cut-glass ashtray. She'd bought the pipe from Incense Peppermints, a head shop that opened up in downtown Pocatello. The pipe was made from blown glass with blue and green swirls.

I pinched bits of moldy hay out of the plastic bag and filled the pipe, careful not to spill any on the green Formica. None of us knew how much it would take for all of us to get high, so I tamped the moldy hay down into the pipe bowl with my thumb, then laid in more moldy hay.

When the pipe was filled, I set the filled pipe in the middle of the green Formica.

Mrs. Cody reached out her hands, palms up. With her left hand, she took hold of Billie's hand, with her right, she took hold of mine. Billie put her hand in mine, and the three of us were a circle.

On the table, in a blue vase, lilacs. The smell of lilacs, the smell of moldy hay, something French, and the smell of chocolate chip cookies. Mrs. Cody was baking chocolate chip cookies.

Mrs. Cody cleared her throat and bowed her head.

Dear God, she said. Her voice was just like Billie's Simone Signoret.

My daughter, Billie, and her friend Rigby John, and I have come here and formed a circle. We think it is good to know the ways of the world, so we've decided to turn on with this marijuana. Please know we wish no harm upon ourselves or others. And we approach this experience with the utmost respect.

Mrs. Cody squeezed my hand and opened her blue eyes on me.

Do you have anything you want to add? she said.

Weird. A Jew praying to God about marijuana. My mom would have to pray a rosary and a fucking litany. But then it never could be my mom.

Billie? Mrs. Cody said.

Billie didn't look at me. If she did, she'd start laughing, so Billie looked down at her hands and shook her head no.

Well then, Mrs. Cody said, dear God, we ask that you grant each one of us a good trip. Please watch over us so that we don't freak out.

I lit the pipe while Mrs. Cody sucked on it.

You're supposed to hold it in as long as you can, Billie said.

Mrs. Cody's blue-gray eyes lit up, and she inhaled and kept the smoke inside her until she couldn't stand it any longer, then blew the smoke out.

Billie and I stared at Mrs. Cody. She still had a bubble of brown hair, blue-gray eyes. Nothing about her had changed.

Then it was Billie's turn. I lit the match again and held the match to the moldy hay. Billie sucked in deep, then pulled the pipe away, then talked like you do when you're holding in the smoke: Thanks, Billie said.

Then it was me. Billie held the match. While she was holding the match, she exhaled a bunch of smoke just as I inhaled a huge toke.

I held my breath. Some part of me started spying on everything I was thinking and doing. What I could see, hear, what I could feel. I was playing I Spy, watching everything I did and every bodily function up close.

Nothing differnt. Everything normal.

So we finished off the first pipe. Just as we finished, a bell went off. We all jumped. Mrs. Cody got up, walked to the oven, and pulled the chocolate chip cookies out.

Right then, Billie looked over at me. Her eyes opened wider, and she seemed to take me in, all of me in for a moment, and in that moment while she was taking me in, she was thinking of just the right way to say what she wanted to say.

It felt good to be looked at so full on like that again. Then I wondered if Billie was doing that because she was stoned.

Billie got up, walked into the front room, and pretty soon some music started. When she came back in the kitchen, Billie was smiling her big smile.

It's *Sergeant Pepper's Lonely Hearts Club Band,* Billie said.

You bought the album? I said.

What a world in that album cover. I touched the album cover all over with my fingers. *Sergeant Pepper* so full of color and shiny things, hats and folds of cloth and jewelry, gold tassels and all sorts of weird new things. Things I'd never known.

Mrs. Cody set a blue plate of cookies on the green Formica tabletop.

We all said, What the hell, and loaded up the pipe again, smoked the pipe empty, set the pipe down, and waited for the Doors of Perception and Heaven and Hell to open up. But nothing opened up.

Nothing differnt. My dream of a new consciousness was only moldy hay.

Mrs. Cody took the pipe, loaded the pipe, lit a match, and sucked in more smoke. She passed the pipe to Billie. Billie sucked on the pipe, then handed the pipe to me. I sucked in a big heap of smoke. We passed that pipe around until it was empty.

We were just going along, just Ho-hum, when is this marijuana going to work? Billie's mom brought in a red candle, lit it, and turned the lights down. *Sergeant Pepper's Lonely Hearts Club Band* playing loud over and over. Billie and her mom laughing and smoking and jabbering away, the whole world just going along, going along.

That's when I looked down at my hands.

Almost seventeen years I'd had these hands.

Just beyond my hands on the table, the flame of the red candle flickered. Across the smooth green plains of Formica, the flame reflected in the blue vase was the color of blood before blood touches air. Up out of the top of the red-blue blood vase, a volcano of lilac flowers billows and billows. And just at that moment, the cut-glass ashtray caught the flame and cast whanged-out angles of light. At the base of the ashtray, the angles of light were the letters of a secret alphabet. Beyond the secret alphabet of light, the blue plate. Upon the blue plate, a mountain of chocolate chip cookies.

My God, chocolate chip cookies.

I was there sitting, watching things, I Spy a guy who'd had his hands for almost seventeen years, watching things go by, go by, on my second, on my third, on my fourth chocolate chip cookie. John and Paul and George and Ringo dressed up in shiny blue and red and gold. I just knew it, at any moment, marijuana was going to crack my world open, and the foreign alphabet would make sense, and finally I would be shiny too and free.

Just as I looked at Billie and her mom, from out of both of them the laughter came from inside and went up and out. Mother and daughter, the same smile, the same teeth, the same way they held their heads but differnt.

Such a weird sound, laughter.

The reason laughter sounds weird is because laughter *is* weird, man. I mean, can you tell me what laughter is?

Then inside me down deep, something inside that had to come up and out, and when it did, my weird sound coming out of me, laughter mixed up with Billie's and Mrs. Cody's, and all of us all of a sudden all sitting in this sound that we were all making from the inside, and we were looking one another in the eyes as we were making the sound. Three totally differnt people, as fate would have it, all sitting together around the green Serengeti Plain of Formica and a red flaming candle and a red-blue blood vase with exploding lilacs and the secret alphabet of light from the cut-glass ashtray, with John and Paul and George and Ringo, Mrs. Cody, Billie, and me in a kitchen in a house in Bannock County.

Born in a trunk in the Princess Theater in Pocatello, Idaho. Every one of us.

Which makes us laugh even harder.

The rest of the night, it's hard to remember. I mean, I can remember everything — I mean, I think I can — but the way of remembering is differnt. Usually when you think back, you think, Well, this happened and then this happened and then this happened. Things happened and then after they happened, you make sense of them. But that night with the marijuana, it wasn't this and then this and then this. It wasn't consecutive. The way I remember it, it all happened at once. You didn't have to wait for it to happen and be over for it to make sense. It was always just happening, and as it happened the sense of it was going on at the same time.

That's why we laughed so much. Because things were constantly making sense, and we didn't have to wait till they were over.

So as the night went on, that was the way it went, more tokes, more cigarettes, more beer. Talking and laughing, everything just going by and going by, making sense. Then all of a sudden, for some reason, Mrs. Cody wanted to be shiny like George, Paul, John, and Ringo. The next time I looked up it was Mrs. Cody in her old wedding dress. She was twirling and twirling to *Sergeant Pepper's*. It made perfect sense.

But that wedding dress, and what that wedding dress contained for me, I had no idea what I was in for.

At first Mrs. Cody's wedding dress was just another white dress. Silky and shiny and the sound silk makes. Twirling and twirling, shiny white, how white can be so many colors in the candlelight.

Then Billie tried the dress on. Billie's boobs, pushed up and out, looked like they were going to burst over the top of the dress, but she got the dress to fit. We were laughing, and Billie was twirling, and white was all the colors you could imagine, and everything was going just fine. Then "Lucy in the Sky with Diamonds" came on, and things started getting weird. Something about Billie in the wedding dress. Shit bunched up in my chest, and I felt like I was going to throw up or shit my pants.

Billie in a white wedding dress, like my sis in a white wedding dress, the way Billie's mother, my mother, was in her white wedding dress.

A simple shiny white dress and all it stood for. All the heartbreak it brought.

In a moment, how clearly I saw: the shiny white wedding dress was a prison, a way for women to make themselves cold and faraway and unhappy, and then, more than anything, above all, make you be the one who has to pay for their suffering.

In nothing flat, the world went away, and I was dizzy and alone with my breath coming fast and my heart beating loud in my ears.

Everything was making sense, but now it wasn't funny.

Be careful what you go after.

I wanted to go outside, get some air, breathe deep, run far away. But I didn't run. I sat. So still. Me on the chair with my fear.

After a while, an eternity, after more smokes, more beers, Billie took the dress off and laid the dress on the kitchen chair beside me.

The next thing I remember was I was in the bathroom.

You have to be careful in other people's bathrooms when you're stoned. There's all those things in a bathroom that have smells and stains in the sink and leaky toilets and shower curtains and bath soaps and creams and makeup and deodorant and medicine, but most of all the mirror is what you have to watch out for.

Don't look in the mirror. Just say, Hello, how are you, nice to see you, glad you're doing fine, then get the fuck out of there.

But that night I was looking for answers. The answer in the mirror.

Staring back at me was a spineless ass, a momma's boy. The guy with a yellow tulip up his ass who wasn't strong and sexy like Chuck diPietro.

In my hands, somehow in my hands, in one hand, the album cover. *Sergeant Pepper* and all the color, blue sky and famous people, dressed up fancy in hats and jewels and shiny dresses. Edgar Allan Poe, Tarzan, Marilyn Monroe, Marlon Brando, John in lime yellow, Ringo in pink, Paul in robin's-egg blue, George in red, everything bright and shiny.

In my other hand, the white, shiny, smooth wedding dress.

Something snapped. My black Converse tennis shoes and white socks and Levi's and T-shirt on the bathroom floor, my big pink feet and my big white hairy Idaho legs stepping inside something so soft and shiny, a bull stepping into a china shop. Then I pulled the dress up, tried to get the dress up above my nipples, but the dress would go only as far as my nipples. No way I could even think of zipping up the back.

The only way the dress stayed up was if I smashed my elbows into my sides.

In the mirror. My mother's steamer trunk. Scintillatingly gorgeous.

See how my son plays.

Differnt. I was differnt all right. Not a man the way most men were. I might as well cop to it. Fuck you and the stud horse you rode in on.

Either I had to change, or that dress had to change. One or the other. I figured it was the other. I was going to take that dress and change the meaning of the dress, break it out of its prison into something completely new.

Into the kitchen, when I jumped out in the shiny white wedding dress, Mrs. Cody, Billie, their blue eyes so open wide, like they were seeing one of the wonders of the fucking world.

Well, they were.

The Wizard of Oz going from black and white to color. I twirled in, shiny white, all the colors in the candlelight. John, Paul, George, Ringo, and Rigby John. Lovely Rita meter maid. He's leaving home. Bye-bye. I was scintillatingly gorgeous.

Billie and Mrs. Cody, my audience at their feet, yelling and screaming and whistling, jumping up and down and clapping their hands.

Liberation. It was a step. If only for one tiny stoned moment.

The way I looked in their eyes, I loved.

Bravo! Bravo!

As fate would have it, then in a moment, Mrs. Cody's blue eyes went dark, the way my mother's go from gold to green. And I could see, Mrs. Cody understood what I was doing. She saw the suffering in that dress. For me, and for her. And before I knew it, Mrs. Cody's hand was around the red candle and the red candle was flying through the air. The red candle hit me in the balls, a big splash of red wax all down the front of the white wedding dress, aimed at my crotch.

Mrs. Cody yelled: This dress ain't no virgin no more!

And there we were laughing again. That strange sound coming up from deep inside. So hard, all of us, laughing, even while I held my balls, laughing like laughing was a place you went off to, a place totally somewhere else, and all you could do was hold your sides and try and breathe.

And from out this place, something else.

The last song on *Sergeant Pepper's* was playing, "A Day in the Life," when the music gets real loud and it isn't music anymore but chaos, noise of a symphony gone haywire.

Mrs. Cody, the way she looked, might as well have been my own mom right then. Migrained, when it was too much and God the Father was settling into her skull. Mrs. Cody, out of the blue, like she was possessed or something, ran up to me and grabbed the dress by the bodice and ripped the dress down off me. She was still pulling, and I managed to step out of the dress. Then Mrs. Cody was screaming *fuck* and *shit* and was running out of the kitchen with the dress into the garage.

Billie and I didn't know what to do. We didn't figure on Mrs. Cody to be the one who freaked out. I quick pulled my pants on and my shirt.

In the garage, I pulled the gas can out of Mrs. Cody's hand just before the gasoline hit the dress.

It took us awhile, but me and Billie got Mrs. Cody settled down. Mrs. Cody kept saying she was sorry over and over, and that it wasn't me that made her angry, it was the dress. The fucking dress.

After Mrs. Cody went to bed, Billie put Simon and Garfunkel's *Bookends* on, and we cleaned up the house.

When everything was wiped down and put away and we'd scraped the red wax off the floor and everything was clean and the lights were back on and I had my shirt back on and my shoes and socks, I stood by the kitchen table and looked at things. Where had that other world with the flickering red candlelight and the green plains of Serengeti Formica and red-blue vases and exploding lilacs gone?

Billie laid the white wedding dress across the kitchen table. The white of the dress was so white in the bright light. The red stain at the crotch bright red.

At the front door, Billie looked tired. She took my chin in her hand and squished my cheeks together.

Rigby John Klusener, she said. There's no one like you.

In Billie's eyes. It was great to be inside there in Billie's eyes again.

I'm glad we're back together, I said.

Billie knew what I meant. Things had been weird since Chuck diPietro.

You know, Billie said, you don't have to worry. I don't want to marry you. That would ruin everything.

No doubt about it. This girl was psychic.

Our good-night kiss was two lips against two lips soft with a kind of suck, tobacco, and the taste of pink. Up in the sky was a place of endless dark. The same damn moon a slice of silver ball up there hanging in the firmament. Stars like you'd paint stars.

I closed the aluminum door.

The C not for *Cody,* but for *cunt.*

Women of weddings, lashed in shiny wedding white, blood of cunts, have mercy on us.

PART III

Thunderbird

8 A Day in the Life

I HAD NO IDEA the events of the summer of my seventeenth year would blow my ass clean out of Bannock County, three hundred miles out of Pocatello, and I'd be out here on Highway 93, alone with the moon, my thumb stuck out, a full feeling in my soul, and my heart broke. So much happened in a year, too much to comprehend. It's only just over a year ago Mom and I'd finished the novena for chrissakes. Then last summer, Flaco and Acho. Then Billie. Not to mention Sis's wedding fiasco and Dad's threat of divorce and Billie going off with Chuck diPietro.

Smoking marijuana.

That's a lot. And it was nothing compared to what was about to come my way.

In the meantime things had settled down. All the shit people had been feeling got stuffed back in the closet, and everyone, as usual, was going about his business as if nothing was up. I was fine with that.

The only thing I knew for sure was it was haying time again. And this summer, it was even more hay than last summer. And this summer, no Flaco and Acho. This summer, the actual haying part wasn't even going to be a family affair. Mom just flat-out said no. Sis was married and pregnant, and Dad always had some other damn business to do when it came to haying. So it was just going to be me and some hired man for both the haying and the hauling.

The first sign that things weren't going according to plan was Dad announced we wouldn't start haying on the Saturday, the day he'd planned. So I had a day off. Didn't know what to do with myself. Then Sunday off too.

Sunday night after supper, when I got the water changed up in the pasture, when I came back into the house, no one was sitting in the love seat in front of the TV waiting for *Bonanza*.

Mom and Dad were in their bedroom with the door closed. That'd never happened in the daytime before, or even early evening. Inside in their bedroom you could hear them talking, sometimes talking loud, but not yelling.

I thought perhaps it was more divorce.

When the *Bonanza* music started, Dad came out of the bedroom. He sat down on the love seat alone. Pretty soon Mom came out. She went into the kitchen, made Dad some tea, and brought the cup of tea in with her and sat down.

It was an episode where the Cartwrights were having troubles with the local Indians. We just sat there, staring at the TV, Dad stirring and drinking his tea. I tried to get a sideways glance at Mom, but she was on the other side of Dad, so I couldn't tell what was going on. Plus Mom was doing her disappearing act, and when she did her disappearing act, it was practically impossible to find her.

Only I could do it. But she and I had to be alone.

Mom was doing her disappearing act because Mom was dead set against hiring who Dad was hiring. And when Mom didn't get her way, one of the things she did was disappear.

That night there was no chance in hell finding Mom anywhere.

Later that night, as I was lying in my bed, Dad's footsteps started down the stairs. You could always tell Dad's footsteps. Dad's footsteps were like the scariest movie. Lead foot.

The turn of the doorknob. The feeling in my arms that means I'm helpless.

My bedroom door opened. Just Dad's silhouette in the doorway with the light on in the hallway behind him. You could see his legs sticking through his blue jammies.

The covers were up around my neck.

Dad's voice. Moses on the Mount. This is the law.

Tomorrow, Dad said, you will be baling hay with George Serano.

He's the only hired man around here I could find. He's promised me he won't be drinking, but you know about Indians. If you catch him drinking, you tell me. I won't stand for drinking. Hay crop or no hay crop.

Dad's legs looked like X-ray legs.

George is a strong buck, Dad said, so he'll be riding the slip.

My eyes stayed on Dad's ankles and knees, nothing up higher.

You drive the tractor, Dad said. I'm counting on you to get some good work out of him, you hear?

Bone silence in the night all around us in my bedroom. I waited to be sure Dad was done talking.

I said: George Serano?

That's right, Dad said, George Serano.

Dad turned and pulled the door back across the hall light. Then the door stopped.

Now for hell's sake, Dad said. We don't want no trouble like those Mexicans last year. We're differnt from those people. Don't go getting mixed up with 'em. Especially George Serano. Believe me, you don't want to know what that man's got going for him. You stay on the tractor, and he stays on the slip. If the baler breaks down, you fix it or come get me. Let him sit on his ass.

To each his own, you hear me?

Promise your mother you'll keep your distance.

You keep your distance, you hear?

Monday morning, Mom was bent over some bowl, hair flying, stirring up a storm. No mush or eggs this morning.

Pancakes.

Pancakes meant Mom was sorry I had to work with George Serano, but she couldn't do anything about it.

I put extra butter and syrup over the pancakes because I knew I could.

Outside, it was already bright. Across the yard, a tall, lanky man in a cowboy hat, Levi's, cowboy boots, and a bright white shirt leaned up against the baler. He lifted a cigarette to his lips, then let his hand fall to his side.

There he was, George Serano.

The battle had begun.

A dark and dreary night, the last time I'd seen this guy. We were in hospital gowns, rolling around in a dark hospital room, hammering on each other.

He was spouting off some shit about a Thunderbird.

The storm of '66.

The screen door slammed behind me. The slam bounced all over the yard. My boots were planted firm on the cement sidewalk. The morning sun was already hot. I pulled my cowboy hat down over my eyes. It was weird. For a while there, I couldn't move.

It's funny to look back on it now.

In his cowboy hat and cowboy boots and Levi's and a white shirt, leaning up against the green John Deere baler. Smoking one of his Camels. George Serano.

Across the yard, in my cowboy hat and cowboy boots and Levi's, my blue chambray shirt, on the cement sidewalk, keeping the sun out of my eyes. Me.

Him and me.

All we needed were the holsters and the six guns and the theme from *Bonanza,* and it would be a Sunday night.

My boots stepped off the sidewalk and started walking. Not toward *him,* toward the baler. I couldn't imagine walking up *to* him, but I had to walk, so it was to the baler I was walking.

The crazy Indian with the spacy eyes, his wild hair, and the weird way he talked, was what I expected.

That sunny Monday morning, though, there was nothing crazy about the man leaning against the baler. Something gentle about his face and the way he moved his hands.

The closer I got to him, the less I knew English.

I didn't shake his hand, didn't say hello. Perhaps on another day, I would have said to hell with Dad and been nice to George Serano, but you got to remember, this was the guy who stole my madras shirt and my wallet.

And my dirty shorts.

I was pissed. Really pissed. I mean, I was trying to be pissed. I never can be pissed at anybody for long.

George was tall and beautiful like Flaco, and when he said good morning, his voice was soft and polite, and he blew smoke out his nose. I wanted a smoke so bad.

When I passed between where he was standing and the tractor wheel to get up onto the tractor, I ducked my head, made some kind of grunt. I almost expected he'd hit me, and we'd start in hammering all over again out there in the broad daylight.

On the tractor seat, I didn't waste any time. I started the tractor up, a big puff of black smoke out of the muffler, the loud John Deere noise. I put the tractor in gear.

The tractor was driving along just fine when something touched me on the back. George was to the right of me, crouched on the tractor's wheel well, leaning up against the seat. It was his shoulder. His left shoulder against my back. And a familiar smell. The part of the to-mato that folds together red into the stem of green.

Both my hands white knuckles on the steering wheel.

George stuck his big hand out.

George Serano! George yelled in the tractor noise and the wind.

His other hand held onto his hat.

George's hand was like when you have a really good tan with smooth black hairs on the back. His white shirt had a western cut and pearl buttons. In his shirt pocket, showing through, a pack of Camels. A white T-shirt under his white shirt.

His dark deep-set eyes. He was smiling.

Full throttle on the tractor. I reached my right hand out, grabbed George's hand too hard.

A big Howdy Doody shake.

Klusener! I yelled back through the tractor noise and the wind at him.

The name's Klusener!

Day in and day out, every day, eight till noon, one till six, every day including Sunday, dry, hot sun and wind, no stopping for a water break, pee break, cigarette break, no breaks at all, eighty acres and two weeks straight, row after row after row, I worked George Serano hard.

If he needed to drink, if he needed to pee, he did it while the hay slip was going. I hardly looked back at him. Once, when I looked back, George was tipping his silver thermos of water up, water spilling dark onto his white shirt, his Adam's apple working. The other times, the cloud of dust so thick, he looked like a yellow dust ghost.

When the baler got to the end of the windrow, I didn't stop the tractor, didn't slow it down, just lifted the baler teeth, shut the power takeoff, and started turning the steering wheel, made the turn, then lined the baler up with the next windrow, dropped the baler teeth, started the power takeoff, and started in on another windrow.

No pause, no slowdown, no rest.

Me, I was getting a suntan.

One time at the end of the field as I was turning, I caught George peeing off the back of the slip. His back to me, the long stream of yellow coming out of him. I turned around quick.

Row after row after row, day after day.

Once in a while, I'd shear a flywheel pin, or I'd run out of twine, and we had to stop. I did just like Dad told me. Let George sit on his ass while I fixed the problem. I left the tractor running for the noise. The hardest part of a breakdown was George's cigarette. Whenever the baler broke down, while I was fixing the baler George sat on his ass on a bale of hay and smoked a cigarette. I would've killed for one of those cigarettes. I had my own cigarettes, but I never smoked in front of George, which means I didn't smoke at all during the day.

I know it's weird. I just didn't want him to know I had human emotions like cigarette smoking.

It wasn't just Dad. Something in me wanted to get even with the man who stole my stuff, and I wanted to punish him for not owning up to it. But even more than that. Punish him for being a drunk, for being a no-account, for being an Indian, for being a queer.

Every day when we quit at six, I unhitched the baler and drove the tractor to the house. George crouched down next to me on the wheel well. He didn't touch me with his arm or his shoulder while I drove.

At the house, we didn't say goodbye or good day or good night or fare thee well, motherfucker. Nothing. I shut the tractor off. He got off the tractor first. Then I got off. He started walking, and where to I didn't know. South. To the reservation.

I went the other way. I got in the pickup and drove up to the feedlot, where I could finally be alone with myself and the radio on and my cigarettes.

Cigarettes those days tasted good. Sitting in the pickup, I smoked two or three, sometimes four cigarettes in a row.

And that other thing that I do: those eighty acres and two weeks of baling with George, I never once whacked off and broke the sixth commandment.

I swear, a new record in modern history.

Sitting in the pickup, the radio on, sometimes even with my favorite song on and my cigarette and my time to feel good just for myself, there was nothing. I looked down at my crotch, and I'd wonder. It felt as if my whole body'd gone dead.

In the mirror in the bathroom before dinner, after washing my hands and arms and sticking my head under the faucet and scrubbing my face and ears and hair and toweling off my hair, the eighty acres and two weeks of baling with George Serano, I stood at the mirror, the water running into the sink. I didn't have my skin fungus this summer because I wasn't in the yellow dust all day. Up close at myself, I looked and looked into my almond-shaped hazel eyes, as if I was somebody I didn't know and I was there looking back at me, trying to find myself.

Mom and Dad and I at the kitchen table. The sign of the cross, the pot roast, the spuds, the gravy, the canned green peas and carrots. Fucking supper, man. You know all about fucking supper. Except now the questions: Is George doing his work? Is George sober? Is he drinking on the job? Are you keeping your distance?

Sleeping. Forgot how to sleep. No longer sleep and dreams and soft pillows and comfort in my bed. Only hot nights and lying in the dark staring at my bedroom ceiling plaster, no exotic beige paramecia for me, only flat olive green.

Not a breath of wind through my open windows. Outside the crickets and the frogs and nights so dark they festered stars.

Wednesday and Friday nights, those eighty acres and two weeks, I didn't tell Billie who I was working with. I knew there was a truth I wasn't telling her, but to save my life I didn't know what it was.

Plus those days, I didn't know what it was about Billie. Something about her was so beautiful, made it even more difficult to talk. One Friday night in particular parked in Mount Moriah, out the window, right behind Billie, was a huge Austrian Copper rose. The way she was sitting, it looked like tiny bright orange and yellow roses were spraying out her head. Those days, everything about Billie was like that rosebush. Her dark red hennaed hair shiny with hairspray. The gold loops in her ears. The slope of her neck. Her skin so milky white and beautiful there, you'd think she was a famous statue. Especially in the sunset light. And her lips too, full and soft and pink. That, and her eyes. No tear duct cancer lately. The blue of them the blue of a late afternoon sky.

I swear, that evening across the cab from me, Billie Cody was quite a picture. Looking back on it now, the way I was acting, I can see how Billie thought I was still angry with her. But I wasn't. All I knew was I was tired. Dead tired.

Billie didn't feel like talking much either, though. The more beautiful she got, the farther away she was. I just picked her up at her house, said hi to Mrs. Cody, got Cokes at the Snatch Out, then drove straight to Mount Moriah. One time, Billie and I fell asleep, my head on Billie's shoulder. So safe I felt up against her, her French smell. I woke us up because I was snoring.

For the life of me, I couldn't figure out why I was so tired. It was hay season all right, but this year I wasn't doing the hard work. George was doing the hard work. I was just driving the tractor.

Weird how you can't see what's right in front of your eyes.

I was fighting a battle. A battle for my life, really. And I didn't even know it.

Still fighting.

As fate would have it, the day we moved the baler onto the last forty acres was when it happened.

The last forty acres was land Dad was leasing from Filo Hess about two miles from the house.

That morning, at the breakfast table, same as ever, I was staring down two eggs and a bowl of mush.

Dad quit stirring his tea, put his teaspoon down on the oilcloth tablecloth.

I hadn't been screwing up, I'd been doing a good job with the baling, working hard, keeping my distance, making good time, so for a moment Dad let his Roosky eyes land on me.

You can pick up George on your way over to Hess's forty, Dad said. He'll be waiting on the road by his grandma's mailbox.

Two teaspoons of sugar, a splash of milk onto my mush.

His grandma? I said.

Grandma Queep, Dad said. Just beyond the Lattigs' place on Rio Vista.

That run-down old place off the road under the Lombardy poplars? I said.

You've been by there a hundred times, Dad said.

George Serano lives *there*? I said.

With his grandma, Dad said.

The old cabin just on the other side of the swimming hole? I said.

That's the place, Dad said. He'll be waiting.

The mailbox was old, rusted through, holes of buckshot. The red flag was down, and above the red flag in painted-on black letters: QUEEP ROUTE I NORTH BOX 86. I pulled the tractor and the baler off the road and looped into the entrance of the lane. I didn't pull into the lane because I'd have to back out of the lane, and I never could back the tractor up with the baler attached. Things always went haywire, and the tractor and the baler ended up cramped up together in some hellacious way God couldn't figure out.

On the road, across the road, up the road, down the road, walking down Grandma Queep's lane, under the Lattigs' elm trees, under the whole bright morning sun, no George Serano nowhere.

I shut the tractor off, sat there in the quiet on the tractor seat for a while. Figured it was a good time for a smoke, so I lit me a smoke. Half the cigarette gone, and still no George. I could just imagine Dad pulling up in his pickup, squealing brakes, the loud metal-to-metal pop of the door, Dad's dark Roosky Gypsy eyes, his wrist on his hips, hiking up his Levi's, yelling: The hay, the hay, the goddamn hay!

There was only one thing to do. I couldn't risk driving the tractor and the baler down Grandma Queep's lane because there might not be a place to turn around.

So I started walking.

During the past two weeks I hadn't said boo to George, hadn't even looked at him, and here I was walking up to his front door. What was I supposed to say? Good morning? I hope you're feeling well? Nice weather?

It was all too much to figure out, so I just kept walking, and since I was walking, I just said, What the hell, you might as well smell the roses.

Grandma Queep's lane wasn't graveled or paved. It was just two dirt tire tracks with a line of grass down the middle. Puddles of water in the low spots. The way my boots sounded on that kind of dirt was nice. On either side of the lane, a post every eight feet, and between each post, sagging strands of barbwire. High grass along the fence lines, in some places stands of tansy, clover here and there, differnt places some purple blooms of alfalfa, and yellow blooming chamomile. A couple low-growing Russian olives. Asparagus gone to seed. Bull thistles.

The cigarette was finished by the time I got close to the house. I threw the Viceroy down, stamped it out on the dusty ground.

The post there at the end of the lane had a sign on it. The sign painted on wood in black letters said: NO TRESPASSING.

On both sides of me, all around, the barbwire sagged between the posts following the Lombardys through the rectangle.

It's a good thing I didn't take the tractor. I would never have made it out of there. The yard was barely big enough for George's '49 Ford and a blue International pickup.

Inside in the rectangle yard it was dark and cool. Still a lot of shade even though the Lombardys were half-dead. Gusts of high Idaho wind shook the trees and the leaves. The sound was some great high-up sigh. On the ground and on top of things, the sun and the shadows spun around fast. Magic light and dark on everything. Everything covered in hallucination.

Straight ahead was an old gray, wood, slope-roofed barn, and then another shed, looked like a chicken coop. Chickens poking around in the yard. The house, if you could call it a house, was off to the right. There was a smaller tree in front of the house, an apple tree, or a pear tree maybe.

So quiet. Only the wind in the trees.

Grandma Queep's house was bigger than the Mexican house by half. Same old gray wood. When I got up closer, though, I could see the house wasn't a house; it was a log cabin. Stumps of old Lombardy trees for steps.

The screen door was painted dark green. I put my fingers through the door pull and pulled slow. The *Inner Sanctum* squeak. My fist was up, ready to knock. The wood grain of the gray front door in front of my eyes, a swirl of lifelines.

About that time, a dog started barking. A big dog.

Thank God the dog was inside.

Before my fist had a chance to knock on the gray wood swirls of the door, the door opened. Woodsmoke and coffee and frying grease were the smells. Buckskin. And something else, maybe peppermint or some kind of herb.

The woman who opened the door opened it only enough for her body to fit. Behind her the big dog's big, deep bark. Then, through her legs, the dog's nose was gray whiskers.

Shut up, Bonanza! she said.

Then to me: You're the Klusener boy. Come in.

The old yellow dog stopped barking. He turned around and limped over to the woodstove. A Majestic, green enamel. Next to the stove, an old smashed-out pillow covered with a blue and red Pendleton blanket covered in dog hair.

When the screen door slammed behind me is when I realized I was inside the house. Grandma Queep closed the big wood door. My breath. I was having trouble with my breath.

Grandma Queep was no more than four feet tall. Lots of gray-to-white hair braided in a big braid and rolled around in the back of her head in a bun. A red bandanna handkerchief tied around her head, but still strands of hair stuck up like cobwebs all around her face. Her skin was real smooth and leathery, and around her eyes thousands of tiny wrinkles. Two deep wrinkles in her forehead that dipped down between her eyes. Bushy white eyebrows, and underneath the eyebrows her red-rimmed eyes were dark and clear and looked at you the way a child looks at you, direct contact, her eyes and your soul, like there was nothing in between.

I crossed my arms over my heart.

You're lookin' for my grandson, she said. He ain't good for shit, that boy, but I love him.

Grandma Queep had no teeth. Her cheeks sunk in under her cheekbones. She turned her eyes across the room.

On the planked shiny wood floor, a large braided rug in front of an old trunk at the bottom end of a brass bed. Over the braided rug a step was a half-open door. Sunlight and shadows swirling around coming in through the door.

George! she yelled. Get your ass out of bed! The Klusener boy is here. You're late for work! It's a new day, son! A new day!

A thud in the next room. Grandma Queep looked up her dark eyes at me. You could feel the place inside you where they landed. Just below my breastbone in the middle. Her thick, dark lips lifted up on one side, a smile, her pink gums.

Firewater, she said. That's what you white folks think we call it, don't you? Firewater. Hell, it ain't no firewater he's been drinkin'.

The lifted lip was no longer a smile, it was a snarl.

It was a Wild Turkey, she said. And him and some other damn souse drank the whole bottle.

Coffee? she said to me. Her eyes.

It'll be awhile, she said.

No, thank you, ma'am, I said.

Name's Queep, she said, not *ma'am*. Call me anything, but don't call me ma'am. I ain't no madam. My name is Hazel Queep. You can call me Granny, or Grandma Queep. Won't answer to nothin' else.

Grandma Queep walked to the table, a round oak table with carved oak feet. On Granny's feet was a pair of Minnetonka moccasins, the kind you buy at J. C. Penney. A blue and green bird beaded on the top. On her legs were dark tea rose nylons rolled up midcalf.

She pulled out a wood chair with a high back.

Sit down, she said. Cream or sugar?

My legs and feet, two giant steps across the room. Beneath my steps, the solidness of the house.

Sugar, I said. Two teaspoons.

Granny reached down to the pieces of cut wood in front of the cookstove, picked up a piece, opened the door to the oven and slid the wood in, closed the door, then started moving things around on top of the stove.

In one room about twelve by twenty, from where I could see, besides the green enamel Majestic cookstove, was a small window with four panes above the sink. Curtains on the window, white cotton print with rickrack, the same cloth as Granny's dress. Then one of those old refrigerators with the motor on top. Looked like an alien had come down here and landed in an old Indian woman's house.

At the other end of the room, an armoire. Dark like the wood in Saint Joseph's Church. Below the armoire, the braided rug, then the door to George's room. A big trunk with a curved top like the armoire, a red, white, and green Pendleton folded over it. Then the brass bed, a big white quilt with the same kind of blue and green bird as the one on Granny's Minnetonka moccasins. That whole wall covered with photographs. The old-fashioned oval kind of photographs with strange-looking old people in suits and ties and white dresses in them. Another window with lace curtains. A Singer sewing machine, the treadle kind. A white doily across the top of the sewing machine stand. On the doily a kerosene lamp.

Out of the door of sunlight and shadows, George poked his head around the corner. He didn't look too good. Big purple circles under his eyes, hair all a mess. Black stubble beard. I thought Indians didn't have beards.

Morning, George said.

When I said morning back to George, I knew in my heart I'd never yet said morning to him.

George's eyes had a little bit of the storm of '66 in them. He wiped his mouth with his sleeve and stepped into the room.

I'll be right with you, George said. Just wait outside. I'll be right out.

What about his coffee? Granny said. I made him a cup of coffee.

That's when the other man, a tall white man in a cowboy hat, walked out of George's room. His belt buckle a huge piece of turquoise.

My breath in, my breath out. Things got real slow.

George's fist in the air, its shadow, came down, down, down, onto the table.

Bam.

The china sugar bowl, the silver salt and pepper, the silver butter dish, jumped up off the table a good inch.

Grandma Queep's eyes, her deep brown eternal eyes, not a blink.

The words out of George's mouth slow, long, loud, one word at a time.

He   can   drink   his   fucking   coffee   outside!

I was drinking my coffee outside, when Granny's swirled wood door burst open and the green screen door went flying back. George was about ten feet tall coming out the door. His boots hit the top stump, then the bottom stump.

The coffee burned my mouth, then I spilled my coffee.

George didn't look at me, just kept walking straight ahead down the lane. I didn't know what to do with the cup. When I looked over, Granny was standing in the door. She made a motion with her hand to put the cup on George's car fender. So I set the blue pewter cup down on the gray fender. Shadows and light, crazy hallucinations all over on everything.

Halfway down the lane, when I caught up to George and my stride matched his, I turned around, pulled my hat down over my eyes. There was Granny in the shadows and light, waving from her door. I waved back, then looked over at George, then wished I hadn't waved.

Hess's field was the last forty acres to bale, and a field so big it took up the entire fucking planet. Hot sun, blue sky, wind, and brown-looking rows of green hay row after row after row.

Besides being so big, the only other thing differnt about Hess's forty was in the top-end corner — a big old weeping willow tree in a low sloping patch of green pasture grass by the ditch.

No pause, no slowdown, no rest, I hit the field with the tractor in a fury, baling hay the way I'd been baling hay for the past two weeks. At the end of a windrow, I lifted up the baler teeth, shut off the power takeoff, turned the steering wheel around, lined up the baler teeth with the new windrow, dropped the teeth, turned on the power take-off, and started in on the new row. Back and forth, back and forth, one long, uninterrupted movement around and around, the baler just eating up hay. Yellow hanging dust.

All morning. Broke for lunch at noon.

At one o'clock, started back in all over again.

The day was a particularly hot day even for June. The sky wasn't blue, it wasn't a color at all, just bright. Low to the ground ahead of me, waves of heat were mirages on the hay. Puddles of water where there weren't none. My hands, my arms all the way up to my cutoff sleeves at the shoulder, dark, dark brown, almost black with red. The Snickers candy bar in the toolbox totally melted.

In the middle of a windrow, in the middle of the field, in the middle of the afternoon, I heard the scream.

At first, I didn't know what the hell. A sound, a horrible human sound. George getting chopped up into little pieces. Impaled by a spinning sprocket. Fan belt gone mad about his neck. His arms and legs mangled in the power takeoff. The hydraulic hose strangling him to death. The earth opening up. The heavens descending.

Whatever it was, it was my fault.

The universe has always conspired to fuck me up.

The scream got inside my head, in my breath, a huge fist squeezing on my heart. I was pulling on levers, pushing buttons, turning knobs. When everything was shut off, the scream was still inside me and outside me. I covered my ears and jumped from the tractor seat over the tractor wheel. My boots hit the ground running. I was past the baler, right up close to George. He was standing alone on the hay slip, his one hand holding on to the iron bar. He was bent over, looking down. George was screaming at the ground.

The storm of '66. I thought it was the storm of '66 again. George had the DTs. He'd been drinking last night, and now today he was crazy drunk again, and he had the DTs. Only this time, there was no doctors or nurses. Just me and George in the middle of a hay field.

Everything in me said, Run like hell.

Yet something weird, something I can't explain.

The sound coming out of George was a sound I'd never heard.

But it was a sound I understood.

My hand floated through the yellow dust and settled on his shoulder, the muscle under his shirt.

George? I said.

I'd never spoken his name in front of him before.

What looked up from under his cowboy hat, through the yellow dust, was dark, wet eyes. Like Granny's eyes now, full and deep with everything, nothing in between.

His lips shiny too and wet like his eyes. Wet eyes and wet, red lips under a thick mask of yellow dust.

A gust of wind blew around my ears. The world so quiet without the tractor and the baler.

The whites of George's eyes were red. Within the red, solid dark rounds. From out of the dark rounds, a light. Bright, sharp as the sun.

His lips, rubber lips like my lips when I was full of hate and tried to speak.

Why are you doing this to me? he said.

Why are you treating me this way?

More wind and quiet.

In no time at all, the bones of my body were hung all together wrong.

Of course, I had no idea what he was talking about.

And that's what I said. I said: What are you talking about?

George stepped back, let go of the iron bar. His body fell back against the stack of hay. Yellow dust flew up all around.

My head bone connected to my elbow bone, elbow bone connected to foot bone.

Guilt. I mean, I can see it now as guilt, guilt mixed with fear. Or fear mixed with guilt.

Back there on that day, though, I couldn't name it. Bones all haywire. A scared feeling in my chest. My heart beating fast. Breath I couldn't find.

You see that weeping willow over there? George said.

Yah, I said.

Well, you and I are going over there, George said. And we're going to sit under that tree. And we're going to have a drink of water. And we're going to take a rest.

In my mind, I could see it all. George and I loafing on the job. Dad driving up in his pickup, his Roosky eyes, him yelling and waving his hands.

Keep your distance.

Oh no, I said. We can't do that.

George reached up, took his cowboy hat off, beat his cowboy hat against his Levi's leg. Yellow dust floating up, swirls of yellow dust.

The hell we can't, George said.

George's black hair sticking up. The line across his forehead. Above the line, sweat and hair and cinnamon brown skin. Below the line, cakes of yellow dust, wet, red eyes, lips.

Come on, let's go! he said.

My feet couldn't move.

I can't, I said. My father.

George's hand undid the top button of his white shirt. Then with a hand on each side of his shirt, he grabbed each side and pulled. The pearl buttons snapped open all the way down the front. Yellow dust. On his white T-shirt, yellow, wet stains in his armpits. One long yellow wet stain down the middle to the top of his pants.

George's lips were no longer rubber. They knew they were talking, and they knew what to say. His eyes, the sharp bright light gone soft like his voice soft too, the way the first day in the yard leaning against the baler he said good morning.

Sure you can, he said. And fuck your father.

In the dark firmament of my haywire bones, something hard and brittle gave way.

Your father is a mean, dry drunk, George said, who hates niggers and injuns.

Through the yellow dust, across the hot, wavy air, I could see it coming.

George's open hand clapped down onto my shoulder.

Come on, George said. You can do better than that.

Through the hay stubble, over the mounds of windrows, I followed George. At the barbwire fence, George pushed his hands down the top strand of barbwire, swung one leg over the top, then the other.

George made a grunt and sat down on the grass next to a big weeping willow root.

I crossed over the barbwire fence same as George, stepped over the ditch. Already on my skin, I could feel the water in the ditch and the cool green grass in the shadow of the tree.

George unscrewed his silver thermos and then tipped the thermos up. His Adam's apple going, water coming out the sides of his mouth, George took a long drink, stopped drinking, burped, then lifted the thermos and started drinking again.

It took me awhile to find the right place to sit. I didn't want to sit too close to George, but then I didn't want to sit too far away either. I decided on a place a little over an arm's length away from George's knee. I had my thermos too. I poured the water out of my thermos into its red plastic cup.

George went on as if I wasn't there. He capped his thermos, burped again. About the time I sat down, he stood up, pulled his arms out of his white long-sleeve shirt, then shook out the shirt. Man, that yellow dust is nasty stuff. You don't realize how nasty it is until it's floating over you while you're sitting in the shade on soft green grass.

George let his shirt drop, tossed his cowboy hat on top of his shirt.

Then something I wasn't ready for at all.

In one long motion, George pulled his T-shirt up and off his stomach, the thin line of black hair there, up over his chest, the black hairs of his chest and around his nipples, up off his arms pointed up to the weeping willow. The underneath parts of him, the naked places people don't see — the black hair of his armpits, the paler undersides of the muscles of his arms — all of him, the top half, that is — right there in front of my eyes.

Heart stopping, that moment. Heart and somewhere else down low. A catch in my breath. The water in my red plastic cup I was tipping up and into my mouth went in my throat down the wrong pipe, went up my nose, went everywhere. I was coughing, holding on to my throat, making a spectacle, spitting water up all over myself.

The whole while I was coughing, though, inside me something was differnt. Differnt and new and perfectly still. Water and a big, cool shadow and green grass where usually there was only hot bright sun.

George wadded up his T-shirt in his hand, took his T-shirt with him as he walked. Just outside the line of shade, at the ditch, George knelt down, then lay down on his belly. He stuck his whole head in the water.

From where I sat, George's boots, his long Levi's legs and big, round butt, the shine of the sun off the smooth hard muscles of his back and shoulders. His head gone down into the ditch.

His head stayed in the ditch so long I began to worry. Then the splash and his big inhale of air.

Water dripped off his black hair down his shoulders and back.

Come on, now, George yelled over. He was waving his hand.

You try it, he said. It feels great.

There was nothing on earth I wanted to do more.

But you know me. Instead I sat there, holding on to my thermos for dear life.

No, I said. I'd better stay here.

My voice was high. I hated that my voice was high.

No, I'd better stay here, George said just like I'd said, the high whine of my voice.

Get your tight ass over here, he said. Jesus Christ, Klusener, you need to give it up. Relax! Have some fun!

Something I came to know about George. What George was saying and how he was saying it were often two differnt things. He could tell you to go fuck yourself, but sometimes the way he said it made you want to smile.

I was over at the ditch before I knew it, kneeling, then lying down an arm's length from George. The smell of mud and ditch water, moss, and the sun on George's skin.

The first time I lay next to him was in the hospital during the storm of '66.

This was the second time, by the ditch next to the weeping willow.

There would be more times lying next to George.

Take your T-shirt off first, he said. You can use your T-shirt like a towel.

My whiny voice wanted to say *no*.

I pulled my T-shirt off.

That moment, the way George looked at me, my arms, my chest and belly, my neck, my nipples, my naked skin, was my first time ever. All those years doing what I was not really doing, whacking off and breaking the sixth commandment — getting off only on my body getting off — all of it always internal, isolated, in my head. An imagination of sex that went on within that had nothing to do with the world.

That day, though, when George's black eyes landed on my flesh, it was the first time ever sex was outside. Sex was what I saw in George's eyes.

Everything differnt. Differnt and bright.

What always happened when I was half-naked never happened, though.

Instead, near my heart, a sharp pain. A pitchfork stuck in a bale of hay.

I shoved my head into the ditch.

The cool water all around my head, my eyes, my nose, my cheeks, my jaw, my forehead, water in my hair. Even on my lips I felt the water touch me. Bubbles in my ears.

I was doing fine, hanging out, no problem, everything was cool. No pain in my heart with my head in the ditch.

Then something happened people who have trouble with breath never want to happen.

George's flat, full hand was at the back of my head, pushing my head down.

The breath. There was no breath.

My head, my face, was pushed farther down, down into the water, into the mud.

My arms pressed hard against the earth, pushing against the hand at the back of my head.

Breath. The pain in my heart spread to all over in my chest. Down into my belly. Up over my shoulders. Down my arms.

Moments and moments and moments like forever.

Then George's hand slid away. The place on my head where his palm had been the outline of it in my mind. The splash, the rush of air, coughing. The air. Breathe the air.

On my hands and knees, I was still coughing, sputtering. My ears were trying to hear, I was trying to see, still trying to get my breath.

Serves you right, George said. You shouldn't ever trust somebody like that.

My lips, rubber lips. Tears stuck in my eyes. The pain in my chest, in my belly, up my shoulders, down my arms.

Was hate.

Finally I said: *You* did, I said. You trusted me.

My voice was way high.

I'm an *Indian,* George said. Didn't your old man ever tell you you can't trust injuns?

George was still lying across from me, leaning up on his elbow. I never once saw that man smile. His body just a leg's length away.

Spontaneous combustion. My leg and foot came up, and my boot heel landed square into the wet sod of George's nuts.

George doubled over. He was yelling loud.

All the times I'd hated and all the times I'd stopped the hate. All the people I'd hated, wished dead, plotted to kill. All the while the feeling in my forearms that meant I was helpless. Spineless ass, spineless ass, spineless ass.

Spineless, helpless, whiny.

It was too much.

I made my hand into a fist. I clenched the muscles of my forearm, my upper arm. I leaned in from the shoulder. Hit George a John Wayne punch from out of the movies. Square in the face.

I was up and running for the fence. Mid-ditch, midair, my jump stopped. George's hand was a hard grip around my leg. I went down fast, my knees and legs and boots, splashing into the ditch.

You little cocksucker, George yelled.

George's arm reached down and grabbed me around the middle. Just like that, I was up in the air on his shoulder, kicking and yelling.

My flailing arms got in one good smack to George's nose and a couple to his ears.

But early on it was clear. Despite the fight I put up during the storm of '66, as George flung me off his shoulder and onto the solid, solid ground that day under the weeping willow, it was clear. I was no match for George Serano.

No sooner had my back hit the green pasture grass than George Serano's body was smack down on mine. There went my breath again. George's hands were around my wrists above my head.

His face so close to my face, his black eyes, blood inside his nose, his sandpaper whiskers.

Tiny veins, little red lightnings in the whites of George's eyes. From out of the dark rounds, bright, sharp light.

Beyond his face, above, the wind a slow move through the willows.

You white, tight-assed little shit, George said. You think that you can work me all day out in the heat without a rest? What gives you the right to treat me like that?

Out of George's nose, a drop of blood, down to his lip. George's teeth, the red pink inside his mouth, his hot breath, tobacco and toothpaste so close to my face.

Mad dogs and Englishmen, George said. I'm not the fucking Englishman, am I?

George's thick black body hair against my chest and belly. His armpit hairs almost in my nose. The overwhelming smell of him, sweat I could taste, buckskin and flint in the back of my throat. The part of the tomato that folds together red into the stem of green.

Pinned down. Man, I hate being pinned down. It's as bad as losing your breath.

Breath. It was a miracle. Somehow my breath was back, and I was breathing.

Every breath I took, I hated George more.

I swear, if I'd had a gun, I'd have shot the son of a bitch.

The trouble was, I couldn't get to my hands.

Prick! I yelled.

Spit came out my mouth, flew through the air, and landed on his face.

You stole my wallet, I yelled. And my new madras shirt. And.

And and and. My mouth couldn't speak the other and.

For a second, the sharp bright light in George's eyes went soft. For a second, his grip on my wrists let off, and for a second there my hands were free. Then George had them pinned down again.

What wallet? George said. What the fuck you talking about? George said. What shirt?

George was just like Sis. How convenient. All of a sudden wasn't going to remember.

In Saint Anthony's Hospital, I yelled.

I wasn't yelling. I was screaming.

Your crazy drunk DTs, I screamed. And your bologna breath.

Just then, the way George's eyes were looking at me, I was the one who was nuts, not him. George pushed his shoulders up, pulled his neck and head back.

Bologna breath? George said. I do not have bologna breath.

I was still screaming.

Don't play dumb, I screamed. You were out of your mind. The thunder and lightning. Don't say you can't remember, I screamed. You were trying to kill me. I'd be dead right now if the nurses and the doctor hadn't given you a shot. Plumb nuts, crazy bastard! You were screaming and yelling, The wind is Thunderbird breathing, you said. Thunderbird can take any form, you said. Human, plant, animal. Thunderbird has no shape, you said, but he has four legs or two legs or a fin with hooves, and the hooves have claws.

George let go of my hands, pushed himself up away from me quick, up on his arms.

I was still screaming.

Thunderbird's wings cover the world, you said. His wings are clouds, the beating of his wings brings the thunder. Thunder is the sound from deep inside his throat, you said. Although he has no head, there's teeth in his beak, and the teeth are wolves' teeth. He has one eye, you said.

George was back up to standing. Crouching standing, backing away slow. The blood from his nose, down onto his chin. George wiped his face, and his hand came back blood. In his eyes the old storm of '66.

Screaming, I was still screaming.

Lightning comes from that eye, you said. He sees everything, you said. He flies through the sky, you said. Searching to cleanse the world of filth.

Filth was the word, the one single word, the smoldering word, for all the days and nights of hate I'd felt and never spoke.

George's boot caught on the big weeping willow root. He fell back on his ass.

I didn't miss a beat. I was a long leap up through the air landing right on top of him.

My legs straddled George's chest. My hands were slapping, slapping him across the face. Blood flying with every slap.

I was still screaming.

Then in the morning, I screamed, you were gone from the hospital and so was my wallet, my new madras shirt, and.

And and and and and, I screamed.

And.

And my pair of dirty undershorts!

The world quiet all around. The wind in the willow tree, Thunderbird breathing. Thunderbird, the water in the ditch. My back was flat on the grass. My chest so fast going up and down, up and down. Out of my eyes, beyond the weeping willow, all I could see was blue, one little bright cloud.

The sound coming out of George was a horrible human sound. The earth opening up. The heavens descending.

It was a sound I understood.

Inside first down deep, something inside that has to come up and out, and when it does, it is such a weird sound.

George was on his knees, holding his sides. His hands pounded the grass, his feet kicking. His whole body thrashed around, rolling across the ground. A high wail, snorts, sounds like only animals make.

I'd never seen anyone laugh so hard.

Laughter so hard it was all I could do not to laugh too.

It wasn't long at all, and no matter how hard I tried, there I was making sounds just like George. Inside me, the force up and out of me, I started twisting around, the earth opening up, the heavens descending, trying to make room for what was coming through me, the weird sounds coming out of me.

Weird thing, laughter.

I loved God so much right then.

That night while my parents watched TV, I called Billie. Billie and I hardly ever talked on the phone, so I didn't know what I was going to say. I just wanted to hear her voice. Mrs. Cody answered and told me

Billie'd gone out for Cokes with her girlfriends. Right off, Mrs. Cody lit a cigarette and started in talking, talking about one thing, then another, then about our marijuana night. Just when she got to the wedding dress, Dad came in the kitchen, turned on the light. The drut look. Sister Mary Cowface. He pointed to his watch. I told Mrs. Cody I had to hang up.

I snuck one of Dad's Viceroys and walked out the kitchen door. It was a big, hot Idaho night, crickets and frogs chirping and croaking. The sprinkler going razzle razzle on the front lawn. The only other sound was my boots on the rough gravel. Tramp came running up and poked his head in my crotch. He was so happy I came out he stood up on his hind legs and put his front legs on my arms. The two of us did a little jig, his pink bologna tongue hanging out. An endless source of amusement, that dog.

Into the night, past the machine shop and the granaries, out past the spud cellar. Darker and darker, like in the olden days, just Tramp and me and the yellow moon. Stars, hard bits of diamond light. A safe place. I was looking for just the right one.

The grain elevator poked up into the moonlight. When I stepped up onto the first flange, the moon shined on the slick bottom all the way to the top. Tramp made a low noise in his throat and lay down. A stairway to the stars, I kept walking up and up, the rattle of my boots on the flanges. Just past halfway, when the grain elevator began to tip, then farther out, when I hit perfect balance, I sat down careful and lit the cigarette.

That afternoon under the weeping willow, after the strange sound had come up and out of me and George, after laughing so hard like that, there was something else that happened with George. And since it happened, I didn't know what to do with myself.

The laughter had gone on so long and hard, it had to change. It was quiet under the weeping willow. Just the wind. I sat like an altar boy, an arm's length away from George, keeping my distance. I was worried any minute Dad would come driving up, yelling and waving his hands. Even worse I had my shirt off, and Dad didn't like me to take my shirt off. Especially since George's shirt was off too.

My right hand was on the green grass, a fist into the earth. For a moment, I closed my eyes. And in that moment George reached his big hand out and laid his hand on mine. I quick went to move my hand, but that's exactly what Dad would do. And because I'd laughed with the man and met his granny, I broke the rule. I did not keep my distance and I did not move my hand. Above us, the blue sky real blue, the long green wafts of willows, Thunderbird breathing.

What happened next, in my whole lifetime, there was nothing to prepare me for what happened next. It was a sound, a strange sound coming up and out of George, but this time the sound was not laughter.

Snot coming out his nose, big sobs like burps, George wept deep and hard and as long as he had laughed. The same way Dad cried at Russell's funeral. The way I'd cried when I found Russell's grave. But more. I'd never known someone to weep like that. His head bent all the way over his crossed legs, his face right up against the ground, his back muscles jerking, his big hand smashed on mine, George wept so hard, he was screaming at the ground.

The grain elevator bobbed up and down. I smashed the cigarette out on the bottom of my boot, stood up, and walked off the deep end of the descending staircase. When I stepped off, the grain elevator snapped right back up. A crash and bang that made Tramp jump.

In the safest place, in the hayloft of the barn, at the back end, the moon shining in silver onto the gold straw, I pulled the straw up all around me and Tramp. The barn was full of its spirits.

And something more. Something large and dark out in the night I didn't know. Thunderbird.

In my bedroom, both windows were open and not a sign of breeze. The sheets were hot and stuck to my legs. A train whistle off faraway.

I put my hand that George had touched, the back of it, against my nose and mouth. Smelled my hand, rubbed my knuckles across my lips. I wondered about George. Why was he crying? Did he know why he was crying, or was he like me, at Russell's grave, and he was surprised too: How he could carry pain around like that and not even know.

That first morning after the day under the weeping willow, George wasn't at the mailbox, so I walked up Granny's lane again. With each step of my boots on the powdery dirt, the closer and closer I got to George Serano, the faster my heart beat. I told myself to breathe and smell the roses. It was the same lane I'd walked the day before, but today I hardly recognized the place. The barbwire fence still sagged between the posts, the patch of tansy, the chamomile, the low-growing Russian olives, purple blossoms of alfalfa. Asparagus gone to seed. Bull thistle.

Into the shade of the Lombardys, magic light and dark on everything. Hallucinations on the ground, on George's '49 Ford, on the skin of my arms and all over on my body. Was like water walking into water, my body. The green screen door. Bonanza barking before I knocked.

As soon as Granny opened the door, there was the red bandanna tied around her head, the strands of hair like cobwebs around her face, her bushy eyebrows. Around her eyes, thousands of tiny wrinkles.

Her red-rimmed, deep brown eyes looked me up and down.

It was all in her eyes.

Her brown-rope hand reached out, grabbed my arm, let go, then grabbed my other arm.

Anything broke? she said.

Her fingers on my arms, slick as leather.

Broke. There I am in an old log cabin on the rez, deep inside the magic shadows of big old Lombardys, looking down at a four-foot Indian woman who was so old her face looked like lava rock. The only thing near me that had anything to do with the twentieth century, the single bare light bulb hanging down above the table. I am waiting for her grandson, a man who I'd twice had to defend my life against. A man who had stolen my wallet, my madras shirt, my dirty underwear, a man who had shoved my head down into the water and mud. A man who I had already laughed and cried with more than any other human being in my life so far, a man who when he came walking into the room might just make me fall over in some kind of conniption fit, and this old woman, Grandma Queep, her eyes as deep a wound as any broken heart, is beating her gums, asking me, Is anything broke?

Broke. Everything was broke. I was at that very moment breaking.

I'm fine, I said.

The two deep wrinkles in Granny's forehead that dipped down between her eyes got deeper.

Didn't expect you back, Granny said.

Bonanza raised his head up and let out a loud bark. On the shiny wood floor, Bonanza's old white paws were standing between Granny's Minnetonka moccasins and my old haying boots.

My arms were folded across my chest. I unfolded them. My mouth tried to say some kind of shit, gave up. I folded my arms over my chest again.

That was quite a snafu you had with my grandson, Granny said. He's got a black eye, and his face looks like he tangled with a porcupine.

Granny's dark, dark eyes, nothing in between.

You two got it in for each other, don't you?

That's when Bonanza poked his nose up into my crotch. Not just a nudge. More like a punch. I quick put my hand down there in front of me, stepped away.

My rubber lips. I swear, if I could breathe and move my lips the way I wanted, I'd be a fine human being.

Not anymore, I said. George and I are cool now, I said. No more hassles.

Granny walked over to the stove, started moving things around on the stove. Bonanza, his toenails little clicks on the shiny floor, made it to his Pendleton pillow and then fell over.

Surprised your daddy didn't can George's ass, Granny said. You want some coffee?

Then: George! she yelled. It's the Klusener boy. You're late for work! It's a new day, son! Brand-new!

A thud from the other room.

Another Wild Turkey? I said.

Grandma Queep turned. Her red-rimmed eyes, always her eyes, like they were full of tears.

No, Granny said. He's sober. Can't tell you why, though.

I didn't tell my father, I said. What happened yesterday was between George and me.

Granny took two quick steps across the shiny floor. Bonanza was up in no time, barking loud.

Granny stuck her face right up close to mine. She was moving her lips over where her teeth used to be. Her eyebrows, like one eyebrow all the way across her eyes.

Direct contact.

What did you say your name was? Granny said.

I haven't said yet, I said.

Well, say it then, she said.

Rigby John, I said, Rigby John Klusener.

In her deep brown eyes, ribs of gold.

Right, Granny said, I know the Klusener part. What I was looking for was the Rigby John.

Granny's eyes went off a little bit and looked at something else. Something inside.

Son! she said. You take milk with your coffee, don't you? Milk's good for your bones. My grandson will be right with you.

Then me and my big mouth. All of a sudden, words came out of me out in the world I wanted to swallow back up.

Is he alone?

For a moment there, I thought maybe I'd spoken soft enough so Granny couldn't hear.

But no such luck.

George! Granny yelled. Are you alone in there?!

Oh my God, my breath.

How many cowboys you got in there with you?!

Granny's thick, dark lips lifted up till her gums showed, big smile, pink gums all the way around.

Noises out of George's room. Drawers opened, closet doors banging.

No, Granny! George yelled out. It's just me and the tumbling tumbleweeds!

The rest of that day and the next day and the next, neither George nor I knew what to do with ourselves. Our eyes didn't know where to look. Our lips didn't know what to say. Neither one of us knew what the fuck. George's one eye was dark blue with a little green right under the eye, and his cheek was scratched and scratches on his forehead too.

Things are so much easier when you hate somebody.

At the ends of the field, I took the baler a lot slower when I turned around. I shut off the power takeoff, lifted the baler teeth, cut the gas, made the turn long and slow and always looked back at George to see if he was OK before I started in on a new windrow.

We stopped for breaks. A couple of times in the morning, and three or four times in the afternoon. But we didn't go back under the weeping willow. We stayed out in the field in the sun. Just long enough for George to drink some water and have a smoke.

We'd made such good time baling so far, my dad wasn't coming around.

It was tough during the breaks. The tractor was off and there was just the wind in our ears where there used to be a lot of noise. George sat on the slip on a bale of hay. I stayed on the tractor. The smell of his cigarette driving me nuts. It wasn't like we were ignoring each other like before. We were both real polite, saying things like: Did you get enough to drink? and, It sure is hot out here today, and, That last bunch of hay was full of quack grass.

On the fifth day, we finished up Hess's forty, and with Hess's forty finished so was the whole hay crop.

As fate would have it, the last bit of hay to go through the baler was at the top end of the field, just across the fence from the green pasture grass, the ditch, and the weeping willow.

When the last bale of hay came out of the baler, George lifted the hay bale above his head, pumped the bale up and down, then tossed the bale onto the pile of hay on the slip. I kept driving long enough for George to put the iron bar in the ground and unload the stack of hay. I shut the baler off, then the tractor.

I jumped up, stood both my haying boots on top of the yellow tractor seat, stuck both my arms into the air, and yelled as loud as I could yell: Far out! The fucking hay is done!

The sky wasn't blue it was so bright, and between my arms and my hands outstretched, one piece of cloud, a little brighter than the rest of the bright sky, moved east between my hands.

Then that quick, I felt stupid for standing up and yelling. The bones of my body were hung altogether wrong. There I was, a dumb kid, a showoff, making a spectacle of myself.

Plus I'd said that word.

My arms stayed stuck up in the air for a while. I was afraid to look down, afraid to look at George. What I expected to see was my father's Roosky eyes. Eyes that hated me and were ashamed.

Then what do you know. I hear a long, loud yell. More like a whoop than a yell. A sound like you hear the Indians make on television, and I look over at George, and just as I look, his arms go up in the air, then down onto the ground, and George is three perfect cartwheels around and around and around to the fence, and the last one he lands on his ass.

The fucking hay is fucking done! he yelled, then whooped a loud Indian whoop.

George with his ass in the hay stubble, his hat gone crooked, in that moment, a pain next to my heart, something like an arrow going through me.

I loved God so much right then.

Loved George.

Then George was over the fence, and I was off the tractor and over the fence, and George's hat was off, and his shirt, and his T-shirt was off, and he was lying his long body out along the grass, his head stuck in the ditch. The smell of mud and ditch water, moss, and the sun on George's skin. I came up on him from behind, put the flat of my hand against the back of his head, pushed his head down into the water.

Then it was water splashing all over, and George was up and on his feet, and he started in after me, and I ran to the weeping willow, and George was chasing me around and around the weeping willow tree, and I was laughing so hard I kept stumbling, but he couldn't catch me because I could run so fast.

When he did catch me, just like that, I was up in the air, on his shoulder again. I was kicking and yelling, but it was fun this time, and when I hit the solid, solid ground, it was not so solid.

George's body was smack on top of me. The hair of his chest and belly up against my T-shirt. My legs spread, my arms and hands pinned down above my head. Same place, same two people, same position, differnt day, differnt feeling altogether. Water from George's hair dripping in my face. George's breath, tobacco and toothpaste. From his body, his armpits, the smell on the back of my throat, flint and buckskin.

That moment.

The pain near my heart spread out all over inside my chest.

Breath was fast in and out of George. In his eyes, he was still chasing me around the willow tree. In his dark eyes, ribs of gold.

Above his head, Thunderbird was a long, slow breath through the willows.

Then everything stopped. His wrestling body stopped. His grip on my wrists stopped. His breath. George's eyes went soft like Jesus.

I wanted to close my eyes but didn't.

Perfectly still. George's eyes and my eyes, only the blue sky in between.

George sat back, turned around, crossed his legs like Buddha. I sat up too. After a while, I scooted my butt around so that I sat next to him, cross-legged too a little too close. My knee touched his knee. I pulled my knees up, put my arms around my knees.

George and I sat like that for a long time. We didn't look at each other, didn't talk. The wind in the willow tree was Thunderbird. All around our ears, breath through the willows, a sound like the tree knew everything about George and me and, like us, didn't know what the fuck, so all afternoon, all it did was sigh and sigh.

Sitting like that makes your butt sore, so I lifted up one cheek, then the other. My knee brushed up against George's knee again. George reached over and picked up his shirt. Out of his shirt pocket, he pulled out his pack of Camels. He tapped a cigarette out, put the cigarette in his mouth. The wind in the willow tree, another big sigh.

George took the cigarette out of his mouth, let the cigarette lie in his hand. With his palm open like that, the cigarette in his palm, George swung his hand around to me.

That cigarette was between my lips in no time. The butt was a little wet. What had been on George's lips was now on my lips.

George lit his own cigarette, then lit mine. There never had been a better cigarette, and there will never be.

How'd you know I smoked? I said.

The Viceroy butt you left in the lane that day, he said.

That's what makes Indians such good hunters. They notice shit like cracked twigs and cigarette butts. I thought maybe I'd say something about Indians being good hunters, but I didn't know how it would sound coming out of my mouth, so I said something I didn't have to worry about.

All this hay still has to be hauled in, you know? I said.

My voice wasn't high. My voice was clear, and it sounded the way I wanted it to sound.

That's ten days, maybe two more weeks of work, I said.

George's shoulder was inches from mine. My sunburned arm was so much darker than his skin.

George took a long drag on his cigarette. When he spoke, smoke came out his nose and mouth.

I don't know if I'm up for it, George said.

The wind in the willow tree was so loud right then, I needed to shout.

Don't you need the job? I said. Don't you need the money?

One good weekend, and that money's gone, George said.

I wasn't hugging my knees anymore, and my knees were starting to drop.

Before what I said next, I took a deep breath. Held it in. Made sure there was plenty of breath. Still, though, trying to coordinate my breath with my rubber lips, plus the cigarette, it took me awhile.

Finally, really soft and really, really slow, I said: Don't you ever want to stop drinking?

From the side, George looked totally differnt. His nose was bigger and had a hook. His lips lifted up on the side, like Granny's lips.

All the time, George said.

My cigarette was hot-boxed, I was smoking so hard.

Then why don't you? I said.

What's there to do then? George said.

You could save your money up, I said. Buy your own place.

George turned his head. In his black eyes, something sharp.

Settle down? George said. Raise a family?

George took another drag. He could French-inhale better than anybody I'd ever seen.

Besides, George said. I already have my own place.

My French inhale went up just one nostril.

Granny's place? I said.

Nope, George said.

George pounded his open palm on the pasture grass.

It's right here, he said.

You don't need to buy it to own it, George said. If you own yourself, you own the world.

My knees were slowly moving down and down. If my right knee went all the way down, it would rest on George's knee.

Another deep breath. A deep breath and another long, deep drag.

Really soft and really slow: How can you own yourself, I said, if you can't stay sober?

George laughed his chest up just one laugh.

That's the problem, George said. What to do while you wait?

Boredom is a bitch, he said.

Waiting for what? I said.

With his hand, George pushed the wet hair off his forehead, smoothed his hair. He leaned back on his elbows. Picked a piece of cheatgrass and put the grass in his mouth. George stayed leaning back like that. He chewed on the grass and looked out at the hay field, at puddles of water where there weren't none, as if what was in the hay field was what he was looking for.

I don't know how to say it, George said.

For Thunderbird? I said. You're waiting for Thunderbird.

Yah, George said. You could say that.

Another perfect French inhale.

More than likely it will take *some* kind of storm, George said.

You're waiting for a storm? I said.

George hacked up. His spit was dry, and he spit it out away from me. This time his laugh was hard and wasn't really a laugh.

Thunderbird's a Ford Motor product, George said. My cousin's got a pink one.

I tried to let it pass. I figured the whole Thunderbird thing was just not for me to know. I looked at the afternoon sky. The sky was going from only bright to blue. I looked at the hay field. The shadows from the tractor and the baler were long, dark spots on the ground. I knew it was best to keep my mouth shut, but there I went again.

Jeez, what's the big deal about this Thunderbird? I said. I only wanted to know.

Something slow the way George lifted the cigarette to his lips. That, plus the quick way he wanted to jump at me then. Any second, George's fist was going to come flying around, and my nose would be broke again. I was thinking how to block the punch, where I could run, maybe I could get up the willow tree.

George looked straight at me. His lips, rubber lips like my lips when I was full of hate and tried to speak.

Well, maybe there's some things you're not supposed to know, George said. The white man can't know everything. Let me keep of mine what's left.

White man.

I stubbed my Camel out into the pasture grass. The wind in the willow tree was another big sigh. My heart beating in my ears. I couldn't hear myself think. The breath, the breath, the breath.

What I said next, I don't know where it came from. Maybe Thunderbird made me do it, made me keep talking. Since the night of the storm of '66, I hadn't been able to stop thinking about that damn bird. Plus, you know what? My father, Scardino, all the men in the world you needed to tiptoe around. I was getting tired. The world is full of tough guys. Maybe I wasn't one of them, but twice now I'd fought back and came out of it alive.

White man, I said. My father is a white man. Not me, I said. I'm differnt.

Tiny veins little red lightnings in the whites of George's eyes. His lips pulled back against his teeth. Smoke was pouring out his mouth and nose.

Yah, different, George said. You're *different* all right, George said. And the little faggot ain't got a fucking clue.

In all of my time on this earth so far. That moment, I could feel every part of my body and how it was that every piece fit.

What pulled me together in one particular place so quick was George's spit.

Spit on my face. *Faggot* in my ears. The sharp pain all over in my chest.

Faggot like *fuck*. The first time you hear it, you know.

But you know me. I didn't know.

I just couldn't know yet.

I should have cried, let it out and cried and cried. But I didn't know George yet. Not like I know him now. So I just sat there, my arms wrapped around my legs. Quiet. The way you are when your breath is knocked out. So quiet you disappear.

A long time with nothing happening. A truck went by on Quinn Road. The water in the ditch. The sun pushing shadows out of the tractor and baler. The wind in the willow another big sigh.

George tapped another cigarette out of his pack. I expected the cigarette to go into his mouth, but there was his hand again, with the cigarette lying in his open palm.

I picked up the cigarette without touching George's hand. Let him light it.

It took awhile. George tried a couple times to speak. But he couldn't speak. Rubber lips. He knew what he had done.

George lit his cigarette. Three perfect French inhales, a long sigh like the wind in the willow tree, then something I didn't see coming.

George reached out his hand. His hand went all the way from him, all the way over to me.

I didn't move away, didn't flinch, just sat.

For a moment, George's hand, just two fingers, touched the top of my head. Then his fingers down slow behind my ear, to my neck, from my neck to my chest.

And then he pulled his hand away.

Don't you ever wonder who you are and what you're here to do? he said.

Yes. I wanted to say yes. But all I did was blow out smoke and move my head up and down.

Don't you wonder what all this is all about? George said.

George's eyes looked up and all around. The gold in them. His arms went out and made a big circle around him like a ballerina.

Don't you wonder about the mystery that is always around us and in us? George said.

Then: Yes, I said.

George pulled his feet up in close, put his arm around his legs.

A person can't do it alone, he said. He needs a vision. An intent in his life to fold his life around.

George's eyes, the sharp light gone soft like his voice soft too. His lips, thick and full and cinnamon red. Smoke coming out of them. Out his nose.

There's all kinds of ways, George said, to go about finding what your vision is. Some people go to sun dance, some to sweat lodges. Some go to the Four Square Baptist Church. Some people go to Mass. There's all kinds of ceremonies out there you can go and do. Even getting drunk is a way. At least by getting drunk you can feel what it's like to have the power touch you.

A long pull on his Camel, the sound of his breath as he pulled the smoke inside.

But booze is just another lie, George said. It makes things look like a vision, but it ain't.

My breath. A deep, deep inhale, all that smoke.

Then, slow, really, really slow, I said: Then why do you do it?

You do it, he said. Why do you do it?

For a moment there, no words came out.

It's fun, I said.

And it's not fun for me? he said.

It's differnt, I said.

You mean you're not a *drunk*? George said. Fuck you. I'll give you twenty years.

My thought right then was I'd love a beer. I'd love to smoke some weed with George.

George's hand was back up, coming at me again. This time his hand stopped. His Camel pointed at me little jabs.

You might say Thunderbird is God the Father, George said. Big Daddy. Zeus with his lightning bolt, or Moses's burning bush.

Thunderbird is the force in life that makes life alive, George said. The power of the storm is no different from the power that pushes up a blade of grass. It's all life. It's all what makes life alive.

George's Camel at me, little jabs.

Shoshone people believe this life force, George said. This power can touch you. When power touches you, you receive a vision. You don't have to go to the mountain. You don't have to go on a quest. You don't have to make a novena. You don't have to petition the Lord through prayer. Vision can happen to anyone anywhere, anytime. When you go home, your dog could walk up to you and talk to you, tell you what you need to know. Or a crow. Or a seagull. Or maybe the way this tree is talking to us, if we sit here long enough we will hear.

The wind in the willow tree, another big sigh.

George's Camel at me in little jabs.

All you have to do is wait, George said. Wait and smoke. For Shoshone people, smoking is praying. No matter what you are doing, no matter what is coming down, the secret is to keep smoking and never forget that you are waiting.

George's inhale was smoke like you've never seen traveling from a mouth up into a nose.

What I'm doing, George said, is waiting.

Just me and the tumbling tumbleweeds, George said.

I'm not baling hay. I'm not hauling hay. I'm not driving my car. I'm not getting drunk. I'm waiting for when the power is ready to touch me, George said. To give me the clue, the missing piece, to tell me what it is I'm supposed to do, or the way I'm supposed to be.

That night, the back of my hand against my nose and mouth, I rubbed my knuckles across my lips. My legs were tangled up in the bed sheet. Outside my open windows, Thunderbird was not breathing. Not one breath. Quiet, too, the way it was quiet after George had quit talking that afternoon. I'd taken my last drag on the cigarette just as George did too. Together in the same spot on the grass, we stubbed out our cigarettes. Our hands pushing the butts into the earth that way made them look like they were dancing.

The sky rich blue, the sun going low. No more puddles. Things leaning into themselves into the sun, long black shadows into the gold.

Quiet, like you've disappeared quiet.

The wind in the willow tree, a sigh. Deep and quick. The way you catch your breath. Before something happens. You can't do anything to stop.

9 Downtown

By THE END OF JUNE, everything about me was going haywire. I wasn't hungry. I couldn't sleep. Smoking cigarettes like I was a chimney. My thumbnail I'd bit down all the way to blood.

Nobody noticed anything differnt, though. Then Mom one day reached over and put her cool, rough, red farm hand on my forehead. Her almond-shaped hazel eyes, high-beamed headlights, looked right into mine.

Are you wearing a hat out in that heat? she asked.

Billie too, she did the exact same thing, put her hand on my forehead.

Rig, are you OK? she said. You're burning up.

I was burning up all right. Way up on the grain elevator, I knew I had to keep still and keep balanced, but this time when I finally stopped climbing and took a look around, I was dizzy. Real dizzy, but something in me wanted to keep going up, up into the sky and never come down.

But it don't work that way. Ask any Flying Wallenda. Never coming down ain't possible.

Out in the hay field, we were hauling, not baling hay, and baling hay George was always fifteen feet away in a cloud of yellow dust, and the tractor and baler were loud. Hauling hay, George's leg was right there next to the gearshift, and his arm on the back of the seat came almost to my shoulder. The only noise was the truck, and most of the time the truck wasn't running.

Out in the hay field, all that silence and propinquity to deal with, like to drive you nuts.

At the supper table, always Dad's questions. How far, how much, how many bales, how long before you finish? Mom's almond-shaped hazel eyes always looking for some nuance. Is George drinking? Is he keeping up his end of the job? Are you keeping your distance? How many days before we can lay him off?

Then there was Billie. Parked in Mount Moriah one evening, I finally managed to get it out my mouth that the guy I was baling hay with was George Serano, and by the way he was the Indian guy you saw me wrestle with in the hospital during the storm of '66.

Billie didn't bat an eye. She just said: As fate would have it.

Then: Does he still go on about that bird?

That was Thunderbird Billie was talking about, and knowing George he'd have a shit fit if I said anything about Thunderbird, so I just told Billie, no, that George didn't talk much about himself or his religion except for a couple of things. And of course then Billie wanted to know what those couple things were.

Well, I said, he's half-Italian. His mother's Italian and lives somewhere in Italy. His father's half-Shoshone, half-Apache, and is a Mormon and spends his time in Mexico. While he works, he hums a song. *Drifting along with the tumbling tumbleweeds.*

And something else about George, I said, is George don't live his life like us white people do.

Billie touched her gold chain and the Hand of Fatima around her throat. Her blue eyes opened up wide. Something far off in Billie's voice right then.

Us white people? Billie said.

He's not goal-oriented, I said. He's not into achieving anything. He's not working or making a living or planning for the future. He is waiting.

Billie reached in her Marlboro pack, pulled out a cigarette. She pushed in the cigarette lighter.

What's he waiting for?

Of all the things I could have said. What came out of my mouth right then, I had no idea.

For love, I said.

The cigarette lighter popped out.

Billie lit the cigarette, took a deep puff. She turned all the way around and looked at me in the eyes. Her blue eyes opened wider, and she seemed to take all of me in for a moment, and in that moment, I swear, Billie'd put two and two together and saw all the way into my dark heart. I tell you, this girl was psychic. Couldn't put anything past her.

Billie handed me the cigarette. I watched her face real close, for all the ways I could know her face. But Billie's face was just Billie's face, and she didn't say anything or let on in any way that she knew.

I was taking a long drag on the cigarette.

Smoking too is differnt, I said. Smoking isn't like smoking is to us. For George, smoking is praying.

Billie's voice Simone Signoret.

Then let's pray, Billie said.

So we prayed, Billie and I, smoking our cigarettes. Pretending we were Indians. Not out loud, but Billie in her head, me in mine. With my inhale, I prayed that Billie wouldn't ask me one more thing about George. With my exhale, I prayed that she'd ask me to tell her everything.

Like to drive you nuts. Sweltering summer. Hot days, hot nights. Still no sleep, or not much. No whacking off, still. Tension in my muscles like a wild animal ready to spring. Something in my belly too. Whenever I took a dump, it was shit spray. Then Mom asked me again if anything was wrong. I said no. But I looked my eyes away as fast as I could because Billie Cody might have been psychic, but my mother was the grandmother of all psychics. At least with anything that had to do with me.

Then the morning, a morning like any other morning, except it was my seventeenth birthday, breakfast was mush and a glass of milk and fried eggs. Only thing differnt was that Mom was somehow more deliberate as she put down the food in front of me. And that she kind of stayed hovering around as I broke the yolks. They were perfect. Dad was sitting in his chair smoking a Viceroy, drinking his tea with two sugars. He was reading the *Idaho Catholic Register*. Then for no reason, out of the blue, Dad shook the paper, folded it, and put the paper in his lap. He looked over to Mom and gave his tea a couple of stirs with his spoon.

It didn't take long to realize that Dad's Roosky Gypsy eyes had moved from Mom to me. Really, I can't tell you the times when Dad let his eyes light on me. When he was mad, maybe. He looked straight at me when he was mad. But this morning he was looking and looking, and he wasn't mad.

Dad cleared his throat before he spoke.

I just wanted to say, Dad said, you've been doing a good job handling Injun George.

Handling.

Fuck.

Thank you, I said.

Fuck.

In Granny's yard, magic light and dark on everything. Granny's green screen door made the *Inner Sanctum* squeak. The wood grain of the gray front door in front of my eyes, a swirl of lifelines. Bonanza barking before I knocked.

Granny opened the door. Woodsmoke and coffee and frying grease. Buckskin, something else, maybe peppermint, something sharp, Granny's red handkerchief. Strands of white hair stuck up like cobwebs all around her face. Her red-rimmed eyes so bright always, like they were crying. Nothing in between.

Rigby John, Granny said. You look like hell.

Shut up, Bonanza! she said.

Bonanza, his toenails little clicks on the shiny floor, made it to the Pendleton pillow and then fell over.

Granny's old brown-rope hand pointed over at the table, then pulled out the wood chair with the high back.

Here, she said, sit down. You want some coffee?

No thanks, I said.

When I sat down in the chair, Granny's eyes and my eyes were at the same level. Her red-rimmed eyes were looking at me, nothing in between.

Something happened to you this morning, she said.

Sweat from my forehead dripped down into my eyes. I wiped my face on my sleeve.

It's my birthday, I said. I'm seventeen.

Seventeen makes you sweat and turn your skin green? Granny said.

My hands were shaking, so I put my hands in my armpits. Sweat rolling down my armpits.

I'm all right, I said. I just ate something bad.

What was it? Granny said. Dog shit?

Direct contact. All there was in the world right then was Granny's eyes and my eyes.

*Horse*shit, I said. I ate some horseshit.

Granny's pink gums all the way around. That smile of hers was so big, her whole face collapsed into it.

George! Granny yelled.

Granny had to stop and get her breath, she was laughing so hard.

Rigby John is here! she yelled. He's green as a toad!

He's been eating horseshit! she yelled.

That really cracked Granny up. She was holding her stomach, making all those weird sounds you do when you laugh.

It's his birthday! she yelled. He's seventeen! You're late for work! It's a new day, son! Brand-new!

A thud in the next room.

Granny smacked her lips together, sucked her lips in over where she didn't have any teeth, took a deep breath.

He's alone, Granny said. And he's sober.

Don't ask me why, she said.

Granny's one eye gave me a big wink.

Happy birthday, she said. Many happy returns.

The brown-rope palm of her hand pressed against my forehead.

Granny's eyes, tears in them, like she was always going to cry.

Now and then, she said. We all have to eat shit, she said. Just don't go making it a habit.

Granny's hand was cool and slick like a crooked tree branch across my eyes.

Just so happens, Granny said, I've got a special remedy for horseshit. Just give me a minute.

That's about the time George stepped out his door. Even with a hangover, George Serano was a beautiful man. But without one, he was dangerous.

Granny's special remedy was a tea that tasted like mud and sticks. But I drank the whole cup. And I took my time. There was nothing better than sitting at Granny's table, under the 'lectric light with George and his coffee, the log house cool all around me.

Like in *The Wizard of Oz* when the black and white turns to color. Ain't no place like home.

At the supper table that night, I just wanted to eat the damn supper, then get my ass out of there. Billie had something special planned for my birthday, and I couldn't wait to see her. At Granny's house this morning drinking mud tea, knee to knee to knee with George and Granny, is when I finally knew it in my bones. It was time. High time to tell Billie the truth about George. The trouble was, I still didn't exactly know what was true.

Dad was just as usual sitting at the table with his legs crossed, stirring his cup of tea, reading the *Idaho State Journal*. But Mom was a bit differnt again. She had her hair fluffed out and her eyebrows were on and she was wearing her new shade of lipstick, Red Cherries. Her big plastic glasses were on the table next to the butter dish. When I looked into Mom's almond-shaped hazel eyes, her eyes weren't tired-looking. And she was smiling. Usually Mom smiling meant the world to me, but that evening Mom's smile was wasted on me.

I sat down in my chair same way as I always did. When I looked up, I couldn't believe my eyes. Mom was carrying a plate with a rib-eye steak on it and fresh creamed new peas and potatoes. My favorite food next to hamburgers.

Even Dad was smiling.

It was strange.

For dessert, a yellow cake with chocolate frosting and vanilla ice cream.

There was a birthday candle on top of the cake, and Mom started out singing the "Happy Birthday" song in the right key. Dad joined in with his high, squeaky voice. When they finished singing, I blew out the candle.

My wish right then was I was out of there and next to Billie and telling the truth like we'd always promised.

Mom sat down in her chair and folded her hands on the oilcloth tablecloth. She put her big plastic glasses on and looked over at Dad. Mom unfolded her hands, folded them. The way they were rough. Lots of little wrinkles. The cut-to-the-quick fingernails.

Dad and I wanted to do something a little special for you today, Mom said. Just the three of us.

Mom pushed her glasses up on to her nose. She was looking at Dad again. Like they had this all practiced.

Dad made a sound in his throat, let the newspaper drop. Then his eyes again. As he spoke, his dark Roosky eyes stayed right on me.

You done a real good job in the hay this year, Dad said. You got that hay baled in record time.

Dad looked away quick, shook his paper up, started in to reading again.

My breath. No breath.

Mom stayed sitting. She leaned in farther on her elbows.

Dad, she said.

Dad didn't look over. He stayed looking at the paper.

Mom's big plastic glasses were pointed right at him. She leaned in more.

Dad shook the paper again. He didn't look up.

You had a good day of hauling today too. How many loads you get?

Seven, I said.

Mom took a deep breath, leaned in more. Her rough, red farm hand on the oilcloth tablecloth inching toward Dad.

Dad let the paper fall onto the blue and white tiles of the floor.

Dad rumbled in his throat some more.

Then: This morning I told you about George. What a good job you're doing. But I didn't say all I wanted to say.

Sunlight coming in the window. Onto the kitchen table, on the yellow plastic and chrome chairs, onto Dad's newspaper on the blue and white squares of tile on the floor.

In my life, same as ever. On my right was my father in his Levi's shirt and his Levi's and leather belt with the silver buckle and his cowboy boots. His smashed-down black hair the way his cowboy hat fit. His dark Roosky Gypsy eyes. The smell of him, Lava soap, horse sweat, and sauerkraut.

Same as ever, on my left was my mother. Her hair fluffed out, her Red Cherries lipstick, eyebrows each a perfect swoop. Her big plastic glasses. Her shiny, red, rough, wrinkled, farm hands. Cut-to-the-quick fingernails. Her cotton-print rummage-sale blouse. Her denims. Her white Keds. Her new perfume.

Above the table, the bright light that pulled down. My two hands, the same two hands I'd had for seventeen years, palms down on the tabletop.

Then the air cracked a little bit. A crack like in cement, ants crawling in and out.

Dad said: You've been a good son to me, and I'm proud of you.

The crack was inside me now. And the ants.

Fuck.

Mom pushed off her elbows, sat up straight, took a breath. She pushed the cake plate toward me.

Her almond-shaped hazel eyes.

Happy birthday, Mom said. Have as many pieces as you want.

The Snatch Out was hopping. The end of June, a warm summer Saturday night, everybody was there. The double line of parked cars parked in the Snatch Out went all the way to Ashby Street. I gave Billie the Cokes, put the pickup into first gear, eased up on the clutch, and turned the pickup down the middle of the two lines of cars.

I never did like driving through the Snatch Out. Everybody was looking at you, and you had to pretend everybody wasn't looking at you. Made you feel like everything was wrong about you, everybody looking at you like that. Dad's old beat-up '63 Apache pickup, the banged-in door, the dirty windshield, hay leaves and dust sifting out whenever you hit a bump.

Still I had to do it, though.

I stayed in first gear down through the line of cars, the pickup idling a slow roll, the tires cracking on the gravel. Shiny car after shiny car on the right. Shiny car after shiny car on the left.

I couldn't wait to get out of there, couldn't wait to get to Ashby Street, where, like always, Billie and I turned left, not right, and Billie and I would start yelling, Screw you! at the cars in the Snatch Out as we hightailed it over to Mount Moriah. Couldn't wait to get close to Billie so I could hold her and tell her what that true thing in my heart was I wasn't saying.

But that evening was going to be differnt than I'd planned.

Differnt as things could get. I got nowhere near the truth.

On second thought, I got my nose rubbed in it.

One step too far on the grain elevator, and my face was in the dirt.

Halfway down the line of cars, Billie saw an empty parking space.

Rig! Billie said. Park in there!

I looked at Billie like she'd gone plumb crazy.

I want to go to Mount Moriah, I said.

Just give me a minute, Rig, Billie said. I got something I need to do.

Executing a three-point turn into in between two shiny cars isn't easy. Especially with a Coke in your hand, especially with everybody watching. Especially in the Snatch Out. I gave the Coke to Billie, put in the clutch, put it into reverse. I told myself to just think of it as backing up between two stacks of hay. I was doing fine, everything was fine, and then the horns started honking. On the left was a blue and white '58 Chevy, on the right was a root-beer brown '57 Pontiac. Both of them were honking.

It's all right on this side, Billie said. You've got plenty of room, she said. They're just flipping you shit, she said. You're doing fine.

I eased the pickup into the parking place, my front end lined up with the Chevy and the Pontiac. I shut the pickup off.

Cheers and clapping from inside the Pontiac.

Smooth move, Ex-Lax! someone yelled.

Billie rolled up her window.

On my side, in the '58 Chevy, two seniors from Pocatello High. As far as I knew, nice guys, into hot rods.

Billie handed me my Coke. Before I could say anything, Billie stuck a cigarette in my mouth, lit it, then lit hers.

Billie's cigarette was a circus. A Ferris wheel, then the Tilt-A-Whirl.

Rig, Billie said. Look, I know this place freaks you out, but just listen to me for a minute. Just a minute!

Something about Billie was differnt. Her hair was differnt. It was still ratted, only it was parted down the middle with a pigtail on each side. She was wearing a fuzzy pink sweater with pearls on it. It was loose knit, the sweater, and you could kind of see her bra underneath. She was wearing hip-huggers, bell-bottoms, something I'd never seen her wear before. You could see her bellybutton. A new small pink satin purse with a gold clasp. Her earrings were hippie earrings, Indian beadwork in the shape of a bird. Every time she moved her head, those birds flying, flying. No blue eye shadow. The only thing the same was the pink lipstick, her Midnight in Helsinki nail polish, and her white-strapped sandals.

Me, I was no differnt. Same old Levi's, my chambray shirt, my black Converse tennis shoes. All of them clean.

Billie took a sip of her vanilla Ironport Coke with lots of crushed ice. Chewed on the ice. Through the window, behind Billie, in the root-beer brown Pontiac, two girls from Highland High.

In her best Simone Signoret: Rig.

It's your birthday, Rig.

Billie's sip on the Coke, the crunch of the ice on her teeth.

There was something about Billie's eyes. Maybe it was the no blue eye shadow. Simone Signoret: And it's Saturday night, and you can do whatever you want, Billie said.

Something rolled over in my stomach.

I laughed my chest up a quick laugh.

What do you have in mind? I said.

Billie's cigarette, spurt spurt spurt, then razzle razzle razzle, back to spurt again. Billie's eyes opened wider, and she seemed to take in all of me for a moment, and in that moment while she was taking me all in, she was thinking of just the right way to say what she had to say.

Tonight's my treat, Billie said. Let's do something completely different!

Like sit in the Snatch Out? I said. Come on, let's go. I want to talk.

Billie lowered her eyes to her shiny pink satin purse with a gold clasp. Billie's little fingers, her Midnight in Helsinki blue fingernails. Inside in there in her purse, a plastic bag.

Billie lifted out the plastic bag.

In the plastic bag were six joints rolled fat.

Really different! Billie said.

That quick I had no breath, just cigarette smoke inside me. My heart banging in my chest, in my ears.

I quick grabbed Billie's hand and pushed Billie's hand back down into her purse.

What are you doing?!

I was whispering, but I was yelling too and I was coughing.

I quick looked over at the two guys in the '58 Chevy. They were cool. Then on past them, up the line of cars. Across the Snatch Out, the line of shiny cars in front of us all the way from Pole Line

Road to Ashby. Then over to Billie's side, at the root-beer '57 Pontiac and the two Highland High girls. On down the line of cars past them.

When my eyes got back to Billie, in Billie's blue eyes it was Midnight in Helsinki.

When I got a breath between coughs, I said: What the hell are you doing with *joints* in your purse!

Billie's cigarette was in her mouth. When her lips moved, the cigarette went up and down.

Oh, don't have a *cow!* Billie said. It's just a couple of joints.

We're going to smoke six joints? I said.

No, silly, Billie said. I'm going to *sell* them.

Sell them? I said. Are you crazy? What if there's a narc?

Billie's eyelids went halfway down over her eyes. Whenever her eyelids did that, Billie started acting like my sis or my mom.

Billie's cigarette was a windshield wiper, then a straight dive to the ashtray. She leaned over, kissed me a quick peck on the cheek.

It's your Catholic sense of doom again, Billie said.

There's no narcs, Billie said. What I'm doing is completely safe. What time is it? Billie said.

Billie's fingers were back into her pink satin purse again. She moved the plastic bag aside, reached in, and pulled out a man's wristwatch.

Eight o'clock, Billie said. On the nose. Any second, it's going to start happening.

Start happening? I said.

Billie's hand reached up to the rearview mirror. She pulled the mirror around and looked in the mirror. Out of her pink satin purse came her gold lipstick tube. Billie pulled the tube open. That little pop of air. As she turned the bottom of the tube, the pink lipstick rolled up and out and was on Billie's top lip in the middle. One pink swipe down her lip on the right. Then the lipstick was up top on the left, the pink swipe down the left side. Then across the bottom lip, starting from the left corner, the pink lipstick tube stayed in place as Billie moved her bottom lip across.

Just act like everything is perfectly normal, Billie said.

The she rolled her lips against each other like after putting on lipstick.

Billie put the lipstick back into her purse, pulled the plastic bag out, folded the bag, put the bag in my shirt pocket. She patted her hand on my shirt pocket three times.

Who was this girl?

Billie gave me a big smile. A smile like I was the only boy in the whole world.

Just reach in and pull one out when I tell you to, Billie said.

Relax, Billie said.

This is *different*, Billie said.

Happy birthday, Billie said.

It wasn't long, and the two girls from the '57 root-beer brown Pontiac got out of their car. One of them, the one with bleached-blond hair with a flip, knocked on Billie's window. Billie rolled down the window.

Come in and sit, Billie said.

Billie scooched over, and the two girls slid into the pickup. The girls and Billie were talking a mile a minute. I didn't get what they were talking about, so I just watched the shiny cars pass by. After a while, Billie looked over at me. That same smile, like I was the only boy in the whole world.

Cheryl, Karen, Billie said. This is Rigby John.

Both the girls were real cute. Probably really popular. The way they smiled was nice but you could tell they were checking me out. Cheryl and Karen both said, Hi, Rigby John, together, and the way they said my name, they sounded like they were singing, so they started laughing.

Then they were off again, the way girls do, talking, talking. So comfortable with each other. Their long hair and their perfume smells and sitting close, touching each other.

Sometimes, I think I could watch girls all day. Not in a bad way, like looking to screw them or something. Just looking. How their hair is, how they smell. Jewelry on them, how bracelets fall down their arm, or an earring catches the light. The way they start moving when they get around you because you're not like them.

Then Cheryl said something about the Senior Summer All Night Party. They all talked and talked some more, but it wasn't long, and Billie and Cheryl and Karen were all looking at me again.

Billie laughed that laugh of hers that started in her chest, then moved her whole body.

So, Rig, Billie said. You want to go to the Senior Summer All Night Party with me?

A flash of heat in my cheeks. It took me awhile to speak. You know, the breathing thing. Which was weird because I think it made me look cool, the way I was silent. But underneath I wasn't cool. My mother. I knew my mother wouldn't let me go to an all-night party.

Sure, I said.

More talking and laughing. Cheryl flipped her hair. Karen touched the peace symbol that hung from a piece of leather around her throat. Billie got out the cigarettes, passed the cigarettes around, and we all took a cigarette. I lit a match, and there was the joke about three on a match and there we were four, all of us crammed in the pickup. On the radio, the Box Tops were singing "The Letter." Outside the windshield, headlights and exhaust fumes, an endless parade of kids in their cars.

So, do you have the stuff? Karen asked.

How much is it? Cheryl said.

Billie patted her hand on my shirt pocket.

Two dollars, Billie said.

Two dollars for one joint? Cheryl said. Or two dollars for two joints?

Two dollars for one joint, Billie said.

That's cool, Karen said. We each want a joint.

Here's four dollars, Cheryl said.

Billie looked at me, her eyelids down halfway. I reached into my shirt pocket, pulled out the plastic sack, unrolled the plastic sack. My fingers weren't shaking. I pulled out two joints and handed one joint to Cheryl, one joint to Karen.

That moment, handing out the joints like that, the way Cheryl and Karen were looking at me, something stirred in my balls.

Billie saw it too. In my face, Billie saw what was happening in my balls.

There were three more girls that night. Two together at once, then another one alone fifteen minutes later. I don't remember their names, and they didn't come in and sit with us and smoke like Cheryl and Karen. Billie knew all three of them. Seemed like Billie had a lot of close friends. They all stood outside Billie's window, and Billie talked to them for a while and then Billie patted my shirt pocket and her eyelids went down halfway, and I reached in my pocket and pulled out the joint and handed the joint to Billie and then Billie handed the joint to the girl.

The three girls were all real differnt. One was tall with short black hair. One was heavyset with braces with a stick-on red star on her forehead, and one was a black girl with an afro who Billie kissed on the cheek. Three differnt girls, but each girl, it was the same way. When they saw me go into my pocket for the joint, they looked at me like I was the coolest guy they'd ever seen.

Billie opened her pink satin purse with the gold clasp. In her purse was the man's watch, her lipstick, and ten one-dollar bills. Billie took the bills out, fanned the ten dollars out in her hands.

Yummy! Billie said.

Then: Here, Billie said. Put this money in your wallet.

The ten one-dollar bills in my wallet with the couple I had looked like a million.

There's one joint left, I said.

And with that I started the pickup, put the clutch in, put it into first. As Billie and I were driving out of the Snatch Out, two cars honked their horns and waved. Just as we pulled up to Ashby, out of the '57 root-beer Pontiac, Cheryl and Karen yelled: Wooo! Right on! Billie and Rigby John!

Instead of turning right, Billie and I turned left.

On the radio, the Buffalo Springfield was singing "For What It's Worth."

Billie had that smile on. I was the only boy in the world.

I shifted real smooth from first into second.

Happy birthday, Rig, Billie said.

Let's paint the town red! I said.

Let's paint it pink, Billie said.

The rest of that night was something like a circus ride, something like a dream. Billie and I smoked our joint parked in Buddy's Pizza's parking lot. I was scared at first smoking out in the open like that, but

Billie wasn't, so I figured if Billie wasn't scared, I wasn't going to be scared. Plus, I kept thinking of how all those girls had looked at me that night. The guy with a pocketful of joints.

The grass hit us fast, and my head was spinning, but I felt clear and strong.

Out of Billie's pink satin purse came another surprise. My birthday present. Billie had made me and her plastic laminated fake IDs.

My kiss to Billie was two lips against two lips soft with a kind of suck, tobacco, and the taste of pink. Billie fit in just right under my arm.

I'd never felt so close to her as I did that night. Something in me was differnt, I don't know what, but I felt I was all brand-new. I'd completely forgot all about George Serano, and the truth I needed to tell Billie. At that point I couldn't even remember what it was I was going to say.

We put our cigarettes out, and then the loud metal-to-metal pop of the driver's door, and Billie and I were out in the warm night and high, right in the middle of Saturday night. The wind blew from the west, and the wind was warm, and the way the wind hit our faces, we were invincible.

Hand in hand down East Fifth Street, Billie and I walked to the corner of Fifth and East Center. The other side of the tracks. The *other* side of Pocatello. Where the old Pocatello House used to be. Black people. Indian people. Mexican people. Neon lights and all kinds of people on the streets everywhere. The world so strange and new, especially while we stood waiting for the light to change. I wondered if we might see Flaco and Acho. It was like Billie and I were in a big town like San Francisco or something.

There was a line to get in the Blind Lemon.

Billie and I held on tight to each other's hands. Just before we got to the bouncer, Billie pulled out her pink satin purse with the gold clasp and pulled out a cigarette. I lit the cigarette. Billie took a couple puffs, handed the cigarette to me. Our fingers touched.

Praying, Billie said.

Smoking is praying, she said.

The bouncer was a college guy in khaki pants and a white oxford button-down. His glasses were horn-rimmed and he had a crewcut. He looked like one of the Kingston Trio or one of the Brothers Four.

He was sitting on a high stool behind a podium. There was a lamp on the podium. Bugs in the light of the lamp. A frat ring with a blue stone on his finger.

The door to the Blind Lemon was open, and the music was loud, and the place was packed, everybody drunk and yelling. Communists, the lot of them. Smoke pouring out of the open door out into the night.

Something about the light inside the bar was something I'd never seen before. Everything was glowing with a purple glow.

When it was my turn, I stepped up to the podium. I handed the bouncer my fake ID. Usually, I would've been scared shitless, trying to find my breath, but the grass had kicked in. When you're stoned, you don't have to wait until it's all over for things to make sense. As they happen, things make sense. Ordinary things, like looking, make so much sense.

The sleeve of my chambray shirt turned into some kind of day-glo purple brightness. It made so much sense, this brightness.

The bouncer saw me staring at my shirtsleeve.

It's a black light, the bouncer said. We just put them in, he said. Makes everything look weird.

The bouncer hardly looked at me, handed me my ID back. When I opened my wallet up to put my ID back in, the black light coming out of the Blind Lemon made the dollar bills, my hands, look like we were on another planet.

Planet Blind Lemon.

So much sense.

Then it was Billie's turn. Billie wasn't a lot taller than the podium. Her little hand, her tiny Midnight in Helsinki fingernails. She handed her ID to the bouncer. With her other hand, Billie grabbed my hand and squeezed. Billie's hippie earrings, the Indian beaded birds, flying, flying.

The bouncer looked hard at Billie's ID. He checked the corners. He turned Billie's ID over, looked on the back side. Pulled his glasses down his nose.

I couldn't figure out why he was spending so much time on Billie's ID. I was the one who looked like he was seventeen years old. Billie could pass for twenty-one any day. And Billie's ID was the same as mine.

Then it hit me. Another, even deeper sense of meaning. A true marijuana moment.

The bouncer looked differnt with Billie. A way he didn't look with me. He was making himself look tough, like he was a real hard-ass.

When I looked over at Billie, I could see. Billie wasn't worried a bit.

The guy was flirting with her.

It blew my mind, it made so much sense.

Then something else. Billie's boobs.

The bouncer was really looking at Billie's boobs. Billie said she was used to it, and I was used to it too, in a way, the way people, I mean, men, looked at her breasts. But that night with the bouncer, that moment, just before Billie stepped into the black light, he was *really* looking at her boobs. I mean, he was gawking.

It made so much sense.

Billie's boobs under her loose-knit pink sweater, in the black light, that bra of hers was going to pop out like the Star-Spangled Banner.

The bouncer gave Billie's ID back to her, and Billie was putting her ID back into her pink satin purse. Just before Billie took the step, out of darkness and into the light, so to speak, I put my hand on Billie's arm.

You know, Billie, I said.

Right at that moment, Billie's head was still outside, but her boobs were inside. Inside, that is, in the black light. The bouncer's eyes bugged right out his head. I thought he was going to have a conniption fit.

Billie looked down. There they were. Each one as big as my head. The two enormous day-glo white D cups that were her breasts.

Billie squeezed my hand so hard it damn near broke the bones.

Oh shit, Billie said.

What happened next went smooth and made sense.

I pulled my shirttails out, unbuttoned my shirt, took my shirt off, and handed my shirt to Billie.

If ever I was sure there was a time that Billie really loved me, it was right then.

In her blue eyes. So much sense.

Billie took my chambray shirt and pressed her face into my shirt.

Billie's big smile, like I was the only boy in the world.

My God, you smell good, Billie said.

Inside in the crowded smoky loud Blind Lemon, my T-shirt glowed.

Billie's teeth glowed. We kept pointing and laughing at each other because of our teeth. All over on the both of us, tiny little specks of
things that glowed. My chambray shirt on Billie was glowing. Billie's
hippie earrings, those birds were glowing too. Glowing and flying.

All around us, people with glowing teeth, everything that was
white, glowing purple-white. Everything dark, especially dark. Everything dark covered in glowing specks. A weird purple light in people's
eyes. *Come on, baby, light my fire.*

Couldn't hear yourself think.

Everybody yelling and laughing.

Planet Blind Lemon.

Billie and I in the middle of it all. Billie in my shirt, and for some
reason I was holding her pink satin purse. Smoking the same cigarette. My arm was around Billie's shoulder. Billie so close. Like we
were one being, attached at the hip.

After a pitcher of beer and about an hour in the Blind Lemon, Billie
and I felt like we were tripping on acid. There was this one woman
who had put Murine in her eyes, and the Murine in the black light
made it look like her eyes were leaking green shit.

We moved on to the next bar. It had regular lighting and a good
jukebox, called Juck's. Then after Juck's, there was the Emerald Club,
then the Office, then a basement bar close to the railroad tracks called
Satan's Cellar. Each bar, each time, the bouncer checked our IDs,
looked us over, let us in as slick as snot.

Satan's Cellar had a cover charge because there was dancing. One
dollar a person. After all the beer we drank — I should say *I* drank —
there were still five one-dollar bills in my wallet.

Mostly hippies in Satan's Cellar. I didn't know Pocatello had so
many hippies. The dance floor was no bigger than ten feet square, so
it was real crowded.

"Monday Monday," "To Love Somebody," "Baby I Need Your
Lovin'."

The top of Billie's head right under my chin. Her breath through my
T-shirt onto my chest. Her French smell. Both my arms around her.
Billie had her hands in the back pockets of my Levi's. Warm and close
and slow, Billie and I were smooth dancing.

*If you're going to San Francisco. Be sure to wear some flowers in
your hair.*

Right there that night on the Satan's Cellar dance floor. The first time I heard that song.

You might say that song changed my life.

Back out on East Center Street, we were feeling no pain.

Billie and I stood ourselves on the sidewalk under a lamppost. Just Billie and I in a bright spot on the sidewalk. We had our hands on each other's shoulders. We were looking at each other in the eyes. We were laughing and talking and laughing. I can't tell you what all we were talking about or what made us laugh so hard, but whatever it was, it was making so much sense, and the way it was making sense made Billie and I laugh our asses off.

Eleven-forty-five by Billie's watch. The night sky was a mess of stars. A big gust of warm wind blew our hair back. Even Billie's hair with all her hairspray. Her earring birds flying, flying.

Billie and I started walking, just walking along, her shoulders under my arm. Billie was trying to take steps as big as my steps.

Another big gust of warm wind. Out in the dark night, the wind blew through the leaves of a tree, the high sigh on top, and Billie and I turned to look. In the branches, a large bird. A crow maybe, or a raven. All we could see was the bright in its eyes.

The tree was a scrub elm growing by the side of the underpass where the cement sloped down.

That part of town my dad called Niggertown.

Billie's eyes lit up as if the high sigh of the wind and the bright eyes of the bird had made her remember something.

I've got a great idea! Billie said. Let's go to the Working Man's Club!

Something big and sharp in my heart then. Breath. There was no breath. My hand on my throat, then my hand on my chest, I laid my palm flat.

Billie's elbow, locked in my elbow, pulled me forward.

Come on! she said. Let's do something *really* different!

Walking was a dream of walking.

So long ago that Sunday after nine o'clock Mass, the first time I heard the word *nigger,* and the word *nigger* landed on the dark side of my heart. How old was I then, five or six? One of the very few times my family did anything differnt. A detour on the way home from church, my father behind the wheel. He had turned his face and smiled his black eyes across the front seat of the '48 Buick Special into Mom's almond-shaped hazel eyes, the net of her Sunday hat a shadow onto her forehead and her glasses.

Slumming, Dad had said. Just thought we'd see how the other half lives.

The other half, the dark half, that part of Pocatello, especially the two bars Dad pointed out that Sunday to us, his loving Catholic family locked safe inside their big green Buick, Sis squeezing my hand so hard. The two "dives," as Dad called them, the Working Man's Club and Porters and Waiters, the bars' long, sad windows with the paint peeling off, the rusted, broken-down cast-iron fence, the garbage overflowing in the two garbage cans, a skinny yellow dog peeing on a dead bush, the two sets of front stairs up to the first floors, a woman with dark skin in a yellow dress and red high heels sitting on the front steps, the little neon blue moon in the cracked window, WORKING MAN'S CLUB. Next door above the door, the painted red sign with fancy gold letters, a sign like you see in the train station, PORTERS AND WAITERS. The slow, sinful saxophone jazz playing out from somewhere inside in there, enormous and dark.

Those two dives and the basement door in the alley behind the two dives and what I was still yet to find behind that basement door.

Even back then, five years old, to me the world on the other side of my rolled-up window, beyond the stuffy locked-up Buick, was Scrooge and the Ghost of Christmas Past, something shocking, differnt, a pain down low in my pants I wanted more of.

The part of Pocatello that exists only in a Judy Garland song.

Niggertown.

Looked like the Princess Theater to me.

Or *The Wizard of Oz* when it goes from black and white to color.

Magic.

Billie's hand was around my arm, and she was shaking my arm. We'd walked two blocks down East First Street and were standing on the sidewalk across the street from two old buildings. We were in the dark, next to a big, square, metal dumpster painted dark blue. Behind us, weeds growing up, the cyclone fence, pieces of garbage and tumbleweeds stuck in the fence. Beyond the fence, the wide, empty, dark expanse of shiny railroad tracks that went through the middle of town.

Rig, Billie said. You are so stoned. Are you all right?

There was something like San Francisco about the old buildings. The long, sad windows with the paint peeling off. The rusted, broken-down cast-iron fence. The garbage overflowing in the two garbage cans. The two sets of cast-iron stairs up to the first floors.

Slumming, I said. Just thought we'd see how the other half lives.

Rig? Billie said.

The neon blue moon in the cracked window. WORKING MAN'S CLUB. Right next to the WORKING MAN'S CLUB, another set of stairs that led up to a door. Above the door, the painted red sign with fancy gold letters, a sign like you'd see in the train station, PORTERS AND WAITERS.

Slow, sinful saxophone jazz playing out from somewhere inside in there.

Then and now. Enormous and deep. In my body, a gust of Idaho wind got inside and was blowing me around.

None of this made sense. Everything made sense.

I put my hand on the dumpster, leaned my body against it. The dumpster smelled of new paint. When I spoke, my voice sounded like a faraway train.

What's that thing that happens to you, I said, when you feel like something's already happened to you?

Billie was right there on my arm, ready to hold me up.

Déjà vu? Billie said. Is that happening to you? I love it when that happens.

A skinny yellow dog ran along the street. Right in front of Billie and me, he stopped, raised his leg. Peed on a dead bush.

Billie nudged in close to me against the dumpster. She wanted to *déjà vu* too.

I put my fingers to my lips.

Sshh!

I stuck my head around the dumpster, and so did Billie. The lamp-post was a spotlight down onto the stairs and the sidewalk. My eyes went right to the top of the stairs, at the dark door of the Working Man's Club. I knew what was coming next.

The Princess Theater.

The slow turn of the handle, the low screech of the door. Black and white turned to color. Out of the door stepped a pair of strapped red high heels and a long yellow dress. The woman was dark-skinned, tall. A strapless, yellow, shiny dress, the slit in her yellow dress all the way up to her thigh. Long, straight black hair to her shoulders. Red, red lips. She was holding a purse like Billie's, a red satin purse. She walked sideways down the steps, placing each high red heel exactly on the step. Slow and red and yellow in the neon light of the blue neon moon, the woman stepped down, each step careful, each step the sound of the red high heel against the cast-iron step. At the second-to-the-bottom step, in the middle of the lamppost spotlight, the woman in the yellow dress reached down, pulled her dress up a bit with her fingers, bent her knees, and sat down. The wind, a big gust, blew her hair. From out of her purse, she pulled a green bottle. She unscrewed the cap of the green bottle, tipped the bottle up, and swallowed. The strong muscles of her neck. The woman set the bottle on the step next to her. It was a bottle of Thunderbird. She screwed the lid back on. Out of her red satin purse, her large hands with dark fingernails pulled out a pack of cigarettes. She lit the cigarette, inhaled. The best French inhale you ever saw.

Billie whispered: Smoking is praying.

A long, warm wind blew slow waves through the yellow dress.

The brown, broad shoulders, the cut of the chin, her thick lips, her deep-set eyes that looked like Jesus. The thick black hair on her chest. The hair on her legs, hair on up to her thigh. Italian hair.

Buckskin and flint on the back of my throat.

As fate would have it, George Serano.

Differnt happens when you least expect it.

Billie's shoulder under my arm moved in closer. She squeezed my hand.

Wow, Billie whispered. He is such a beautiful woman.

The neon blue moon on George's hair made his hair black-blue. George crossed his legs, pulled the skirt of the dress up over his knees. In the spotlight, his one red strapped high heel bouncing.

Scintillatingly gorgeous.

A pain down in my pants I wanted more of.

Billie kissed me on the cheek, her breath.

Billie whispered: What do you think he's doing?

The slow, sinful saxophone jazz was playing a Judy Garland song.

George took another long drag on his Camel. His French inhale was perfect. He leaned back, his elbows on the second step up. Another drag. George lowered his head, looked down at the top of the yellow dress. With his thumb and index, George pulled at the top of the dress, adjusted himself.

Billie's whisper: He's smoking. And I think he's waiting for someone.

Billie was still raring to go. The beer, the marijuana, the warm night wind, she was flying. I was flying too, but not like Billie. The loud, fast everything making sense, everything so much fun, had turned into something else. A huge headache between my eyes and a chest full of sour smoke.

Billie grabbed my arm and started to pull me away from the painted blue dumpster. She was headed across the street to the man in the yellow dress.

Come on! Billie said. Let's ask him where he got his shoes!

There was no way I was going to move one step closer to George Serano.

There was nothing else to do but close my eyes and let my body fall. In nothing flat, I was sprawled out on the sidewalk, my head and shoulder up against the blue dumpster. I was holding onto my chest.

And there you have it. I couldn't blame it on fate, or blame it on the universe.

Only me. I'd rather pretend to faint than face the truth.

Billie fell for it. She knelt down and put her arm around me. Her cool hand on my forehead.

Rig! Billie said. Are you OK?

I waited a while to speak.

I said: I think I'm going to puke, I said. I don't feel so good.

Oh, Billie said, I know just how you feel.

Billie drove. Both the windows rolled down, the wing windows open, the night air was a dark wind that blew our hair and was warm against our skin. I leaned against the pickup door, slouched down, my face right in the window in the wind. I didn't talk. Couldn't. My insides had disappeared. All I could do was stare out at the passing streetlamps and the stars way off, out and beyond. After a while, I closed my eyes. The wind against my closed eyes.

I figured Billie was taking herself home, so I was surprised that when she shut off the pickup, when I opened my eyes, we weren't at her house. We weren't at Mount Moriah either.

The big round neon sign yellow and orange with red neon blinking. THE SUNSET MOTEL.

What are we doing here? I said.

Happy birthday, Rig, Billie said. I've rented us a room.

The headache between my eyes went through my head to the exact center of my brain.

In a *motel*? I said. What are we going to do in a motel?

The loud metal-to-metal pop of the pickup door. Billie got out of the pickup, slammed the door, walked around the front of the pickup, opened my door. I just sat there on the seat. I couldn't move.

Come on, Rig, Billie said. Her best Simone Signoret.

It's twelve-thirty, I said. It's late, I said. I got to get on home.

My voice was high.

Billie's eyes opened wider, and she seemed to take in all of me for a moment, and in that moment while she was taking me all in, she was thinking of just the right way to say what she had to say.

Billie put her hand on my hand that was on my leg. I tried not to jump, but in her hand it was like lightning.

Rig, Billie said. It was a joke. Cheryl and Karen got the room for us. For your birthday. I told them they were crazy, that a motel room wasn't for us. I told them I loved you and that we were friends, but a motel room just wasn't for us. Not yet. But some things have happened, and I do, Rig. I need to be close to you. Tonight at the Blind Lemon when you took off your shirt is when I knew. I needed to be naked with you and lie down and be held by you. And there it was in my purse, the Sunset Motel key, room fifty-eight.

Billie opened her pink satin purse, reached in, held up the key between us. The green tag of the key with the white numbers, 58. The tag spun around in the wind and shined with the neon sunset.

Then Billie leaned in the door, her head against my belly. She was crying hard. Big, deep sobs and snot. Her deep breaths through my T-shirt.

Up the twelve cement steps, along the cement walkway, I walked on the outside. When you walk, the man is always supposed to walk on the outside.

Room 58 was a green door. Billie unlocked the door, pushed the door, and the door swung open. Inside, it was darkness. Billie reached up, put her hand into the darkness, and flipped the switch.

Bright ceiling light was the headache between my eyes, where God the Father lives.

Everything in the room had down-low shadows.

Behind me, when the door latch clicked in the door, there was no breath.

The lamp next to the bed, the light through the lampshade was a softer light. I turned off the overhead.

The bedspread was red with raised ribs of red. The carpet orange and red shag carpet. The smell of Pine-Sol. A smell underneath the Pine-Sol, mold, diarrhea, puke.

I've got to pee, Billie said. I'll be right back.

Freezing in there inside the air conditioning. Across the room, the window was a red curtain. Behind the red curtain, an aluminum window. The only way to open the aluminum window was to break the window.

The toilet flushed. When Billie stepped out of the bathroom, she was rubbing cream on her hands.

Fuck, Billie said. It's freezing in here.

Fuck.

Billie took my hand. Her hand was slick.

We sat on the edge of the bed. It was warmer on the bed by the light. Billie and I both tried to get close to the warm light. We laughed a little. It was funny trying to get warm in Idaho when it was July.

In Billie's blue eyes, I looked in her eyes so close right then. I found what I wanted to find.

Midnight in Helsinki. I was the only boy she'd ever loved.

I pulled my T-shirt up over my head. The cold air on my naked chest, my nipples, my arms. Billie let her blue eyes rest on my skin. Goose flesh. My skin was pretty clear. The tan line of my T-shirt with the sleeves cut off.

Billie's eyes were red, dark mascara teardrops out the corner of her eyes. She unbuttoned the chambray shirt, took it off, let the shirt drop on top of my T-shirt on the floor on the red and orange carpet. Then Billie was unbuttoning her pink sweater with the beads on it. Her white skin such a differnt white from her bra.

I put the heel of my right boot against the toe of my left and pried my boot off. Then the other boot. My white socks saggy and stretched out and strange white. Billie unbuckled her white strapped sandals. Her tiny toenails. A smell in the room like earth.

My hands around my Levi's tops. I unbuttoned one button at a time. One pant leg, then the other, and my Levi's were in the pile.

My shorts like my socks. Low-hanging sags and washed so many times they were transparent.

In the room, all around us, forced cold air.

Billie's hip-huggers were so tight, I had to help her pull them off.

We had to laugh. Really, it was so absurd when I was pulling at the cuffs of her pants and my balls were bouncing in my huge elongated transparent shorts.

When I laughed, my aching head.

Billie reached around behind and unclasped her bra.

My God, the surprising weight of her breasts, their full white flesh. The way they moved, large, glowing fish underwater. The nipples, not pink like mine, but soft brown.

Then my socks were off, then my shorts. Then Billie's pink bikini underpants.

Canal water, moss, mud, horse piss, lemon grass.

Buck-naked.

The dark brown hair in Billie's crotch.

That cock of mine, lying on top of my balls.

I was trying to have a very good parade, but it wasn't working.

Billie made a little scream, and between the thin yellow sheets Billie dived in first. Then me. For a moment, we lay there frozen, the both of us, not touching, looking up at the flat white ceiling, one long crack, the covers pulled up around our necks.

I reached over to shut off the light.

Billie said: Leave the light on, Rig.

I turned my head, let my eyes open.

There she was, Billie Cody.

I don't want to lose you in the dark, she said.

Warm and naked in a cold bed, how two bodies fit. All around us, cold, cold and weird, things slipping in and out of the dark. Shivers in my body like I was standing next to death.

Billie's warm, smooth hand along my arm, on my ribs, across my chest.

Two lips against two lips soft with a kind of suck, tobacco, and the taste of pink. There I was with Billie, Billie Cody, my girlfriend, the girl I could kiss and kiss and kiss, and we'd become a dream.

I pulled the covers down. Billie's nipples were goose flesh and sticking up and hard. My hand touched her nipples, and although my hand touched her nipples, I wasn't there in my hand.

Kiss me there, Billie said.

Heartbeat all through my head. Sour smoke in my chest. My heart, sore, deep in mucus. In my mouth, Billie's hard tit lolled around my tongue.

The long arch of my hand that landed on the hair of her crotch. How smooth her hair was down there, smooth and slick.

As soon as my hand landed, Billie jumped a foot off the bed.

My hand was cold. Everything was cold. Fucking freezing.

Billie opened her legs.

My hand slipped down through hair, down and down into endless folds of dark, wet flesh.

In my mind, *fuck* and *cunt* and *pussy* and *hard-on* and *put out* and *going all the way* and *queer*.

Something awful.

The something awful that had been trying to get into me since George Serano on the steps in a yellow dress.

Fear can wear just about anybody's face.

Billie Cody, my best friend, in the Sunset Motel in a frozen room 58, turned into something awful.

It's only now, looking back, I can even talk about it.

The something awful was all over Billie on her skin, on her big poking-up nipples, on the C that stood not for *Cody* but for *cunt*.

Billie smelled funny and she had cigarette breath and mascara drips and her tiny fingernails and her stupid hippie earrings and her ratted hair all smashed against the pillow stupid.

Billie was someone who wanted me to do stuff I didn't want to do.

But I did.

I wanted to.

It's just that I couldn't.

Then I couldn't stand it that I wanted to get away from her.

I got up fast, put my feet on the orange and red shag carpet. My skin was blue, it was so cold.

My elbows on my knees, my back to Billie, the muscles in my back spazzing, I put my sore head in my hands.

Billie, I said, Billie, I'm sorry, but I just can't do this.

Sunday morning, I got out of bed too fast. The room was at a slant and wouldn't stay still. I made it to the bedroom wall and up the stairs and into the bathroom. I pulled the door closed behind me and leaned up against the door. Locked it.

I clenched my hands around the bathroom sink.

No way I was going to look in that fucking mirror.

The worst thing was in the mirror.

Fuck.

The night before, I'd got in late, two-thirty-in-the-morning late, and Mom and Dad knew it. Mom's almond-shaped hazel eyes looked everywhere but at me. The wrinkles around her lips had multiplied. Dad was milking it for all it was worth. Cussing under his breath and honking the horn of the Buick. It was Sunday morning and time for church.

Inside the Buick, Dad smelled of too much Old Spice. Mom in one of her goofy hats. As ever, Dad drove, Mom sat in the passenger seat. I sat in the back.

The headache of George in a yellow dress and red high heels, the headache of not being able to fuck Billie in room 58 of the Sunset Motel, the headache of my tight-assed Catholic sex-hating mother and father that Sunday morning was a God the Father headache so bad I could barely open my eyes. Any minute I was going to barf.

In the church, morning sun shafts of God light through the yellow gold, the verdant green, the my-blue-heaven stained glass of the windows. At the holy water font, I put my fingers in the water, made the sign of the cross. Past the choir stairs, on the left, the confessional. Dad's black Roosky eyes, Mom's almond-shaped hazel eyes, her little wrinkles around her mouth. By the looks on their faces, I'd better get in the confessional fast before I went to hell.

The little red light bulb above the door was on.

The Monsignor is in.

My cock a tiny burning piece of shame.

The confessional door closed behind me. When I knelt down, I heard the red light bulb outside my door click on. Hot inside the dark.

Sweat drips going down the insides of my arms. My headache, the drunk hangover, my tortured soul.

Out of the dark, on the other side of the screen, the outline of Monsignor's hooked nose.

Bless me, Father, for I have sinned, I said. My last confession was two months ago. These are my sins.

Slow, sinful saxophone jazz playing out from somewhere inside in there, enormous and dark. Mortal sinful. The wave of warm wind through the yellow dress. Red strapped high heels carefully placed on each step down and down. Black hair up his leg all the way to the thigh. Black hair on his chest. Like Dad's black hair. George's cigarette, his achingly perfect French inhale. Smoking is praying, smoking is praying is waiting. The taste of buckskin and flint on the back of my throat. My stiff cock.

Two lips against two lips soft with a kind of suck, tobacco, and the taste of pink. Billie, my beloved Billie, the girl I could kiss and kiss and kiss, and we'd become a dream. Kissing venial sin, hugging venial sin, everything else is mortal sin. Stuck on Billie's body these mortal sinful parts, mother's parts, sister's parts, soft, wet parts, parts that are hellfire and damnation and contamination to touch. My limp cock.

Blood filling my cock full, and me stuffing my cock in a big wet cunt and fucking the shit out of it.

Fuck you, Father, for I have not fucked and sinned.

Yet I've committed the gravest sin, sinned exceedingly.

My body is ugly. The casket for my smashed-flat roadkill soul.

Monsignor's ear was pressed up against the screen.

My T-shirt and my white Sunday shirt were soaked through. My sweat smelled like sour tobacco, German beer, Billie's cunt.

The words in my throat that wouldn't come out. Words stuck down there in all that phlegm. I swallowed, cleared my throat.

Father, I said.

Down in my voice box, I hacked and cleared, trying to get the words through.

How could I confess about George and Billie? How could I confess about me?

Monsignor was waiting. I was waiting.

Waiting is praying.

What came out of my mouth next were words I didn't expect to hear.

I broke the ninth commandment, Father, I said.

The ninth? Monsignor said.

The ninth, I said. Not the sixth.

I committed the sin of bearing false witness, I said. Once.

False witness? Monsignor said.

The tone of his voice — you could tell, he expected the sixth, the other, more interesting, sin.

Only once? Monsignor said.

Only once, Father, I said. They're all one big once.

Monsignor's hand was up to his mouth, then just his index finger against his lips.

To whom did you bear false witness? Monsignor said.

My lips were dry. I licked my lips.

A friend, I said. I bore false witness to a friend.

My first confession in four years that wasn't about the sixth commandment and self-abuse and the details of self-abuse.

When I finally opened my eyes, Monsignor was mumbling through the prayers, making the sign of the cross with his hand. I was totally surprised. I expected a lecture, an argument, at least a discussion. Maybe he was late for Mass, and there wasn't any time.

Three Our Fathers and three Hail Marys and three Glory Bes. I swear you could say I fucked Christ on the cross in there, and that's what you'd get. Three Our Fathers, three Hail Marys, three Glory Bes. Maybe five. Certainly at the most, it would be five.

During Mass, I hated God.

Mass was long and hot, and I yawned once so big, my throat made that stretching sound. During the sermon I did a drift, snap, drool. Wiped my mouth. Took a deep breath. Mom's sharp elbow jabbed me in the ribs. Her wrinkled, wrinkled lips. Her almond-shaped hazel eyes straight into my heart.

Fuck.

After Mass, Mom and Dad go down for coffee hour. I'm standing alone on the steps of Saint Joe's, trying to figure out what the fuck, when all of a sudden it's Sis who's got a hold of my elbow. She's wearing a fall with a lace prayer cap on top and a blue dress the size of a house. In her Roosky eyes, I've never seen in Sis's eyes, her be so happy.

I guess it was just being close to Sis again. I felt them. Two big tears rolled down my cheeks.

Sis grabbed my hand, the way she'd always grabbed my hand when we were kids. I snuffed up, wiped my tears. Sis's eyes stayed right on mine as she pulled the Marlboro out of its pack, lit it. She took two puffs, looked around, then quick handed the cigarette to me.

I was on my first puff.

Sis whispered: Sorry about Billie.

My French inhale was good, but then the smoke went all wrong, and I started to cough.

Billie? I coughed.

Sis took the cigarette, took a long, long puff. Sis flipped the fall like it really was her hair.

Yah, Sis whispered, you know — Billie!

Jeez, this was a small town, but how in the hell could Sis possibly know already?

What? I said.

Sis looked around, leaned in close, handed the cigarette to me. Grabbed my hand that way again.

My deep inhale. Smoking is praying.

Sis's hand went up to my forehead, pushed back my hair.

Smoking is praying is waiting.

Billie's pregnant, Rig, Sis whispered.

I know all about it, Sis said. Chuck diPietro is at the house half the time, she said. Him and Gene, they're like *brothers*. It's like I didn't marry one man but *two*.

Into my sour-smoke lungs, more smoke. The inhale deeper and deeper.

Chuck is the father, Sis whispered. And that's the God's truth. And the bum won't marry her.

Smoke blew out my lungs like I was on fire.

Air, air all around, yet not a drop to breathe.

Sis took the cigarette. The ashes on it were hanging off all weird. Hot-boxed.

Sis's inhale, then deep-sigh-exhale, old Marlboro smoke.

Men are such assholes, Sis said. Really fucked up.

Sis's eyes and my eyes. Roosky and hazel. Dad's eyes and Mom's. She reached up, put her thumb and index around my chin.

You need a shave, she said.

Then: You know, Rigby John, Sis said. You're such a sweetheart, Sis said. What this world needs is more men in it like you.

10 Hey There, Georgy Girl

A GRAY, HOT SUNDAY after church, my head thick with hangover, my lungs full of sour Marlboros. I went into my bedroom, closed the door, and threw myself on the bed. The smoldering fire inside. The delicate balance on the grain elevator one giant step too far. I was going down fast. I was the most disgusting human being in the world. I was ugly. My dick didn't work. I couldn't fuck my girlfriend. And the guy I'd been haying with turned out to be a female impersonator. I was stuck in my bedroom, stuck in a Sunday, stuck with my parents, stuck in the house. There was nowhere to go to get away to because I was the one I needed to get away from.

The universe had conspired, and there I was, stuck with myself.

When my parents were both finally out of the house I called Billie. Just made a bigger mess of everything. My whole body was shaking. There was no breath, and when I went to speak, something jumped out of my throat and started screaming.

I called her a little whore and asked who else she'd fucked.

Fucking great, Billie said. Typical fucking male.

Fuck you, Billie, I said.

No, fuck you, Rig, Billie said.

I was in the middle of yelling another *fuck you* when Billie hung up.

I wanted a cigarette but couldn't bear the thought of another cigarette, so I just walked out the door. The gray had burned off, and the day was late-afternoon gold sun. I didn't want the sun. I wanted a cold rainy day. I walked along with my shadow. George always said you can tell how you're doing by how your shadow looks. My shadow stayed close around my feet, too ashamed to show itself. Tramp and I went to all my safe places. First on top of the granaries. Then in the spud cellar, then crawled up on the grain elevator. Didn't even try to hit balance, just walked up one end, then walked down the other, smacking the elevator down. Scared the wits out of Tramp. On top of the railroad cars, there were no faraway places, there was only me.

The pain that day inside me, I'd never felt the likes before. Pain kept pulling my head down like I was a sinner before an angry God. But I wasn't a sinner, I was still a virgin. Moments from the night before crowded up in my head. The Sunset Motel, freezing in room 58. Flashes of Billie's breasts, her cunt, her soft hair down there, the way her hands had touched my skin. How could something so natural be so frightening?

Differnt. I was differnt all right. A fucking freak.

But most of all, even more than not being able to get it up, the hardest thing to face was Billie and Chuck diPietro together, fucking their brains out.

Billie had betrayed me.

Tramp and I were curled up in the straw in the hayloft of the barn. I'd run the Billie and Chuck scenario over and over in my mind so many times, I can't tell you. Then lying there on the straw, I reached my hand up and brushed my knuckles across my mouth and I remembered George.

Only the day before, when I pulled up to the first stack of bales in the field, I'd just shut the truck off, when George leaned up and went to put his Camel out in the ashtray.

I had my eye on that half-smoked Camel.

George's dark eyes looked at his cigarette, then he handed the cigarette to me.

Thanks, I said.

The cigarette that was on George's lips was on my lips. I took one puff, two, three, hoping I wasn't hot-boxing. I handed the cigarette back to George.

The look on George's face when I handed him the cigarette back. Really, I don't know how to describe it. Shocked, I guess, and maybe a smile under the shock.

George sat there with that look on his face and stared at the cigarette.

You can have your own cigarette if you like, George said.

Oh, I said, it's just.

Like most of the times with George, I didn't know how to say what I wanted to say, so my mouth just started talking.

Last summer, I said, Flaco and Acho. We hauled hay. We shared cigarettes.

We were best friends, I said.

Just like that, George's eyes went red-rimmed and wet like Granny's eyes. Eyes so full of Jesus right then.

Slow, George's big hand reached out and took the cigarette, put the cigarette in his mouth. His black eyes differnt, even darker, not so much Jesus.

He inhaled the smoke, blew smoke out his nose and mouth, handed the cigarette back to me.

Then we can share cigarettes too, George said.

The sore place next to my heart where I smoke. It wasn't just Billie, George had betrayed me too. In a way I wasn't sure how exactly. But somehow a good friend doesn't parade around town in a yellow dress and red high heels showing off, making a spectacle of himself. I mean, not if he's a man. I mean it was embarrassing.

Fuck.

The train wreck of George Serano.

Boy, did I have a lot to learn.

The hay, the hay, the goddamn hay.

Monday morning, I was slamming things around. I didn't eat my mush. Didn't eat the hard fried eggs. I didn't drink the glass of milk. I went straight for Mom's pot of coffee and poured myself a cup. The coffee was terrible. It tasted like half the amount of coffee there's supposed to be. Why was I surprised? Why should coffee be any differnt from anything else of Mom's? She'd probably reused the coffee grounds.

I spit the coffee out in the sink. I'd have a cup at Granny's.

Flying down Tyhee Road in the hay truck, Monday morning early,

Saturday night George all dolled up, dressed up like a girl sitting on the steps was something I couldn't bend my head around. How was I even going to *look* at George, let alone spend the day hauling hay with him?

What's worse was my lungs were still too sore to smoke. I tried, but my old buddy Viceroy tasted like horseshit. It was all horseshit. Everything was horseshit. The whole fucking world, one big pile of fucking horseshit.

In Granny's yard, the magic light and dark was only the goddamn sun coming down through a bunch of old dead trees. The high sigh on top of the trees was only the wind. Granny's green screen door made the same old *Inner Sanctum* squeak. The wood grain of the gray front door in front of my eyes, swirls and swirls. Bonanza barked before I knocked.

Granny opened the door. Woodsmoke and coffee and frying grease. Same old, same old. The smell of buckskin and Prince Albert.

Then it was Granny's red handkerchief. Strands of white hair stuck up like cobwebs all around her face. Her red-rimmed eyes so bright always, like they're crying. Nothing in between.

When her eyes looked into mine, Granny saw right into my soul.

That quick, everything changed.

It took all I had not to cry.

Rigby John, Granny said. You don't look no better than the last time I saw ya. You still eating horseshit?

Shut up, Bonanza! she said.

Bonanza, his toenails little clicks on the shiny floor, made it to the Pendleton pillow and then fell over.

I bit my upper lip. Breathed hard through my nose.

Still eating it, Granny, I said.

Granny's old brown-rope hand pointed over at the table, then pulled out the wood chair with the high back.

Here, she said. Sit down. You want some coffee?

Granny's high-backed chair, me in that chair, my elbow on Granny's table, the light bulb hanging down shining on the wood table. In the red rez, I was not in yellow Bannock County no more. One of the safest places in the world.

When I sat down, the way I was sitting was just like Mom and

Dad. My shoulders up around my ears. I looked around for George.

Sure, I said. Love some coffee.

Granny's hand was on the back of my shoulders.

Relax, Granny said. I'm not going to bite ya.

My shoulders came down an inch.

Do you have any of that other stuff? I said.

What other stuff? Granny said.

Your special remedy for horseshit, I said.

Granny smacked her lips together, sucked her lips in over where she didn't have any teeth. That smile of hers so big, her whole face collapsed around it.

She had to stop and catch her breath, she was laughing so hard.

Stars and garters, Rigby John! Granny said. You sure do make me laugh.

Granny's Minnetonka moccasins with the blue beaded bird were a soft scratch along the shiny wood floor. At the green porcelain Majestic, Granny leaned over, picked up a piece of wood in the pile by the stove, opened the iron door, and stuck the piece of wood into the stove. On top of the stove, she started moving things around.

The curtain on the window above the sink had a big brown scorch on it. I was thinking about that scorch. George had told me Granny always set the kerosene lamp in that window at night.

Every night, George said, rain or shine, you can bet your life on it. That light is on and in the window every night.

Why is that? I'd asked.

The ancestors, George said. Our ancestors live in a sacred tree. The Shoshone ones. Granny wants to honor them after the sun goes down.

Trouble is, George said, sometimes she gets the lamp too close to the curtains. One of these nights she's going to burn the damn house down.

A brown scorch on a white curtain. Funny what little things can mean if you look close at them.

Then it was Granny's refrigerator. The refrigerator door was open and inside the refrigerator it was empty and dark.

What's happened to your refrigerator, Granny? I said.

Granny slid a pan across the stove.

Broke, she said. Motor's dead.

Twenty years now, Granny said. That damn thing wasn't ever worth a goddamn, Granny said. Now it's broke for good.

Granny set the blue pewter cup of coffee down on the table, then another cup, a white cup with a broken handle, and a can of Sego Milk.

You going to get a new one? I said.

Plan to, she said, when the eagle shits.

Then: Milk's good for ya, Granny said. Put some in your tea. Build your bones.

Granny's coffee with the Sego Milk and one teaspoon of sugar was the best thing you could want to taste in the morning. I drank the coffee like I was eating candy. When I got done with the coffee, I went to the horseshit remedy. With Sego Milk and a teaspoon of sugar, the horseshit remedy was almost as good as the coffee.

Granny sat down across the table from me. I'd never seen Granny sit before. She was so slumped over, her head just barely cleared the table. With the empty refrigerator behind her and under the hanging-down light bulb, Granny looked old in a way I'd never seen her. She folded her brown-rope hands, her wood-stick fingers together.

She moved her lips over her gums a couple of times before she spoke.

Rigby John, Granny said. I'm sorry to tell you this. But George won't be hauling hay with you today.

A big gust of Idaho wind blowing around in my chest. So pissed. Then scared. Scared for myself somehow. Then I was scared for George.

Granny watched my face go through all this.

What's up? I said.

Granny's rope hands, her twig fingers, her brown arms branches of trees.

He'll get over it, Granny said. I'll doctor him up good. Then you can work his ass off for him. Give him something to do.

Part of me wanted to start slamming things around some more. Light the kerosene lamp and start the curtain on fire. Kick the refrigerator. Maybe go stomping out the door. Then there was the other part.

Is he all right? I said.

Granny put her brown-rope hands, her fingers crooked twigs, on top of her red bandanna, then let her hands slide down her face. White spider webs flying out all around her face.

All there was in the world right then was Granny's red-rimmed eyes and my eyes.

He's a little under the weather, Granny said. Why don't ya come back tomorrow and see how he's doing?

That day and the next day, I hauled hay by myself. I hated George, but I hated Dad worse.

I stacked and loaded and drove, the whole shootin' match. By myself. Don't think I ever worked so hard. Didn't once let up. Never rested one minute. Rested when I was driving. Part of it was, it felt so good. It felt good to push myself, to do the work of two men. To push and push and push at something in the world, hay, bales of hay I could move, progress I could see, see I could make a differnce. Plus, if I worked hard I didn't think about Billie, or George. Plus, Dad didn't know. I loved it that I was hauling hay alone, and Dad didn't know.

I got away with it for a while. At least I thought I did. It was about four in the afternoon on the second day, Tuesday, I guess. I was about ten loads left from finishing Hess's forty, when I looked up just as Dad pulled the pickup alongside the truck.

The loud metal-to-metal pop of the driver's door.

Where's your helper? Dad said.

I was on the back of the truck. I picked up a bale of hay, walked with it, set the bale down on the rack floor, kicked the bale. There were two more bales to stack. I wasn't going to stop moving.

Breath. I took a deep breath.

He wasn't feeling well this afternoon, I said. He'll be back tomorrow morning.

Dad pushed his cowboy hat up. Roosky Gypsy eyes. He put his wrists on his hips and hiked his Levi's up with his wrists.

He knew I was lying. And I knew that he knew.

I wasn't going to budge.

I picked up another bale, carried it, put the bale on top of the other bale.

How long you say he's been sick for? Dad said.

Just this afternoon, I said.

I picked up the third bale.

Funny, Dad said. I ain't seen him come through the yard with you for two days now.

I carried the bale to the stack, lifted the bale up with my knee.

The tops of my lungs, the breath thing starts there.

That right? I said.

I punched the bale with my gloved hand, punching the fucker secure into place.

That's right, Dad said.

Hay dust in my throat. I coughed hay dust.

Well, I said. You must've missed him. Six loads yesterday. On our fourth load today. Right on schedule.

Then: Stomach cramps, I said. George took some Alka-Seltzer. Had to get out of the sun.

Don't you worry, I said. He'll be back tomorrow morning bright and early.

No more bales on the truck. I jumped down onto the ground, to the stack of hay, so I could throw up some more bales.

Just as I went for the bale of hay, Dad stepped across, stood himself between me and the hay.

He'd better be, Dad said. Or I'll kick both your asses.

The sun was behind me and was in Dad's eyes. He was squinting and looking up at me. Up. Maybe it was just how we were standing, but right then I was taller than him, and Dad was looking *up* at me.

Suit yourself, I said.

Dad laughed his chest up one short laugh.

Pretty tough, ain't ya? Dad said.

That place in my chest at the top, the Idaho wind kicking around. I just stood. Made myself taller, didn't say anything, looked into my father's squinting eyes. The feeling in my arms that means I am helpless. But I kept standing tall, didn't show it. Made my face look like it knew it was being looked at.

Idaho wind. Flies buzzing. Somewhere far away a train whistle. Dad and I stood like that, him and me, for some time.

Then Dad stepped away.

I closed my eyes. Took a big breath but a breath he couldn't see.

His boots walking through stubble. The loud metal-to-metal pop of the driver's door. Dad started up the pickup.

I started throwing hay bales onto the truck. I made like I wasn't watching him, but I was watching him.

Dad put his arm up on the back seat, turned to look behind, and he backed up some. Then he put on the brakes. Shut the pickup off. Dad just sat in the pickup looking at me.

Something was up.

I bucked a hay bale up onto the truck, then turned around for another bale.

Rigby John, Dad said.

Yah, I said.

I told you to keep your distance with these people, Dad said. Last year it was those Mexicans, and look what that got us. Burned our straw stack down. Now this year. I told you about George. I told you to keep your distance. I thought I could be proud of you, but here you are, doing a goddamn Indian's work for him and then lying to your father about it. It don't make no sense. What's so damn difficult about letting people be? You always got to go get all messed up in them. And they ain't worth it. All's they'll do is stab you in the back.

I picked up a hay bale, threw it on the truck.

Dad took his foot off the clutch, and the clutch made that clutch sound.

My nigger-loving son, Dad said. I swear I don't know where you come from.

I was bent over another bale, my gloves around the strings. I let go the strings and stood myself up back to my tallest.

Dad, I said, don't use that word. It's disrespectful. *Blacks* is what you're supposed to say.

My voice was high.

Did I ever tell you about the time, Dad said, that me and Jimmy Weis took that nigger out of the Golden Wheel Bar in Blackfoot?

Dad let out a big heehaw.

Jimmy put the gunnysack over his head from behind, Dad said, and I hogtied his feet. Boy, you should have heard that nigger yell. Jimmy and I threw him in the back of Jimmy's pickup, and we took him all the way up to Johnson Creek. We told that nigger we was going to lynch him, but we didn't. Just scared him, you know. Nigger shit his pants. Jimmy and I laughed and laughed at that nigger, walking around bumping into trees with that gunnysack tied around him with shit in his pants. Damn near laughed our asses off.

*　　*　　*

So many times, I wished I had a pitchfork in my hand that day. We'd see how scared somebody could get.

But there was no pitchfork.

And I wasn't ready yet.

Plus, there he was. He was my father.

So I just stood. You might say froze. Out in the Idaho sun, July, the heat bearing down, puddles where there weren't any, big old flies buzzing.

Froze.

Froze even more than the Sunset Motel.

And that's saying something.

An old ignorant redneck bragging about being a bully.

Honor thy father.

I mean, really.

Fuck.

The next morning, sitting in Granny's high-backed wood chair. I was staring at the scorched curtain, staring into Granny's dark, empty refrigerator, sipping on a cup of hot coffee with Sego Milk and a teaspoon of sugar, and a cup of horseshit remedy, when I heard George's footsteps come out of his room.

Part of me was going to get sick. Another part was leaning back to land a punch like I did under the weeping willow. Another part couldn't stop staring down at the wood of the table.

George stood at the table for a while. Out the corner of my eye, all I could see was his crotch. Finally, I turned my head, looked up at him.

I couldn't believe my eyes.

One side of George's face looked like a busted-up watermelon.

Big bruises and cuts on his hands.

You ought to see the other guy, George said.

Inside the truck, after George got in, slammed his door, and was sitting next to me, before I turned on the key and pushed my foot on the starter and started the truck, George and I sat there for a moment, the shadows and light swirling all around on us. I went to say something, something about his face, something about his yellow dress, just something. But I didn't know how to say what I had to say. Plus there was so *much* to say, and where in the hell did you start?

George reached into his shirt pocket, pulled out a cigarette, lit it. Two or three magnificent French inhales, then George handed the cigarette to me.

It's weird. It was just a cigarette. In a hay truck in the red rez under a bunch of half-dead Lombardy poplars, one man hands another man a cigarette, and the other man says no. A simple act. Not a big thing in the world with Vietnam and civil rights. But that morning, in my life, that particular cigarette meant all the differnce in the world.

My excuse was that my lungs were sore.

Some things, when you look back on what you did, you wish you'd never done them.

Puke Price, for instance. I mean Allen.

That morning with the cigarette was another one of those times.

The truck engine roared big all around us. I put the clutch in, put the gearshift into reverse.

George's cigarette in his bruised hand, his torn knuckles, George still held the cigarette out to me.

Moments of gesture.

I waved my hand between me and the cigarette.

I looked straight ahead, didn't look into George's eyes.

No way I can smoke that, I said.

We were back onto Quinn Road before George put the cigarette back to his lips. The truck engine seemed loud. I thought the muffler was going.

But the muffler wasn't going. The engine was loud because it had to cover up what had happened with Billie. I mean, what didn't happen.

It had to be loud to cover up George in his yellow dress, his red shoes.

It had to be loud so I couldn't think.

George didn't do anything. He didn't take a deep breath. He didn't say anything. There was no indication. George just kept smoking the cigarette like it was just another cigarette.

But that cigarette was differnt. That cigarette was more than it was.

I did not want to smoke, did not want to wait, to trust, did not want to pray with George Serano.

I was getting as far away from that guy as I could.

*　　*　　*

George got out, unhinged the gatepost to Hess's forty. He threw the gate into the weeds up against the fence. I heard him jump onto the back of the truck.

In the mornings, George always got back in the cab after opening the gate. We'd smoke the rest of the cigarette, talk some, and then start in to work.

That morning, when George jumped onto the hay rack instead of getting in the cab, it was sore in my chest, not cigarette-smoke sore, but sore in my heart where George used to be.

I pulled the truck alongside a stack of hay, shut the truck off.

My breath. Lots of deep breaths.

When I opened the door and stood outside in the field, George was on the back of the truck trying to get his gloves on over his beat-up hands.

I tried to think of something nice to say. Couldn't think. I put my gloves on too.

George's face in the morning sun wasn't just black and blue. His face was every color you could think of.

Well! George said. Let's haul your fucking hay!

The top part of my lungs, the breath.

It's not my hay, I said. It's my dad's.

Then why not let him haul it? George said.

The hay dust inside in the fingers of my gloves.

When I looked up at George, inside in the whites of George's eyes, little red lightnings.

No doubt about it. George and I were in for another round.

I picked up a hay bale, bucked the hay bale up to George.

George picked up the bale, walked to the front of the truck.

Why don't you and I say fuck it, George said. And go for a hike up Scout Mountain? It's a beautiful day. What do you say?

George's lip was bleeding.

All I wanted was to bend over and hold my chest and my stomach.

A hike? I said. What, are you crazy? We've got hay to haul.

I bucked up another bale.

George gave the bale a kick, then picked it up.

The hay, the hay, the goddamn hay, George said. Your whole life, that's all it is is hay.

Another bale up.

But, I said, my dad.

George picked up the bale, walked with the bale, stacked it.

Don't blame it on your dad, George said. You're a grown man, George said. Why don't you do something for yourself once?

Another bale up. Hay dust blowing back into my face.

I hacked up, spit hay dust.

I can't just up and leave, I said.

Why not? George said. You're not a slave.

I am till I'm eighteen, I said.

Then what? George said. Get drafted and go to 'Nam?

George picked up the hay bale and threw the hay bale the length of the truck bed.

Great! George said. Just great! From a hay slave to a war slave. Fucking great!

The feeling in my arms that means I'm helpless.

I'm not going to Vietnam, I said.

My voice was high.

George shook his shoulders and wiggled his butt. He made his voice sound high and like a girl's, like mine: *I'm not going to Vietnam.*

I bucked another bale up onto the truck.

George picked it up, threw the bale back into my face. My arms went up just in time, but I was on the ground.

What the fuck you got to say about it?! George screamed. You do *everything* you're told! Of course you'll go to Vietnam! If they tell you to go, you'll go!

Red blood so red on his lips. Blood stretched over his white teeth.

I was back up on my feet as fast as I could get.

What do you know? I said.

You're an ignorant, dutiful redneck, George said. The army's full of them. What the fuck else is there to know?

Redneck? I said. I'm not a redneck.

My neck was red, my face was red, I'm sure.

George's feet were planted square underneath him. From where I stood, he was twelve feet tall.

Redneck pussy, George said. You wouldn't say shit if your mouth was full of it!

Keep away from those people. They only mean trouble for you.

Me a pussy! I screamed. Look who's talking!

George's leap from the truck was like Superman landing. He landed right next to me — a little too close for me to take a swing, but still I thought I'd better. I was taking a swing when George's gloved hand caught my arm. George's body pushed my body up against the stack of hay.

You'd better take a good look at yourself! I said.

George put his face right into my face. He was spitting blood.

And what is it I would see if I looked, huh? George said. What is it, huh?

George's hand was bringing my arm down slow.

You're the pussy! I said.

George's dark eyes, the gold bars in them. The red lightnings in the whites.

Tell me what makes me such a pussy, George said.

My arm was down all the way down. George's hand on my arm pressing into my crotch.

It was roiling in my gut and up and out my lips before I even knew it.

I don't parade around town in a yellow dress and fancy red high heels! I said.

The wind blew George's hair back off his forehead. For a moment, I thought George would smile. But he didn't smile. George never smiled.

My arm was clenched, and my hand and George's hand were pushing deep into my crotch.

George's breath was cigarette smoke and toothpaste and blood.

Up close, his bad eye, his left eye, was yellow and weeping.

No accounting for taste, George said. Now, is there?

I lifted up my other arm slow. For a moment there, I thought I'd just lay it on his shoulder. Instead, I grabbed the back of George's hair, knocked his hat off, pulled his face up.

At that angle George was some Picasso painting.

At least I'm not hiding, George said. It kills a man's soul when he hides.

My hand in George's hair was pulling as hard as I could. George's hand on my hand pushed into my crotch was lifting me off the ground.

I wasn't going to let go and neither was he. Grunts and groans, cursing and swearing, there we were again, George Serano and me, kicking up dust, round three.

A gust of wind, a hawk, some large bird flying low, in a moment, something collapsed. George and I were falling, falling. On the ground, in the stubble, next to the truck tire, we landed.

Our arms around each other, our legs.

George was trying to catch his breath. My breath was in and out of me too. It ain't like on TV when you fight. You have to stop and catch your wind.

Our deep breaths. The buzz of flies. Wind.

Things got slow.

George's voice in my ear: I saw you, George said. You and your girl-friend. That's why I came out the door and down the steps. I wanted you to see me. I wanted to freak out the white boy.

George's chest up against my chest, the quick laugh.

Guess my plan worked, George said.

Arms and legs and arms. I untangled myself, I pushed myself away. Scooted my butt across the ground, leaned against the truck tire.

George let his head drop onto his arm. He lay in the alfalfa stubble like a nude with his clothes on. He reached into his shirt pocket, pulled out his Camels, tapped one out. He lit his Camel with a new blue Bic lighter. The perfect French inhale. After several puffs, he did not offer the cigarette to me.

When he finally spoke, George's voice was quiet, deep, down low.

It's true, George said. I got a great big pussy. But I do what I want.

Even Grandma tells you what to do, George said. Sego Milk and a teaspoon of sugar, and what do you do?

I'm not at all like you, George said.

George wiped the bloody spit from his mouth onto his sleeve.

In your whole fucking life, George said. Have you ever done any-thing that somebody hasn't told you to do?

Right then and there, I'd have slapped George good just to prove I could, really, prove that I was a badass and I could hit a man smack where it hurt the most, right in his bloody wound. But there was the blood on his lips and blood coming down his chin and his blue and green and yellow swollen eye. Blood on his cigarette.

I couldn't do it.

Fuck you, I said.

No, George said. Fuck you.

Don't ask me how, or why, but George and I finished out the day hauling. It wasn't our regular seven loads, only five, but still.

That next morning, driving the truck to Granny's house, I never in a million years figured to see George. Thought he'd be off somewhere *waiting*. But there he was, seven-thirty A.M., standing at the side of the road.

George got in the truck, didn't say good morning or fuck you. Didn't look at me. Same way with the rest of the mornings. George was shut down like a steel trap. A total stranger. And meaner than ever. Even after his lip healed and the green balloon that was his eye went down, we still didn't talk. George never once looked me in the eye. Smoked his cigarette alone.

Which was just fine by me.

I'd bought my own cigarettes. Pall Malls.

I wasn't no better. Just about everything was pissing me off. If a hay bale broke, or the stack on the truck shifted, or if the truck didn't start right off, I took it as a personal offense. One time, the vehicle registration and the proof of insurance that was clipped to the driver's side visor fell down while I was driving over the corrugations. Those fucking little pieces of paper falling down like that pissed me off so bad I took those papers and crushed those papers in my hand, then stuck them in my mouth, and I was ready to gnash them into oblivion before I regained my senses.

Just let any little fucking thing go wrong, and I was ready to tear into it.

My girlfriend was knocked up. I was the laughingstock of Pocatello. And the man I was hauling hay with painted his fingernails.

The truth hurts, man, and here's something even more true.

George was right.

I couldn't even get it up to knock my girlfriend up.

I swear, every day, every day, every day, thousands of screaming magpies gathered in the sky and dived at my head.

On and on and on, one hay-hauling day after the next.

George always showed up. Every morning, there he was, seven-thirty, leaning against Granny's mailbox.

One morning I asked him.

George, I said. Why don't you go for a hike up Scout Mountain? You're so free. What are you turning into, a slave to hay?

George's perfect French inhale. He knew that would get me.

Granny needs a Frigidaire, George said. A couple more weeks, and I can buy it for her.

There was something else, though. Another reason why George was sticking around. But he didn't tell me about that until later.

We finished up Hess's forty and moved on to the home place. That meant George showed up at my house in the morning. That meant I didn't get to see Granny no more. By the end of the week, we'd finished hauling in two-thirds of the crop.

Every morning at seven-thirty, George and I bucked hay till noon. George ate his lunch out in the barn. One o'clock, we'd start in all over again. Ninety degrees in the shade. At six o'clock, I drove George up into the yard, then let him walk home.

The truth is, George wouldn't *let* me drive him home.

Fine by me. After the first day, I never offered.

When the weekend came, I didn't ask Mom and Dad for the pickup.

That's just what I wanted to do. Drive through the Snatch Out. Show my face in town.

On Sunday, I was fit to be tied and was beside myself. I couldn't stand it, out there alone on the farm with just my mind.

I called Billie.

Billie answered the phone.

It took awhile for me to speak.

Billie, I said, I'm pretty messed up. Can we talk?

Silence on the other end of the line.

For a moment, this was all a stupid mistake. All we had to do was talk, and everything would clear up.

Then: Let's be sensible, Billie said. I'm pregnant, and you're not the father. What's there to talk about? That I'm a whore, or you're a damn fool?

My chest was going to explode. In my stomach, lots of farts.

Billie, I said, what about our promise?

Promise? Billie said.

That we'd be friends no matter what, I said.
Another silence. A pregnant silence.
Sorry, Rig, Billie said.
And Billie hung up the phone.

It was in the second week. George and I were bucking hay in the field next to the derrick. I was on the truck stacking. Something shiny caught my eye, and I looked. Dad's pickup was parked at the top end of the field. I pulled my hat down, squinted my eyes for a better look.

Dad was standing against the fence looking through a pair of binoculars. At George and me.

I can't believe it, I said.

George threw a hay bale up onto the truck.

George said: What?

The old man's got the binoculars out, I said. He's checking us out.

George said: I'm so glad we're not fucking.

That moment. The sun was beating down, I was thirsty and hot, hay dust all over on my sweaty back, and I couldn't believe my ears. In front of my eyes, all I could see was Granny, her mouth open, pink gums all around, laughing her ass off.

What do you say to something like that?

Billie too. Billie would have laughed too.

Fuck.

I pretended I hadn't heard.

I puffed up my chest, put my hands on my hips, looked down at George. I never could pretend to be Dad.

What did you say? I said.

Only the top of George's cowboy hat. George threw up another bale. Not a trace of a smile on his face.

Say what? George said.

Another day the end of that week. We were on the last twenty acres, the field that borders Tyhee Road, at the bottom end of the field, almost a half mile from the house.

I heard it first. Music.

As it happened, it was my turn to stack again, so I was on the truck.

A car, it was a fancy car, a new Lincoln, a brand-new '67 white Lincoln. The car was parked on our side of Tyhee Road. The windows were rolled down, and as far as I could tell, there were three guys in the car, two in the front and one in the back.

The music was loud. Where George and I were standing was about five truckloads away from the car, and still you could hear the music. And the guys laughing.

I stopped stacking and I stood and listened. George bucked up a bale of hay. He saw that I'd stopped and was standing and look- ing out.

Is your dad playing peeping Tom again? George said.

It's a car, I said, a fancy new Lincoln. And three guys.

Listen! I said.

It took me awhile to figure out the tune. Then when I realized what the tune was, it took me awhile for it to register.

Hey there, Georgy Girl! Why do all the boys just pass you by?

I looked down at George's face, just as the words of the song went *a new Georgy Girl!*

George's dark eyes. Even though I wasn't up close, I knew. Tiny veins, little red lightnings, in the whites of George's eyes. From out of the dark rounds, bright, sharp light.

Motherfuckers! George yelled.

In nothing flat, George running to beat hell, then there he was jumping over the fence.

The three guys all opened their doors and got out of the car.

It's funny how easy it is to tell about something after it's over, but while it's happening it's all just one thing after another flipping past your eyes.

My leap off the truck had me flying through the air. I think I flew the whole way to the fence. Then I was jumping over the fence, run- ning up through the barrow pit.

The Lincoln's license plates were from Idaho Falls. The guys looked like they were from Idaho Falls too. Long hair and beads. Bell-bottom pants. Guys from Idaho Falls are weird.

All three of them were taking punches at George, but George was holding his own. None of them saw me coming. Not even George. I still had my leather gloves on. I hit the first guy I came to square in the jaw. Didn't even look at his face before I hit him. The guy went sprawling out onto Tyhee Road.

When the other two guys looked around and saw me, they freaked out. It wasn't three to one, it was three to two, and looking back on it, I think those guys could tell. Those weeks, and that week especially, neither George nor I was putting up with any shit.

In no time at all, that hot-rod Lincoln was leaving rubber on Tyhee Road.

Then it was just a little white speck of white Lincoln on the horizon.

George and I stood on the pavement, both of us, leaning against our knees, looking down at our shoes, trying to catch our breath. Fights ain't like you see on TV.

The sky was starting in with blue, not just bright. The sun already on its way to down. Gold starting up, and the long shadows. George started to say something, then stopped.

Were they the guys who beat you up? I said.

George stayed leaned over, breathing hard.

Thanks for the help, he said.

Then: Where'd you learn to land a punch like that anyway?

That's when it happened. That weird sound that comes from inside and goes up and out.

My chest, my shoulders, everything about me, started moving weird, strange snorts and shit coming out my mouth.

Laughter is so weird, man.

Pretty soon, I'm on my hands and knees, slapping the pavement. Dark and deep and weird the way laughter comes up like that. So much like weeping. Tears are coming out of my eyes, and I can't talk. I'm just kneeling in the middle of the road having a conniption fit.

What is it? George said. What's so fucking funny?

One long, long moment of no sound coming out at all. My mouth was moving, but it was no use.

George took a step over to me, pushed my shoulder.

Georgy Girl, George said. What's so fucking funny about *Georgy Girl?*

Still, I couldn't speak. Only weird sounds. You can't do anything about laughter, you just got to let it run through you.

It's a movie, George said. It's a good movie.

I wanted to say, *I saw the movie.* I wanted to say, *You're right, it's a good movie.* I wanted to say, *That's not why I'm laughing.*

But I couldn't say any of that.

What I finally said, what finally came out of my mouth after howling like a damn dog and rolling around on the pavement, finally, finally, finally, I said:

I'm so glad, I said.

I'm so glad we weren't fucking.

Driving into town, I had to stick my head out the window and take deep breaths. In my mind, I was practicing what I was going to say to Billie. Then I started saying things out loud, then screaming them. Lots of fuckers and fuck-yous and fucked-ups.

At the Snatch Out, Billie climbed in the pickup, slammed the door like a true Idaho girl. There was no breath inside me and a world of farts.

Billie looked almost scary-differnt. Her face was full and round, and she'd gained a lot of weight. Plus she had tear duct cancer, and her eyes were red. She wasn't ratting her hair anymore, and her hair was longer than I'd seen it. She was wearing my black T-shirt, which was huge on her, and a pair of black stretch pants, and black strapped sandals with a low heel. Her Midnight in Helsinki blue toenails and fingernails. She wore no lipstick, no eye shadow, no mascara. Hippie earrings that were turquoise Indian beads.

Wednesday night, Saint Francis De Sales night, Billie Cody and I, at the Snatch Out drive-through window, picking up a cherry Coke Ironport with extra crushed ice, a regular Coke, and a large French fries. We drive through the Snatch Out parking lot, which was thankfully pretty empty, then left on Ashby. Billie and I didn't say much. We just said the French fries were good and stuff like that. Mostly it was Billie who said stuff. I was playing it cool. I made especially sure when I reached for the French fries, I didn't get the ketchup cup.

As we drove, the warm wind was blowing through the cab, blowing through Billie's long, loose hair. The radio was playing the top-ten hits. My hands were fists around the steering wheel. I didn't look around, only stared straight ahead.

Parked next to Russell's grave, out the windshield the moon was a half-moon and was sitting on top of the huge American elm. On the radio it was "All You Need Is Love." Billie sat across the cab from me. We both stared ahead.

In a moment, when I smelled Billie's French smell, my breath came back.

Across from me, sitting on the pickup seat, was my friend, Billie. My pregnant friend. A life was growing inside her. She wasn't married, and that had to be tough.

Still though, no matter what, Billie was the one who had to start the talking.

When the radio started playing "Ode to Billie Joe," Billie reached over and shut the radio off. She pulled her legs up and sat like Buddha. Her cigarette was a three-ring circus.

I got a lot to say, Rig, Billie said. A lot. I need you to listen to me, OK?

I did one of my coolest French inhales. Tried to make my face like James Dean would look if his girlfriend slept around.

Billie closed her sore eyes and inhaled deep on the cigarette, then leaned back.

I called you, Billie said, so I could talk to you face to face. You deserve that.

Billie looked up and out of the window when she spoke. Billie always did that when she didn't know what to say.

This is not an easy thing to do, Billie said.

But it's authentic, I said.

Billie looked up and out the window again.

Rig, I am sorry, Billie said. Her best Simone Signoret ever.

In a moment, all the fuck-yous, all the practicing over and over in my head, stopped. If I moved my hand, my hand would touch Billie's knee.

Billie scooted so her back was against the door. Her legs were up on the seat, her feet curled under her. She slurped her cherry Coke Ironport with lots of crushed ice, set the cup on the pickup floor.

I slept with Chuck the night of your sister's wedding, Billie said.

The sharp pain next to my heart. I made my hand into a fist and slammed the steering wheel.

Fuck, I said.

Please listen, Billie said.

Billie's hands were on my arm. I wanted to pull my arm away but didn't.

I don't know why I did it, Billie said. I was drunk. I wanted you. I was pissed you took your mother home. There's all kind of excuses, and I'd do anything now to go back and change things, but I can't.

As fate would have it, I said.

I knew those words would hurt her. But I was glad.

Billie looked up and out the window. Silence like only in a cemetery. Silence only like when you talk like this.

Then: Those weeks when you were trying to get a hold of me, Billie said, I had three dates with Chuck. I just met him, and we mostly just drove around. He was older and cool. He's got a job. I'd never gone out with a guy who had a job. I liked his car.

Billie's long drag. That cigarette was hot-boxed already.

I did a perfect French inhale.

We did it a second time, Billie said. Because the first time it hurt, and I was curious.

I made my hand into a fist and slammed the steering wheel.

Fuck! I said.

Rig! Billie said. Please listen.

All there was was my cigarette and me smoking, smoking, and the whole time Billie was talking, but I didn't hear a word. When I checked back in, Billie was saying this:

After that, though, it was like we were married or something. He started telling me to do things. Telling me how to dress. He told me I shouldn't smoke and cuss.

Billie's blue eyes were all red around the rims. Her tiny hands were shaking.

And you know, Billie said, he's not very smart. Chuck and I can't talk like you and I talk.

The goddamn moon. Wind in the very top of the big old elm tree.

I knew I was pregnant after the second time, Billie said. I was throwing up in the morning, my boobs were getting bigger, they hurt. I was a real bitch. I mean, all the signs were there.

But I was like your Indian friend, Billie said. I was smoking and waiting for the big bird to tell me which way to go.

Rig, Billie said. How could I be so stupid?

Billie's eyes, the clear blue inside all the red. Man, they looked so sore. Billie looked up and out the window.

I've wondered about the sex, Billie said. Why you never wanted to go any further than we did. But I understand. At least I think I do.

The feeling on the top of my lungs. No way I was going to cry.

Catholicism, Billie said. Your sister, Billie said. Rig, I'm sorry you have such a mother.

The breath thing. Oh, jeez, I was in a lot of trouble.

Pretty soon Billie's hands were back on my arm.

What's so weird, Billie said, is I really didn't want to go all the way with you either. I just wanted to sit and kiss and talk with you and look in your eyes. I love it when your eyes are gold.

Billie slid across the seat. I raised my arm and in no time Billie's face was against my chest. My arm across her shoulders, I pulled Billie in so close. Billie's French smell.

That night at the Sunset Motel, Billie said. Fuck.

Fuck, I said.

Billie's chest started going up and down, and she was sobbing big sobs, snot coming out her nose. This crying when she couldn't cry could really plug up her eyes.

If I could change anything, Billie said, it would be that night.

I knew that motel room wasn't for us, Billie said.

Room fifty-eight, I said.

But there you went, Billie said, and gave me your shirt at the Blind Lemon. Such a generous thing to do. I don't know if you realize how *considered* I felt. Through all this pregnancy stuff, with my mom, with my dad, with Chuck, I never once have felt considered.

Billie sat up, reached into her black leather purse with the silver clasp, pulled out a Kleenex. All the while that she said this whole next part, Billie was blowing her nose and talking her voice wobbly, then blowing her nose and trying to catch her breath. All the while, her eyes redder and redder, not one single tear.

That night we had such a great time, Billie said. It was your birthday, and the world for once seemed bright, Billie said. I just loved you so much. Plus Cheryl and Karen had given me the keys.

You're the only one I can talk to, Rig, Billie said. And there I was hiding from you. It was breaking my heart.

That's really all I've ever wanted, Billie said, is to be closer to you. I wasn't trying to trick you into being the father, Billie said. Rig, that's the last thing I would do.

You got to believe that, Billie said.

Dark all around us. The trees of Mount Moriah, darker shadows than the sky. Billie and I sat like that, her face against my chest, my arm around her, Billie's French smell. The moon, the goddamn moon, down through the branches of the elm. The wind blowing the branches, flickers of shadows and moon onto Billie's face.

Then, so weird, my voice in the silence:

I suppose, I said, you're going to get an abortion.

Billie snuffed up, pulled in closer, tried to crawl inside me.

More silence. Only the wind and breathing.

I don't know, Rig, Billie said. It's not so easy when it actually happens to you.

More silence.

What about Chuck? I said. Do you love him?

Billie looked up out the window.

I hate him, Billie said. I don't love him, Billie said. Yet there's something between us, something strong.

What's growing inside me, Billie said.

When Billie said *what's growing inside me,* there's something that happened, I don't know if I can say.

Our two bodies closer than ever. Our breath together in and out. The wind just then, a gust, the Thunderbird breathing. Within the gust, Billie and I, for a moment, we were the same person.

That's when it hit me. In that moment of being so much the same, I understood something that made so much sense.

Billie and I weren't the same.

Most of all she wasn't *mine.*

Even better, I wasn't hers.

I didn't have to make myself be differnt to be her friend.

So alone in that moment right then, so terrified, yet I felt free.

Maybe, if the child in her were mine, I would not have felt our differnce. The child would be how Billie and I were even more the same.

But the child grows and becomes again someone completely new.

Maybe that's what George had meant.

If I haven't ever been somebody, how could I possibly do anything on my own.

Back at the Snatch Out, Billie was looking up and out the window. Waiting for Godot. It was the moment when a boyfriend and a girlfriend kiss.

Our hands held tight to each other's. I didn't ever want to let her go.

Friends, Billie said. Always. I promise.

On Pole Line Road, the buzz of a siren and a cop car flashing red and white.

Friends, I said, I promise.

Everything the same, everything differnt.

Billie slammed the pickup door hard, then poked her face into the window.

What you doing Saturday night? Billie said.

No plans, I said.

Would you like to go to the Senior Summer All Night Party with me? Billie said.

Red and white flashes on the world, headlights, dark.

What about Chuck? I said.

Billie's big smile all over her face.

Just because I screwed him, Billie said, don't mean I go out with him.

From deep down in my belly up, a weird sound out of my mouth. Billie Cody could make me laugh.

Yah, I said, but won't he be pissed?

He could give a shit, Billie said. Besides he's got a date with your brother-in-law and Joe Scardino.

At that moment, a dust devil whirled up dust, napkins, paper sacks, from the gravel of the parking lot.

The cop car flashed red, flashed white, red, white, red, white, red, white.

I'd love to go, I said.

As fate would have it, just before noon on Friday, George pitched the last bale of hay off the truck. I picked the hay bale up and shoved it in place into the stack. Neither George nor I jumped around and yelled fuck and did cartwheels like when we'd finished baling. I guess because we were both tired. At least, that's what I thought.

The sky was gray overcast, gray and bright, and the wind was blowing hot from the southeast, not the northwest, where the wind usually blows from.

Feels like rain, George said.

That's what people do in Idaho, they talk about the weather instead of talking about what they want to talk about.

With our feet, George and I scraped the hay dust and hay leaves off the truck bed and into the feed manger. At the head board of the truck bed, I dug out the smashed-in hay leaves that had piled up in the corners. Inside the cab, George picked up the candy wrappers and the empty cigarette packs and Coke bottles.

Let's face it, we were both trying to find things to do.

The end of something and before the beginning of something else.

The cleaning up was done and the haying was over, and we weren't going to work another day in the hay, and our time together was over, and we weren't going to see each other again except for maybe pass each other driving on Tyhee Road or Philbin Road or Quinn Road.

So there we were, George and I, standing behind the truck. Two men face to face, not looking the other in the eyes. Both of us trying to find what to do with our arms and our hands. We knew this was it, but neither one of us said a thing.

George took his hat off, smacked his hat alongside his thigh, then jumped up on the back of the truck. He sat on the truck bed, his legs dangling down. George looked up at the sky, let out a big sigh, said:

Cigarette?

George stuck out his hand. George's strong hand in front of my face for me to grab hold of. I almost didn't take it, I almost ignored his hand and hiked myself up alone. Then before I knew it, George'd reached down, put his hand around my forearm, and I put my hand around his forearm, and George pulled.

Going up, I thought I was going to hit the sky.

Little laughs from inside the both of us. Our arms had touched, and our bodies had to laugh. George's touch was still all over my arm when I sat down. I sat an arm's length away.

My hand went to my T-shirt pocket and patted.

I don't have any today, I said.

We can smoke mine, George said.

George pulled a Camel out of the pack, just one Camel, lit it. Two perfect French inhales.

George handed the cigarette to me. Our fingers did not touch.

The wet on the filter, that was George's lips.

So, I said, you got enough money to buy Granny her refrigerator?

Went to Sears Sunday, George said. Bought her a nice one.

I handed the cigarette back to George. Our fingers did not touch.

We sat there, our legs hanging down. The cows were starting to crowd up to the manger.

I was going to say something about how dumb cows were or something like that, something about the weather, some Idaho shit.

Then George said: Me and you, George said, we've had our ups and downs, George said. I want you to know I wish you well.

Quick lightning in my veins, in my chest a big gust of wind.

I loved God so much right then.

When I went to speak, I couldn't. No words inside me. Then all at once, something hit, and my lips started moving. I didn't know what I was going to say.

I never have seen Flaco and Acho again, I said. Not ever.

I toked on the cigarette, didn't even try a French inhale, handed the cigarette back to George.

The gold bars in George's dark eyes. Jesus in George's eyes.

Then George looked up and away, the same way Billie'd looked up and out the window. When things are difficult to say.

It's probably best that way, George said.

Breath. All that was empty was everything.

Two guys sitting on the back of a truck. The truck parked between a haystack and a feed manger. All around them dark gray sky. A bunch of damn drut Hereford cows staring up.

I didn't know what to do. I figured it was best to get it over with, so I took a deep breath, put a smile on my face, stuck my hand out.

Well, goodbye then, I said.

Then: I hope what you're waiting for comes to you.

When George's palm touched my palm, I was ready to give his hand a big so-long-pardner pump, but his hand just rested there in mine, letting me hold it. Big, rough, calloused hands. My palm so white, the back suntanned brown, thin and long.

George's voice was soft, like that first day in the yard when he spoke.

It'll come, George said. Whatever it is.

When I went to pull my hand away, George's hand stayed tight around my hand. George pulled, and just like that we were chest to chest, and my face was in his neck. The part of the tomato that folds together red into the stem of green.

Our cowboy hats poked into each other. Knocked my hat clean off my head.

Buckskin and flint on the back of my throat.

George's lips moved slow against my ear: Shoshones don't have a word for goodbye, George said. We just say *Happy trails* or *Keep on tumbling like a tumbleweed.*

Then that quick, George pulled me away from him the way he'd pulled me in and then let go.

George jumped down off the truck.

He handed me up my hat. Our fingers did not touch.

Tell your old man I'll be by tonight to pick up the rest of my check, George said.

I'll walk home from here, George said.

One last toke on the cigarette, a wicked French inhale, then George's fingers crushed out the butt onto the bed of the truck.

George was halfway down the mangers, almost to the end of the feedlots.

George! I yelled.

George stopped right in his tracks. Turned around quick.

From that far away I could see his dark eyes.

Yah? George said.

I didn't say *don't go away.* I didn't say *come back,* I didn't say *please stay.*

As usual, I didn't have a clue *what* I was going to say.

Then: Can I bum another cigarette? I said.

George started a slow lope back along the mangers. The sky behind him was gray to pure white to charcoal in the east. The cows all moved away because of George. At about ten feet from the truck, George stopped, took the pack of cigarettes out of his pocket, tossed the pack an arch into the air. The Camels landed exactly in my hands.

Keep the pack, he said. I've got more at home.

Then George turned around.

George had his own way of walking. Long legs slung out slow, hip and shoulder syncopation, riding low in his own saddle.

At the end of the haystack, just as he turned.

Happy trails! I yelled.

Keep on tumbling like a tumbleweed! I yelled.

That quick, George was gone.

I was on the back of the truck, my arms wrapped around my middle. The place on my arm where George had grabbed me.

Just me and the cows.

And Tramp, his pink tongue hanging out, a wet piece of bologna.

Tramp, I said, looks like it's just you and me.

Tramp got that look on his face. His paw started poking, poking the air.

I leaned over, picked up George's crushed-out cigarette. Put the butt to my lips.

After supper, I changed the water in the pasture. When I got in the pickup to go back home, the gray clouds in the west were showing off orange and pink. By the time I drove into the yard, it was night.

The lights on inside the house, the television, the rosary, my bed, my hot sheets — I couldn't face it. I started walking.

At the swimming hole, the white water flowed down the outcropping of lava rock. The air was hot. The moon on the silver water, the coolness of the water, the music. But I didn't take off my clothes. I went to the bolted-down two-by-twelve, jumped across to the slick, dark lava rock, and landed, my black Converse tennis shoes suction cups. My hands and feet found their way up the side of the mossy, wet, dark lava. On top, the flat, dusty earth was hot even through my shoes.

I leaned against the barbwire fence, the fence between yellow Bannock County and the red rez. Granny's Lombardy poplars were darker than the night. The wind in the tops of the trees, a roll and swirl. In Granny's kitchen window, the kerosene lamp. A tiny bright square of light in all the dark. Granny's ancestors were out here in a special tree looking in on that light just like me. So bright the little flame in the lamp.

A gust of wind started me thinking about Thunderbird and God and spirits and what happens to us when we die. I wondered if you had to be Indian to hang out in a tree when you're dead.

That would be about the best.

Being a tree, or sitting in a tree, was a fine idea of heaven.

I squinted hard to see if the kerosene lamp was burning the curtain. I stayed silent, listened hard like a coyote or a wolf. Frogs and crickets, the wind, a faraway train. No fire.

No George.

George was probably out. Mom'd paid him his last paycheck, and for sure George was out on the town in his yellow dress and red high heels having himself a ball.

That's when it hit me. I turned around slow.

The wind in the cedar tree, a sweet sound, and sad too.

The scrub cedar by the swimming hole, all these years, the tree where Granny's Shoshone ancestors lived.

Granny's sacred tree.

I sat down right there on the dusty earth, and maybe for the first time ever, I took a good, long look at the tree.

The sweaty body smell of it. The trunk came up out of the ground maybe a foot thick. The boughs didn't begin until about where my head was as I sat. Ten or twelve feet tall, not as wide. Full and green and dense. Compact like the way you draw trees as a kid, except for one branch up at the top that took off all by itself.

At eye level, an arm's length away, was the lowest of the cedar boughs.

I wondered then in all the years if I'd ever touched the tree.

I reached my hand out to touch the bottom limb. My fingers were right there, ready to grasp. Then I thought about what George had said. There were some things for the white man not to know.

Sacred things.

That night in my dream, Granny's ancestor tree was a yellow submarine filled with Indian people laughing and dancing and singing.

PART IV

Purple Haze

11 The Great Escape

WHEN BLACK AND WHITE turns to color. I've searched my whole life for that moment. When a big gust of Idaho wind turns to Thunderbird and all that is ordinary falls away. In an instant you're in the gaze of another, and for whatever reason — the universe, fate, or just dumb luck — all of a sudden things get perfectly clear, it's magic, one soul is touching another, and there is love.

That first bright morning with Flaco and Acho, when I shook Flaco's hand, and he didn't shake my hand, but held my hand in his. I shaded my eyes and took the chance, looked quick, and in his eyes was Jesus.

Then Billie, how hard we laughed, waiting for Godot, the goddamn cigarette lighter, my body a forty-pound block of extra-sharp Cheddar cheese. *Like you? I think I love you.* The way our kisses could make a dream.

And George. Mom and me in the Buick and the Buick spinning out of control and out there in the sunset field a naked man holding his hands open to a drop of rain.

So many moments I've stood close to the fire.

But I always stepped back. Dared not step beyond the safety of the fulcrum point. George says you have to wait, to trust, for the moment spirit touches you.

What I've just figured out is that if you're not there, ready for spirit, ready to take the plunge, to jump, to fly, you're shit out of luck.

You have to step up too, and not just up to, you have to take the step that's just beyond.

Maybe spirit will greet you, maybe not.

In any case, you have to take the step alone.

And despite all odds, do something completely on your own.

Little did I know the Senior Summer All Night Party was going to provide me the opportunity to take my first step.

I didn't have a clue what was ahead of me. That Saturday evening, the only problem I could see was how to get out of the house.

I figured the best thing to do was lie and just say I was going to some kind of prom. But in the middle of summer? Everybody knew about the Senior Summer All Night Party. Even Mom. Two years ago, she wouldn't let Sis go.

Like always, though, things were worse than they seemed.

There was a lot more to worry about than the *all night* part of the Senior Summer All Night Party.

The universe has always conspired to fuck me up.

No wonder there were storm clouds gathering.

Then something in a moment. Something you'd least expect.

I was sitting in the pickup smoking one of George's Camels, trying to figure out how I was going to finagle past my mother, get out the door and into the pickup, in a suit, when a song came on the radio. A new song. I turned the radio way up.

"Purple Haze" by Jimi Hendrix. As soon as I heard the first beats of that song, weird how you can know when something is totally new and differnt before anybody tells you. And right then, listening to "Purple Haze," the sky above me was a kind of purple too.

"Purple Haze" didn't feel like a new song, or any song at all. "Purple Haze" felt like a new part of my soul.

No doubt about it. Something new was going on in the world. Something new, but I didn't know what yet.

All's I knew it had everything to do with putting on my suit, walking out of the house, getting in the pickup, and driving out of the yard.

'Scuse me while I kiss the sky was on my lips when I opened the kitchen door.

Mom was in her denims and pink rummage-sale blouse, her back to me, her hair hanging down in her face. Oatmeal cookies or peanut butter cookies or chocolate cookies or pound cake, eggs and flour and sugar, there she was bent over a bowl, beating things into shape.

I closed the kitchen door. Said: Hi, Mom. Then walked down the stairs to my room. The shiny brown suit Mom bought me for Sis's wedding would have to do. I took the suit off the hanger and laid the suit on the bed. There was a wrinkle in the pants where it had been hanging on the hanger, but otherwise it looked fine. I had a new, thin, shiny red tie I was going to wear and a white shirt with a tab under the collar. The shirt needed ironing. The shoes were black, worn every Sunday for a year. Nothing fancy.

I stepped into the shiny brown suit pants and buttoned the top button, zipped up. I guess I'd grown some since April. The waist was a little tight and the pant cuffs were just below my ankle. I figured if I wore dark socks, no one would know the differnce. Then the jacket. My wrists were definitly hanging out.

I spread the *Idaho Catholic Register* out on the floor — the page where it listed the condemned movies — I put my shoes on top of that page, then opened the can of Kiwi black. I opened the door a crack and watched Mom while I put black shoe wax onto my shoes. Somehow I had to get the steam iron and the ironing board out of the broom closet and get them downstairs without her seeing.

I was spitting onto the toe of my second shoe, I was reading about condemned movies, *Lolita, Loves of a Blonde,* when I looked up just as Mom put the cookie sheet into the oven. She closed the oven door, set the timer on the stove, then opened the kitchen door.

Through the kitchen door window, I watched as Mom put her gardening gloves on. She picked up the short-handled hoe and pushed out the screen door, and the screen door slammed.

Out of the broom closet, I got the ironing board and the iron and the pressing cloth. It felt weird to be in my underwear in the kitchen. It was an immediate hard-on. Shit.

That's when the phone rang.

It was Billie, and she sounded freaked out and she was whispering.

Rig, Billie whispered. Thank God I finally got you. Your mother kept answering, and I had to hang up. Look, don't pick me up at the house. Dad is being very weird. I'll meet you at the Snatch Out, seven-thirty.

Snatch Out, I whispered too. Seven-thirty.

Three giant steps across the blue and white kitchen tiles, I peeked around the kitchen door and looked through the window. No Mom. Three lunges down the stairs, I was back down in my room.

When you're raised with a sister, you learn how to do things like sew and iron and cook and wash dishes. I pressed the pants — just the wrinkle out of the middle of the legs — then started on the shirt.

I had to make another trip upstairs to get the spray starch under the sink. My cock was still hard, but I was ignoring it. In the kitchen, the smell of oatmeal cookies. The green bowl was half filled with cookie dough. With one hand, I grabbed a chunk of cookie dough, with the other, I reached under the sink.

Just then, the timer on the oven went off.

Then the screen door slammed.

I shoved the cookie dough into my mouth.

The chunk of cookie dough was so big I could barely get it in my mouth. Mom was taking off her gloves. I quick looked over to the green bowl. Shit. You could see just where the huge chunk was missing. Mom was going to have a fit. For a moment there, I thought I'd spit the cookie dough back out and try and smooth it back into the rest of the cookie dough. But there wasn't time. Plus there I was with my shorts sticking out in front. I ducked and ran down the stairs and closed my door. My door closed at the same time the kitchen door opened. Just in time.

I leaned against my bedroom door, gulping down oatmeal cookie dough as fast as I could. Upstairs, I could hear Mom take the cookie sheet out of the oven and set the cookie sheet on the stove.

I waited with bated breath.

Only the sound of the steam bubbling in the iron.

After a couple minutes, I decided the coast was clear. Somehow Mom hadn't noticed the cookie dough. Three quiet giant steps across the room, I walked behind the ironing board and stood. I put my hand around the iron's handle, picked up the hot steam iron.

I'd just put the iron down onto the collar point when there was a big crash in the kitchen. Then it was Mom's footsteps coming down the stairs.

There was no lock on my door, and she never knocked. Mom just walked up to my door, opened the door. There she stood, Mom Klusener, my mother, her hair not yet done up for Dad, her face not on, just stubs of eyebrows above the inside corner of her eyes. Her big gray plastic glasses. Her pink rummage-sale blouse, her denims, her white Keds. Her hands were on her hips. Not a good sign.

What the hell is the big idea! Mom said. How many times have I told you not to eat the cookie dough! I work hard to have something nice to eat around the house and what do you do but go and shove it all in your mouth. All I do is work around here, and for what?

Me me me, Mom said. That's all you think about is me me me.

I lifted the iron, pointed the flat of the iron at my mother.

The steam in the iron bubbled. Puffs of steam blew out.

Mom looked over on my bed. There was my brown shiny suit laid out. There was my red tie. My black belt. There were my polished black shoes on top of the *Idaho Catholic Register.* There I was in my underwear ironing my white shirt.

What are you doing? Mom said. Where are you going in a suit?

Mom started walking toward me and the ironing board, but halfway she stopped.

Put your damn clothes on, Mom said.

Then she pointed at my shirt and flipped her fingers.

You're not doing that right, Mom said. Let me iron that for you.

If Mom got a hold of the iron, the battle would be lost. I put the iron down on the collar, pressed.

No, it's OK, I said. You're making cookies, I said. I can do this.

What's left of the cookies is in the oven, Mom said. All five of them, Mom said.

Good Lord, Mom said. Why not eat the whole bowl?

It's a sin to steal, Mom said. The eighth commandment, Mom said. Thou shalt not steal. It's a mortal sin to steal.

The wrinkle in Mom's forehead went all the way from her hairline to the top of her nose. Mom took a deep breath, and as she huffed out the breath, she looked at the iron and the ironing board as if it were the first time.

Just where do you think you are going, young man? she said.

Young man. Not good.

I wasn't looking at her, only looking up now and then. I made myself engrossed in ironing my white shirt. The seam on the shoulder, the top button, the second button. Mom took a couple more steps. My naked chest was burning up. When she got to the ironing board, she touched the ironing board. The ironing board was her place, not my place.

Mom's almond-shaped hazel eyes. That close they weren't green or gold. They were gray.

I *said,* Mom said, where are you going in a suit?

Mom's big plastic glasses had slipped down her nose. On each side of her nose was an oval red sore from the nose pads of her glasses. Without taking her eyes off my eyes, with her index finger, Mom reached up, pushed her glasses back up her nose.

My eyes were starting to burn, but I was not going to blink first.

I'm going to a party, I said.

In a suit? Mom said. What party?

Just a party, I said.

While Mom's eyes and my eyes were in the stare-down, the whole time Mom's hands were down below us somewhere trying to get the iron. I kept moving the iron back and forth so she couldn't grab it.

In a suit? Mom said. In the middle of summer?

I looked down. The iron was on top of the second and third buttons.

Then: You're not going with that Billie Cody, are you?

I let go of the iron, stood up tall, then leaned my fists down onto the ironing board. Mom was like that too with her fists. Me on one side, Mom on the other. The steam iron steaming up in between.

Head to head, eye to eye, with Mom like that, it was a standoff. The spotlight behind Mom's eyes had me, the deer in her headlights.

For a moment there, everything stopped.

It was in that moment, some part of me took a look around my room. The olive green walls, the paneling, the olive green matching bedspread, the lamp. I couldn't believe it. I might as well have been standing in a room in the Holiday Inn. There was nothing in my room that was truly mine.

A big deep breath.

Mom, I said, I *am too* going with Billie Cody, I said. To the Senior Summer All Night Party.

The look on my mother's face. I don't think I'd ever seen that look up so close. The hundreds of tiny wrinkles around her mouth were thousands. The way she set her jaw. The ripples along her jaw, the grinding of her teeth.

When she spoke, deep and gravelly, Mom's voice sounded like it came from hell.

For God's sake, Rigby John, Mom said. The girl is pregnant.

Pregnant like *shit* or *fart* or *fuck* or *cunt* or *faggot*.

Who told you that? I said.

That girl, Mom said, is a common slut. She has an illegitimate child in her womb and a mortal sin on her soul. And now the bitch is parading around at all-night parties.

Mom's chest filled up. She lifted her mighty chin.

Well, Mom said, not with my son she ain't.

The breath. Jeez, the breath. Where was it?

I'm not the father, I said.

My voice was high.

You sure as hell ain't, Mom said.

The breath, the breath, the breath.

But Billie needs a friend, I said.

Friend! Mom said. What kind of damn fool are you? That girl is a little whore.

Something was burning. I looked down. The iron was burning a dark brown iron point onto the shirt collar.

Now look what you've done! Mom said. Your new Sunday shirt!

What happened next, I didn't see coming.

Mom's open hand slapped me hard across the face.

You spineless ass, Mom said. You're not going nowhere.

Mom could pack a wallop. I stepped back a couple steps, saw stars. I must confess, though, it felt good to get hit like that. After a hard slap in the face, I woke up. Something else kicked in, and it was a whole new ball game.

Mom shoved the ironing board, knocked it clean over. I quick grabbed the iron. Then Mom dragged the board to the doorway, then this truly amazing thing — Mom picked up the ironing board like it was a spear or a javelin and with a grunt from deep inside her *threw* the ironing board into the air and out the door. The ironing board bumped up the stairs and crashed loud down onto the kitchen floor.

Mom's hair was flying, and her glasses were crooked, and she was screaming. Not any words or anything you could make sense of, just weird sounds like a dog or a cat that had got run over by a truck.

I remember saying to myself: This woman is a crazy maniac.

When Mom stopped, she was standing in the doorway, her hands, her feet, pressing into the doorjamb on each side.

And me. I was standing alone in my bedroom in my shorts with a hot iron in my hand. My white shirt, its burnt collar, lying on my feet.

Just like that, Mom walked over, ripped the cord of the iron out of the socket.

Unplugged.

You're not leaving this house tonight, Mom said.

With that, Mom grabbed the iron. The iron was hot as hell, but still she grabbed the iron, from the bottom, and ripped the iron away from me.

Mom's almond-shaped hazel eyes had gone completely stone gray. Not a trace of green or gold. Her hair was gray too. Mom's hair wasn't brown, it was gray.

Upstairs, the timer on the oven started to ding.

I'll be back with the rosary, Mom said. You and I are going to kneel down *right here* and pray the rosary. If not for your soul, for your family's good name.

Ding ding ding upstairs.

Mom took a couple of steps toward the door. Then stopped and turned.

Get your damn pants on, Mom said. And kneel down and examine your conscience. We've got a rosary to pray.

Mom walked out the door. Ding ding ding ding was all I could hear. Plus my ears were ringing. I didn't have time to stop and think, or even breathe. In no time at all, she'd be back with her rosary.

Praying the rosary was out of the fucking question.

In no time at all, I had my white shirt on, had it buttoned up. I slipped on my dark socks, one foot and then the other. Stepped into my shiny brown suit pants, stuck my shirttails in. Buttoned. Zipped. The oven timer stopped dinging by the time I had my suit jacket on. The oven door closed when my hands looped my belt. I looped the red tie around my neck. The cookie sheet was on top of the stove when I put my wallet in my pocket. I stepped into my shoes, bent down, tied one and then the other.

I was up the stairs two at a time. Mom was at the broom closet making the sign of the cross. When she looked up at me, she looked like she'd seen Satan himself.

You're going to hell! she screamed. You're going to hell!

Mom was like a big cat on my back, scratching and screaming. Her teeth against my scalp, in my hair, trying to get a bite.

It's easy to tell about something after it's over, but while it's happening, it's all just one thing after another flipping past your eyes.

Mom was doing some serious damage to the sides of my head. I didn't know what to do, so I ducked my head and ran into her bedroom and toward the bed. At the bed, I stopped fast, bent down at the waist, and Mom went flying off my back, ass over teakettle onto the bed — the smooth, perfectly made bed. Mom bounced once, then went flying off the bed, down the other side, and smack onto the floor.

Mom was back on her feet in no time.

By the look on Mom's face, there was no doubt about it. This was a battle to the death.

Then I was running. I ran through the kitchen, my feet over the blue squares and the white squares, past the kitchen table, the chrome chairs with the yellow plastic seats, past the sink, the oven, the five oatmeal cookies. I thought, What the hell, if I'm going to hell I might as well be eating oatmeal cookies. I scooped up the five oatmeal cookies, opened the kitchen door, ran down the four steps, ran into the garage, opened the garage door from the inside, got in the pickup, dumped the oatmeal cookies on the seat, started the pickup, and put the gearshift into reverse. I'd just turned my head and was ready to back out of the garage when all of a sudden, there was Mom, the scream of her, outside, pulling down the garage door.

The slam of the garage door was a slam deep down in my heart. Where there was light, now there was darkness.

What's the use. I was trapped. I'd never get away from her.

The sharp pain next to my heart. I know it sounds weird, but my mind went totally blank. I shut off the pickup, got out of the pickup, walked back up the stairs into the kitchen, then down to my bedroom. I sat down on the olive green bedspread, leaned over, and looked at my polished black shoes on the brown flowered carpet.

In no time at all, Mom was standing in the doorway.

Mom was screaming. The world was screaming. My ears were ringing. Thousands of screaming magpies gathered on my bedroom ceiling and dived at my head.

You're going to hell, you're going to hell, you're going to hell, you're going to hell.

Screaming and screaming and screaming.

You do as you're told! You're not leaving this house! You get that suit off you! You should be ashamed of yourself! Just wait till your father gets home! You're going to hell, you're going to hell, you're going to hell, you're going to hell!

There was no way out.

Then something out of nowhere.

A gust of wind, a hawk, some large bird flying low, in a moment, something collapsed. I looked at my hands, I lifted my hands up and looked at my hands.

How did this happen? How did I get there back in my bedroom, my mother in the doorway, the human barricade, a crazy maniac between me and the rest of the world?

The feeling in my arms that means I'm helpless. I cupped my hands over my ears.

Jesus loved Mary Magdalene. Jesus would have gone to the Senior Summer All Night Party with Mary Magdalene.

With that, I was up. I walked to my mother. I didn't know what I was going to do.

Those steps, four or five steps to her, my black shoes on the brown flowered carpet, closer, closer. The closer I got, the more my mother did not move. She was a block of cheese, she was concrete, she was lead. I was still only inches from her, and still I didn't know.

My hands went around her waist and lifted. Just like that, as if my mother was a bale of straw, I set her aside. She was claws and screams and scratching, trying to get at me, but I held her away with my hand. Then I ran again.

Up the stairs, out the kitchen door, down the four kitchen steps and into the garage, I opened the garage door from the inside, got in the pickup, started the pickup, put it into reverse.

I turned my head to back out of the garage, and there she was again, something dark out the corner of my eye, from out of nowhere all of a sudden, there was Mom again, outside, closing the garage door.

The slam of the garage door. The darkness where there was light. My impulse was fuck it, to gun the engine anyway, bust through the garage door.

My mother would always be lurking there when I least expected her.

I shut off the pickup, got out of the pickup, made noise running up the four kitchen steps, then jumped back down the steps, landed soft, quick ran back into the garage and hid behind the garage door.

Through the garage door window, I saw Mom's gray hair go past and up the kitchen stairs. On her fourth step, I came out from behind the garage door. Mom was just starting down my bedroom stairs when I tiptoed up the four steps, reached in, turned the lock in the kitchen door, and pulled the kitchen door closed quiet.

The garage door opening was thunder-and-lightning loud. I ran to the pickup, started the pickup, put it in reverse, turned my head to back out of the garage. No crazy maniac mother. I gunned the engine, leaving rubber on the cement floor of the garage. I half expected the crash of the garage door coming down, but there was no crash. No darkness, only light.

When I hit the driveway, gravel was flying. I backed out into a three-point turn. I put on the brakes, put the gearshift into first, hit the gas.

Mom came bursting out the screen door wielding a broom in her hands.

You're going to hell, you're going to hell, you're going to hell.

Gravel was flying, and the pickup was fishtailing. Mom was running down the sidewalk at me. Tramp was running behind her, barking. Just where the sidewalk ends and the driveway begins, Mom and me in the pickup met.

It was scary how Mom looked. Mom didn't even look like Mom. The skeleton of her face was poking through.

I started rolling up the window.

Mom smacked the kitchen broom hard down onto the hood. So hard her big gray plastic glasses went flying off. I pushed the pedal all the way to the floor. Another smack of the kitchen broom hit the top of the cab. I looked over just as the broken broomstick came down and poked in through the top crack in the window. I cranked hard on the window handle.

Just in time. The sharp end of the green broom handle poked into the cab. The jagged piece of splintered wood was pointed straight at my head.

When I looked back in front of me, it was time to turn right onto Tyhee Road. There was no way in hell I was going to stop and look for drunk Indians or hay trucks or Mormon families in their Ford cars. So I just started turning the wheel. The pickup leaned a dangerous lean. The tires were spitting gravel. Dust was flying. For a moment there, I thought for sure I was going to end up rolled over in the neighbor's front yard.

But we made it. Me and the Chevy Apache made it around the corner. Then there we were on the tarmac heading down Tyhee Road. In no time at all, the speedometer was hitting fifty-five. As fate would have it, it's the damn truth, on the radio it was "Purple Haze." I was jumping up and down in the seat. I was yelling and laughing and screaming like the cowboys on TV — Yee-ha! Ha! Ha. Yee-ha-ho!

I grabbed the sharp edge of the broom handle, rolled the window down. Took the broom handle in my hands.

Better than a poke in your eye with a sharp stick.

The broom handle, with its jagged point at the end, was just big enough to fit in the palm of my hand. Something nice the way it fit. I slipped the broom handle end into the inside pocket of my suit jacket.

My cigarette was lit, "Purple Haze" on the radio. If this was going to hell, then bring it on. I was escaping, showing off. I was eating her oatmeal cookies. I was making a spectacle of myself. I was Rigby John Klusener, and *I* was *hauling ass*.

The sky was big, dark, gray rolling clouds. Thunderheads. A couple of raindrops hit the windshield. When I turned on the wipers, the wipers screeched and the windshield became one big smear.

In the Snatch Out, Karen's root-beer brown '57 Pontiac sat off by itself. When I pulled up alongside, the driver's window rolled down. It was Billie behind the steering wheel. She was wearing new rose-colored John Lennon glasses.

My heart was still pounding. I couldn't wait to tell Billie about Mom. But when I got a good look at Billie, I didn't say a word. Something was up.

Did anybody follow you? Billie said.

I looked around for crazy maniacs. The Snatch Out was pretty empty.

My mother hadn't followed me.

No, I said.

Then: Let's not talk here, Billie said. Follow me.

Billie took off, and I followed the root-beer brown '57 Pontiac through the parking lot to Ashby, then left on Ashby. People I passed by in their cars looked at me weird. I felt like Illya Kuryakin in *The Man from U.N.C.L.E.* About five blocks away, on West Herzog Street, under a big silver maple, Billie pulled the Pontiac over and parked. I pulled in behind her and got in the Pontiac.

Billie was wearing her mother's wedding dress. Weird, seeing that dress again. The splooge of red wax at the crotch. But I didn't say anything. I pulled out George's pack of Camels. A Camel for me, a Camel for Billie. But Billie shook her head.

I can't, Billie said. Cigarettes are making me sick.

Weird not smoking with Billie. I rolled down my window, lit my cigarette, blew the smoke out the window. So much I was bursting to tell Billie, but what did I say?

It looks like it's going to rain, I said.

Idaho, man, you can't get away from it.

From out of the ignition, something caught my eye. Connected to the ignition key was a large key ring with a bunch of keys. And something else hanging down. Attached to the key chain was a piece of lava rock.

Billie's tiny fingernails were painted red. She was rubbing her hands around and around. I thought it was because she needed a cigarette.

Maybe this wasn't such a good idea, Billie said.

What? I said.

Billie's hands, her little red fingernails, around and around.

My father is really drunk, Billie said. He wouldn't let me leave the house. He locked me in my room, Billie said. I managed to call Karen and then I crawled out my window.

Billie's voice was a deep Simone Signoret, and it sounded far away.

What a sight, Billie said. Can you imagine? A pregnant woman in this dress trying to make it out her bedroom window.

Billie's mother's wedding dress.

White shiny silk. Billie's boobs about to bust over the top. The red glob of red wax in the crotch. Red wax drips all the way down the front of the dress. The dress was big and took up that whole side of the car. I reached over and touched the folds of skirt, a long drip of red wax. When Billie moved, the slick sound of silk. Something once so shiny and clean, now shockingly dark and bloody.

It's a good metaphor, Billie said. Don't you think?

Can you really wear that dress to the dance?

It's all I could find to wear, Billie said. Before I jumped out the window.

Billie looked down at the dress, the red wax splooge. She pulled her belly in, then put her hands up on the bodice. Billie moved one breast around and then the other.

I swear, Billie said, I feel like any minute my nipples are going to boing out for the whole world to see.

Billie's red-lipped smile wasn't much of a smile. The gray evening light, the way it hit the John Lennon glasses, mirrors of rose-colored clouds.

Just then, above us, the silver maple went crazy. Wind, big gusts, blowing hard. A blast of hail, hail so loud you couldn't think. Billie and I looked at each other, hail pinging off the Pontiac, and for a moment, all there was in the world was hail and the roar of hail. In no time at all the ground was covered. That quick, the hail stopped.

Through the windows, the breeze was cool and smelled weird like burnt flowers. A magpie was making a fuss.

Rig, I'm afraid, Billie said. I haven't told Dad who the father is. Mom tried to tell Dad it isn't you, but he won't listen.

Shit, Billie said. He's so drunk.

Billie wiped her eyes and blew her nose. Her nose was as red as her eyes.

Dad thinks the father is you, Billie said. And he knows your pickup.

He'll be out tonight looking for us, Billie said. I just know it.

Billie slumped down and a big sob burst out. I scooted across the seat, put my arm across her shoulders. Billie's French smell mixed in with silk and the smell of wax.

For a long time, we sat like that, Billie and me, raindrops spitting on the windshield. I thought about the time in the Shanghai when Billie'd cried, and because she cried she'd turned into something ugly and needy and it freaked me out.

Billie was crying now. I didn't feel freaked out, and crying didn't make her ugly.

Boyfriend and girlfriend hasn't got much to do with friends at all.

Billie snuffed up, blew hard into her torn-up Kleenex.

I'm so sorry, Rig, Billie said. I didn't mean for this to happen.

Billie hadn't really looked at me since I'd sat in the car. Her eyes were swollen and red, and she thought she looked ugly so she hadn't looked.

Just then, though, Billie looked up, and her eyes blinked, and the blue in them flashed out bright from inside all that red.

What on earth happened to you? Billie said.

What? I said.

Billie reached up, pulled the rearview mirror around.

Look at yourself, Billie said.

In the mirror, blood under my nose, three big scratches on my cheek, a big bruise growing on my cheekbone, my hair sticking up like some guy crazy.

What a sight.

Into the mirror: Hello, Mother, I sang, hello, Father.

Billie's smile was smack all across her face. I loved it that Billie was smiling.

Your mother and father did *that*? Billie said.

Only mother, I said.

Your father's not the only one out looking for us tonight, I said.

Oh fuck, Billie said.

Oh fuck is right, I said.

My money's on Mom doing the most damage, I said.

Right then, I wanted to tell Billie all about how I'd escaped from Mom. But I didn't. She was too freaked out.

A long Idaho moment with so much to say and saying nothing.

There we were: Billie Cody and Rigby John Klusener.

As fate would have it, all Billie and I were trying to do was go to the prom.

Jeez, Billie, I finally said. Look at you and me. I swear, we're so weird we're moving into the ludicrous.

Into the absurd, Billie said.

The resemblance is phenomenal, don't you think? I said, We look exactly like Yves Montand and Simone Signoret.

Billie and I do exactly the same thing at the same time. Inside us first, down deep, something inside that has to come up and out, and when it does, my weird sound mixes up with Billie's weird sound, and then both of us are sitting in this sound that we are making from the inside, and we are looking at each other in the eyes as we are making the sound.

Weird thing, laughter.

Here Billie and I were again, a year and some months since we met, still laughing, holding our stomachs, our bodies slamming around inside the Pontiac, arms flailing, feet kicking, high screams laughing like a couple of damn fools.

Billie's whole body is rolling, rumbling, trying to accommodate the weird sound coming up and out, and sure enough, wouldn't you know it, boing, out pops one nipple, then, boing, out pops the other nipple. Billie's laughing so hard, she can't even put her nipples back in. She just sits there, these massive, soft pink mounds of flesh, two brown nubs, two beings, bouncing up and down, alive themselves.

My God, the laughter. Sore belly. Snot and saliva, then coughing because of cigarettes. Then just because we're Billie Cody and Rigby John Klusener, because we're so Yves Montand and Simone Signoret, as fate would have it, just to make the cycle complete, wouldn't you know it, one of us has to fart. It was me this time. The oatmeal cookie dough. My fart was abrupt and real loud. Made a tent in my suit pants and traveled down my leg. Thank God it didn't stink.

It was too much.

Really, the way Billie and I laughed, wasn't like we'd ever laughed before.

And I tell you, since then, nothing, never, nothing ever has made me laugh for so hard, so long. Never.

I met Billie Cody laughing.

And that evening, in the root-beer brown '57 Pontiac, under the silver maple on West Herzog Street, hailstones covering the ground, laughing is how we parted.

And despite all the shit that came down later on that night, that's how I plan to remember it.

Remember her. Billie Cody.

The problem was, when we quit laughing, we still had the problem. Billie was still pregnant. Billie's father was out to kill me. And my mother was out to crucify Billie and suck out my blood.

Then there was the problem of the joints.

Billie had promised a bunch of people she'd have joints to sell them that evening before the dance. The problem was she told them she'd meet them in the Snatch Out.

If we stay in this car, Billie said, we should be safe. My father doesn't know this car, and neither does your mother.

*　　*　　*

Saturday night, the end of July, heat lightning and intermittent rain and hail, Pocatello, Idaho, the Snatch Out. It's about eight-thirty, and the place is buzzing.

Billie and I are parked in the root-beer brown '57 Pontiac. Billie's behind the wheel, and I'm sitting on the passenger side. Billie is back to wearing the rose-colored John Lennon glasses. She's also wearing a wide-brimmed felt cowboy hat, and I'm wearing a porkpie hat. We got the hats from Karen.

Karen and Cheryl are driving Cheryl's parents' white Buick Riviera. They've come and gone and bought two joints.

Still to buy joints are four people, all girls. Liz and Diane and Kathy and Carrie.

I don't know any of them.

The joints are in my shirt pocket.

By this time, Billie is smoking. Her cigarette is a windshield wiper. Then a straight dive to the ashtray.

Billie, I say, so far we've seen two cop cars.

Rigby John, Billie says. It's your Catholic sense of doom again. Everything's going to be fine. What we're doing is completely safe.

Just act like everything is perfectly normal, Billie says.

Perfectly normal, I said. We look like Laurel and Hardy, and everything's perfectly normal.

At least it's different, Billie said.

Differnt, I said. It's pronounced *differnt*.

Then it's rain so hard you can't see out the windshield. It was like when you're in a car wash, the windows. The neon of the Snatch Out sign, the headlights of cars, smeared ghostly lights, running in together.

A knock on Billie's window.

Billie looks over her glasses at me first, then rolls down the window slow. Under the black umbrella is a girl in a red shiny dress. Her hair is black, and curly like the girl on the good ship *Lollipop*.

Hi, Billie, she says, can I get in back till the rain stops?

Sure, Billie says, and reaches around and unlocks the back door.

The dome light goes on, and the girl with the black hair ringlets and the red dress collapses her umbrella and gets in the back seat.

Liz, Billie says, this is Rig. Rig, Liz.

Liz and I say hi. Liz is wearing lots of mascara and auburn eye shadow. Her hair bounces every time she moves. She looks at my porkpie hat and the iron burn on my collar. My untied red tie. She looks at Billie's Hoss Cartwright hat.

I thought you guys were going to the Senior Summer All Night Party? Liz says.

We are, Billie says. We're incognito.

I turn my head around.

My mother, I say. Her father.

Oh! Liz says. Right.

This Liz person doesn't know what the fuck, so she says: How much was it for one joint?

Two dollars, Billie says.

Billie goes to pat me on the shirt pocket, but I already got the joints out. I unroll the plastic sack. My fingers aren't shaking. Seven fat joints lying in the palm of my hand.

Liz looks at me like I'm the coolest guy she's ever seen.

Take your pick, I say.

Liz points with her index. Her fingernail, red, the same red as her dress.

I'll take the fattest one, Liz says. The one in the middle.

Two dollars? Liz says.

Two dollah, Billie says.

Another knock on the window. This time it's on my side. The rain is still coming down hard. There's no way I can see out.

A flashlight shines in the window. The flashlight beam is right on my crotch. I quick close my palm over the joints.

A man in a dark hooded coat with shiny gold buttons is standing outside the window. My heart is pounding so hard I'm sure that Liz and Billie can hear. A squeaky noise out of Liz in the back seat. Billie whispers a low *shit*. I don't look at Billie because my heart has stopped beating.

The breath. When I roll the window down, it's loud rain.

And it's Diane.

Billie says, Diane! so I know it's Diane. Diane is wearing a man's black hooded parka with gold buttons over her prom gown.

Groans and moans all around.

Jesus Christ! Billie says.

You scared the shit out of us, Liz says.

It's just a flashlight, Diane says.

Then: Any illegal drugs in here? Diane says.

I reach around and unlock the back door on my side.

When Diane gets in, the dome light goes on. She pulls off the coat. Her hair is short and brown. She's wearing a diamond tiara. Her prom gown is silver white with spaghetti straps.

Love the hats, the dress is appropriate, Diane says. Anybody got a cigarette? I've got a thermos here of gin and tonics.

Diane unscrews a black thermos of gin and tonics, hands the thermos to me. I take the thermos, tip it up, take a long swig.

Gin and tonics with lime in the summer, you can't beat it.

I take out George's pack of Camels, offer one to Diane, one to Liz. Billie takes one too. We all light up, four on a match, and there's the joke about three on a match and we're four. We're smoking, passing the thermos around. Billie isn't drinking. Billie turns the radio on. "Purple Haze" comes on, and we all scream a little. We all say, *Ooh, this is my favorite song.* We all sing, *'Scuse me while I kiss the sky* real loud.

Outside the windshield, headlights and exhaust fumes. The rain has stopped. Everything wet and shiny. Passing by is an endless parade of kids in their cars.

I have my hand out with the joints in my palm. Diane has just taken her joint, just laid the two dollar bills in my hand and is looking at me as if I'm the coolest guy in town.

Just as Diane says Carrie wants to know if you got any hash, there's a loud cough out of Billie.

When I look, Billie's white as a sheet. Her hand is covering her mouth.

In front of us, the endless line of cars. Behind a white '60 Chevy that's just inched past, there's a white pickup truck with CODY PLUMBING on the side of the door. Billie's dad is honking his horn, and yelling really loud, *Fuck you, you little cocksuckers! Get the fuck out of my way!*

Billie pulls her hat down, ducks low, quick puts out her cigarette. I put the joints in my shirt pocket, duck down too.

Who is that asshole? Diane says.

My father, Billie says.

Oh! Liz says. Then: Well, I got to go. My date is waiting.

When Liz opens the door, the dome light goes on.

Billie can't go down any farther because her belly's up against the steering wheel.

Fucking Liz! Billie says.

Holy shit! I say.

Billie's dad looks across the cab right over at us. For a moment, my eyes and his eyes meet and stay locked on each other. I swear Billie's dad has got me nailed.

Liz slams the door. The dome light goes off.

Bye-bye, you guys! Liz says.

Time for me to go too, Diane says.

Diane goes to open the door.

The dome light! Billie and I jump to stop Diane.

Ha-ha, Diane says, her diamond tiara twinkling. Fooled ya.

Then: You don't have to worry about that old fart, Diane says. He can't see past his nose.

Billie's dad opens the door to his pickup and gets out. When he comes around the front of his pickup, one hand is on the front hood of his pickup and his other hand is on the back end of the '60 Chevy. The bald spot on the top of his head. As he walks between his pickup and the Chevy, the headlights of his pickup are bright once, then twice, against his red T-shirt. He manages to take three steps our way, then falls flat on his ass. Horns start honking, and everybody's headlights go on. Kids are pointing at this drunk guy who's on the ground. Across the seat from me, Billie is not Billie. She's a photograph of Billie. She's not moving a muscle, not making a sound. Mr. Cody gets himself back up. When he's standing, he isn't looking our way. All the headlights of the cars flashing on and off make him look like a zombie. His red T-shirt is up, and his butt crack is poking out. Mr. Cody starts yelling and waving his arms. He picks up some gravel, starts throwing gravel around. Horns honking, headlights flashing. Plus, now the white CODY PLUMBING pickup is blocking all the traffic.

A red and white flashing light on Pole Line Road gets Mr. Cody fast back into his pickup. In no time at all the pickup's gone, and Mr. Cody's gone, and Billie and I are breathing again.

Did he see us? Billie says.

I don't know, I say.

He didn't see shit, Diane says.

What about the cops? Billie says.

Your dad's OK, Diane says. They were pulling someone over on Pole Line Road.

When Diane leaves, I reach over, take a hold of Billie's hand. Billie and I sit there trying to get our shit together. Neither one of us can speak. I light a cigarette, one for Billie, one for me. My hands shake while I hold the match to Billie's cigarette. I figure I should say something nice to mellow things out.

He's gone now, Billie, I say. Your dad's too drunk. He won't come back.

That's when in a moment, something else.

On Pole Line Road, past the flashing cop car, the Buick drives by. Mom's driving the Buick, and she's on the other side of the four-lane highway. Just as I look, the Buick's in front of the driveway to the Kraft cheese factory. Mom's head is stuck out the window. Her hair is flying, and she doesn't have her face on.

I don't say a word to Billie. Billie and I just keep sitting and smoking, trying to get our hearts back inside our chests. We smoke our cigarettes, put out our cigarettes, light two more. Billie's got her Kleenex out again, blowing her red nose. She's no longer breathing like she's going to bust a placket. My breath, of course, is something else.

Where's Kathy and Carrie? I say. We've got a dance to go to.

Billie opens her mouth. She's telling me something about Kathy and Carrie, but I don't hear a word she says.

Out of the frying pan and into the fire.

Out the back window of the Pontiac, I see hair poking up, I see Mom. She's walking between the Snatch Out fence and the backs of the cars. She looks in the back window of the green '54 Mercury on Billie's side of us.

Mom comes around the back fender of the Mercury and heads straight for Billie's window. I quick lean across Billie, push down the lock on her door, then the door lock in the back.

My hand bumps into Billie's Hoss Cartwright hat. When Billie looks around, I smile and say: Just in case.

I lock my side too, front and back.

Mom is walking past the Pontiac on Billie's side. There's nothing I can do. My heart pounding. Where's the breath? The feeling in my arms that means I'm helpless, I go fucking catatonic.

My hand is on the door pull. At least I can keep her away from Billie.

Something happens, though. Outside Billie's window, Mom's face moves in close to the glass. Mom's eyes look straight into Billie's eyes. Then straight into my eyes. Mom's not wearing her big plastic glasses. She's as blind as a bat without her glasses.

Billie doesn't move. I don't move. We look right back. Smoke curling up from our cigarettes.

Fuck, Billie whispers.

Fuck, I whisper.

Mom's face stays framed in Billie's window. She just keeps staring in. The wrinkle in her forehead that starts at her hair and goes to in between her eyes isn't there. Her jaw isn't clenched, no ripples in her jaw. Even the wrinkles around her mouth look gone. Someone so young, a mother of long ago, looks in. Her almond-shaped hazel eyes are flecked with gold.

Mom walks on around to the front of the Pontiac, then over to the black '58 Chevy sitting next to us on my side. She bends down, looks in the window. Then on to the next car, and the next car, and the next. All the way down the line of cars.

Rain. Another cloudburst, raining pitchforks.

In the smeared ghostly light, walking in the rain along the cars in the Snatch Out, Mom doesn't look like a zombie or a crazy maniac.

Mom looks like a woman walking in the rain.

She looks lost.

Who knows how long Billie and I sat staring straight ahead. I mean it was like an acid trip. Body rushes. Mind warps. Jeez, I thought for sure my body had merged with the Pontiac cushions and all I was was a head sticking up like a headrest out of the front seat.

Finally, when it was long enough to know for sure that Mom was good and gone, finally, my mouth said: Fuck this waiting for Carrie and Kathy, I said. We got to get out of this place.

But as fate would have it, Billie and I would have two more visitors that night.

Carrie and Kathy, they were not.

The universe has always conspired to fuck me up.

*   *   *

Into the empty space on Billie's side, a red and white '59 El Camino backs in. Billie doesn't see the El Camino. She's too busy smoking, staring into space. It's Joe Scardino's El Camino. Scardino's driving, and somebody's with him. When the El Camino has backed in all the way, when Scardino shuts off the car, I look and there's the curly dark hair, there's his thick neck, there's the big shoulders.

Billie is sitting four feet away from Chuck diPietro.

The feeling in my arms that means I'm helpless.

Billie goes to turn her head to the window. I squeeze her hand hard.

Don't look now, I say. But Chuck is parked right next to you.

It's a blow straight to Billie's heart. Or a blow within her belly. What holds Billie up, stops holding Billie up. Billie closes her eyes and curls into the steering wheel, her arm across her belly.

In that moment, I understand so much in that moment.

It is a blow of love.

Billie Cody is in love with Chuck diPietro.

In a moment that lasts forever, all around me the world is a car wash, smeared ghostly lights and echo sounds. The top of my head is a dirt gray mushroom cloud. The rest of my body is a thick mud hole, dark midnight and mud deep and far away. I can't climb out.

Jealousy sucks.

When I climb out, my cigarette is hot-boxed. Then, after I get my breath back, something else.

I want to slap her, hit her with my hat, open the door, kick her butt out the door. Yell at her. I want to yell at her and call her all the names my mother had called her, all the names my mother had called me, plus the C that didn't stand for *Cody* but for *cunt.*

But a man isn't supposed to do any of those things to a woman, let alone a pregnant woman.

And Billie isn't just any pregnant woman. Billie is Billie. My friend.

Then what happens? I get a whiff of Billie's French smell.

Then there is her hand, Billie's hand with the tiny red fingernails. Her hand is trembling.

Billie? I say.

Under her Hoss Cartwright hat, over her John Lennon glasses, Billie opens her eyes.

Rig? Billie says. What am I supposed to do, Rig? We can't just up and drive away now *they've* pulled in here.

Why not? I say. We can drive away.

It will look like we're running away, Billie says.

What we look like.

Joe Scardino and Chuck diPietro on one side.

Billie and I on the other.

Joe and Chuck are tough and cool and hip. They have it all, beauty, balls, and confidence.

Billie and I are differnt. We're puffy-eyed, pregnant, gawky, and limp-dicked. We are afraid of our fathers and our mothers. We are wearing stupid hats.

Fuck.

That moment. That's when it really started to happen.

Fuck as philosophy. Fuck as a possible way to address the world.

More precisely: Fuck you.

Plus, you know what? All the men and all the women in the world you need to tiptoe around. The world is full of asshole bullies, evil bitches. But five times now, I'd fought back and came out of it alive.

Billie, I say, come on. You're going to be fine.

Simone Signoret, I say, you can win the Academy Award for this one.

Now turn around and look diPietro in the eye.

Billie's face. That song "Funny Valentine," that's Billie's face. The smile that goes all across. Her cheeks go up, and there's almost a dimple.

Billie puts her cigarette out. She blows her nose, snuffs up, sits back.

Beyond Billie, in the El Camino, diPietro and Scardino are talking to a girl standing at Scardino's window.

Billie is saying *fuck fuck fuck* under her breath. Billie pushes the rose-colored John Lennon glasses back up her nose. She reaches up, pulls the rearview mirror around, gets the gold tube of lipstick out of her purse. The red lipstick rolls up slow out of the gold. Red first on the top of her right lip, then down. Red on the top of her left lip, then down. Then Billie holds the tube of red in place as she slides her bottom lip across. She rolls the red back into the gold, caps the lipstick, puts the lipstick into her black purse, closes the silver clasp.

Billie cocks her Hoss Cartwright hat a little to one side. She puts the cigarette in her mouth, rolls down the window, leans out.

Billie looks across to Chuck diPietro, she gives the horn a toot.

It takes a while for Chuck to look around. When he does look, Billie tips her hat. Her cigarette bouncing on her lip, Billie says: Howdee do? Billie says, Nice evening, ain't it?

My God, then what Chuck diPietro does, blows my mind. Fear and surprise in his eyes, Chuck quick ducks his head, turns around. He totally loses his cool.

For diPietro too, it's a blow.

Billie's not the only one in love.

In no time at all, Chuck has his door open, he's out of the car, he's not looking at Billie, he's looking down at the ground, he's got the car door closed behind him, and he is almost running toward the Snatch Out takeout window.

Even I, I think, could learn to like this guy.

Billie and I kiss each other on the cheeks. We're saying *Right on* and *Cool,* and we're slapping on our knees. I've just tapped out another cigarette. I've just lit the match and stuck the match to the cigarette, when all at once, there he is, Joe Scardino at the window. Billie jumps. I jump. Thank God I don't scream.

It's been a long time since I looked into Joe Scardino's dark eyes. I'd seen him now and then, usually in the Snatch Out or in the Dead Steer, but always in his car and just in passing. I didn't see him at school. He'd dropped out of school. I'd heard enough about him, though. He was Pocatello's James Dean.

But I had not forgotten. The last time I'd been that close to Joe Scardino was the day he'd stuck a yellow tulip up my ass.

Hey, Billie, Scardino says.

The Joe Scardino smile.

Hi, Joe, Billie says.

Then: Hey! Klueless! How's it hanging?

Scardino's hand at the end of his big arm comes into the Pontiac past Billie's face. Some kind of scratched-in tattoo on the inside of his forearm. Billie turns and looks at me look at Scardino. The gold hoops in her ears catch the light.

The feeling in my arms that means I'm helpless. It takes me awhile, but finally my hand reaches up and shakes his hand.

Scardino, I say.

Scardino leans his arms down onto the window ledge. His hair isn't a duck's ass anymore. It's like the Beatles'. He's wearing Levi's and a black T-shirt. Puka shells around his neck. He's checking out Billie's Hoss Cartwright hat, her red cunt–splooged wedding dress. He's checking out the cleavage. He's checking out my porkpie hat, the iron burn on my white collar, my short pants, my wrists sticking out of my jacket.

His dark, deep-set eyes, his skin. He looks so much like George.

Where's your truck? Scardino says. His hand patting the top of the Pontiac. That truck's a real beater, he says. You stock-race it?

Quiet. It is time for me to talk, and everything is quiet.

Then: No, I say. That's my dad's truck.

Scardino flips his shaggy black hair out of his eyes. Before he speaks, he raises his index finger, points his index finger at me.

I see you've taken up smoking, Scardino says.

His thick red lips, one side snarled up.

I put the cigarette to my mouth. I do a passable French inhale. The way my heart is beating.

You want one? I say.

From my shirt pocket, I pull out George's pack of Camels. I tap a cigarette out for Scardino, reach across Billie. Scardino takes the cigarette, puts the cigarette onto his lip into his snarl.

Scardino lights the cigarette, sucks the smoke in. He's every tough guy you've ever seen smoke.

Scardino keeps his big arms on the window ledge. He squats down, puts his chin on his forearm. That smile. His one tooth there that is sharp.

Hard to imagine, Scardino says. Klueless smoking cigarettes. Last time I saw you, you were diagramming sentences.

Now look at you, Scardino says. Smoking, drinking, running around with wild women.

Scardino's brown eyes roll over at Billie.

Something always going on behind Scardino's eyes.

Makes you worry what that something is.

Scardino flips the shaggy black hair out of his eyes.

Don't try and fool me, Scardino says. You can't fool me.

Just look at you two, Scardino says.

What? Billie says.

What? I say.

You can fool everybody else here, Scardino says, but you can't fool me.

Howdee do, Scardino says. *Nice night, ain't it.*

Scardino hacks up, turns his head, spits. Bounces up and down on his haunches.

The weird hats, the weird clothes, he says, I mean, really, what the fuck. Nobody normal just starts doing shit like that.

Scardino sticks his tongue out, crosses his eyes.

You guys are doing acid, Scardino says, ain't you?

Billie and I look at each other. We look at each other like we are doing acid looking at each other. The hats, the glasses, the red cunt–splooged dress, the jacket, the pants, the iron burn. It all fits. That quick, both of us are laughing.

All the while I'm laughing, though, it's Scardino. The way he's looking at us. The way he's smiling. What makes you worry about Scardino's smile is it's never really a smile.

What kind is it? Scardino says. Where'd you get it?

What's been going on behind Scardino's eyes, what's been covered up by his smile — it's all there now, in full bloom all over his face.

I'm not surprised. That recess years ago, the way Scardino'd hit me, knocked me back against the incinerator. I sat down or fell down. I remember I didn't cry until I put my hand to my lips and saw the blood. And as fate would have it, for whatever reason, here he is again, Joe Scardino back in my face in the window of my life. His arm is pounding up and down on the window ledge. His face is bright red, his lip is curled, his sharp tooth. Something inside me gets cold.

What the fuck! he says. Dealing acid out of your car in the Snatch Out! he says. Where'd you score?

Billie is surprised.

She laughs a laugh I've never heard from her.

Acid! Billie says. We're not dealing *acid*. We're just selling a couple joints.

Scardino's fist comes down hard.

Don't lie to me, Cody! Scardino yells. He points his two fingers at his eyes. You're tripping your tits off!

How many hits you got? he yells. What is it?

Billie goes to say something.

But there's no use in saying anything.

There never was any use.

Once Scardino wants something, there's no stopping him. Scardino's going to get it.

The way I put my hand on Billie's forearm makes Billie look down at her arm, then up into my eyes. I *really look* into Billie's blue eyes so she knows the story I'm telling with my eyes has something to do with the story I'm about to tell with my mouth.

My mouth don't open at first. The fear high up in my chest. Under the fear, though, across my middle, something that is old, something solid and full, moves slow.

The jig is up, I say.

Thank God my voice isn't high.

Billie looks at me like, What the fuck are you talking about? She's freaked. She knows what Scardino is for me.

The jig? Billie says.

Yah, I say.

I lean around Billie, make sure that Joe Scardino can see all of Rigby John Klusener's face.

We got one hit left, I say.

One hit? Scardino says. What is it? Purple barrel?

Windowpane, I say.

What? Billie says.

You're shitting me! Scardino says. A hit of windowpane? You can't get windowpane in Pocatello! Let me see it!

I go to move, but there's nowhere to move to. I open my coat, look at the lining. The color orange in the cloakroom. It had been a miracle.

I needed a miracle.

Billie sits there. I sit there. Scardino squats there. The only thing that happens happens in our eyes.

How much do you want? Scardino yells. Ten? Twenty?

In a moment, Billie reaches up, puts her hands behind her head. She lifts her chest and stretches out long. Somebody needed to do something.

Billie's breasts hang there between Scardino's eyes and my eyes.

Scardino leans his body closer in. His eyes are on Billie's breasts. Then his eyes go up and lock in on my eyes.

Sweat down my armpits.

From behind Scardino, I see him come around the El Camino —

Chuck diPietro. His hands are full of Cokes and hamburgers and French fries and napkins and Coke straws. He's still looking at the ground.

What holds Billie up stops holding Billie up.

I swear Billie Cody is so predictable.

Hey, Chuck, Scardino says. No onions on mine, remember?

Then, loud enough for Chuck to hear, Scardino says: So who's kid is it, anyway? Scardino says.

Chuck diPietro stops. Everything about him stops. He's a forty-pound block of cheese. He's concrete. He's lead.

Joe, Chuck says. Let it alone!

That quick, Billie leans forward and starts the Pontiac. She's got it in drive, and her foot is on the gas pedal. We're just about to tear ass out of there.

That quick, I reach down and shut the car off, take the keys. The key chain and the lava rock in my palm is heavy.

Billie's sore blue eyes on me, they can't believe I did what I just did.

Billie looks all around her every which way. But all around her, she's trapped and there's no place to go.

Billie slumps down and a big sob bursts out.

It's *my* kid! Billie yells. Fuck all of you!

Yah, yah, Scardino says.

Joe! Chuck says. I'm warning you!

Scardino leans in, his big arms crossed on the window ledge again.

But why is it, Klueless, Scardino says, that it's diPietro here who's fucked your girlfriend?

That there was the moment right there in all my life.

The universe conspired that moment. Just for me.

Although, for a while there, I didn't know what the fuck to do with it.

My helpless arms, you know, the breath, the pain next to my fucking heart, big farts rolling around my belly. The whole shebang, it was all going on.

Things got slow. Things got fast. Things got far away. Things got like in a car wash. There was thunder, lightning, all of a sudden there was pouring rain. You name it. Everything you can think of happened. My bare butt getting beat by my dad. Mom catching me whacking off. The rosaries, the novenas, the litanies. Fucking litanies, man. The eternal humiliation of the Catholic Church. Slave labor on a hay baler. All of it. The fucking tulip up my ass. The whole ball of red-cunt wax.

Of all the things I could or couldn't have done, could have said, should have said, didn't say, coulda woulda shoulda, this is what I did.

I raised up my finger. Not my third finger, my second finger.

I said, Scardino. I said, You see this finger here? On the end of this finger right now is one of the purest pieces of windowpane in the world. The possibilities of ecstasy and insight you can't fucking imagine. And just because you're such a fucking prick, I said, this is where it's going to go.

That's when I stuck my index finger in mouth. On my face a look that would have put Theresa of Ávila and Saint Sebastian to shame.

When I pulled my index finger out of my mouth, I held that finger up, so Joe Scardino could see. That's when I raised the other finger, the third one, pulled my second and fourth fingers down around it, and flipped off Joe Scardino with one righteous fuck-you flip of the bird.

In nothing flat, Scardino is around the Pontiac in front, coming around fast to my side. Something deep in me knows this is my worst nightmare.

Everything I've ever known to be true, every place in my body — all the fear, the hate — the place in me that has always wanted to kill this motherfucker, I reach inside deep into the muscle and bone, and call upon.

Scardino's heading fast for my door. His hand reaches out for my door handle. That's when I push. One hard slap of the door.

The door hits Scardino square. Mostly in his chest and stomach, but somehow with everything going by so fast, I know it's also hit his head.

Scardino slams against the fender of the black '58 Chevy behind him, then goes flying over the hood.

Headlights in the Snatch Out start flashing on and off, and people yelling.

Rain. My hat goes flying off, and I'm out the door. I'm just around in front of the Chevy, when out of nowhere, Scardino is a leap from up and out.

I don't even think.

I let go an overarm pitch that sends the key ring and the lava rock flying smack between Scardino's eyes.

Immediate blood down Scardino's face. He holds his hands over his eyes and stumbles away from the Chevy into the passing-by line of cars.

Thousands of screaming magpies gather in the sky and dive at my head.

I'm right after him. I lean in and, with all my weight, hit Scardino hard, fist against teeth, skin, muscle. An awful sound that makes me sick. A terrible pain in my hand.

Scardino is down, lying in a mud puddle. Headlights on and off, on and off. Rain spits and pieces of hail. People all around yelling.

Chuck diPietro's yelling: Break it up, you two! Break it up!

DiPietro tries to grab me. Billie tries to grab me. But no one can touch me.

I jump, a Flying Wallenda, and land on Scardino's stomach. Something cracks. Out of Scardino, vomit and air. Weird cries like my brother, Russell, coming out my mouth. I'm sitting on Scardino's chest. I hit him once, hit him twice, my fists against his face.

Then in a moment, it's so quiet. Only rain. Flashing headlights and rain.

I am breathing hard and holding my chest. It ain't like on TV, fighting.

It's easy to tell about something after it's over, but while it's happening it's all just one thing after another, flipping past your eyes.

Someone running, something fast. I turn, and it's diPietro.

He's coming at me for the tackle. I roll over, splash into the puddle. DiPietro goes flying by.

Then Scardino's on top of me. The tattoo on his inner arm is a Playboy Bunny. His fists are flying, but they're not really landing. With all the blood, he can't see. Scardino does land one on my ear. The same ear sore from Mom. Then bam! Smack into my old broken nose.

Everything goes black, but the next thing I know, I'm back on top again, whaling on Scardino. DiPietro's got me by the shirt collar. The collar's tight around my neck. The breath. The top button pops off, then the next button.

The miracle inside my jacket. The broken end of Mom's broom handle in my hand is a good fit.

Let go of me! I yell, or I'll shove this up his neck!

The sharp end of the green broom handle in my hand is under Scardino's chin. DiPietro lets go my collar.

Quiet. Everything so quiet. Only the headlights and the rain.

In the puddle next to Scardino's bloody face, a flash of lightning. Raindrops hit the puddle.

Blood bubbles from out of Scardino's nose.

On my right, diPietro's on his haunches, he's moving his hands slow, he's talking quiet to me. He's looking me in the eyes, he's saying something. Billie's standing next to him. She's crying and saying something too.

Headlights on and off, on and off.

The sharp end of the broom handle, all I'd have to do is give it a shove.

I give it a shove, just enough to break the skin.

A stream of blood runs out and down Scardino's neck.

Just like that, the pointed end snaps, a thick sliver of wood breaks off and sticks out under Scardino's chin.

A gust of wind, a hawk, some large bird flying low, in a moment, something collapses. I look at my hands. I lift my hands up and look at my hands. The broken-end broomstick in my hand.

Somehow I am standing above Scardino. The headlights are bright all around me, the whole world is bright, bright and so quiet, only rain.

On my face, on my hair, my eyes, soft rain.

Scardino is a shadow on the ground, holding up his hands. Open palms, spread-out human-being hands, the universal sign to stop.

Fuck you as a possible way to address the world.

My voice is clear and calm and not too high.

Fucking Scardino, I say. You selfish prick. I've had enough of you.

Quiet. Nothing in the world but quiet, bright headlights, rain.

Scardino's up and running through the rain and bright lights. DiPietro runs after him. When Scardino opens his car door, Scardino stops. He yells: I'll get you for this, you little fairy! Your ass is fucking grass!

Below me, in the mud of the Snatch Out parking lot, my thin red tie. I reach down, pick up the tie, tie the tie like an Indian around my head.

Yah? I say. Well, your ass is whipped!

Quick lightning in my veins. In my chest a big gust of warm wind.

I reach down and pick up my porkpie hat, put it on.

I loved God so much right then.

Scardino dives into his El Camino. DiPietro grabs the hamburgers and Cokes sitting on the roof. Before diPietro gets in the car, he looks over to Billie. Billie looks back, and Billie smiles. In the silence and the rain and the bright lights, I'm standing there, and I watch, and Billie and Chuck diPietro smile at each other.

The 409 dual carburetor Positraction whatever-the-fuck super-charged shit the El Camino is roars into the silence. The squeal of tires as the El Camino reverses, then slams into the Snatch Out fence.

Laughter. All around, kids in their cars, it's laughter.

Then it's an all-out rubber burn forward, the El Camino fishtail-ing out of the parking space. Into the line of cars, there's just space enough between a Rambler and a Corvair. The El Camino makes it through the space, but when it turns toward Pole Line Road, the back fin of the El Camino takes out the left headlight of the Rambler.

Then it's only noise we hear. The El Camino jumping the curb. Horns honking all four lanes up and down on Pole Line Road. The Kraft cheese truck pulling out, blaring on its horn.

Then a crash that sounds like World War III.

By the time I get through the cars to the sidewalk, the wheels of the Kraft cheese truck in the air are still spinning. The bed of the truck is lying on top of the crushed-flat El Camino.

Across all four lanes of Pole Line Road, boxes all over broken open.

Scattered from here to kingdom come, little packets of Parmesan cheese.

At the emergency entrance to Saint Anthony's Hospital, there were cop cars in front and cops standing all around.

Billie and I parked the Pontiac, then walked up the steps of the main entrance. Through the big wood doors, in the hospital corridor, every kid in Pocatello was there. It was so crowded, there was no place to walk. Billie wasn't wearing her hat. I was, though. That porkpie hat wasn't going to leave my head for a long time. Tied under it, my thin red tie.

I pulled down my hat. Kids pushing and crowding. Policemen trying to get people to go home. By the time Billie and I got to the receptionist, it was confirmed.

One of the two of them, either Scardino or diPietro, was dead, and the other was in a world of hurt.

Weird, at one point in all the commotion, I looked down at the shiny brown-tiled hospital floor. That's when I remembered. The blue overnight case that looked like a purse. Surrounded by a hundred people, there we were, Billie and I, standing in the exact spot where we first met.

There were two policemen posted by the reception desk. Nobody was getting past the two policemen. No matter what.

Billie did, though. Billie and me.

At first, the policeman, when he saw Billie's red cunt–splooged wedding dress, wouldn't let her anywhere near.

Then the next thing I knew, Billie was standing on her tiptoes, leaning in and whispering in the cop's ear.

The policeman had an Italian name. On his badge: RICCI.

Officer Ricci's face went soft and he closed his eyes when Billie told him.

He pointed down the hallway, told Billie to go down the hallway, down two flights of stairs to Emergency.

When I stepped up, Officer Ricci stuck out his club. His Italian eyes looked hard at the red tie around my head, my porkpie hat, my beat-up face.

It's all right, Billie said. He's with me.

He's my friend, Billie said.

Billie and I were the only two people in the Emergency waiting room. I lit a cigarette, one for Billie, one for me. There we were, still smoking George's Camels. Billie's tear duct cancer looked worse in the fluorescent light.

I spread my right hand out wide. My other hand held it at the wrist.

On the green wall, the black and white clock at ten-thirty-five, and Mr. and Mrs. Scardino walked in. Mr. Scardino was short and had thick glasses and was smoking a cigar. He was wearing his pajama tops and pants with suspenders and wingtips and a gangster hat. Mrs. Scardino was old as ever, all in black. She looked tall next to her husband. Her white hair like spiders around her face. In her hands, a long black rosary. The two of them walked slow, Mrs. Scardino leaning into her husband, through the swinging double doors, EMERGENCY ROOM NO ENTRY, their arms around each other.

Ten-fifty, Mrs. diPietro came running in. A cigarette in her hand, and her face was red. Short, white hair sticking up, an old army jacket, faded jeans, and sneakers with the heel backs broken in.

No Mr. diPietro.

Billie didn't know if there even was one.

An hour later, just one of George's Camels left. The swinging double doors opened, and a Benedictine nun walked out. Billie grabbed my hand.

It was Sister Angelica. Lots of black eyebrows.

Is your name Billie Cody? Sister Angelica asked.

Yes! Billie said, and jumped up quick.

Sister Angelica stepped back, put her hand over her mouth. She stared down at Billie's red–cunt splooge.

Charles diPietro would like to speak to you, she said.

My eyes went straight for Billie's blue eyes.

Billie looked up and away. There wasn't a window there, so she looked at the clock.

When things are difficult to say.

Billie's hand lets go of my hand.

Down the hallway, Sister Angelica walks, then Billie walks.

Billie has her own way of walking. Short stride, fast steps, the click of her black strapped high heels. The slick sound of silk.

Through the swinging double doors.

That quick, Billie is gone.

12 The Back Door

ALL I WANTED was a place to be quiet and alone.

There was only one place. The swimming hole.

I drove in the back way, from Quinn Road. Opened the gate with my sore hand, drove through, closed the gate behind me. Drove the pickup up the side of the ditch bank and onto the narrow road. I cut the headlights. From their bedroom, Mom and Dad could see the headlights.

Even during the day, the canal bank was a narrow fit for the pickup. On one side, it was the dark water of the canal, on the other a twenty-foot drop. I kept my bearings by driving slow, by keeping my head out the window. The left front wheel always just a foot or so away from what I could see of the solid dirt before it sloped into ditch. The lightning helped.

Mom always said to stay in the car if you're caught out in this kind of lightning.

What Mom always said.

My clothes come off easy. I untie the red tie from around my head, take off the porkpie hat. The wind on me naked. The warm sandy earth up through my bare feet. Now and then my body lights up a bright strobe of lightning.

I take off running. In the air, warm wind all around me, a bird flying, flying. Lightning cracks open the sky. I plunge my sore and aching body into the moon silver rapids. The sudden whoosh of water, and I'm a fish. Swimming through wet dark. Cool water on my nose, my ears, my eyes. Cool water on my bruised cheek. Tangles of moss around my legs. On the bottom of the canal, thick, slimy mud. I grab the mud, squeeze the mud through my fingers. My right hand feels less stiff.

Up for air, I climb the bank. The night air cold on my body. I walk barefoot on the gravel to the pickup, slip on my T-shirt, my brown suit pants, tie the thin red tie around my head, put on the porkpie hat. I grab the matches and George's pack of cigarettes, one Camel left.

From the two-by-twelve, my feet push off, my legs stretch out, and I'm across to the slick, dark lava rock. As I climb the rock, the sky above flashes one thin, bony hand of electric light.

The white-water rapids below, I sit down in the same dusty spot I sat last night, look up at Granny's sacred tree. The wind in the tree. Its sweaty body smell. I've got George's last Camel in my mouth, trying to get wet matches lit. I tip my porkpie hat to Granny's ancestors.

Good evening, I say. A lot's happened since I last saw you.

Then in a moment, a sound. A branch snaps or something like it. Maybe the water stops, and it's the silence I hear. Whatever it is, I'm all goose flesh.

From within the tree, a French inhale. The unmistakable sound.

George? I say.

Is that you, George?

A flash of heat lightning.

Whatever is in the tree, it is not George.

A dark bird startles up, a bird as big as the tree. The flutter of wings, wafted air against my face, my heart. I am standing in the wind. I have to hold on to my porkpie hat. Slowly the bird rises. Above me, Thunderbird is long, black, slow strokes up and up. In the sky a crack of lightning. Thunder boom presses deep inside my sore ear. Thunderbird's black wings, its beak, the tail feathers, an outline of lightning all around. Thunderbird is as big as the southern night sky.

With the dark, the huge wings disappear, and Thunderbird becomes the night.

Another flash.

Just below, my eyes settle on the dark rectangle stand of Lombardy poplars, then the clump of dark inside the dark. Granny's log cabin. The high sigh of the wind. Wind a differnt sound in the poplars than wind in the cedar.

Inside in there, Granny's kitchen window is dark.

Rain or shine, you can bet your life on it, George had said, that light is on every night.

A gust of wind, a feeling in my bones, instinct, whatever you want to call it. I knew.

It wasn't easy getting from the swimming hole to Granny's cabin. Down the canal bank, in the triangle field of tall grasses, there were gopher holes everywhere. Then there was the barbwire fence and the extra darkness under the Lombardys. All that dead wood lying on the ground, and I was barefoot. When I got to the pounded-down dirt by the outhouse, I was sailing.

Granny's dark green screen door. I put my fingers through the door pull and pulled slow. The *Inner Sanctum* squeak. Bonanza started barking. I knocked once, then again louder. No Granny.

I pushed the latch down and opened the door, Bonanza going nuts, but not at the door. From the sound, he was on his Pendleton bed.

Only dark night light through the windows. Flashes of lightning.

One flash and I see Granny's legs, her rolled-up tea rose nylons, her Minnetonka moccasins, sticking out from behind the kitchen table.

My bare feet could feel the shine on Granny's wood floor. When I got to the kitchen table, I reached for the light, turned the old switch, and electric light went on all over.

I was down on my knees by her head. I put my ear next to her mouth, but it was my busted ear, so I couldn't tell.

Granny's hand, the old brown rope, the long, thin fingers. I put my hand on Granny's hand, loose, thin skin on knobby bones. Her hand was warm.

Granny's eyes opened. Gold bars in her dark brown eternal eyes.

George? she said.

Then something in Indian.

Granny? I said. It's me, Rigby John Klusener. Are you all right?

My butt went down onto Granny's shiny wood floor. I put my hands under her head and shoulders, lifted slow. I moved my legs under her so her head was lying in my lap.

Her heartbeat was in her hands, her heart beat the way she moved her head, her whole body was her heart beating.

Granny's eyes looked straight into my eyes. There was nothing in between.

Then a whole long thing that Granny said, all in Indian, nothing I understand, but looking in Granny's eyes, I understood a lot. Said the same things over and over, like the rosary or a litany you might say. How the morning light came in her kitchen window. The shade of the Lombardys. Hallucinations, the shadows the leaves made on the ground. Her damn dog, Bonanza. All the dead people in the photos above her bed. How much she loved her grandson. The recipes for what ailed you, when you ate too much horseshit, when your grandson came home all bloody and broken and drunk. Coffee and sugar and Sego Milk. The cedar tree, the tree of her ancestors. Her kerosene lamp at night in the kitchen window was the way to keep company with your dead.

Those things and a lot more things I could never begin to know.

Then Granny lifted her arm, made her finger into a pointer. Her heartbeat in the way she pointed.

My pipe, she said. Get my pipe on the table.

Heartbeat in Granny's voice.

I sat up high, my eyes just table height. Next to the covered silver sugar bowl and silver salt and pepper shakers and the silver butter dish, her corncob pipe.

And is my tobacco up there? she said. Prince Albert in a can?

Next to the corncob pipe, the red can of Prince Albert. Some old guy with a mustache and weird hat standing up straight.

Yah, I said.

Well, let him out, she said.

I managed to reach the pipe, then slid the can of Prince Albert over slow.

I got the can open, filled the pipe, all the while Granny's dark eyes in the electric light, nothing in between.

Help me up, she said.

Granny sat up slow, mostly me helping her up. She leaned against the smooth green Majestic just above her head. The bright electric light shining down on her face. Her long hair undone, white hair falling down her shoulders, all the way to the floor.

The heartbeat in Granny's hands as she reached for the pipe. Granny puffed and puffed, smoke rising, the sweet sharp smell of Prince Albert.

Just tell me one thing, Granny said.

What's that? I said.

Who the hell are you again? she said.

I'm Rigby John, I said. You remember. Klusener. George and I buck hay together.

Oh hell! Granny said. You're Rigby John. The boy George is in love with. A real sweetheart, that boy, coming from that family. Got a nice ass too. Never seen my grandson so smitten! George don't know what the hell to do with himself!

A gust of wind. In a moment, something opens up. Out of Granny's lips, the word was a blow in my chest and love spread out all around over on my body.

Granny held the pipe to her mouth. Her heartbeat in her hands. Big puffs of smoke billowing up.

Then something I wasn't expecting at all.

Granny took the pipe out of her mouth, turned the mouthpiece toward me, and handed me the pipe. The pipe on my lips was wet and hot.

Moments of gesture.

So beautiful Granny right then, her eyes big, round, and dark, bars of gold, red rims all around. Like a child's eyes. Full of life. Nothing in between.

So careful, I laid the corncob pipe back into Granny's open palms. The heartbeat in her palms. The pipe between Granny's lips, puffing, puffing.

You got to go tell George I'm dead, Granny said. He ain't going to like it.

The feeling in my arms that means I'm helpless.

You're not going to die, I said. Do you have a telephone?

Tell him it's a brand-new day, Granny said. Brand-new, son!

You don't have a telephone, do you?

George is out tonight, Granny said. He's more than likely at the Back Door. Do you know where the Back Door is?

Let me help you into bed, I said. I'll run get the pickup and call an ambulance.

Granny put her hand to her mouth. I thought she was going to cough or cry. She started making a weird sound.

Of course you know where the Back Door is, Granny said.

No, I don't, I said.

The weird sound coming up and out of Granny, her eyes closed, her mouth open, the line of pink gums all the way around.

Well, you're sitting on it! Granny said.

Laughter so hard out of Granny, it was scary. Laughter so hard, she could snap in two.

And you know me. I can't be around laughter like that without catching it too.

So there we are, Granny and me on her shiny wood floor, smoking a corncob pipe, laughing our asses off.

That's how I plan to remember her, Granny, laughing.

Then Granny went off again speaking Indian. A long line of words that made no sense. But the way Granny was saying the Indian words, the way she was looking at me and laughing, all's I could do was laugh.

Hooting and hollering, Granny and me, so hard Bonanza started barking.

Shut up, Bonanza! Granny said.

Then that quick, the laughter in Granny stopped.

Granny's old rope hand went up to her neck. Her head slid slow in an arch down the green enamel, her long white hair trailing.

Bent over on the floor, Granny was only a pile of bones.

I put my hand on her hair. Her hair soft and smooth, like when you pet a bird. I put my face down on the floor, right across from Granny's face.

Her heartbeat in her lips.

The door in the alley, Granny said. Tell them you love flowers.

Tell my grandson his name was on my lips.

Granny said one word, an Indian word, and then even though her wide, round, dark eyes were open, even though the gold bars were in her eyes, even though everything else in the world didn't change, that quick, Grandma Queep was gone.

The other half, the dark half, that part of Pocatello, the two dives, the Working Man's Club and Porters and Waiters, the part of Pocatello that exists only in a Judy Garland song.

Niggertown.

Looked like the Princess Theater to me.

Or *The Wizard of Oz* when it goes from black and white to color.

I was standing in the shadows, next to the big square metal dumpster painted dark blue. Behind me, weeds growing up, the cyclone fence, pieces of garbage and tumbleweeds stuck in the fence.

Something like San Francisco about the old buildings. The long, sad windows with the paint peeling off. The rusted broken-down cast-iron fence. The garbage overflowing in the two garbage cans.

The neon blue moon in the cracked window. WORKING MAN'S CLUB. Right next to the Working Man's Club, another set of stairs that led up to a door. Above the door, the painted red sign with fancy gold letters, a sign like you'd see in the train station, PORTERS AND WAITERS.

Slow, sinful saxophone jazz playing out from somewhere inside in there.

I put my hand on the dumpster, leaned my body against it. The dumpster still smelled of new paint.

Slumming. Just here to see how the other half lives.

I thought if I stood there long enough, George in his shiny yellow dress, in the neon light of the blue neon moon, would walk out the door, step sideways down the steps, place each high red heel exactly on each step, the high tap of the heel on each step. Then at the bottom, George on the second step, George would sit down, reach in his red silk purse and pull out his Camels, tap one out, and light it.

On the street, people all over the place, Mexican people, Indian people, black people, even some white people, up the stairs, down the stairs, into the doors and back out, drunk, dancing, the smell of marijuana.

A yellow dog lifted his leg onto the cast-iron fence.

Everything was there but George.

The door in the alley, Granny'd said.

I started walking. Rain pouring down on cement and pavement. The alley behind the Working Man's Club and Porters and Waiters was dark shadows, darker than the rest of the night. Two-story buildings on each side. No streetlamps. Big potholes in the alley, puddles of water in the potholes.

I pulled down my porkpie hat, pulled up my suit jacket lapels to close around my neck. I took a deep breath. A low light far away on the left.

An intent in your life to fold your life around.

Love.

I put my eyes on that light, didn't let my eyes go anywhere else, kept walking. For the longest time, all there was was only dark and rain and the crunch of my black Sunday shoes on gravel. My breath in and out. My heart.

The light bulb above the door was covered by a piece of tin. Three cement steps went down to a burnt red steel door. On the steel jamb above the burnt red steel door, just under the light bulb, written in yellow Magic Marker, letters only an inch high: THE BACK DOOR.

Of course you know where the back door is.

I knocked once. Then once again, only louder. Then again real loud.

Rain on my porkpie hat, rain on my shoulders. My black Sunday shoes, standing in a puddle of rain. Under the light, I lifted my right hand to the light. The knuckles were bloody again.

I knocked with my left hand this time, the butt of my fist banging, banging on the burnt red door.

So quiet. Nothing. Only rain.

The door opened a crack.

Light behind a tall white man. No lipstick, and I had to look up to his lips.

What do you say? he said.

George Serano? I said. Is George Serano in there?

What do you say? the man said.

He's an Indian guy, about thirty-five years old, I said. He's tall, got black, shiny hair.

The door slammed closed. I leaned up against the door, pushed all my weight against it. Pounded and pounded on the door.

For God's sake! I yelled. Open the door! He's George Serano, and he loves me!

The door opened a crack.

Yes, the tall man said. But do you love *him*?

I squared my shoulders, took a deep breath. I cleared my throat so my voice wouldn't be too high.

OK, I said. I love him too.

That's *so sweet,* the man said. Now, look, in order to get in here, you got to say something. So say it already, and I'll let you in.

You know, he said. Roses . . . daisies . . . lilacs.

Flowers! I said. Fucking flowers! I said, *Of course* I love flowers!

The light inside went out when I walked in the door. I couldn't see a thing. The door closed behind me, steel into steel, the locks latched. The tall man wore English Leather. He lifted my arms and patted me under my arms and down my body. Then from my socks on up inside my legs. He stopped just short of my balls. He took off my porkpie hat, then put the hat back on my head.

His big hand on my shoulder gave me a firm push. In front of my face, something soft hanging down. The tall man opened the velvet curtain.

One large L-shaped room. Knotty pine walls, brown-and-green-tiled shiny floors. No bright lights. Only light from lamps. The lamp nearest me, on a low wood side table, cowboys on the lampshade. Below, lying on the shiny tile, a braided rug. Along the walls, couches and sofas, standing lamps. Paintings like in the thirties and forties. A tall ship with white masts on the ocean. A Lassie dog in a snowstorm who'd found a baby lamb. Exotic paintings of Egypt.

Off to the right, a pool table under a hanging colored-glass lamp.

Behind the pool table, a corner bookshelf made of knotty pine, wood sconces across the top. Books on the bookshelves.

Straight ahead, in the center of the L, the bar was knotty pine too, with four or five stools. Behind the bar, no bigger than a wardrobe closet, bottles stacked up. Wooden tables and chairs all around. Early American. Ashtrays like wagon wheels on the tables. To the left, beyond the bar, the jukebox and the dance floor.

It was quiet and warm. Only the music on the jukebox and low talking. Pool ball crack. Twenty, maybe thirty men. Most of them old men. Forty and fifty. Almost all of them were dancing. Paired up. Men dancing slow like a man and a woman. Dean Martin was singing, "You're Nobody Till Somebody Loves You," and everybody was singing along low.

When the song was over, the men thanked their partner, went back to their tables, had a drink, lit up a smoke. When a new song started, "How Much Is That Doggy in the Window?," the men got up again, got another partner, or the same partner, and started into dancing again, singing low.

George wasn't wearing a yellow dress. He was wearing a white shirt and a red bow tie and dress pants with suspenders. George was an Italian man. He was dancing with a man who, from behind, I swear, looked exactly like my father.

George was leading.

When George looked up and saw me, when he looked across the smoky room into my eyes, in that moment, I closed my eyes, tried to look away, but I could not. A gust of wind, a hawk, some large bird flying low. A feeling in my bones, instinct, whatever you want to call it. George could see it in my eyes.

Billie Holiday started singing the song KSEI radio always played before it went off the air weeknights at nine-thirty.

I'll be seeing you in all the old familiar places.

George walked across the room, took hold of my hand, my sore hand, led me out to the dance floor. All the men on the dance floor, the men at the tables, even the bartender, stopped and watched. George put his right hand on my back, held my left hand in the air.

There I was dancing with a man, dancing with George.

My shoulders up around my ears. My eyes were like they weren't mine. I couldn't make them look where I wanted them to. They were off staring into space at some goddamn knotty pine, and I wanted to look at George.

What I had to say to George, I had to look at him to say it.

Granny's eyes, the way they looked at you, there was nothing in between.

I closed my eyes tight, took a deep breath.

George was in front of me.

Shiny black hair, suntanned dark cinnamon skin, his dark eyes. The gold bars in his dark eyes. Thick lips the color of the rest of his skin. His sweat, buckskin and flint on the back of my throat. The part of the tomato that folds together red into the stem of green. Vaseline hair tonic. Old Spice.

I knew all these things about George but never up this close.

Our hands were palm to palm on my right, my fingers in between his fingers, or his fingers in between mine. My hand so thin and pink inside his big brown hand. My thumb, how it lay against his thumb. Our forearms touched too. His skin, my too short brown suit jacket and my white shirt poking out.

The slow roll of the dance, now and then the brim of my hat touched his head. My brow and cheekbone, his cheekbone and jaw.

Under my chin, my left thumb was on his red suspender. My thumb was trying to get underneath the suspender. I made my thumb stop.

Under my left palm, starched white cotton and George's shoulder.

The low lamplight on his cheekbone. George's ear. The breath from my nose into the hole of his ear. My nose only inches away from the place where his neck skin and white shirt collar met.

My lips were even closer.

The smell of starch and iron and cotton. Warm breath, tobacco, gin, and lime.

George's hand on my back, his little finger just there at the top crack of my ass. We were touching all along the whole left side of me, the whole right side of him.

The slow roll of the dance, on that side our thighs touched, they came apart, our thighs touched.

And something else down there, loose and full.

I'll be seeing you in every lovely summer's day.

Just me and George and Billie Holiday dancing slow and close.

I saw it coming from a long way off. His head was so still, his eyes on my lips. His lips stuck together as they came apart. Such a slow and graceful descent, the way his lips landed just right on my lips, round and firm-soft too.

Whisker rub. His tongue in my mouth, a perfect French inhale. It was a kind of swoon. Something in George collapsed too. Or we both did. Who knows, at that moment, you couldn't really tell us apart.

It was the longest kiss I'd ever kissed.

Then his lips slid off my mouth, on up my cheek, all the way up to my ear.

George's tongue was in my ear. We were heart to heart, hip to hip, thigh to thigh, two very good parades.

I pulled my head back, put my forehead on George's forehead.

His dark eyes filled up. Two big tears rolled down his cheeks.

Rig, George whispered.

Then: Do people call you Rig?

You know I loved my Granny very much.

My heart pounding. My breath. You know me. Rubber lips. There was everything to say, but I couldn't say a word.

Eye to eye, as I was speaking, my lips touched George's lips.

Granny told me, I whispered, to tell you, I whispered, your name was on her lips.

Your Indian name.

On the dance floor, in the Back Door, Billie Holiday, there was no doubt, I was the only thing holding George Serano up.

An intention in your life to fold your life around.

I stood tall and strong and let him fall. His face against my chest. I reached down, put my arm under his knees, his legs dangled over my arm. One big heft, and I was holding George high in my arms.

There was nowhere to go, no place I knew, no solid, silent place in all the world. So I stood, held George, knotty pine everywhere I looked, men staring. Just stood. Put that solid, silent place in the world inside me and stood.

Stood and stood, held George, held his whole body, until he was quiet.

At Granny's door, when George reached for the green screen door, when he pulled it open by the latch, Bonanza didn't bark. Inside, the light bulb was a bright shine.

George's shirt so white.

George walked around the table. His footsteps, the Italian shoes on the wood planks. I was right behind him. I set my porkpie hat on the table.

Granny lay on her shiny wood floor, folded over onto herself.

George dropped to his knees. So slow the way George put his hands on his grandmother's shoulders, lifted her shoulders, leaned her body against the green enamel of the stove. So slow he reached out, put his hands on Granny's cheeks. His long fingers brought her head up straight.

Behind Granny's head the green enamel of the stove. Majestic.

White hair flying all around her face. George spit on his hands, placed his hands on Granny's head, combed her long white hair away from her face.

George's dark eyes were bright and shiny, the way a child looks, nothing in between. He started singing low. An Indian song that sounded a lot like crying.

At the moment when George started singing, the night was so quiet, I swear I could hear the wind in the cedar tree.

George put his hands under Granny's arms, I grabbed around her Minnetonka moccasins, and we lifted. Skin and bones and a cotton dress. We laid Granny out on the wedding ring quilt of Thunderbirds on her big brass bed. Laid her arms out straight. Laid her legs out straight. Smoothed out her hair.

From out of the trunk at the base of her bed, George pulled out a blue and red and yellow Pendleton blanket. I helped George fold the blanket over Granny. George smoothed the blanket out, lifted her arms out so they lay on top of the blanket.

George lit the kerosene lamp, opened the kitchen window, then set the lamp in the window. George opened the door, opened the window above her bed. He walked through the door into his room, opened the window in there.

Then something else from out of the trunk. A bundle of herbs that George lit, and when I smelled the herbs, I smelled sage. All around the house, George carried the burning sage. He was singing in Indian and wafting the smoke over everything in Granny's house.

When he got to Bonanza, George stopped.

Bonanza in his Pendleton bed looked like he was sleeping. But he was not sleeping. George put his hand on Bonanza's head.

George went down right there on the floor. Long howls and wails out of him like under the weeping willow that day. Sounds I didn't know a human being could make.

I made it to the tall-backed kitchen chair. Pulled the chair out. Sat down at Granny's table in my favorite place in all the world.

With crying like that, you just can't help it. I was crying too.

It took George a long time, but when he was done crying, he was done. George got up, wiped his eyes and blew his nose, and walked out the door. When he came back, his arms were full of cedar boughs. He laid cedar boughs down all around Granny's body. Candles too. A candle on the sewing machine by her head and a candle on the trunk at her feet.

Granny was really beautiful lying on her brass bed under the blue and red and yellow Pendleton. All the cedar boughs, branches of her ancestors, lying all around her. Above her, on the wall, the photographs. The reflection of the candles on their faces, in their eyes. The smell of cedar and sage smoke.

George's eyes had gone soft. I mean, he was differnt. It felt like a whole new person standing next to me. Somebody I hardly knew.

*   *   *

On the other side of the wall from Granny's bed is George's bed. It's an iron bed, single, with a black and gray Pendleton on it. In the room, besides the bed and the window, is a dresser. A blue glass ashtray on his dresser. On the wall a round mirror. Another bright light bulb hanging down.

George sits down on his bed. The bedsprings squeak. He sits leaned over, his elbows on his knees. I don't know where to go, what to do. All I know is I want to be close. I sit down on the bed too. An arm's length away. The bedsprings squeak. In my jacket pocket is George's pack of Camels. Still one cigarette left.

I light the cigarette, take a drag, hand the cigarette to George.

Smoking is praying, I say.

George takes the cigarette. Through his lips, up his nose, a beautiful French inhale.

Thanks, George says.

I love you, George says.

George hands the cigarette back to me.

Our fingers touch.

The smoke, the prayer in my lungs, I love God so much right then.

I know, I say. Granny already told me.

Really? George says. What else did she tell you?

She was laughing when she died, I say.

For a moment there, I think George is going to go off again. But he doesn't cry. His chest gets big, and his eyes get wet, but he doesn't cry.

When he speaks, his lips are rubber.

It's a hell of a deal, he says. Being like you and me. Men loving men. I've hated it all my life. Tried to kill it. Nearly killed a couple women trying to kill it. I'm sorry for you, Rig. It ain't going to be easy.

I don't know, he says. Maybe I can help.

George takes a deep drag on the cigarette. The smoke goes up to the light bulb. The smoke on the light bulb is a whole new smell in the room.

The only thing harder than being born Indian, George says, is being born queer.

George reaches his arm out and takes hold of my shoulder. He pulls me into him like he did that morning, just two days ago, on the back of the feed truck. The bedsprings squeak. In no time at all, I'm sitting right next to George, as close to him as I was when we were dancing.

Under the bright light, all over on my shoulder where George's arm touches me, is a deep warm. My face up close, my nose, my lips, his starched white shirt, the smell from his armpit, buckskin and flint on the back of my throat, all the smells, that part of the tomato, Vaseline hair tonic, Old Spice, our breath, the cigarette back and forth, the circle of our talk. If this is queer, then queer is a prayer.

I didn't know that men could love other men, I say. Not until Granny said it. When she said that you loved me, as soon as I heard her say it, I knew.

I don't stop to think. I just go ahead.

I love you, I say.

George takes hold of my leg, lifts my leg over onto his leg.

I know, George says.

How do you know? I say.

At the Back Door, George says. The whole bar heard you.

Fuck, I say.

Then I'm laughing, but George doesn't laugh. Doesn't even crack a smile. George could laugh, but he never smiled. Granny died laughing.

My thumb is under George's suspender. I pull the suspender down.

George reaches up, puts the cigarette out in the blue glass ashtray.

You got any more smokes? George says.

In my jacket pocket, the plastic sack of joints.

No, I say. But I got these.

George picks up a joint, holds it in his hand, rolls it around between his thumb and third finger, drags the joint under his nose. His one eyebrow goes up.

He hands the joint back to me.

No thanks, George says. I quit smoking dope, George says. Quit drinking too.

When did you quit? I say.

Just now, George says.

You sure? I say.

I'm sure, George says.

How do you know? I say.

Thunderbird, George says. I was waiting and waiting and finally it happened. Thunderbird flew right through me and showed me what I was waiting for.

George takes his open palm and beats his palm once on his chest.

I felt Thunderbird right here, he says.

When? I say.

Just now, he says, in the kitchen with Granny.

George's face, something broken open about him.

George reaches over, opens the top drawer of the dresser, sticks his hand in, searches around, comes out with another pack of Camels. I open the pack because I want George to have both his hands. I tap out one cigarette. George's blue Bic lighter. The flame on the tip of the cigarette.

George inhales, passes the cigarette to me.

Praying.

Waiting.

Trusting.

Why you got that red tie tied around your head? George says. You going native?

My French inhale is long.

I might have run into Thunderbird myself today, I say.

George's eyebrows and his eyelashes and his hair are all the same color black. Except for the gold bars, his eyes are that black too.

An intent in your life to fold your life around, I say.

Then: You know, I say, I think today I was a warrior too. And this red tie came along just when I needed it.

I pass the cigarette to George.

Our fingers touch.

My hands are undoing George's red bow tie. I pull the red tie through his collar.

George and I look down at my hands. I've got the red tie stretched tight across from hand to hand.

I reach up, wrap the tie around George's head, tie a knot in the back.

George touches his forehead, touches the tie.

George's eyes, Granny's eyes. Jesus. They're looking way deep inside me.

Solitary warriors of love, George says. We meet at last.

The words sound true so I say them too.

Solitary warriors of love, I say.

The rest of the night, arms and legs draped over each other, everything half-undone, everything making so much sense, just across the wall from death. Every breath is important, every word, every way we move, has meaning. Buckskin and flint on the back of my throat. Kisses like to burst my heart. George and I fall asleep like that, cuddled in together under the light bulb hanging down, in the back room of Granny's cabin, on George's skinny bed.

When I woke up it was morning, but not the next morning. I had slept through an entire day. I leaned up on my elbow and looked around. A square of sunlight was coming in a room. I was alone. On the other side of the door, the strange rolling sound of people talking Indian. Lots of people. I couldn't understand a word.

I put my clothes on. The door squeaked open, loud, just a crack when I pushed. That quick, all the Indians' voices stopped. Those I could see through the crack in the door were looking over at me. George was sitting at Granny's kitchen table. I didn't recognize him at first. His head was shaved. His red tie was still tied around his head.

George's black eyes. He lifted his chin the way truckers nod hello.

I'll be in in a minute, George said.

It wasn't long, and George brought me a cup of coffee with Sego Milk in it and two sugars and a blue plate with two glazed doughnuts on it. George didn't look too good. Big purple bags under his eyes. Plus he looked weird without his hair. When he handed me the cup and the plate of doughnuts, his hands were shaking something fierce. It scared me because all at once I felt like I didn't know him.

When George didn't look me in the eyes, when he didn't touch me, and when he sat down clear at the other end of the bed away from me, I was sure his heart had turned, and that I had become invisible to him.

The morning after. Or the morning after the morning after, and the days that followed, there was so much happening with George, I didn't know what was going on. I don't think George knew either.

George was rocking back and forth, staring at the piece of sunlight. Tomorrow we're burying Grandma, George said. Then there's the giveaway.

George just sat staring ahead at the patch of sunlight. I couldn't help it, I kept looking for some sign that he hadn't forgotten we'd said *love* out loud to each other. If he'd only look at me, I'd have an idea what was going on. But George wouldn't look.

Friends. George and I were friends.

We Indian people believe that when a person dies, George said, that every possession of theirs must be given away. That way their spirit won't want to stick around. What isn't given away has to be burned.

So if there's anything of Granny's that you want, George said, you best tell me.

Soon as George said that, I knew exactly what I wanted.

Granny's corncob pipe.

I went to speak, though, and my lips wouldn't say.

Instead I said: Does everyone shave their head?

No, George said. Only those who were closest to her. And people usually don't shave their heads. They just cut their hair off.

I reached up. I was real careful the way I touched him. Slow, like a friend, I laid my hand on George's head. The shine of it in my palm. The red tie.

I loved Granny, I said. Could I shave my head too?

That's when George turned to me, his black eyes with gold bars in them red all around his eyes like they were fire. George's trembling hand reached over and clamped down hard on my hand on my knee. What he said next, he said in one big breath, like if he didn't say it fast and all at once, he'd never get it out:

What happened the other night, George said, I was drunk. But I'm not drunk today. And if there's any time in my life I need a drink it's now. But I'm not drinking. My granny was all I had, Rig. My heart is broken. Those people in the next room are my uncles and aunts and cousins. They're here to help me. We're going to bury Granny in a traditional way, and that means there's going to be a lot of people around here day and night for the next couple days.

George took a quick breath, looked away at the spot of sunlight. When George looked back, he looked straight into my eyes. Nothing in between.

What we said to each other the other night, George said. Now in the daylight, hung-over as shit, it's all just as true for me. Every fucking word, Rig. Solitary warriors of love, George said, you and I. After all this time finally we've met. We've touched. I've kissed your mouth. And now I'll never be the same. Rig, it's been you I've been waiting for. Before you, I was dead and buried, and now there's life and I'm free. My God, Rig, you are beautiful. I know you got a life, George said. Things to figure out with your mom and dad and your girlfriend. I got shit I got to figure out too. All these years I've waited, and now here you are, and I can't think straight. I can understand with the funeral and all that you'd want to leave. And I won't try and stop you. But I'm telling you right now. I'll do whatever it takes. I'll get on my knees and beg. Rig, please stay close to me, George said. At least till Granny's buried, until it's time we have to go.

As quick as George had started talking, that quick he stopped. Then he slapped his knees, stood up, and walked to the door. The door squeaked open loud. George stood at the door, between his world and me, then said to me: I'd like you to meet my family.

Then to the Indians in the next room: This here's Rigby John, George says.

I stood up, adjusted myself as best I could, put on my best Catholic boy smile, walked to the door. George reached his arm out and took hold of my shoulder. He pulled me in to him. My friend, my lover, the guy who was going to break my heart. I walked into the room.

Granny's body was no longer on her brass bed. The pictures on the wall were gone. There were people sitting on the bed. Indian people. Indian people at the table, and on the floor in front of the new refrigerator, by the armoire.

No one said hello, or how are you, or nice to meet you. They all just sat and looked at me. One man with one front tooth smiled so much I wondered what was so funny.

In no time at all I was sitting at Granny's table. In the high-backed chair that was my favorite place. On the table, there was Granny's pipe right where I left it, next to my porkpie hat.

George picked the pipe up with both hands. He kissed the pipe. George bowed a little forward, lowered the pipe up and down four times, then handed the pipe to me.

There it was. Granny's corncob pipe in my hands. Somehow George knew.

Thank you, I said. My voice was high.

George untied the red tie from around my head, then wrapped a green towel around my shoulders. The buzz sound of the clipper and my hair getting clipped. Brown and gold hair falling down. I held Granny's pipe, my pipe, close in, next to my belly.

All around me in the kitchen, Indians. Men and women, mostly old. The men wearing Stetson hats, western-cut pearl-button shirts. Levi's and silver belt buckles and cowboy boots spit-shined. Beaded pendants hanging around their necks. One guy, a younger guy, his long hair in braids. The women with red, yellow, purple, blue, scarves around their heads. Shiny colorful shawls like peacock feathers. Flowered dresses. Turquoise earrings and silver bracelets and beaded chokers around their necks. Beaded moccasins. Everybody was smoking.

George got out the can of Barbasol, shook the can, then sprayed white foam across my head.

All the people in the room, when they got a load of me, just like that, life burst through. The sound coming from deep down inside them up and out. On their faces, wrinkles, squinty eyes, open mouths.

Such a weird sound, laughter.

George slapped some Old Spice on my head, retied the red tie around.

Then in front of God and everybody, George kissed me on the mouth. A kiss that stayed awhile, lips to lips. Then George was off again, and I didn't see him for the rest of the day.

By sunset, in Granny's kitchen, everything in the room was covered with food. On the counters, on the table, on Granny's sewing machine. On Granny's bed, the wedding ring quilt was gone and a piece of plywood lay on the bed. Set on the plywood were big pots of beef stew, plates of bread that looked like puffy tacos with sugar on them. On one plate on Granny's bed was a boiled cow's tongue. Lots of other pots with some kind of stews I didn't know. A big bowl of mashed potatoes. A big bowl of corn on the cob. On Granny's green enamel Majestic stove were a bunch of pies and cakes. On Granny's table, a basket full of candy bars and a big bowl of some kind of purple pudding. A coffee percolator plugged into the hanging-down light bulb. On the sink counter, paper plates and paper cups and plastic knives and forks and spoons. In the sink, on ice, cans of Shasta. In the refrigerator, the whole thing full of Cokes and Pepsis and Nehi Orange Crush.

Over by the door, next to a big plastic garbage can, sat an old man I didn't see right off. His black beret had a beaded navy blue and white pendant on it. He was leaning on a cane. It was the same old guy smiling with the one tooth.

Better to eat now, he said.

He nodded his head to the people outside the door.

When that crowd gets in here, he said, there won't be nothing left.

Then he pointed his cane at the green Majestic stove.

Chocolate cake, he said. Get me some. Ice cream's in the freezer.

The way this guy smiled, I couldn't figure him out. I cut him a big piece of cake, put a big scoop of vanilla ice cream on the plate, got him a plastic spoon and a paper napkin. His one tooth was a front tooth. Pink gums all the way around like Granny when I handed the plate to him.

On my paper plate, it was beef stew, red Jell-O, and a piece of yellow cake. I sat on the floor across the door from the old man. The food on my plate disappeared in nothing flat. I was just sitting there, staring out the doorway, at the tipi, at the Indian people and the sky and the fancy evening colors. Just half a mile away Mom was making dinner.

The old man's cane tapped my leg. He said something, but he spoke so low I couldn't hear a thing. So I knelt down next to him, up close.

His face so close like that, the old man's smile wasn't just a smile. It was the way he had to hold his face because he was in pain.

Goddamn legs, he said. They want to cut my feet off.

On the floor, both his feet wrapped up fat and round with Ace bandages.

Would you mind, young man, he said, getting me a cup of coffee?

His voice was so soft, for a moment there, I thought he was a woman.

No sugar, he said. I can't have sugar.

I went to say something about the cake and ice cream, then didn't. I figured it wasn't my place. So I got up, grabbed a plastic cup, put the cup under the spigot, poured the cup full of coffee, and then poured in a half inch of Sego Milk.

The old man's hands were crooked, fingers and bones poking out every which way. I let go of the plastic cup only when I was sure he held the cup firm.

Thank you, thank you. You're a lovely boy, he said.

The old man spoke so low he was almost whispering. I knelt down again, scooted in close. It was the only way I'd ever hear.

Are you OK? I said. Why are you whispering?

The old man sat up straight, his shoulders back. Made his lips go tight.

An old man speaks how he wants to speak, he said. Where is your respect?

All the breath went out of me.

I'm so sorry, I said.

Then the old man was holding his crooked hand over his mouth with his one tooth and he was laughing.

Oh, Lordy! White boys! he said. God love 'em.

This time when he spoke, he cupped his hand over his mouth, leaned in closer to me, exaggerated his whisper.

It was a ruse, he said, to bring you near me.

He was up so close, I could see the sorrel brown of his eyes.

Tell me, he said, do you ever go to a cocktail lounge called the Back Door?

The old man's face looked like a piece of lava rock. His jaw, his cheekbones, his forehead, flat surfaces. Everything else was vertical cliffs.

Yah, I said. Well, one time.

It's a heavenly place, isn't it? he said. Out of this world. I used to go there in my younger days. Do they still have Billie Holiday, "I'll Be Seeing You," on the jukebox?

Just danced to it the other night, I said.

Oh! he said. That's my favorite song, he said. Next to Patsy Cline, that is.

"Crazy," the old man sang. A voice so deep you could hardly hear it.

I love Patsy Cline, he said. That's what they called me at the Back Door.

Crazy? I said.

Patsy, he said.

Of course, he said, my real name is Matthew Owlfeather. What's your name again?

Rigby John, I said. Klusener.

So nice to meet you, Rigby John, he said. I like your hat.

And I like yours, I said.

On his Levi's shirt, silver tips on the collars with a design like two lightning bolts, the same design on his silver bolo tie.

By any chance, are you related to Joe Klusener of Tyhee Road? he said.

My breath was deep.

He's my father, I said.

Really?! Owlfeather said.

The skin hanging down over his eyes lifted up. Inside in the sorrel brown, a flash.

Your father was quite a handful in the olden days, he said.

You knew my father? I said.

Big Bad Joe, he said. Not biblically. But he did hang around the Back Door.

My father was in the Back Door? I said.

Always making trouble, he said. Him and his cousin. What was his name?

Jimmy Weis, I said.

Yes, he said, Jimmy Weis. The Terrible Twos.

That's one of the reasons it's got a steel door now, he said. Your father and his cousin. The Back Door does still have a steel door, doesn't it?

Did my father sleep with any of the men? I said.

Oh! Owlfeather said. I never tell tales out of school. Especially about kin.

Owlfeather's lips on the coffee cup. On the coffee cup a lipstick stain.

Mr. Owlfeather, I said. Please tell me.

His perfect French inhale.

I don't know why, I just did it, leaned down and kissed Owlfeather on his cheek. My lips on the rock of ages. Owlfeather's smile was really a smile.

Well then, he said.

On his Camel, more lipstick. Dark, dark red.

Technically no, he said. At least no one I was acquainted with.

But you know what they say? he said.

A bully does before all the world what he is incapable of without witness.

What? I said. Say that again.

Bluff, Owlfeather said. A man hates most what's in his own heart.

Why go to the Back Door if you hate fags?

About that time, all kinds of people started coming in the door. Somebody must have rung the dinner bell. It was a stampede.

You see, I told you, Owlfeather said. It's a good thing you ate.

His old crooked hand reached out, grabbed a hold of my hand.

Do me another favor, he said. Will you?

Sure, I said.

My hand inside Owlfeather's, slick and smooth.

When you sleep with George tonight, he said, love your body.

What Owlfeather said next he could barely say because he was laughing so hard.

What? I said.

Go for it while you got your youth and spirit, he said. Fuck yourself silly.

Outside all around, people were sitting in chairs, standing around. The moon on bits of silver, white teeth, white feathers, white beads in earrings and chokers and necklaces. Inside the tipi, the fire was low and the shadows were long. The line moved from left to right. Granny's coffin was at the north end surrounded by flowers. At the south end was a group of people sitting in chairs. George was one of them. I could barely see him through the crowd. He was in his Italian suit, the red tie tied around his shaved head.

The woman just ahead of me in line reached down and touched Granny's hands. She said some things to her in Indian. When it was my turn, I touched Granny's soft, smooth hair.

The only part of Granny's pine box that you could see was around the bottom. On a stand by her head was a candle and a tall vase filled with wildflowers — daisies and chamomile, wild mustard, bull thistle, daffodils, syringa, wild yellow roses, Indian paintbrush, white sage, and lilac. More flowers too, a wreath of red roses on a stand and a ribbon that said WE LOVE YOU GRANDMA. Granny's hair was tied back in a bun. She was wearing a buckskin dress. Beaded roses just below her collarbone. Inside, all around Granny was her wedding ring quilt, the design of the wedding rings made up of the stylized bird, the Thunderbird. Across the lid of the pine box, a yellow and brown and orange Pendleton blanket and a shawl with blue fringe with knots in the fringe. Nailed to the lid were Granny's photographs. A man in buckskin wearing a war bonnet next to a woman with her hair tied back and a shawl over her head. A photo of a little girl in front of a log cabin. I looked close, and it was Granny's log cabin. The Lombardy poplars were only knee-high. Two or three people who looked like they were dead. A photo of Granny sitting on the Lombardy poplar stumps in front of the green screen door.

The way the candlelight hit her face, if you squinted your eyes just right, Granny looked like she was smiling.

When I got to George, I stuck out my hand. George stood up off his folding chair, gave me a quick bear hug, then stepped back. George put his hands on my shoulders. Under George's eyes, his skin was a circle of white outlined in dark purple. Maybe it was just the light from the fire, or the shadows, maybe it was his shaved head. Whatever it was, George looked pretty bad.

You look real tired, I said.

I look sober, George said.

That night late, I woke up out of a deep sleep. George pulled the Pendleton back, got in bed next to me, skin to naked skin. It was a hot night, and he was freezing cold. His body was shaking. George curled his body into mine, nudged in under my arm. In the east, the morning light was just starting in.

Just hold me, Rig, George whispered. Hold me tight.

I moved in close to George, made spoons. I started in talking about the day and all the stuff that happened to me that day, but in no time at all George's breath was deep and slow and George was snoring.

His leg up across my legs, his arm over my chest, his cock and balls against my thigh. Such powerful magic being close to a man, to George. His slow in-and-out breath. Yet as I lay there, I knew George was more than just asleep. He was way far away.

Where my friend George was I couldn't tell.

All night, the wind through the cedar tree, Granny's ancestors, singing and crying and singing. I didn't sleep a wink.

At daybreak, the chickens and the rooster started in. Pretty soon you could hear people talking and laughing, coughing. Somebody farted real loud. About seven o'clock, when the sun was in our eyes, George rolled off my arm, sat up quick. The whole long naked back of George all the way down to the crack of his ass. From in the kitchen, the smell of bacon and coffee.

The red tie around George's head was on all screwy. The skin under his eyes was a half-moon of white circled around in purple. The whites of his eyes were red.

You any good with a shovel? George said.

George looked at my hands, then back up into my eyes.

Good, George said. We got us a grave to dig.

At the crossroads of Quinn Road and Tyhee Road, if we turned right, in a half a mile we'd be at my parents' house. Mom in the kitchen in her red housedress stirring something in a bowl. Dad out in the machine shop with his Stetson off working on the combine. But George and I and our shovels, in the back end of somebody's old pickup, didn't turn right; we turned left onto Sheepskin Road, then followed Sheepskin around to where it comes to the plateau and the earth falls into the bottoms.

George and I got out in the middle of nowhere. Not a tree. Only sand and sagebrush and now and then a bitterroot. Jackrabbits everywhere. The August sun and the Idaho wind. George in his cowboy hat, his Levi's, cowboy boots, and a backpack. Me in my porkpie hat, my T-shirt, my suit pants, and my Sunday shoes. Shovels over our shoulders.

There we were, George and I, alone out there in the middle of the rez, in the middle of all that red, in the middle of Idaho.

At a barbwire fence we stopped. George opened up a wire gate, and we stepped through. He pushed the post of the gate in with his shoulder, looped the wire over the post, and the gate held tight. George knew all about gates.

Don't let the spirits out, George said.

As we walked I began to see. Piles of rocks, shiny beads, now and then a marble headstone. George and I were in Sandy Hill Cemetery.

Right next to one of the biggest sagebrushes I'd ever seen, taller than me the sagebrush, George dug his shovel in, turned up the sandy dirt. George stepped off two long steps west, then dug a hole there. One long step north, another hole. Then two long steps east and one long step north of the first hole, he dug another hole, and with that, George had the grave marked out.

We went right to work. We didn't talk. George dug on his side, I dug on mine. We threw the dirt to one side, the south. The sides of the hole we scraped vertical with the back end of our shovels. When I was digging, George was throwing. Digging, throwing, digging, throwing. We went on and on like that for the longest time. Like it was the Olympics for hole digging, and George and I were on the Idaho team. I forgot all about my sore hand. Something so good to push yourself like that. Earth in my nose and my own sweat, and George, glorious George, buckskin and flint on the back of my throat. Shovel for shovel. We dug. We threw. Faster and faster.

There's nothing better in the world than digging yourself a hole.

Finally, when we were about three feet down, I had to stop.

I leaned up against my shovel. I was breathing like a racehorse.

That's when I saw it, the rectangle of earth where Granny would lie for all eternity.

Granny for all eternity in that hole. No wonder George was so far away.

The sun was high, and the only shade was from the sagebrush, and that shade wouldn't be on the grave for at least another hour. George's T-shirt was soaked through. All around George, on the ground, drops of sweat.

I took my hat off, wiped my head. The sun on my shaved head was hot.

My deep breath.

What about your father? I said. Is he coming to the funeral?

George's shoulders jerked up, but he didn't stop. He stuck the shovel blade into the earth, stepped on the shovel, pushed it down, then he leaned down, scooped up the earth, threw the shovelful of earth onto the pile.

Four feet down and going.

No, he said. It's not a Mormon funeral, so he ain't coming.

Jeez, I said.

Shovels of dirt flying, flying, out of the hole and into the pile.

Are you going to see him then? I said. After Granny's funeral?

George kept digging. Didn't stop for a second.

The feeling in my arms that means I'm helpless. It was like our days in the hay field. Only it was George this time pushing to get the work done.

Then: That old man with one tooth, I said. Matthew Owlfeather, I said. He told me my father used to hang around the Back Door.

That stopped him. George leaned up against his shovel.

No shit? George said.

It scared me how much I wanted to see George smile. No doubt about it, something was up.

My turn, I said.

And jumped into the hole.

No, George said, thanks. I need to keep moving.

George was moving. All over his whole body his muscles were twitching.

I put my hand on George's twitching shoulder.

How long does it last? I said. After you've quit drinking?

George's eyes looked away, looked down, looked at everything but me.

Days, weeks, George said. A lifetime.

But this shaking, I said.

George raised up his hands, looked at his hands.

Don't know, George said. I've never done this before. At least I've never seen myself do this.

In the hospital, he said. Was I shaking like this?

I didn't even stop to think.

Worse, I said. You were plumb loco. Screaming and crying.

George leaned back onto the side of the hole.

No wonder you hated me so much, George said.

Just the wind. Sand along the ground, the sound of sand. Behind George, a white-tailed rabbit jumped into a clearing. Jumped out.

The first time that afternoon we heard the thunder.

Did you bring some water? I said.

George didn't say anything for a while. Just stood leaning against the wall of the grave. His hands a hard grip on the shovel handle.

Then: It's in my backpack, George said.

Inside George's backpack, a green glass jug with THUNDERBIRD on it. The place next to the lip a round of glass where you could put your finger through. I unscrewed the lid, smelled inside. Tipped the jug up. It was water.

George took a long drink, water dribbling out the sides of his mouth. How many times I'd watched his Adam's apple go up and down.

When he was done, I took a drink. Cool water. I was praying to the cool water. Praying to Granny's ancestors. Praying to Thunderbird. Help me with my friend.

I wiped my mouth, screwed the lid back on, set the green Thunderbird jug under the sagebrush shade. I walked off a ways like I was going to pee.

My knees on the ground, I reached down, picked up a handful of earth. I made the sign of the cross.

Just in case.

If Thunderbird didn't listen, maybe someone else would.

Saint George, I said. Slayer of the dragons, I said. Pray for us.

George was still digging like a maniac when I got back to the hole.

George, I said, how about a cigarette?

George stopped shoveling. Stood up, arched his back, looked up at me. The level of the hole was at his armpits.

The way we were standing, I was about five feet taller than George.

George stuck the shovel blade into the earth, stepped on the shovel, pushed it down, then leaned over, scooped up the earth, threw the shovelful of earth onto the pile.

More thunder. Down so low I could feel thunder in my feet.

A long breath and really deep.

George! I said. Tell me where you're at.

The way George curled up his lip. How easy it was to fear this guy. George's shovel went flying out the hole.

Sit down, George said.

I, who have been accused of doing everything he is told, didn't sit down, just stood there.

Sit the fuck down! George yelled.

From inside the grave, George tapped his hand next to my feet, right at the edge of the hole. I sat so that my legs dangled into the grave.

George took off his hat, pulled my legs open, put his chest in, wrapped his arms around me, pulled me in close. I loved God so much right then.

George and I stayed like that for a long time. The shakes going through George's body into mine. Then George lifted up my T-shirt with his teeth, pressed his lips. His tongue and his lips on my belly. With every round of his tongue, I lost another breath.

The hairs on George's head were rough just like his whiskers. Sweat was pouring down my neck, down my chest, down my armpits.

When George finally spoke, his forehead was on my bellybutton, his chin and mouth lay on my crotch.

I'm not shaking just because I'm sober, George said. For the first time in my life I'm afraid.

It's Granny all right, George said. And it's this fucking hole we're digging. It's all the people and the funeral.

But really, George said, it's not knowing what's going to happen next.

I never used to worry about that, George said. I was cool. I was going along smoking and praying and trusting whatever the fuck happened next just happened.

I was sure of myself, George said. Didn't have a care. I knew what I was doing. I was waiting for Thunderbird. Just me and the tumbling tumbleweeds.

But now that Thunderbird is here, George said, now that spirit is passing in and out of my heart, everything is different. Everything is so fucking.

Fragile, George said. I'm a wreck because of you.

Now that I love you, George said, there's so much to lose.

As soon as I woke up this morning, George said, I knew you and I would be alone out here. What joy, at first. Then I was terrified.

Rig, George said, I've never had sex sober. I've never had sex when I loved. And having sex with you will make it impossible, George said. Yet I know I got to leave.

Thunderbird gives you what you want, George said. My heart is pounding. I can't catch my breath. Thunderbird keeps passing and passing and passing through, and all I can do is tremble.

The tiniest things — clouds, spit, dirt — are little miracles.

Sometimes the world is so beautiful it hurts.

There are moments when I look at you I think I'm going to die.

Which makes it all the worse, George said.

You and I fucking won't be just sex, George said. You're like me. This will become your way of life.

It's a rat's ass, Rig, George said. A life I wouldn't wish on a dog.

Half of me wants to devour you, George said. The other half wants to run and hide. But I don't do either.

All I can do is shake, George said.

Come in my mouth, George says.

My Sunday shoes are off. George pulling off my socks. I unbutton my pants, zip down the zipper, George yanking at my pants. My T-shirt's over my head. George's T-shirt is over his head. My thumbs go inside my jockey shorts. When I sit back down, my bare ass is on the sandy dirt.

I don't close my eyes.

My cock goes into George's mouth. The world gets thick and full. My cock all the way down his throat, then back out, his lips and tongue on the very tip. His sucking makes the raindrops start. Bright sun on George's head, I hold his head, a crystal ball. The whiskers on his lips and chin. Rough and smooth, sun and rain. I press my ass into the earth.

I arch my back, my legs go round and cross behind his head. Slow, it's so slow, my heartbeat, my breath, the thunder roll, his tongue round and round, the lightning that cracks the sky.

I'm not sure I should tell him. What's coming from down low and up. And how much and how fast.

Then the earth moves, and I look, and I'm not on the earth, I'm in the air on George's shoulders. My hands, which have held his head so tight, fly out like a big bird flying. A screaming bird. The way my hips pump George's face pushes him against the side. I go flying, flying to the south, and land in the mound of earth. The dirt is dark wet just on the surface. I'm covered with mud. I let myself roll and roll and fall into the grave on top of George.

George's skin is wet, his face, his head. I'm laughing so hard. That strange sound coming up. I put my mouth to George's mouth and put my laugh into him. I'm straddling his chest and when I look down, my cock is still dripping. Behind my cock, behind my balls, George's cock is big and hard and pointing at my ass. I know it will hurt, and I want it to hurt, and I put his cock head right there inside and push.

Maybe it's the mud and rain. George's cock goes in steady, slow, inside all the way. The bird is a screaming bird again. I slap George hard across the face, one cheek then the next. He's pushing hard and hard and hard. Fire in the ass. Rain on my face. My fingers scrape mud along the walls. Nothing better in the world than digging yourself a hole.

George's face is wild and open and full of joy and free. He's almost smiling.

I can feel him inside the pulse that makes his body jerk.

Just knowing George is coming, I start coming too. One long stream out of my cock that shoots up and splats against his neck.

Finally, I've nailed his Adam's apple.

In the bottom of a grave, in an inch of water, in a puddle of mud. Some of the mud smells like shit. The rain coming down is soft like the whole world is soft. Arms and legs and arms and legs. My hands cup George's balls. There's nothing in between. George and I are eye to eye.

Alone at last, George says.

And we're not baling hay, I say.

We're fucking, not fighting, George says.

Make love, not war, I say.

Solitary warriors of love, George says.

All these summer storms, I say.

Thunderbird ain't through with us yet, George says.

What's going to be left of us when he's through? I say.

An eye is opened that now must look, George says.

You really do have to go, don't you? I say. There's nothing left here for you now.

Then: Me too, I say.

But where can we go now? George says. Now that we are here?

Thunder and lightning all around. George and I stuck together in the bottom of a grave. Only our breaths in and out.

Your father in Apacheland? I say. Or you could visit Italy and your mother?

And what about you? George says.

I lay my head back, try to keep my eyes open as the rain hits my eyes.

If you're going to San Francisco, I say, be sure to wear some flowers in your hair.

I expected the funeral to be wild with Indians in traditional outfits, singing and dancing the hoop dance and banging the drum. But it wasn't anything like that. Two guys walked up to Granny's casket and closed it, with Granny and everything of hers in it. How simple it was to close and lock the lid. Took my breath away.

Matthew Owlfeather, smiling with his one tooth, lit some white sage and a cedar branch. He lifted his face to the sky, held his arms out wide. The song he sang was one more human breath to breathe through the cedar boughs of Granny's ancestor tree. Sweet and sad. Above, the sky was big with silver and white billowing clouds. On the undersides of the clouds, strips of yellow. Light rain on and off. Every once in a while, sun poking through.

All along Sheepskin Road, a line of cars parked. Maybe a hundred people standing around in Sandy Hill Cemetery. Granny's pine box was in the back of a new yellow Ford pickup. The pickup pulled into Sandy Hill Cemetery, made a three-point turn, then backed up to the grave. George pulled the tailgate down, and he and five other men pulled the pine box off the pickup, carried the pine box to the grave.

Lowered the pine box down with ropes. The hole was just big enough for Granny's box. Room to spare all the way around.

Then another pine box, low and square, an old yellow dog named Bonanza in the box, set on top of Granny at her feet.

When we threw the earth into the grave onto the pine boxes, I couldn't help but think of Granny smiling down there where George and I had fucked. All the life and love and sweat and tears and come inside the hole.

My wish was for a resting place like that.

Back at Granny's house, the giveaway was just that. Every pot and pan of Granny's, her coffeepot, the pewter cups, every stick of furniture — her bed, her box spring and mattress, her sheets, her pillows, her table and chairs, her sewing machine, the picture of the flowers, the armoire, all the linens and blankets in the armoire, Granny's trunk, all the Pendleton blankets in the trunk. Bonanza's Pendleton blanket. The kerosene lamp. Granny's new refrigerator. Her green enamel Majestic stove. The curtains on the windows, the curtains under the counter of the sink. George's bed, his dresser, the round mirror on his wall. The blue glass ashtray.

The chickens, the eggs, Granny's two bales of straw, the porcelain pans hanging on the barn.

Everything. Even the two light bulbs.

The tipi was dismantled, the canvas rolled up, the poles stacked onto a pickup, hauled away.

As people left, taking with them Granny's worldly goods, George stood where the tipi had set, next to the smoldering fire. In his hands, a big roll of dollar bills. He peeled off a dollar bill for every person. George saved the last dollar bill for me.

By sunset it was just me and George in Granny's empty house. The light through the windows on the shiny floor. The places where her pictures had hung. The stovepipe, crooked, hanging down. The scrapes on the floor where the table and the chairs had sat. The four dents that had been her bed.

George walked through the rooms, close along the walls. He touched everything he could. When he got to the electrical box next to the front door, George opened the metal door, reached in, and unscrewed the fuse. He put the fuse in his pocket, then closed the metal door.

Then out of nowhere.

Would you get the broom for me? George said.

The broom? I said. There's nothing left.

It's in the back of your pickup, George said.

In the back of the pickup, an old broom, its bristles worn down to a fist. And a suitcase. One of those old kinds of suitcases, leather, that look like a valise.

George swept the house, every corner. The little pile of dust he swept up, we picked up with our hands. Carried the dust out to the smoldering fire, threw the dust onto the fire.

We made sure all the doors and windows were open. In the middle of Granny's room, George took my hand. His hands weren't shaking. George in his Italian suit, his white shirt, his Italian shoes, and cotton socks, the red tie tied around his bristly head.

I took my porkpie hat off. Adjusted my red tie. My hair was bristly too. My Sunday shoes were scuffed, my suit pants were bagging out, the suit jacket wrinkled, the burned iron spot on the collar of my white shirt. Underneath, my crusty shorts and a three- or four-day-old T-shirt. I was ripe all right, but not the worse for wear.

The Shoshone prayer from George's lips was soft and high and sounded like Idaho. Silver and gold in the sunlight, wind in the poplars a high sigh and scratch, dry June grass. Heat lightning storms in the night sky. Pickup trucks backing up and a pine box bumping down into a grave.

Outside, George took the fuse out of his pocket, bounced it up once in his hand, then threw the fuse as hard as he could into the tall pasture grass.

Where the tipi had sat, the fire was ash and embers. George pulled up the knees of his pants, sat down like Buddha. I sat down across the fire from him. He laid the broom bristles into the fire. With some poking around, the fire was up and spitting again.

George reached in his pocket, pulled out his pack of Camels, tapped one out, lit it. His French inhale. George handed the cigarette to me.

Is there anything left, George said, that you can think of, that we haven't given away or burned?

My mind went over all the places in the house, in the barn, on the barn, in the chicken coop, in the outhouse.

I hope there's toilet paper left, I said.

George almost smiled, I swear.

Anything else? George said. I packed up my suitcase, we've swept the house. As soon as this broom is burned, I think we're done.

There was something else. I reached into my inside jacket pocket, pulled out Granny's pipe, set the pipe on the ground.

No, George said. I gave that pipe to you.

It's not the pipe, I said.

Then, from inside the same pocket, I pulled out the plastic bag of joints. I rolled out the plastic, picked up the joints, and put them in the palm of my hand.

Threw the joints in the fire, then the plastic bag.

The smoke smelled of broom handle and burnt plastic and marijuana. I went to sniff up the smoke, then didn't.

The wind in the poplar leaves, a wind scattering up high. Old, dead wood croaking. George's dark eyes.

You didn't have to do that, George said. I'm the one who's getting sober.

And I helped, I said.

Then: What about your car? I said. That's a possession, isn't it?

Fuck! George said. My fucking car. It's still parked in town!

What's left to tell about George and me? Not much.

George pulled out his wallet, opened it, and from inside a fold George pulled out a shiny black arrowhead.

George carved his initials into the apple tree first: GS.

Then I carved my initials: RJK.

George carved in the heart around our initials.

For supper that night, we ate nothing.

At the cedar tree, George and I held onto each other's hands and jumped. We were one flying whooping hollering screaming shits and giggles, one long smooth uninterrupted naked thrust through the night sky. Suspended in the air, arms, legs, cocks, a ball-out splash, the whoosh down deep into cool, muddy, green water.

No swimming suit, water all around me touched me deep the way water goes wherever it can go. My legs, my ass, my cock, my balls, waterfall rushing water against me, better even than air. Floating low, my body a slide along dark rocks and mud, tangles of moss, gliding like a seal, some kind of sea animal, I was sprouting gills, breathing water. In the dark turbulence, my hands found one human leg and then another, and I grabbed the legs and pulled, and from somewhere up above in the breathing-air world was a holler, a high-pitched yell that turned into bubbles.

George's face right up next to mine through the dark, muddy green, George all his teeth. His dark eyes turned devil, George grabbed me, but I was too fast. I was out of the water in one long lunge, the deep breath of air glory in my chest. In no time at all, George's arm around my neck. Then his other arm scooped me up under my knees.

We could not stop. I swear we fucked ourselves so silly, the old two-by-twelve almost snapped.

That night, under the poplars, then up and beyond them, the moon and the stars. Lying in our bedroll, George and I, we couldn't stop touching.

In the morning, there's no chickens, no rooster, no smell of coffee or frying bacon. No porcelain pan to watch the sunlight in. There's just enough toilet paper.

The loud metal-to-metal pop of the pickup door. I get in, George gets in. I turn on the key. The pickup starts, no problem. I put it into reverse. We drive out Granny's lane, past the tansy and the burdock, past the bull thistle, the chamomile, and the purple-head alfalfa. Turn right on Quinn Road, then left. George and I drive past Hess's forty.

It's the first time in a long time I think about my dad.

At the Sinclair station on East Fifth Street, I've got enough money to fill up the tank. I make sure I don't spend George's dollar. George goes in to take a shit. Then I go. The smell of the bathroom after he's done. The smell like his come tastes, like his armpits smell, buckskin and flint on the back of my throat.

When I get back in the pickup, George has two cups of coffee, two glazed doughnuts, and a newspaper, the *Idaho State Journal*. George tosses something into my lap.

I reach down, pick it up. It's a map of Nevada and California.

Then it's a yellow daisy George slips behind my ear.

Be sure to wear some flowers in your hair, George says.

On Pine Street, in front of a small white house, George's '49 Ford is parked.

I flash back to the day, so long ago, when Mom and I were headed for devotions. Just in time, Mom hit the brakes and cranked the steering wheel. Directly in front of us, the old gray '49 Ford parked barely off the road. All around my ears was a loud screech. The Buick spun around for a long time.

God spins you around like that only once in a while. Thank God.

Mom was cussing a blue streak.

Just as I looked and before I quick looked away, that moment, a big fat drop of rain slow from a cottonwood leaf in the last light fell, the splash in his hands, crooked light.

George. Naked in the field.

Those Indians and their goddamn queers.

George leans across the cab, kisses me right there in broad daylight on a Pocatello street. Then he gets out, slams the door, walks around the front of the pickup.

The red tie around his head in the bright day of Pocatello, something about the red tie on his naked head in Pocatello scares me to death.

At my window, George's dark eyes, the sunlight in them, bars of gold.

I love it when your eyes are gold, I say.

George's long, beautiful fingers touch my hand.

I'll see you back at Granny's, George says.

Out of the back, George picks up his leather suitcase, carries his suitcase to his car, opens the trunk, puts the suitcase in the trunk.

I put the pickup into first gear, let out the clutch. I make it a couple blocks before I pull over and stop. Out the rearview mirror, I try to get a look, but George's car is gone.

George is gone.

That quick.

Then I can't do anything. I'm crying too damn hard.

At Russell's grave, I'm spread-eagle under the huge old elm. I tell Russell, the elm, the cemetery, the sky, the whole world, all that's gone on between me and George. It's surprising how long the story goes on. It starts with a spinning Buick and a naked man in a field in the rain and ends in the middle of a day, on a Pocatello street, Pine Street, in front of a white house, his fingers on my hand.

Then: Russell, I say, he took his suitcase. He told me he'll see me at Granny's house. But he took his suitcase.

Only minutes later, as I pull out of Mount Moriah Cemetery. On East Fifth Street in front of the Fanci Freez, I hear the siren. In the rearview mirror, a cop car. Its flashing lights are red and white.

13 As Fate Would Have It

THE COP HAULED his big self out of the cop car and walked up to the pickup. In the side mirror, it wasn't long and the blue of the cop's uniform took up the whole mirror.

The cop was a big guy, big belly, but the rest of him was as big as his belly. He was like you took a normal person and pumped him up with air. So much flesh on his hands, you wondered how he opened and closed his hands. Pink skin and red hair with freckles. Sergeant Roscoe.

My pounding heart. The feeling in my forearms that means I'm helpless.

Sergeant Roscoe pushed his hat up, put his hands on his hips. Sweat on pink skin. Belts and leather pouches and leather holster and boots and leather straps all over on this guy.

Pig was the word that came to mind.

Can I see your driver's license and registration, please? Sergeant Roscoe said.

I got my driver's license out of my wallet, handed it to him, then pulled down the visor, slipped the registration out that was always clipped under the piece of plastic.

Our fingers did not touch.

Just wait here, Sergeant Roscoe said. I'll be right back.

The roll of his hips. When Sergeant Roscoe sat down in his police car, the car went down about a foot.

Static on the police radio you could hear all through the bright afternoon.

When Sergeant Roscoe got back, his big pink face and thin yellow-red eyebrows and blue eyes were filling up my whole window.

Mr. Klusener, Sergeant Roscoe said, I'd like you to step out of your pickup.

Leave the keys! Sergeant Roscoe said. Hands up!

Then I was spread-legged, leaning against the front bumper of the pickup, and Sergeant Roscoe was rubbing his billy club up my legs and down.

Put your hands behind your back, he said.

The handcuffs around my wrists, I can't tell you. There was no breath.

Sergeant Roscoe grabbed me by the arm and led me to the back end of his car. He opened the back door of the station wagon, gave me a shove headfirst, and I fell into the caged-in back end. He slammed the door and locked it.

As we drove away, I watched the brown Apache pickup get smaller and smaller and then it was gone.

Just be there at Granny's, George, I kept on thinking. *Just be there at Granny's.*

A long, dark corridor, lined with iron bars. Sergeant Roscoe escorted me by the arm. If he'd had a lariat he'd have hogtied me. A big ring of keys attached to his belt. The sound of the sliding iron gates bouncing off the hallway walls. Way inside down a hall, through rows and rows of iron bars, a black man in an iron-bar room, yelling and screaming. The smell of piss and ammonia.

At the end of a hallway, Roscoe unlocked a gray steel door. Inside was a gray room with a cement floor and one of those windows where you can't see them, but they can see you. I saw it once on TV.

There was a table in the room and four chairs. Everything gray. A gray cement floor. One window up high with bars on the window.

Sergeant Roscoe pushed me down into the chair, undid my handcuffs.

What's with the red tie? he said. Some kind of hippie shit?

I didn't have a chance to answer.

Take your jacket off, Sergeant Roscoe said.

I took my jacket off, handed it to him. Sergeant Roscoe went through all my pockets.

Alleluia. Alleluia. Silently, I thanked the Lord, thanked Saint George, thanked Thunderbird, I'd thrown the joints into the fire.

Take your shirt off, Sergeant Roscoe said. Then your shoes and socks. Then your pants and your undershorts.

I took my shirt off, handed Sergeant Roscoe my shirt.

Roscoe checked in the pocket, stuck his nose in the pocket. Shook the shirt out like when you shake out wrinkles.

Then my shoes. One shoe, then the next.

Sergeant Roscoe stuck his fleshy hands into my shoes, turned my shoes upside down. Tried to pull off the leather heels.

Then my socks.

Sergeant Roscoe turned my socks inside out, stuck his hands up inside my socks. Then my pants.

Sergeant Roscoe checked all the pockets, turned my pants inside out.

OK, he said. Let's have the shorts.

My crusty four-day-old shorts. I took them off, handed them to Roscoe.

There I was standing naked in a gray room, my cold feet on the cement floor. In the window where only they could see me, I could see only a skinny boy.

I couldn't think of anything about me that wasn't wrong.

I tried and tried, but I couldn't come up with anything good.

I'd be a terrible American if communists tortured me.

Just be there at Granny's, George. Just be there at Granny's.

Roscoe took my shorts on the end of his billy club. Held my shorts up in the air between him and the window.

Roscoe's face got even pinker, if that was possible.

Then: Bend over, he said. Grab your cheeks, spread 'em.

Little holes in the cement floor where pieces of gravel had washed out.

Sergeant Roscoe's billy club back there between my cheeks.

You don't have any LSD stuck up in there, do you? he said.

No, I said.

No sir, he said.

No sir, I said.

Then: Put your clothes back on, he said. Sit down in that chair and stay in that chair and don't move.

Behind Sergeant Roscoe, the door slammed loud, and the slam bounced around up and down the hallways.

The clock on the wall was the only other thing in the room. The clock was the black and white kind like in school.

The red hand, snapping off the seconds.

At 3:45 Detective Harold Richardson walked in the room.

Alleluia. Alleluia. Harold Richardson was a Knight of Columbus at Saint Joseph's Church. His wife, Mrs. Richardson, was in the Altar Society with my mother.

Harold! I said.

Detective Richardson, he said.

Detective Richardson, I said.

Detective Richardson was wearing a blue suit and a blue tie. Brown hair, buzz-cut up the sides, a wave in front like Van Johnson.

He set a Coke down on the table and a bag of Clover Club potato chips.

Rigby John, he said, I trust that Sergeant Roscoe made you feel at home.

My chin was moving in a way it had never moved before. It wasn't just rubber lips, it was a rubber lower face.

My hands were shaking. Opening the sack of potato chips was so loud.

What did you and Joe Scardino fight about Saturday night? Detective Richardson said.

The Coke bottle was cool in my hands. It took a while for my chin to settle down. My heart was pounding, you know, my breath. Fuck. One of these days I'm going to just keel over. I took a drink of Coke, swallowed.

Is he dead? I said.

Detective Richardson took a deep breath, put both his hands on the table, leaned in. He looked down at me, and his eyes were brown, and they looked sad.

He is, Detective Richardson said. Were you fighting over drugs?

There was this one time when Patrolman Harold Richardson came to Saint Joe's when we were in the second grade. He talked to us about safety rules, crossing the street and such. He told us to be careful of drunk drivers. Scardino asked him how you could tell a drunk driver. Harold Richardson said that a drunk driver always swerved to the middle line of the road.

No, I said.

Then what did you two fight about? he said.

I never could lie worth a goddamn. So I didn't say a word.

Only silence and the snap snap of the red second hand.

Detective Harold Richardson got up off the table, pulled out the chair across from me, sat down.

He slid his chair in, folded his hands on the table in front of me.

Rigby John, he said.

His voice was low and his lips pronounced every word slow.

I'm going to be straight with you, he said. Saturday night, a boy was killed, a Catholic boy from our parish, and another boy, Chuck diPietro, was put in harm's way.

I want you to tell me the truth, he said. And if you don't tell me the truth, you'll be in serious trouble.

There were traces of marijuana in Joe Scardino's blood, Detective Richardson said. Drug use and drug trafficking in Idaho is a felony offense. You could get thirty years to life, he said. And if you lie about it, even more.

The red second hand, snap snap.

Now, this is the important part, he said. Don't lie to me now. Were you doing drugs with Joe Scardino at the Snac Out Drive-In?

Detective Richardson's face was so close, I could see how the lid on his left eye hung down while his other eyelid didn't.

That's when out of nowhere, for some reason, what the fuck, as fate would have it, I made the sign of the cross.

Harold Richardson blinked his eyes. Both eyelids blinked. No doubt about it, the sign of the cross had made an impression.

I lowered my voice like I was in confession.

No, I said.

Then: Did you talk to Billie? I said.

We have, he said.

That's when I did it. With everything I'd known so far, I looked straight into Detective Richardson's brown eyes. Nothing in between. If I was going to get my ass out of this crack, it was going to take everything I had.

Sometimes the world needs a vivid imagination to make it a more livable place.

Then you must know, I said, Billie and I were dressed up silly. Billie had her mother's wedding dress on that had red wax down the front, and we were both wearing hats. Billie's pregnant, you see, and her father didn't want her to go to the Senior Summer All Night Party, and we were afraid of her father catching us, or my mother, I said. So we switched cars and put on our hats. We were just goofing around.

When Scardino saw us, I said, he thought we were doing acid. I told him we weren't, but he got mean like he always does, and he came after me. I just defended myself, I said. And Billie, I said. Scardino's temper has been something I've had to live with all my life.

And to tell the truth, I said, I'm glad I knocked him down. I should have done it years ago. Then he and Chuck got in his car and he went flying out of the Snatch Out straight into the traffic on Pole Line Road.

That's when I heard the crash, I said.

Snap snap of the red second hand.

Snatch Out.

Detective Richardson unfolded his hands. I took another drink of Coke. The potato chip in my mouth was all that I could hear.

Were you smoking pot in that corncob pipe of yours? he said.

No, I said. You smoke tobacco in that pipe.

Then did you smoke a joint, he said, or ingest marijuana in any way?

My almond-shaped hazel eyes didn't flinch.

No, I said.

Then: So where have you been for the last four days? he said. Your mother and father are worried sick.

Just be there at Granny's, George. Just be there at Granny's.

A deep, deep, deep breath.

My eyes, Detective Richardson's eyes. Still nothing in between.

After the accident, I said, I needed to be alone. This may sound weird, I said, but I've been hanging out in the cemetery, I said. I've been examining my conscience, I said. I've been praying.

It's weird. A kind of glow from deep down. I could feel the glow on my skin and on my face.

Maybe this was what it was like to feel Thunderbird.

And Billie's child? Detective Richardson said. Are you going to do the right thing and marry the girl?

My goddamn chin.

The child, Detective Richardson, I said, is not my child. It's Chuck diPietro's child.

Detective Richardson slammed his hand down hard onto the table.

Aha! he said. You and Scardino weren't fighting over drugs! You were fighting over a woman!

Two or three hours more, Detective Richardson and I went on and on like that. Question after question. I kept on having the right answers, though.

After all, they let me go.

Now that I look back on my day in jail — you know, lying really wasn't that hard.

I was lucky, though.

But mostly I was telling the truth. Scardino's death was his own damn fault. No reason for anyone else to suffer.

Around seven o'clock, Detective Richardson got up, walked to the door, opened it.

By the way, he said. The corncob pipe was clean. No marijuana residue.

I believe you, son, Detective Richardson said. You've always been a good boy. I'm sorry you had to go through this.

I'll call your father, he said.

Then just before he closed the door, he said:

DiPietro broke his leg and his collarbone, he said. And some bruises and scratches. He's lucky he's alive.

I loved God so much right then.

As things turned out, I ended up spending the night. Alone in a cell room with only bars for walls. Just a mattress.

Just be there at Granny's, George. Just be there at Granny's.

The guy in the cell next to me was old and fat. When the lights went off, he pulled down his pants and stuck his cock through the bars.

Want to be my jail bitch? he said.

As fate would have it.

A night in jail, my father said, was just the thing for me.

Nine o'clock, after he got the chores done, my father was waiting in the lobby of the police station.

Same old thing, always too goddamn much work to do.

Dad looked differnt.

After a night in jail, people look only one of two ways.

You either look like you are in jail or you look like you are out of jail.

If you look out of jail, then you look like you are keeping people in jail.

My father was keeping people in jail.

Dad in his cowboy hat, his Levi's shirt and his Levi's, his cowboy boots, his leather belt with the silver buckle. His dark Roosky Gypsy eyes that went a little wild when he saw my shaved head.

Sergeant Roscoe slid open the sliding gate, closed the gate, locked it.

My father shook Sergeant Roscoe's big pink hand. I was standing right there, and my father didn't look at me, and Sergeant Roscoe didn't look at me, and then they started right in talking about the weather.

Idaho.

After a while, when I was getting my wallet and my hat and my thin red tie and my corncob pipe from the secretary with the beehive, Detective Harold Richardson came out a door, and then Richardson, Roscoe, and my dad were talking about the Pocatello Frontier Rodeo.

The insides of my porkpie hat were all torn out.

The corncob pipe was in two pieces. The stem part and the corncob part. I stuck them back together.

Just be there at Granny's, George.

Outside, it is one of those bright mornings, fresh in a way that you can still smell the night.

Down the slope of lawn, the Buick is parked at an angle to the curb. Mom is in the car. Her face is on. Hair done up. She's wearing her old horn-rimmed glasses.

Mom does not look at me.

I tie the red tie around my head, put on my hat.

Dad is still inside shooting the shit with Sergeant Roscoe and Detective Richardson.

Mom hates to sit in the car and wait for Dad.

So do I.

Mom and I wait.

Mom is in jail.

Some cop drives the pickup around and parks it in a parking space at an angle to the curb.

I go up to the police station door, open the door, stick my head in.

Dad, I say, Mom's waiting.

Mom drives the Buick home. Dad drives the pickup.

When the pickup doors are closed and Dad and I are alone in the pickup, before we roll the windows down, the way Dad smells is a lot like George.

Something so deep and important I understand in that moment when I smell my dad.

And that quick. As soon as I understand that George is in my father's smell, I forget.

It will take years to know again what I know in that brief moment.

As soon as we turn off the highway onto Philbin Road, Dad starts in.

Rigby John, he says.

I can't remember if my father has ever called me Rigby John.

You have broken your poor mother's heart, Dad says. She lives and breathes for her children. She works hard and has devoted her life to you kids, and this is the way you treat her.

You should have seen her face when she read your name in the newspaper, Dad says. On the front page of the *Idaho State Journal! Wanted for questioning, Rigby John Klusener!* How dare you drag our family name through the mud!

The only thing I hear of what Dad is saying is the part about the newspaper. That part is new. The rest of it is just more of Dad's same old shit. I don't pay attention to a single word. There is only one thought in my mind, and that is George.

Dad can tell I could give a shit. I guess that's why he reaches over, pulls my hat off, then pulls the red tie off my head.

Look at you, he says. Some sort of circus freak. What the hell did you shave your head for? What are you, some kind of spectacle? A goddamn hippie?

That's when I reach down, turn off the ignition, pull the keys out, then throw the keys out his window.

Jeez, I've never heard my old man cuss like that — I mean I've heard him say it all, but never a string of goddamn-fuck-you-little-cocksucker-asshole-piece-of-shit like that before.

But like I said, I could give a shit.

George is waiting for me and George and I are in love and I'm out of here.

The pickup engine hums down. I grab my hat and my red tie.

Solitary warriors of love.

I jump out of my door, hit the ground running.

Fuck you as a way to address the world.

Dad runs after me for a while. But there was no way he can catch me.

I have my red tie tied back on, I have my hat on, I am under the cottonwoods on Philbin, almost at exactly the same spot where God had spun the Buick around the first time I saw George.

That's when Mom pulls up alongside.

Same Buick, same Mom, differnt me.

You best get in, son, Mom says. You're only seventeen. We could make things real hard for you.

Son.

What, are you going to take a broom after me? I say.

Silence from inside the car.

I walk some more, but not for long. Inside the car, Mom's new perfume smell.

In the rearview mirror, Dad is in the pickup right behind us.

The rest of the morning and most of the afternoon was Mom and Dad and I around the kitchen table under the bright overhead light. The same oilcloth tablecloth with red tulips. Mom and I were sitting. Dad was standing. On the blue and white tile, Dad was walking back and forth.

Where have you been the past four days? Dad said.

With friends, I said.

What friends? Dad said. That pregnant girl?

But I won't say what friends.

You got to keep your distance.

Shame on you! Dad yelled.

Dad put his wrists on his hips, pressed his wrists in and lifted his Levi's. That was the signal. As soon as Dad started hiking his pants up with his wrists, you knew you were in for it. He was just starting in on waving his arms and whipping up a big brouhaha, when I said:

And at a grave, I said.

That stopped him. His Roosky Gypsy eyes.

A grave? Dad said. Whose grave?

Russell's grave, I said.

Russell's grave hit him like a ton of bricks. It was like I'd kicked the wind right out of him. Dad pulled out his chrome chair, sat down, put his elbows on the table, folded his big hairy hands.

When he spoke again, he wasn't yelling.

What on earth were you doing *there*? he said.

He's my brother, I said. What other reason do I need?

Mom quick pushed her chair back, got up from the table, and walked into her bedroom. She came back with her big black rosary. When she sat down again, she made the sign of the cross.

Brimming with tears her eyes, along the bottom lid, brimming.

One big tear rolled down her cheek.

Dad bent his head down into his hands. The top of his head was getting bald.

Quiet. We sat like that, the three of us, and it was quiet.

Then out of nowhere, Dad pounded his fist down onto the table. Over and over again, pounding and pounding his fist.

You're just trying to upset your mother! he yelled.

Yelling and pounding and yelling like he was nuts. I've never seen Dad so exasperated.

Then it was all the nigger-loving hippie communist queers. That's what was wrong with the country. Pretty soon, he was reciting the Ten Commandments. How many of them I'd broke. I was grounded for the entire year. Could never drive the pickup to town again.

Jeez. Hollering and cussing and laying down the law.

And when I graduated I was enlisting in the army and going to Vietnam.

They'll make a man out of you there, Dad said.

Weird, the whole time Dad was going off, Mom was quiet. She didn't look up, she didn't pipe in and say shit. She just sat there in her rummage-sale cotton blouse and her jeans and her Keds. The thousands of tiny wrinkles around her mouth. Her swooped eyebrows. Her gray hair. The ripples in her jaw. Thumbing the beads of her big black rosary.

With those big gray plastic glasses gone, you could see her face.

Almond-shaped hazel eyes. Grandpa's eyes. Brimming.

I didn't say a thing. Just acted like I was listening.

Just be there at Granny's, George. Just be there at Granny's.

One time Dad did go for my hat, and right there and then I let him know real fast.

I didn't block his hand. I didn't hit him. I didn't scream or cuss.

I stopped my father with a look.

It was the same look Mom used to stop him.

And what I said: When's the last time *you* went to Russy's grave?

Dad didn't touch my hat. Or me.

The most important thing, though, that afternoon, wasn't Dad's Moses on the Mount conniption fit.

It was that Mom had made my favorite lunch. Bologna sandwiches with lettuce and mayonnaise and mustard, *two* pieces of bologna. Clover Club potato chips and a hard-boiled egg.

You should have seen the salt I poured on that egg.

Dad was so pissed he grabbed the salt shaker and threw the milk-can salt shaker all the way across the room.

Big deal. So what. Who cares?

Plus there was apple pie. My mother had baked an apple pie.

When I got up and poured myself a cup of coffee, neither one of them said a word.

Any Sego Milk, Mom? I said.

At four o'clock, Dad told me to get the hell out of there and go change the water in the pasture.

I went up into my room, closed the door, sat on my bed. In the same spot I'd sat four days ago, Saturday, when my mother was a crazy maniac, the human barricade at my door.

I looked at my hands. I lifted my hands and looked at my hands.

So much had happened. I didn't even recognize whose hands they were.

From my window, you could see the tops of Granny's Lombardy poplars.

My heart pounding. My breath.

Just be there at Granny's, George.

I quick put my cutoffs on and my tennis shoes and a clean T-shirt. It was a relief to get out of the crusty shorts.

I opened my door, walked down the stairs, turned to walk out the kitchen door. From the top of the refrigerator, I quick grabbed Dad's Viceroys, tapped a couple out.

Just before the kitchen door went closed, Mom said: Rigby John.

I pretended I didn't hear her.

Man, I love my pickup. It's Dad's pickup, but it should be mine. Tramp sits beside me in the cab. He's all smiles and his tail beating hard against the seat. His tongue wet bologna.

Tramp, I say, I missed you, buddy.

Tramp's tongue starts hanging out. He gets that look on his face.

Tramp, I say, would you like to be my jail bitch?

Sure as hell, there he goes, Tramp's paw poking, poking the air.

I put the pickup into reverse, make a three-point turn, hit the gas. Tramp and I are flying past the steel granaries, past the spud cellar, past the grain elevator. At the intersection where you can go left, past the boxcars, then up the road that is the boundary of yellow Bannock County, I turn right, open the gate, drive through, close the gate. In the place between the gates where you can drive fast, I drive fast. Dust rolling up, the sun shining in the windshield, exhaust fumes. I light a Viceroy. My exhale settles my body deep into the seat. Wind and dust and smoke and going fast. There's nothing better in the world.

Just be there at Granny's, George.

At the second gate by the derrick, I open the gate, drive through, close the gate.

Then up the gravel bar that is the natural boundary to the rez. Up the lane between the alfalfa and the barley. To the swimming hole.

I am out and running. Over the fence, Tramp right behind me, onto the ditch bank, then bouncing over the two-by-twelve. My legs stretch out as I jump to the outcropping of slick, dark lava rock. I land, my palms sea anemones, suction cups onto the black, slick rocks. My feet find their way up the mossy, wet lava.

Once on top, I look down.

It is a very good parade.

My feet are across the border, my feet are on the rez.

Planted deep in all that red. Crooked as the wind, Granny's lone cedar tree. In the hot sun, the cedar boughs smell of one more sweaty body. The wind through the cedar, the secret song of the wind in the cedar that moment is something not outside me but down deep up behind and under, a fist balled up inside me opening to a hand waving in the wind.

Over the fence, through Granny's back pasture, past the outhouse, past the barn and the chicken coop, into the middle of Granny's yard.

Poplar leaves scatter. All over on the ground a swirl of hallucinations. Shadows and light, shadows and light.

In the yard, under the apple tree, there is no George's car.

Granny's green screen door is open. All through Granny's house, the doors and windows are open wide. Her shiny wood floors. No sign, no trace of life.

Of George.

A gust of wind, a hawk, in a moment, some large bird flies low out Granny's kitchen window.

Then it's Tramp barking and barking. I tell Tramp to stop barking, but he won't stop barking.

On the apple tree, below our initials with the heart between, there's a piece of paper thumbtacked to the tree.

The paper rattling in the wind.

The feeling in my arms that means I'm helpless.

My heart pounding. My breath.

> Dear Rig,
>   I already miss you.
> Happy trails.
>   Love,
>   George

Hallucinations around me all over on the ground. I sit down right there under the apple tree. My arm around the trunk. My head on wood. In my one hand, the piece of paper. In the other hand, my palm full of sunshine. Above me, all around, the wind's high sigh and scratch.

The universe has always conspired to fuck me up.

Who knows how long I sit there. Who knows how long Tramp barks.

Long afternoon shadows. The blue sky is pink sky is peach sky. Sunset is red.

The piece of paper balled up in my fist. My fist against my chest.

In my fist it is the sharp pain next to my heart.

The thing about poplar trees, if you sit there long and quiet enough, the wind through the poplar leaves is voices. At first, the voices say the usual things. Love songs and poems and shit.

Eleanor Rigby Joan picks up the rice in the church where a wedding has been. Hey there, Georgy Girl. I'll be seeing you in all the old familiar places.

Then poems. Edgar Allan Poe poems, "The Raven," and e. e. cummings's "A Leaf Falls on Loneliness."

Then, after a long time, other people's voices and the songs and poems stop, and the wind is only Thunderbird breathing.

Then a gust of wind, a hawk, some large bird, Thunderbird, flies away, and you're alone.

Then it's just you there with all you don't know and your dog, and you can't cry anymore, and the wind in the poplar trees is just the wind.

That night, last night, when I got home, I opened the kitchen door, walked over the blue and white tiles, straight to the phone. Called Billie Cody. I stretched the phone cord into the bathroom and closed the bathroom door.

Right there on the bathroom floor, without a cigarette, I sat on the black and white tiles in the lavender bathroom and talked to my friend.

Billie was really happy to hear from me. She'd been worried, with the cops and all. She said she was fine. Chuck was fine. She sounded good.

That's about all she had to say.

I started into talking, and then I couldn't stop. I told Billie everything.

*Every*thing.

From start to finish.

I didn't cry. Talked matter of fact, as if the whole thing had happened to someone else.

Me and George, warriors of love, Granny's death, digging the grave, the cops, the night in jail, the note on the apple tree. Everything. Right up to leaving for San Francisco in the morning.

I don't think I've ever talked so long without stopping. To anyone. To Billie or to Tramp. Must have been over an hour.

The knock on the bathroom door was Mom.

Supper's ready, she said.

Then: Billie, I said, got to go.

I'll drop by tomorrow before I leave, I said. Early.

Sis was sitting at the kitchen table where she always used to sit. She had a black eye and two full suitcases in the hallway. It looked like she'd be staying for a while.

Last night.

The night at supper when the perfectness of fuck hit me.

Fuck as a way to address the world.

There I was sitting at the kitchen table. I was sitting under the bright overhead light, in the same chrome chair with its yellow plastic seat and backrest, and there was Sis sitting directly across the oilcloth tablecloth with red tulips on it, her hair done up in a French twist and Scotch tape taped across her forehead holding down her bangs. Just below the Scotch tape, her swooped, black cat's-eye glasses. Her black eye more blue than black.

To my right there was Dad still in his same Levi's shirt rolled up to the elbows and his big hairy hands and forearms smelling of Lava soap. Across his forehead, the line of sunburn straight, red below white above, his black hair smashed down from his Stetson cowboy hat.

On my left there was Mom in her rummage-sale cotton blouse, her jeans, and her Keds. Her almond-shaped hazel eyes behind her glasses, her hair in a hairnet up in pin curls. On her forehead were the lines, three parallel lines across, that in the middle, between her eyebrows, sank to deep folds of skin between her eyes. Her clipped-to-the-quick fingernails.

A rerun of *Lawrence Welk* was on the TV in the front room. Myron

Floren was playing "The Beer Barrel Polka," and there we all were lifting our hands to our foreheads to start the sign of the cross and the bless us O Lord and these Thy gifts, which we are about to receive from Thy bounty through Christ, our Lord, amen.

On the table were the same four slices of roast beef. The same bottle of Heinz 57 ketchup, the mashed potatoes in the green bowl, the orange gravy boat, the canned peas in the blue bowl, the butter plate, and the bread plate with four slices of Wonder Bread on it. The salt and pepper shakers the shape of milk cans.

A family.

We were all of us in jail.

Just last night. The last night, the last supper, I was ever going to sit through.

The four of us sitting around the kitchen table with all that's happened since two years ago last March. Beginning with what happened behind the barn, then Mom's novena to Our Mother of Perpetual Help for my soul, and the altar boy contest and the baseball game between Saint Joseph's and Saint Anthony's. The yellow tulip sticking out of my ass. The blessed summer with Flaco and Acho. The Slit Sisters. Trying to have a very good parade. *Spineless ass.* Billie Cody, our promise. Sis's wedding. Chuck diPietro. Baling hay with Georgy Girl. Smoking is praying is waiting is trusting. Thunderbird.

Then the Grande Finale. The Big Fiasco. *All* the shit hitting the big fat fan all at once. Billie Cody pregnant, the Senior Summer All Night Party, Mom chasing me with the broom. Joe Scardino, the El Camino and the Kraft cheese truck. Grandma Queep going to the other side. The Back Door, where men like flowers. Solitary warriors of love. Granny's funeral, digging Granny's grave, the giveaway, George's long fingers touching my hand on Pine Street. My night in the city jail. George's note thumbtacked to the apple tree.

My broken fucking heart.

Which pretty much sums up the whole story, not necessarily in that order, and brings us up to date with last night.

So with Myron Floren playing "The Beer Barrel Polka" in the front room, we did what we always did. The only thing we knew how to do. We blessed our roast beef, the canned peas, the mashed spuds, the Wonder Bread, with the same old prayer that came out of us like bad breath from a sick dog, then made the sign of the cross again.

Always the meat first, always Dad first, then me, then Sis, then Mom, was the way we passed the food. Then when each of us had our piece of roast beef, each our potatoes and gravy, each our canned peas, then Dad said pass the ketchup. Then Sis handed Dad the ketchup. Then ketchup for me, for Sis, for Mom. Then we all picked up our forks and started eating.

Except for me. I always asked for salt please because it pissed Dad off that I like salt.

No differnt last night.

I said: Salt please, and Sis looked over her swooped black cat's-eye glasses at Dad first, then molded her mouth all pulled together like a sphincter, handed me the salt shaker milk can.

So I started salting the ketchup on my slice of roast beef, my canned peas, my pile of mashed potatoes with a little crater in them for the gravy.

I started getting kind of weepy because now the Champagne Lady was singing some German schmaltzy shit. Weepy too because I was never going to see my family again, see this house, my bedroom, my bed, see the barn, the swimming hole, the Mexican house, see my dog, Tramp, ever again, never see Flaco or Acho, or Billie Cody or Grandma Queep.

Never see George Serano again.

But I didn't cry because it was just too perfect for me to start crying. I promised myself I would rather bite my tongue off, would rather put the salt shaker in my mouth and eat the milk can shaker whole before I ever cried in front of them again. So I just ate my roast beef, my potatoes and gravy, my canned peas.

I finished my supper in one, maybe one and a half minutes.

Like always I was still hungry.

So I said to Mom, Mom, can I have another piece of bread?

Mom didn't say anything, just raised her plucked eyebrows that for Sunday morning Mass she penciled in with her eyebrow pencil, put her fork down, picked up the empty bread plate, got up from the table, walked across the blue and white tiled floor to the bread drawer, her varicose veins running down to her Keds, bent over, opened the bread drawer, took out the loaf of Wonder Bread, undid the tie, took one piece of bread out, retied the tie, put one piece of Wonder Bread on the bread plate, closed the bread drawer with her knee, walked back over the blue and white tiles to the table, and set the plate in front of me.

That's when I said it inside my head: *fuck.*

And *fuck* was the most perfect way to say what I needed to say.

That moment at the table at supper in the kitchen under the bright overhead light. The *fuck* was the perfect way to fucking say it that moment, me fucking me, I was sitting in the yellow fucking chair, my feet on the blue and white kitchen tiles, shoving a piece of fucking buttered Wonder Bread into my mouth.

In that silence. That drut dead quiet of a fucking silence that hung over the table, over our family, hung over our fucking lives, the Holy Fucking Ghost.

The silence so loud against my eardrums since my eardrums realized they could hear.

Bless us O fucking Lord and these Thy fucking gifts, which we are about to fucking receive through Thy fucking bounty, through Christ our fucking Lord.

A-fucking-men!

Fuck.

There's one more thing left. The thing back at the beginning that happened in the kitchen I haven't told you yet. One more story.

Maybe it's the story I should have told you first.

Like Russell, it's the biggest story. The one I wasn't the same after.

This morning, four-thirty, when I wake up, after I go into the bathroom, after I look at myself in the mirror for the last time, after I shut the bathroom light off, open the door, the way the door sticks, and before I leave the house, before I drive to Billie's, when I walk up into the kitchen, there is the smell of coffee, and Mom is sitting in her chair at the kitchen table.

It's dark, but I can tell. She has her face on, eyebrows swooped, her hair done up. Red Cherries lipstick.

I immediately go into a crouch position. I think all hell is breaking loose.

Mom just sits there, though, looks at me. She's smoking one of Dad's Viceroys.

Want a cigarette? she says.

My mouth fumbles over what the hell to say. Doesn't say anything.

Come on, she says. After all this time, you think I don't know you nick your dad's cigarettes?

No, I say. Yes. Then: I don't know.

As eloquent as ever.

Mom pulls out my chrome chair with the plastic yellow seat and backrest. The chair slides along the blue and white tiles.

She flicks the ash into the ashtray she stole from the 30 Club when she was young.

Here, she says. Sit down.

Mom reaches the cigarette across to me.

Take a drag, she says. It's the only cigarette I could find.

I sit down. Take the cigarette.

Our fingers touch.

I do a perfect French inhale.

How do you do that? she says. I never learned to do that.

The morning light is silver light. Her rummage-sale cotton blouse.

When you blow the smoke out your mouth, I say, you suck the smoke up with your nose.

I hand the cigarette back to Mom. Our fingers touch.

Mom's face is weird when she tries to French-inhale. Her face is like when you try to flare your nostrils and you don't know how.

That weird sound from down deep inside of us.

Laughter.

But soft. We do not want to wake him.

Who'd have thought I'd be laughing with my mother on the day I leave forever.

Mom crosses her legs. Her jeans. Her Keds.

Mom hands the cigarette to me.

Here! Mom says. You take this damn thing. I swear I'll never get it.

Our fingers touch.

Then: I go there too, you know, Mom says. To Russy's grave. It's so peaceful. One afternoon I fell asleep right there on the grass in the sun. I especially love it in the fall.

Do you ever miss him? I say.

He was born on December eighth and died on March eighteenth, Mom says. One hundred days and nights he screamed and then he died.

Yah, Mom says, I miss him.

Two silver rounds, moons, reflected light, her glasses.

So, Mom says. You're leaving me.

Yes jumps right out my mouth.

Can't say that I blame you, she says.

Are you going with her?

Who? I say.

Billie Cody, she says.

No, I say, I'm going alone.

My pounding heart.

Good, Mom says.

Quiet for a while. Just my mom's breath, my breath.

I hand the cigarette back to her. Our fingers touch.

I know you think this is just your mother talking, she says, but Billie's not the girl for you.

Then Mom does something she hasn't done in a long time. She touches me. A soft pat on the top of my hand.

Mom's rough, red farm hands. Her cut-to-the-quick fingernails.

Quiet in the kitchen, in the early morning, quiet all around the touch.

Mom pulls deep on the cigarette. The bright orange fire in morning light just short of darkness.

Rig? Mom says. Take me with you, Rig.

Mom hands the cigarette back to me.

Our fingers touch.

Mom? I say.

Mom exhales so much smoke the room fills up with smoke.

Please, she says.

I've got to get out of here, she says. All I do is cook and clean for this man, and he never thanks me, never even looks at me.

I've worn my knees out praying, Mom says. The Virgin said to pray the rosary, pray the rosary, but sometimes when I pray I get this feeling who I'm praying to ain't there.

Besides you, Mom says, the only thing I got's the piano.

And now, Mom says, your sister's home. I'll love having a baby around again. But it ain't worth it. Your sister has no idea what she's in for.

So what do you say, Rig? Mom says. While we got the chance. Before he wakes up and wants his mush.

*　　*　　*

There's something only I can do with Mom, and I can do it only rarely.

The way I do it is I cross my eyes a little, curl up my top lip, and scratch my butt. That's all I have to do, and Mom's busting a gut.

But I don't cross my eyes, curl my lip, scratch my butt.

I hand the cigarette back to Mom. Our fingers do not touch.

My mother's eyes. High-beam headlights, two most sorrowful mysteries, one pitched a little south, the other east.

Every which way the light in them travels right on past, right on through, or hardly ever settles on me at all.

This morning, at the kitchen table, in the silver light, Mom settles her eyes on me.

Almond-shaped and hazel.

Flecks of gold.

Dear broken Mother, here, let me hold myself in such a way that you will see me, and if you see me, if I please you, the trouble will leave your eyes, and your eyes will go soft and be gold.

And I will stay alive.

Outside, in the pickup, I'm talking to Tramp. I'm telling him I've got to go without him.

From inside the house, it's Mom on the piano. The special way her upright piano sounds. Piano wires thrumming inside a thick hardwood box.

She's not playing "The Bible Tells Me So." The song Mom is playing, the song she is singing alone, without me to harmonize with her, is our favorite song she plays.

> Now is the hour when we must say goodbye.
> Soon you'll be sailing far across the sea.
> While you're away, oh, then remember me.
> When you return, you'll find me waiting here.

After Billie Cody's house, out on the open highway this morning, I was doing fine, just fine. The sunrise was orange and yellow and so bright I needed sunglasses. The pickup was running good, I was safe, fine out of there, no problem. My arm was out the window, the wing window open so the morning air was coming right at my face. Wind and dust and going fast, there's nothing better in the world.

Sunday morning radio.

What a bunch of shit.

It was around American Falls when I turned on the radio again.

I found something all right.

As clear as a bell.

If you're going to San Francisco, be sure to wear some flowers in your hair.

So many sad songs.

I cried all the way to Twin Falls.

Parked the pickup on Norby Street. On the corner of Norby and South Sward.

Started walking southwest. Only time I stopped was to pick this daisy.

So that's how I got here. Out here where there's nothing. Nothing but desert. Out here where everything's alive.

My life from before Russell until this moment out here on Highway 93.

Quite a story now that I tell it.

It took awhile. A whole night in the desert to tell the damn thing.

Not since the yellow Buick with the blonde giving me the peace sign or the bird.

Out here on Highway 93 it's cold. I had to put on my Levi's and my other T-shirt and my white shirt with the iron burn on the collar, and both pairs of socks. Goose flesh all over on my arms and legs. I'm shivering my ass off. Should have packed some winter clothes. My porkpie hat has dew on it.

The gravel ain't so pretty now that I'm not stoned.

In the east the sky is navy blue, pink, and a little yellow just on the horizon. What looks like maybe more storm clouds.

Sagebrush. The smell of sagebrush and the cool morning wind and the smell of rain. That and my armpits is what I smell.

A ribbon of pavement shiny to over both horizons.

It's a new day, son, brand-new.

At sunrise, I decide to check through my stuff, make sure I didn't forget anything.

I take out Granny's corncob pipe, lay the pipe down on the edge of the asphalt. Then there's the photograph. Me standing in front of the old skinny white house with my fishing pole. I lay the photograph out on the edge of the asphalt. Put a piece of gravel on the photograph so the morning wind don't blow it away.

Then there's the yoga book Billie gave me.

George's dollar bill.

The wadded-up piece of paper.

I don't unwad the piece of paper yet. I stick the wad of paper in my pocket with the dollar bill.

Theresa Nussbaum's painting is wrapped inside two plastic sacks and tied with rubber bands. I take the painting out of my backpack real slow, then lay the painting next to Granny's pipe. I undo the rubber bands, pull the plastic off.

I touch the painting around on the four edges.

Forest and green mountains where there'd been only a flat expanse of east.

Have you ever seen *The Wizard of Oz*?

The part that turns from black and white to color is my favorite.

Theresa, the artist from Portland, my red-haired maiden aunt Alma's roommate, had smiled. If I wasn't up close, I'd never have noticed that smile.

The forest and the green mountains are inside, Theresa had said. That's what an artist does. She travels the world looking for something inside.

Just over my shoulder, the sun is a beet red ball sitting on top of a blanket of sagebrush. Morning birds, killdeer, mourning doves, red-breasted black birds, sparrows. Slow, rolling wind.

My breath is clear and deep and sucks in the earth, the sun on the earth, the sagebrush, the wind, and the sky.

An intent in your life to fold your life around.

I'm Rigby John Klusener. I'm free and I'm easy and I'm traveling the world looking for what's inside.

Out of my backpack, I pull out my water bottle, my toothbrush, and my Crest. I pour water on my toothbrush, then put some Crest on my toothbrush, then I'm brushing my teeth. Crest has been shown to be an effective decay-preventive dentifrice that can be of significant value when used as directed in a conscientiously applied program of oral hygiene and regular professional care.

Right about then, thunder so loud like to shake your bones.
A crack of lightning across the northwest sky.
Fucking great.
Ten, twenty minutes, I'm going to be soaked through.
Or French-fried by a stroke of lightning.
Fuck.

The photograph I stick in between Theresa's painting and its frame. I quick wrap Theresa's painting with the plastic sacks, wrap the rubber bands around, set the painting back in my backpack. Then in goes the yoga book and Granny's pipe.

Besides the clothes on my back and the red tie around my head and my porkpie hat and my toothbrush and my Crest and my bottle of water and my roll of toilet paper, and Mom's sack lunch with the bologna sandwich and the hard-boiled egg and the milk can shaker of salt and the Clover Club potato chips and the piece of apple pie, all's I got is my wallet and the two hundred dollars.

Mom blessed her ten twenty-dollar bills with holy water. Then handed them to me. Her rough red farm hands. Her cut-to-the-quick fingernails counted out the twenties into my hand until there were ten.

Pray your rosary, she said.
Then kissed my forehead.
Then there's the wadded-up piece of paper in my pocket.
The feeling in my arms that means I'm helpless.
I reach in my pocket, pull out the wad of paper, bounce the wad up in my hand.

What do you do with something so important? Eat it. Shove it up your butt. Unwrap it, sew it onto your heart.

On one side of me the sun is big and bright as it's ever going to get. On the other side, it's a big, black thunderhead.

Another bounce.

If he loved me like he said he did, then he would've waited.

I spin in circles, around and around, winding up for the pitch, twirling, a dust devil, my arms in the air, a dance. I hurl the wad of paper with a sound from inside and deep, a grunt, and the wad of paper sails through the air like a bird flying.

The crack of lightning is a bony hand up from the earth. Thunder, crash.

That quick, George's goodbye note is gone.

On the pavement, it's my shadow.

I lift my chin up, make my head so the shadow of my head looks like my head is an alien being's big round head.

Alien.

You can always tell how you're feeling by how your shadow looks.

That's when I see it on the horizon. Coming from the east. A glint of sunlight on the windshield. A car.

I zip up all the zippers, button up all the buttons, quick put my arms through the straps of my backpack, square it up my shoulders. I pull my hat down, step off the gravel up onto the asphalt, plant my feet firm. This guy's going to have to run me over if he's going to pass me by.

I stick my thumb out.

The car is two miles away, ten miles. Out in the desert, in all this infinity, there's no way to tell. My eyes are squinting, and I have my hand over my eyes. I can't see the car anymore, and I begin to think the car is just one more heat puddle on a hot day. Then just like that, the car pops up out of nowhere. A tiny toy car far away. The sunlight is bright on its windshield again. Only this time I can see two sections of windshield. The center post of the windshield making two sunshine glints. That center post in the windshield only in old cars before cars got modern with the windshield one piece of glass.

The color of the car is the color of the rest of the desert. It's gray or brown or sage green or sandy or beige. Then the car dips down, and for a long time again it's gone.

When it pops up again, the car is close enough for me to see it's an old Ford.

A '49 gray Ford.

I'd recognize that car anywhere.

From behind me, the half of the sky that's dark and full of lightning and thunder and rain is coming at me as fast as George's car is coming at me out of the sun.

Thunderbird, eye of lightning, grant us peace.

Part of me wants to run into the sagebrush and hide.

Another part wants to start running toward George.

Another part says, Hold your fucking horses. That may be his car, but that doesn't mean it's George.

He's probably sold his car to someone else for a case of gin.

Something else, though.

The weirdest thing.

It's uncanny and immediate.

Out there in the middle of nowhere, in the middle of the road, I'm having a very good parade.

So I'm trying to stuff it down inside my pants when George's car comes over the last rise not fifty feet away from me.

It's George all right who's in the car.

He's probably not alone, though. He's probably got some cowboy with him in a big hat and a turquoise belt buckle.

Then I'm crying, and that quick I stop crying. I'd rather die than cry.

It's too late to run into the bush, so I just stand there.

When George pulls up, I look inside.

As far as I can see, he is alone. Around his head, the red tie.

The radio's on. The song is "A Whiter Shade of Pale." George reaches over, with his long, beautiful, cinnamon brown fingers turns the radio down.

Morning, sunshine, George says. Going my way?

Fuck.

My good parade is very good and poking up my pants.

What are you doing here? I say.

What are *you* doing here? George says.

Then I'm kicking in the side of George's door. While I'm kicking his door, I'm not quite sure why I'm doing it.

Then: Motherfucker! I yell. You said you'd wait! You didn't wait! Where the fuck were you?

I don't wait for George to answer, I stomp off in the direction of San Francisco. Wind and rain ahead, you can almost see the line of rain crossing over the desert.

George's car pulls up alongside. The big, black wheels, the engine heat, so close. That quick, the rain hits. It's pouring down in buckets.

George hollers through the car: Rig! George says. Get in! Let's have a cigarette.

Something explodes in me, and I'm pulling off my backpack and I'm around the car at George's window. It's like running through a car wash. Still, I can't figure why it is I'm doing this, but, still, I lean back, and with all my weight my fist heads straight for George's jaw.

And misses.

George grabs my arm, pulls with both his hands, and in seconds flat the top half of me is in the car, the other half, my legs, are outside kicking in the rain.

It's easy to tell about something after it's over, but while it's happening, it's all just one thing after another flipping past your eyes.

The car is still running, and the car is in gear, and the way we are thrashing around, I know we're not on the road. My head is on the floor on the passenger side. From that angle, looking up, George's face is some Picasso painting.

Somehow I get up, and I'm sitting in the seat. There's no way to see out the windows. Sagebrush after sagebrush scrape up against the car. George is yelling at me, but I can't hear what he is yelling. All I'm thinking is the son of a bitch didn't show, and I land a punch smack in his mouth. His head goes back, and blood comes out his nose. I quick go for the door handle. I'm out the door, I'm on the ground, I'm sliding across the mud in the rain. George's hands slap down on my shoulders, and in nothing flat I'm flying. I'm on my back. George has my arms pinned behind me.

George is on top. He lifts his knee and puts his knee on my chest.

Both of us are breathing hard.

It ain't like on television when you fight. You have to catch your breath.

When George speaks, his eyes look away to just above my head.

When things are hard to say.

Rig, George says. What's going on? Why are you treating me this way?

George and I in the rain in the mud. The wet red tie. The beads of rain on his face.

I hate the tears. I can't wipe the tears away.

You said you'd be at Granny's house, I say.

George's perfect dark, black eyes. The gold bars.

I waited, George says. All that day and the night too. When you weren't there in the morning, I took off.

What I say next are words that spit out of me all over George's face.

I would have waited for *you,* I say. I wouldn't have ever stopped waiting.

George lifts his knee off my chest. He lets go of my arms. He sits back on his haunches, looks up into the rain.

I started shaking again, George says. I couldn't stop. I didn't know what to do.

The rain beads up on George's face, rolls down.

You didn't get drunk, did you? I say.

I had a couple, George says.

Two beers, George says. Then I just said, Fuck it, and hit the road. I was in Salt Lake at a truck stop when I opened the *Idaho State Journal.*

Rig, George says. Why didn't you tell me you were in trouble?

That wasn't trouble, I say. You were trouble.

Then: What's with this rain? I say.

Thunderbird, George says. He ain't through with us yet.

What's going to be left of us when he's through? I say.

My hand inside George's brown hand. He gives me a pull up. Mud all over on us.

Come on, he says. Let's get in the car.

The car. Both doors open wide, the windshield wipers going. The radio's on.

George has to rock the car back and forth while I'm on the back bumper, pushing. It takes us awhile, but we get out of the hole. I get in the car quick before we get stuck again. George floors it through the rest of the sagebrush, and once we go into a fishtail I don't think we'll ever get out of.

We do, though.

After I pick up my backpack, we're driving down a shiny black ribbon of road.

West. California. California. San Francisco, California.

George reaches across, opens the jockey box. Inside is a carton of Camels and matches. George gets out a pack, opens the pack with his teeth. He taps a cigarette out. I put the match to the cigarette.

George's perfect French inhale. A couple times. Then he hands the cigarette to me.

Our fingers touch.

I take a deep drag. I wasn't going to smoke no more, and here I'm smoking.

How'd you find me? I say.

Your girlfriend was at the hospital, George says. She said to tell you Simone sends her love. She said to tell you that she'll always keep her promise. And she told me you were on your way to San Francisco.

There's only two ways from Pocatello to get to San Francisco, George says, the short way and the long way. I figured you'd take the short way.

Maybe it's a miracle I found you in the desert, George says. Like the Mormons.

George's face is real serious. Even when you laugh real hard, he doesn't crack a smile.

Outside my window, through the rain, way far out on the horizon, a big old ray of sun.

I'm seventeen, I say. And you're thirty-five.

That's right, George says.

I'm just a kid, I say. Won't be long, and you'll be bored with me.

Or you with me, George says.

I hand the cigarette to George. His drag is long. We're going to hotbox this one for sure.

I'm a minor, I say. And I've already spent a night in jail. The police could be looking for me.

Could be, George says.

I could get you in a lot of trouble, I say.

You already have, George says.

That's when I notice.

George's head is shaved again, slick and shiny. The red tie around his head.

I put my hand on the top of his head, let my palm lie there.

I thought I lost you, George says. At this rate I'll never have any hair.

George hands the cigarette to me.

Our fingers touch.

Moments of gesture.

Things are dizzy, the way they look when your breath is knocked out.

I'm not going to Vietnam, I say. That'll mean the feds will be after me too.

There's a way we can get around that, George says.

Under my hat, there's nubs of hair. I check the knot on the red tie.

You hate white people, I say. I'm white people.

You're more pink than you are white, George says.

I hand the cigarette back to George.

Our fingers touch.

The windshield wiper on George's side is a regular swipe back and forth. The windshield wiper on my side lies there and twitches like something trying to die.

The heat's on too because we're wet. The heater's so loud you can't hear yourself think.

What about your drinking? I say.

What about yours? he says.

I'm not the one who said he was going to stop, I say.

Quiet. Like you've disappeared quiet. Just the windshield wiper dying and the heater.

You're right on there, George says. I fucked up. I won't be doing it again. Promise.

Static on the radio. I'm flipping through, trying to find a station.

George has never lied to me so far.

He hands me the cigarette.

Our fingers touch.

The ash is almost an inch long. I flick the ash off into the ashtray.

I'm free, I say. I'm an artist, and I'm traveling the world to discover what's inside.

Me too, George says.

Then: Don't worry, he says. I'm just taking you to San Francisco.

After all, George says, we're *solitary* warriors of love.

But what about Thunderbird? I say. You said he wasn't through with us.

We'll have to wait and see, George says.

As fate will have it.

Then I just can't stand it any longer. I've been all cramped up in my two layers of pants, hot and wet and hard and uncomfortable. I unbutton my Levi's, undo my cutoffs, reach in, pull my shorts away, pull out my cock.

There it is sticking straight out, bobbing around like it's listening to music.

George's big smile comes up from the right side first. His laugh is just like Granny's laugh, only he's got all his teeth. Never seen him do that before.

On the radio, out of the static, all of a sudden, it's Jimi Hendrix singing "Purple Haze."

Both me and George say at once: Oooh! I love this song.

I reach over, turn the radio up.

George reaches down, puts his hand around my cock.

A gust of Idaho wind gets inside me and blows me around.

Actin' funny, but I don't know why.

George keeps his hand on the wheel. He lowers his head, puts his lips around the head of my cock. Then he's back up, looking me in the eyes. Gold bars in his black eyes. Nothing in between.

'Scuse me while I kiss this guy, George sings.

This guy.

When George smiles, after all this time, when George smiles, it's a miracle what happens in his eyes.

They go a little crazy. One pitched south, the other east.

Another gust of Idaho wind, this time outside the car.

The wind through the windows is a sigh. Deep and quick. The way you catch your breath. Before something happens. You can't do anything to stop.

My exhale settles my body deep into the seat.

I loved God so much right then.